BARRACUDA FINAL BEARING

"Terrific . . . the fighting really goes into high gear." —*San Francisco Examiner*

"A dandy, hell-and-high-water techno-political thriller . . . stunningly effective." —*Kirkus Reviews*

"Those who thrill to the blip of sonar and the thud of torpedoes will relish this deep-water dive." —*Publishers Weekly*

PHOENIX SUB ZERO

"Moves at a breakneck pace . . ." —Larry Bond, bestselling author of *Cauldron*

"A technothriller by a master rivaling Tom Clancy . . . exciting from first page to last." —*Publishers Weekly*

"A good, suspenseful, and spine-tingling read . . . exhilarating." —*Associated Press*

"Powerful . . . rousing . . . for Tom Clancy fans." —*Kirkus Reviews*

continued . . .

ATTACK OF THE SEAWOLF

VOYAGE OF THE DEVILFISH

Also by Michael DiMercurio

Attack of the Seawolf

Voyage of the Devilfish

Phoenix Sub Zero

Barracuda Final Bearing

PIRANHA
FIRING POINT

Michael DiMercurio

AN ONYX BOOK

ONYX
Published by the Penguin Group
Penguin Putnam Inc., 375 Hudson Street,
New York, New York 10014, U.S.A.
Penguin Books Ltd, 27 Wrights Lane,
London W8 5TZ, England
Penguin Books Australia Ltd, Ringwood,
Victoria, Australia
Penguin Books Canada Ltd, 10 Alcorn Avenue,
Toronto, Ontario, Canada M4V 3B2
Penguin Books (N.Z.) Ltd, 182–190 Wairau Road,
Auckland 10, New Zealand

Penguin Books Ltd, Registered Offices:
Harmondsworth, Middlesex, England

First published by Onyx, an imprint of Dutton NAL,
a member of Penguin Putnam Inc.

First Printing, February, 1999
10 9 8 7 6 5 4 3 2 1

REGISTERED TRADEMARK—MARCA REGISTRADA

Printed in the United States of America

PUBLISHER'S NOTE
This is a work of fiction. Names, characters, places, and incidents either
are the product of the author's imagination or are used fictitiously, and
any resemblance to actual persons, living or dead, events, or locales is
entirely coincidental.

For my beloved wife, Patti,
The one true love of my life.
Patti, although I am the Captain of my soul,
You are the Navigator.
I love you.

ACKNOWLEDGMENTS

This book is written in remembrance of and reverence for Dolores Quigley, who left this world far too soon, and yet who continues to live among us. Her influence and love are felt and received gratefully every single day.

Warmest thanks to Richard J. Quigley, Jr., who is a warm and strong father figure to every soul he touches, and he touches many, including me. Thanks also to Kathy Quigley, who has treated me like one of the family. To Rich and Patty Quigley, Terry Quigley, Tom and Deb Quigley, Chris Quigley, Liz and Jeff Brown, and Brian Quigley, I thank you for making me your brother.

Thanks again to the great Nancy Wallitsch, who was a friend when I needed one, a drill sergeant when I needed one, a nurse when I needed one, and a damned good attorney.

Deepest thanks to Chris Allgeier, who believed and took action.

Thanks to Paul Weiss, who made a huge difference and carried me when I was immobile.

Thanks to Craig Relyea, the first reader and an enlightened critic, and to Mike Matlosz, who lended great support.

Thanks to Patricia and Dee DiMercurio, Mom and Dad, who kept the porch light on and never gave up hope.

Eternal thanks to Matthew and Marla DiMercurio, who have given me love, understanding, and wisdom far beyond their years.

And to the late Don Fine, who—whether he knows it or not—made me tough and gave me courage.

"A nuclear submarine fleet is the future of the armed forces. The number of tanks and guns will be reduced as well as the infantry, but a modern Navy is a totally different thing."

—Russian Army Marshal Pavel Gracev,
  former Russian Minister of Defense, 1993

"It is becoming increasingly clear that the next substantial U.S. naval expedition abroad—the next Desert Storm—may well face an enemy with submarines in its order of battle."

—Captain Bruce Linder, U.S. Navy Commander,
Fleet Antisubmarine Warfare Training Center
U.S. Naval Institute *Proceedings*, May 1996

"The location where we will engage the enemy must not become known to them. If it is not known, then the positions they must prepare to defend will be numerous . . . [and] the forces we will engage will be few."

—Sun-Tzu, *The Art of War*

"Ex Scientia—Tridens." (From Knowledge—Sea Power)

—Motto of the U.S. Naval Academy

"Gentlemen, one thing I've learned at sea is that the procedure manuals are written by people who have never been on the business end of a torpedo with the plant crashing around them, with the captain shouting for power, where a second's delay can mean death. The meaning of being an officer in our navy is knowing more than those operation manuals, knowing how to play when you're hurt, when the ship is going down and you need to keep shooting anyway. That's really it, isn't it, men? The ability to play hurt. That's the only way we'll ever win a war. And in fact, that's the only way you can live your lives. Do that for me, guys. Learn to play hurt."

—ADMIRAL KINNAIRD R. MCKEE, DIRECTOR
NAVY NUCLEAR PROPULSION PROGRAM AND
FORMER SUPERINTENDENT, U.S. NAVAL ACADEMY,
ADDRESSING THE ATLANTIC FLEET SUBMARINE
OFFICERS, NORFOLK, VIRGINIA, 1984

"I still have one torpedo and two main engines."

—CAPTAIN MICHAEL PACINO, USS *SEAWOLF*,
AT THE MOUTH OF THE BO HAI BAY, SURROUNDED BY
CHINESE DESTROYERS AND AIRCRAFT

BOOK I

＊＊＊

RED DAGGER

PROLOGUE

The last engine died as the plunging aircraft tilted into a steep dead-stick turn, the crosswind shaking the wings, the view ahead filled only with deep blue ocean. The waves grew alarmingly close, coming impossibly fast toward the windshield. A moment later the plane smashed violently into the water.

The pilot was hurled into his seat's five-point harness, fighting the wheel and the rudder pedals, until the massive four-engine seaplane glided to a halt and began rolling in the gentle swells of the East China Sea. The pilot glanced one last time at the panel and nodded at the copilot. Shrugging off the harness, he moved aft through the flight-deck door and into the large aft cabin. Looking up at him were two dozen pair of eyes, some steely cold, some excited, a few bored, but none anxious.

The pilot turned to the starboard side of the cabin, where a crowded deck-to-overhead console was set against the bulkhead to the cockpit. A small, intense man sat in the console, the panels and keypads and trackballs encircling him. One of the panels graphically depicted the aircraft on the surface, a door opening in the underhull, a ball on a cable lowering into the sea, a set of numbers rolling up as the ball sank into the depths of the ocean. A panel next to the graphic display filled with dots swimming in a darker field, until the dots coalesced into a bright spot moving slowly across the screen.

"She'll pass close in ten minutes, Commander Chu, five hundred meters east. She's slow, at fifteen clicks. That puts mount-up time now, deploy time in two minutes, with three minutes of contingency time. It's tight, but we can do it."

Commander Chu Hua-Feng stepped to the center of the cabin and looked at the men. Each of them was clad in unmarked black coveralls, their belts holding machine pistols, grenades, and daggers.

"Attention, fighters," he said, his voice deep, projecting without effort. Thin but muscular, Chu stood one hundred eighty centimeters, taller in his rubber-soled boots, towering over the crew. He was in his mid-thirties, which was odd in the Red Chinese PLA Navy, where senior officers were inevitably gray-haired. He carried himself with the air of unquestioned authority, as if he had been the oldest brother, used to command since infancy. The unblinking eyes of the twenty-four men stared at him.

"We mount up in thirty seconds," Chu continued. "Rendezvous with the target Korean submarine will be in twelve minutes. Each of you has been training for this moment for the past year. The practice runs are over now. This is it, our operational test." Chu paused, narrowing his eyes to a glare. "The doubting eyes of the Admiralty are on us. They have said it can't be done, that no one can sneak up and steal a nuclear submarine, under way and steaming deep beneath the surface. But when this mission is over, and we prove it *can* be done, the result will change the map of China. And every one of you knows what that will mean." Chu paused again, scanning the faces. His own face crinkled into unlikely laugh lines around his eyes and across his nose. "Very well, men. Good luck to all of you. Mister First, are you ready?"

Lieutenant Commander Lo Sun stood up from the sonar console, stripping off the headset, and nodded. "Ready, Commander."

"Excellent. Platoon, mount up!"

Immediately the men stood and filed quickly aft in the gently rocking cabin to the aft bulkhead hatch. One after another the men ducked into the hatchway, until the compartment was empty except for Chu. He looked forward into the cabin, and saw the copilot in the door of the flight deck. Chu flipped him a salute, glanced around the big plane one last time, and entered the opening, shutting the cabin hatch behind him.

Inside the cramped red-lit interior of the submersible, he made his way past the men to the control console forward. The control couch was a contoured pad allowing the pilot to lie on his stomach with his head, shoulders, and arms protruding into a high-pressure plastic view port bubble. This was completely black, as if it had been painted over. Chu strapped on his earpiece and boom mike, tested the circuit, and gave a crisp order to the seaplane copilot. Immediately bright light flashed into the cockpit as the bomb-bay-style doors opened in the belly of the seaplane, admitting the October afternoon light.

Below Chu, in the view port, the sea lapped steadily against the doors of the bay. Chu glanced up at an overhead console and pulled an orange T-handle, releasing the submersible *Red Dagger* from the seaplane. Chu's stomach flipped as the vessel tumbled from the plane's bay. The waves rose to meet the view port, then splashed over the plastic bubble. As the ten-meter-long ship sank into the water, the view showed only deep blue, becoming darker as the heads-up display indicated the depth of the submersible. Within a minute the view port was again black, the waves and the seaplane now a hundred meters overhead.

The submarine loomed ahead in the powerful spotlights, long and cylindrical and fat and black. The escape hatch was his landing target. The submersible's computer took over on automatic control, guiding them down to the hatch, attempting to match the submarine's speed and bring down their airlock skirt precisely over the hatch ring.

According to the intelligence brief from Mai Sheng, his PLA intelligence contact, the sub was the Korean vessel *Dae Gu,* a Los Angeles 688I-class submarine, formerly the USS *Louisville,* sold to Korea four years ago under an American program allowing U.S. allies to purchase older nuclear-powered attack submarines as long as Americans were allowed to monitor and control the nuclear material of the reactor core. The intel brief had described the escape hatch location where Chu was to make his landing. The airlock led below to the sparsely occupied engine room of the huge vessel.

With a gentle thud the submersible *Red Dagger* touched down on the deck of the target submarine. Chu flooded a ballast tank, making the submersible heavier by a few tons. That would keep it fast to the submarine's deck. A quiet hiss sounded as the airlock at the underhull was pumped down, creating an air seal between the submersible and submarine hatches.

The docking was complete. Chu powered down the submersible, leaving only minimal power on for the interior lights and the computer. Chu pulled himself off the control couch, his muscles aching from the cramped position, and moved aft out of the cockpit. Lo Sun operated the hatch panel. Large steel dogs rotated, and the lower hatch slowly retracted into the submersible hull. Below, bathed in the hot spotlight circle, the black hatch of the submarine was revealed. There was not much to it, only a circular groove cut in the black non-skid paint of the hull, the metal still wet from the seawater.

Chu pulled a T-wrench from the tool bag on the bulkhead. In the center of the hatch below was a small hole with a square metal peg recessed into it. Submarine hatches had been manufactured to ISO standards for the last few decades; that way a sunken submarine could be rescued by any foreign ship happening by. Sub escape hatches could be operated by anyone with a standard salvage tool kit. Chu bent over and spun the T-wrench clockwise until he heard and felt a metallic clunk. He looked up at Lo.

"Set time minus one. Platoon, don equipment."

Chu shrugged into a harness with a dual scuba-type air bottle. Grabbing a gas mask hanging from the hose to the bottles' regulator, he hung it around his neck. Then he belted on two automatic pistols and a bandolier of grenades. Finally, he fitted his earpiece and boom microphone, looked up at his men, and saw that they were ready.

"Mr. Lo, set time zero when I pull up the hatch. There'll be an indication in their control room as soon as we open it. I want the ship taken within two minutes. Insert on my mark. Five, four, three, two, one, now!"

Chu plunged his fingers into a recessed groove and pulled up the hatch. Despite its mass, it was mounted on a counterbalanced spring and came up easily. Chu latched it in the open position, found the ladder down into the escape trunk, and noiselessly slid down the rails into the dark chamber. Switching on a battle lantern to see, he bent low to spin the central chrome wheel of the lower hatch. He pulled it up and latched it. The hatch opened into the brightness of the engine room below. The sound of whining turbines came up from the hatch, accompanied by a cloud of heavy steam.

Chu slid down the second ladder. As his boots hit the deck of the engine room, he raised his AK-80 automatic pistol in his right hand, the long silencer screwed in. He stepped away from the ladderway as his men came down behind him, their boots quiet on the rungs. Chu walked silently aft past the motor control center to the nuclear control space. He looked in the narrow side door. The men inside were deeply involved in a conversation, the Korean syllables melodic in the space.

Chu snapped off three rounds per man, efficiently dropping the nearest at the throttle, the next two at a long console. The officer standing behind the three men looked over in confusion. His expression became a death mask as two bullets silently ripped into his chest. He sank to the floor slowly, his eyes shutting as his face clunked onto the deck.

After Chu waved one of his men into the room, he continued aft, dropping his spent clip and reloading without looking down. The noise grew to a shrieking roar of steam. He saw a figure between the two large turbines. Chu fired and hit the man in the bicep. The man, an older officer, lunged in an attempt to hide, but Chu raced in and squeezed off another four rounds into the man's chest. Blood began to run on the deckplates of the catwalk between the turbines as Chu continued aft.

He found another watchstander aft of the reduction gear and killed him, then ducked down a ladder to the middle level. There'd be one down here too. It took less than sixty seconds to find the man, standing between two turbines with a clipboard, checking a gauge. Suddenly he clutched his chest, blood spurting over his palm. Too late he looked up to see Chu, then sprawled onto the deck.

By the time Chu returned from the lower level, he found his platoon gathered at the opening to a ladder. Lo Sun motioned them to the port side, where he'd located the duct leading to the fan room forward of the reactor compartment, where the air was redistributed throughout the ship. Chu gave the signal, and the men strapped on their gas masks. They checked the seals and valves in their regulators. Chu put his face into his own mask, testing the coppery, dry air. Then he fired four shots, shattering the mesh covering the duct. He took a grenade from his belt, pulled the pin, and hurled it into the duct, waiting to hear it explode. There was no loud report, only a dull thud as the hydrogen cyanide canister burst apart. The deadly gas would now be sucked to the fan room.

The door to the control room was open. As Chu hurried in and looked around, the dead men registered first. They seemed to be everywhere. Considering how choked the room was with equipment, he was surprised that the American technology required so many individuals to run the ship. On his right was a ship-control station, where two men were slumped over airplane-style control yokes. One of his men pulled a Korean helmsman up from his seat, tossing him into the forward passageway, then taking the control yoke himself. Others did likewise, until the passageway was piled with bodies and the men of the Red Dagger platoon occupied every control station. Chu stepped up onto the periscope stand and checked the room. The two men at the ship-control consoles were maintaining depth at what the numerals said 550. That must be feet rather than meters, he thought, recalling the depth of the submersible and the fact that the deck had never taken a down angle during their assault. The speed indicator read 15, which would mean knots instead of meters per second.

Chu craned his neck around a periscope pole to look at the wraparound panel on the port side. He noticed red circles indicating the open hatch aft. The rest of the control room was much less important. With a nod at one of his men, Chu gave the next order—to harvest every technical manual they could find, given four minutes. One man went into the sonar display room, piling up books. Chu found a book cabinet at the chart table, and withdrew a manual marked *Submarine Standard Operating Procedures*. Chu began scanning it—stopping only when he heard a loud explosion behind the periscope stand. One of the men had blown apart the tumbler of a safe. Once the smoke cleared, the contents of the safe were withdrawn and added to a pile on the deck. Other safes throughout the ship would likewise be yielding up their contents.

Time was short, Chu thought, anxiously adjusting his gas mask. Their air supplies would run out in mere minutes. At last he found the procedure he was looking for.

"Turn the engine knob to stop," he called out, his voice distorted through the mask.

The man at the ship-control console rotated a dial with a needle set in the face from the area marked STAN-DARD to STOP. A second needle set into the face clicked to the stop square, ringing a small bell, the answer from the nuclear control room aft. In the engine room Chu's men would be shutting the throttle valves to the steam turbines.

Chu watched the speed indicator as it dropped from 15 to 12, then to 10. He hurried to the wraparound port panel. He scanned through the procedure manual, searching for the hovering system chapter. If he could stop the ship, they could depart without fighting the forward velocity of the vessel. He paged through several computer displays on the main flat panel, finally finding the display for the hovering system, and selected the presets the procedure called for on the checklist.

He looked over the speed panel. The ship's speed was now nearing zero. It would be like stopping the engines on a blimp, he thought. Now they would either sink, pop up to the surface, or tilt forward or aft. It depended on how the ship had been before they slowed. He waited as the ship glided to a halt. He selected the ship's desired depth using a computer control on the display, then squinted at the display to see the ship's actual depth. The two matched. The ship was hovering.

With one rapid twist of the depth-rate dial, Chu commanded the computer to send the ship plunging vertically downward, to sink to her crush depth.

"Extract!" he commanded.

"Go!" Chu hissed. There was no time for him to climb into the control seat. One of the platoon pilots had already climbed onto the view port couch and flooded the hatch skirt, breaking the connection between the two ships. The depth of the two vessels would be at least four hundred meters, not far from the crush depth of the submarine. The *Red Dagger* could descend to almost seven hundred meters before its titanium hull began to fail, but it would do no good for the submarine's hull failure to take the submersible down with it.

The water jets spun up, and the *Red Dagger* accelerated away from the still descending abandoned submarine. The deck of the submersible angled sharply upward as it made its emergency ascent. Emergency, because its atmosphere remained poisoned with the deadly hydrogen cyanide gas from the grenade detonated on the submarine below, and each man's air was running out. Chu could feel his own air supply dwindling. It was getting much harder to pull each breath from the mask. Finally the submersible reached the surface, and the pilot began to ventilate the interior. A blast of fresh air blew over Chu's sweaty coveralls, chilling him. He waited as long as he could, until the bottle gave up, its air completely exhausted. Hoping the submersible was now safe, he pulled off the sweaty mask and pulled in a breath of salty sea air. The other members of the platoon were watching him, waiting to see if he would collapse to the deck. He took a second pull and nodded solemnly at the men. They all pulled off their masks, relief breaking out on their faces.

A violent shriek sounded through the sea around them, then a roaring screech of ripping metal. Quickly it died to a barely discernible groan.

"Sub's hull is imploding," Lo Sun said. "It must have hit crush depth."

Without answering, Chu climbed to the upper compartment hatch, where he looked out a view port revealing the cloudy sky above. He engaged a control, and the hatch came open. Chu put his head out above the hatch ring and looked out over the calm sea. The mostly submerged submersible hull was barely visible beneath him. The small vessel rolled in the swells, a rocking motion that seemed deeply relaxing. Perhaps that feeling was due more to the success of the mission than the beauty of the sea, Chu thought. Off in the distance the sound of aircraft engines could be heard. Their seaplane was coming to pick them up.

Chu ducked back down, shutting the hatch. He leaned against the bulkhead and closed his eyes. Once the Admiralty was briefed on the mission, it would set into motion a chain of events that eventually would restore mainland China to its rightful status. No longer would the rest of the world call it "Red China"—the country's unofficial name, intended to prevent confusion with the eastern rebel nation, which had intentionally named itself "White China." The nation, once reunited, would once again be known by its true name—the People's Republic of China.

Within twenty minutes, the submersible was docked in the belly of the enormous seaplane, and Chu was sitting in the pilot-in-command seat, throttling up the powerful turboprops to take off, on the way to Beijing.

CHAPTER 1

SUNDAY
OCTOBER 13

GREAT HALL OF THE PEOPLE
BEIJING, RED CHINA

The men's room sparkled. Italian marble stall walls gleamed in the warm light of an ornate crystal chandelier. A babbling fountain was set into the polished tile of the floor, and the jets of clear water were reflected in a rainbow shining high overhead on the ornate Indonesian tigerwood carvings in the ceiling. Deeply polished pine planks lined the walls. The sinks were streaked marble, the faucets solid gold. An armed Red Guard stood stiffly at the door.

Commander Chu Hua-Feng saw none of it. He stood before the gold framed mirror and stared at his reflection. The black coveralls of the *Red Dagger* mission had been left behind. He was wearing a black tunic with the gold stripes of his rank of full commander, his four combat medals gleaming. Despite a knock at the door, Chu continued to gaze at his face in the mirror. There was no narcissism in his look, only disbelief. The face staring back at him could have been his father's: the same high, severe cheekbones, broad nose, dark stern eyes, and severe square chin below full lips. His height was within a hairsbreadth of his father's. And though he had worshipped his father, the mirror's image brought not pride but deep regret and sadness.

His father, Chu Hsueh-Fan, had been the admiral in command of the Lushun Northern Fleet. He'd been aboard his flagship, the aircraft carrier *Shaoguan,* when his fleet and his ship were sunk by a group of rogue American submarines trying to break out of the Bo Hai Bay outside of Beijing after one of them had been captured spying and the others came to the rescue. The catastrophic sinking of the *Shaoguan* had happened ten years before, when young Chu had been a mere junior lieutenant aviation officer flying an antisubmarine Yak-36A vertical-takeoff jet. He had had a front seat for the sinking of the flagship. He'd seen one of the submarines fire a supersonic ship-killing missile. The missile had flown out of the sea, the arc of the rocket's flame trail a perfect parabola, leading directly to Chu's father's ship. *Shaoguan* had taken the hit amidships, exploded into flames, rolled over, and vanished into the gray sea.

Young Chu could only watch helplessly, his only depth charge already expended against the evasive criminal submarines. Though his plane was running on fumes, he was determined to remain hovering over the bay to watch the sinking of the American murderers, until the U.S. fleet's supersonic fighter jets had come screaming in, missiles flying. His Yak had lost a wing. Chu had ejected, but his twenty-two-year old weapons officer and friend Lo Yun had not. The one-winged Yak had plummeted to the sea, exploding into a blinding fireball just before hitting the water. Chu had floated in the deep water of the bay for almost forty hours. The waves washing over his face mixed with angry tears of frustration, while somehow he knew that despite the evidence before him, he would not die. It was the middle of a rainy night when rescue finally arrived, in the form of a Udaloy destroyer. There were no helicopters—they had all been downed by the American fighter jet's missiles.

Chu had been lucky, or at least so he was told. He had escaped without a scratch. The remainder of the fleet's sailors and officers had not fared as well. Of the nearly seventy ships of the task force, half had gone down with all hands. Over three thousand men had died that day. All because a wolfpack of murderous submarines had torpedoed their way out of the bay that they had been in spying.

The horror of that day was a line of demarcation across Chu's life, and after watching his father's ship explode and capsize, he would forever be haunted.

When the pain had eased, after over four years, and he felt he could begin to move on with his life, he realized that he had been overtaken by an obsession, a specter that filled his nights with vivid dreams, that made him toss and turn until he was tangled in sweaty sheets. The obsession was with the power of a stealthy nuclear submarine.

When naval power was measured, there was an amazing force multiplier associated with a submerged attack submarine—the way it could hide, invisibly, and reach out to alter history, just as it had in the Falklands war, then in the Bo Hai Bay, and finally in the American blockade of Japan, when a handful of Japanese Destiny submarines had put an entire U.S. battle fleet on the bottom of the Pacific. Four years after *Shaoguan* sank, Chu's naval career had turned away from aviation and toward nuclear submarines.

There was only one problem. Red China was landlocked now that White China had come close to winning the civil war and had taken up the entire coastline from Hong Kong to Penglai. Only Bo Hai Bay east of Beijing remained in Red China's hands, and the approaches to the Korea Bay and the East China Sea were completely blocked by White China. It was a miserable situation, one that Red China would be forced to live with for the foreseeable future—until Chu had formulated his revolutionary plan, the plan that had brought him here to the Great Hall of the People.

The knocking at the door continued, until finally a female voice called out Chu's name. He blinked, finally turning from the mirror toward the door. A frowning woman in a military uniform stood in the half-open doorway. Her uniform was an olive full-length tunic over trousers, with the shoulder boards of a People's Liberation Army officer, a gold cord wrapped around her shoulder as a sign that she was a staff officer to the leadership. She was tall and slim, the uniform unable to take away an impression of gracefulness. Her black hair gleamed in the bright lights of the room. Her face was sculpted and severe, prominent cheekbones beneath almond-shaped dark eyes, her mouth unsmiling. Lieutenant Mai Sheng was looking at Chu intently.

"You'll be late, Commander. Let's go."

Chu nodded and followed her out into the ornate corridor. His mind had already turned to the briefing coming up when something she said over her shoulder intruded on his thoughts.

"You shouldn't spend so much time admiring yourself, Commander. That's my job."

"I'm sorry, what did you say, Lieutenant?" He had come out of his reverie long enough to pick up on the echo of her words. She had spoken tentatively, with the slightest hint of a tremble. He blinked at her, half in surprise, half in eagerness.

"Nothing, sir," she said, smiling slightly.

Chu didn't smile back, not to her face. He had known Mai Sheng for her entire life, since his father and hers were colleagues. For a long time Chu had never really noticed her—she was just a child, a friend of the family, an annoying little sister, and he was busy with his studies. Ten years ago, though, just before the outbreak of the civil war, she had come to an Admiralty function. She was still young, barely in her first year of college, her hair pulled back, her limbs thin and fragile like a young doe's. The war was imminent, and Chu was in no mood for romance, but he had been amused and even flattered to realize that Mai was flirting with him, looking up at him, touching his arm, laughing at everything he said. Absent was the usual young girl's shyness, replaced by the charm of a grown woman. When he had excused himself to have a drink with Lo Yun, his backseat weapons officer, he couldn't help noticing her eyes following him. Only now did he realize he had the beginnings of feelings for the woman, at the most inconvenient time.

He bit the inside of his lip and forced himself back to the present. Ahead was the most important briefing of his life, a briefing that would start a war. With that thought, Mai Sheng became just another military aide, walking him to the briefing theater. Finally they arrived at a dead end in the corridor, where tall, wide, heavy mahogany carved double doors were flanked by two Red Guards. Both came to attention and saluted.

"Here we are, Commander." Her smile was gone, replaced with an iron manner, as if her thoughts had paralleled his own.

One of the guards opened the doors to cavernous darkness. The room's walls were shrouded in dark foam soundproofing material. Thick carpeting deadened Chu's footsteps. The ceiling was black, also covered in the dark rippling foam. Fifty steps into the room, a half dozen overstuffed armchairs faced a screen five meters tall. To one side was a cutaway quarter-scale model of the submersible *Red Dagger*. On the other side of the screen was the actual submersible itself, with a red-carpeted stairway leading to the port hatch and a second one leading to the upper hatch. Inside a building and out of its element, the submersible seemed ungainly and huge. Between the screen and the model was a podium. Chu walked to it and looked down on the console set into the podium surface, unaware of Lieutenant Mai standing next to him.

"I need to talk to you," she said quietly.

"Not now," Chu said, still reviewing his intended speech to Chairman Yang, Admiral Loen, and General Feng.

"We have an hour."

"Why did you call me out of the men's room? I thought we were on for two o'clock." He swallowed, wondering if she wanted to discuss something personal he wasn't ready for, but her face remained set in a military frown.

"The briefing has been moved to three. But I need

the time to brief you on a recent development. You'll need to know this for your presentation. Not even the chairman knows this yet."

Chu stiffened, watching her.

"We've found out about an exercise being conducted by Japan in the Pacific. In ten days the Japanese Maritime Self-Defense Force will put to sea with six submarines of the new Rising Sun class. They are doing their sea trials as a flotilla, and when that is complete, they will move on to a sub-*versus*-sub combat simulation."

Chu almost choked. "How do you know this? How reliable is this information? What exactly is the purpose of the exercise? Will surface ships be involved?"

Mai Sheng smiled, briefing Chu as fast as she could.

Chairman Yang Pow was now in his eighties. He was a big man, his addiction to rich food no secret to his inner circle. On a trip to the United States thirty years ago, he had first tasted a double cheeseburger, and his life had never quite been the same.

But despite his weight and age, he carried himself with the dignity and strength of an emperor from one of the dynasties long past. He walked quickly, with the inexplicable grace of the large, toward the double doors of the briefing theater. Yang had a round and open face, now beginning to show the lines of his age. Beneath his eyes were dark blotches, which had always been there, but were becoming much more pronounced. Above the dark patches Yang's eyes were large and brown and understanding, hiding behind black horn-rimmed glasses. The lenses of the glasses were almost flat, so little did they correct Yang's eyesight, but it was said that Yang was imitating the leaders of the past, and whether he really needed the big black glasses or not, they made him feel more comfortable.

Yang had been in power for almost eighteen years. He had had a nice run of eight years before the imperial aggression of the Taiwanese had flared.

Led by a diabolical general named Wong Chen, the White Army of the New Kuomintang broke out of their

safety on the island and made landfall in rebellious
Shanghai. At first Beijing had not taken the rebellion
seriously, but soon Shanghai fell to the Whites, and the
port was opened to incoming equipment and ships. By
the time the People's Liberation Army could respond,
the Whites had consolidated a growing beachhead on
the Chinese mainland.

The war raged for six months as the Whites moved
deep into Communist China, taking one city after the
next. Yang, under severe pressure, rejected all recom-
mendations to use nuclear weapons on the invading
White forces, insisting that using nuclear devices on his
own land would just force the people into the arms of
the New Kuomintang. As the Whites, with their superior
equipment and training, pushed the PLA back and
north, he came under severe criticism for that stance,
but to this day he stood by it, even if it had resulted in
a divided China.

The end of the war had also come at his insistence,
as he negotiated a truce with Shanghai, allowing them
to retain their land on the east coast. He forced them
to give up claims to a strip of territory to the north and
west, which would have sectioned Red China into two
regions, in exchange for territory as far north as Penglai
at the mouth of Beijing's Bo Hai Bay. In less than a
year, the White Army had seemingly won, forced Yang's
PLA back, and established a Western-oriented democ-
racy on the Asian continent, taking China's most
wealthy cities from Hong Kong to Tsingtao.

Yang had waited for his chance to strike back. He had
given the enemy time, time to get soft and complacent.
He would allow White China to forget about the war
and the past, and when they least expected it, he would
invade from the west and cast them into the sea.

Unfortunately, there was one major obstacle, and that
was the damned East China Sea itself. The rest of the
world would not watch and wait dumbstruck while Red
China attacked White China. The West would come to
help—particularly the Americans, those perpetual suck-
ers for the underdog—and they would bring aircraft car-

riers and troop ships and amphibious landing ships and tanks and paratroopers and helicopters and supersonic jets.

Without a blue-water navy, without control of the seas, he would not win the war against the traitorous Whites. Many decades before a man named Alfred Thayer Mahan had written volume after volume about sea power, and over and over he had preached that the way to win a war was to control the "sea lines of communication," the blood vessels and arteries of sea commerce. In the dawn of the second decade of the new century, the advice held—without control of the sea, he could not control the war.

There was no solution, not in the near term, Yang thought. And he was old now, feeling his age as his bones grew weak and his body infirm. His father and his father's father lay in their graves, and both would be deeply disappointed and saddened by his yielding of land to the rebels. He had consoled himself with the knowledge that White China was temporary, but now he was beginning to doubt himself. Could it really be that he would go down in history as the chairman who had allowed China to be partitioned and violated?

Two steps behind and to his left walked Lieutenant Mai Sheng, his personal aide, an intelligence officer of the People's Liberation Army. Mai had been with him since her first assignment on the Suchow front during the civil war. She had been deployed on the front lines as the White Army tank battalions had forced the PLA back. Mai had been in intelligence even then, and had been captured and injured during the battle. She had proved herself a vicious and resourceful fighter, full of high spirits and fresh ideas. Yet she was much more than that. Yang had known Mai's beautiful and lonely mother, Xu Meng, over twenty-five years ago. Though no one but he and Xu knew of their relationship, gossips had noticed that Mai Sheng looked much like her mother and eerily like Yang himself.

Yang had sworn a dual oath. First, that he would protect Mai's life and her career, and second, that no one would ever know that he was protecting her. But his caution had seemed scarcely necessary, because Mai was at once icily competent and fiercely independent. Protection of her career had never been a problem, but protection of her life had. He had insisted that her orders be cut to be his personal aide, and for the first year she had accepted it, but lately she had shown a desire to return to a combat company. He would not be able to keep her much longer, and perhaps it was time to let her fly with her own wings. But Mai's problems would now have to take a backseat to the matter at hand, the briefing being given by Commander Chu Hua-Feng.

Yang had decided to allow the briefing on his schedule, not because of its importance but because Mai had insisted.

On Yang's right was PLA General Feng Xuk, commander in chief of the People's Liberation Army. On his left was Admiral Loen Dun, the supreme commander of the People's Liberation Army Navy, or what was left of it. When the White Army had taken control of the east coast, there had been only one port to return to— Lushun, the old Port Arthur in the north of Bo Hai Bay. That had effectively bottled up the fleet behind the Lushun-Penglai Gap. Since then few of the ships had been used or maintained. The front-line destroyers, frigates, and helicopter carriers had lain tied up, rusting and decayed. There was no longer any point in even thinking there was any form of PLA Navy.

At the door to the briefing theater, the two Red Guard troops came to rigid attention, both saluting, then one opening the door. Yang and the others walked into the dimness of the theater, the temperature some ten degrees below that of the corridor. As the door shut behind him, Yang found himself in complete darkness. At first he blamed the darkness on the infirmity of his aging eyes, but then he realized that he truly was standing in a blacked-out room.

Suddenly a single spotlight burst to life, shining down on a huge machine towering over his head. It was some kind of boat or submarine. Then Yang realized what the briefing was about—the submersible that the young navy officer Chu had once briefed him on long ago.

A second spotlight flared up on a smaller form of the submersible, but this one cut in half to reveal the interior. As a musical fanfare trumpeted in the back of the room, both spotlights dimmed and the screen came to life, the only view on the screen a photo of the deep blue sea. The view backed up to reveal that the sea was seen through the front view screen of a large airplane. Yang was led by the elbow to a large armchair, sinking deeply into the upholstery while mesmerized by the vision of the seaplane landing. The camera and microphone must have been mounted on the mission commander's head, since all the views seemed to come from the commander's viewpoint.

Yang stared open-mouthed as the movie showed the submersible nearing the deck of the submarine. Men dived down the open hatch, their automatic pistols dropping the crewmen of the Korean submarine as if they were cardboard targets. Then the final minutes as the commander set the ship to begin sinking, rushing to get out of the hull. When the screen showed the submersible hatch popping open to a panorama of the sea, Yang started clapping and cheering. Feng and Loen followed suit, all three bursting into wide smiles of approval.

But the presentation was not yet over. The screen burst to life again. The face of a news reporter from Shanghai flashed up, reporting that the Korean submarine *Dai Gu* had been lost with all hands, the only trace of it the floating buoy that had broadcast a distress signal. The clip again faded to black. Auditorium lights came back up dimly as a spotlight opened on the podium. A navy commander stood there, resplendent in a dark uniform, gold stripes on his sleeves, ribbons on his chest.

"Good afternoon, Chairman Yang, General Feng, and Admiral Loen. My name is Commander Chu Hua-Feng. The last time you saw me I was requesting funding for the submersible you have just seen succeed in hijacking a submerged under-way nuclear submarine.

"I won't bore you with any further comments on the operational test mission of the *Red Dagger*. However, I do want to mention one development to you.

"In ten days six advanced-technology Japanese Rising Sun–class nuclear attack submarines will put to sea out of Yokosuka." Chu looked over at Mai Sheng, who smiled back at him. "I propose to deploy the *Red Dagger* and the other submersible units and take command of the Rising Sun submarines. Once we have captured them, we will station ourselves in the East China Sea, where we will keep the West from assisting the Whites. With control of the East China Sea assured, the ground forces of the PLA should be able to take back Hong Kong and Tsingtao and Shanghai."

Chairman Yang stared at the navy commander, a hard frown coming over his face. As he rose to his feet the frown became a black thundercloud. He walked slowly, menacingly up to the podium. To his credit, the commander returned the Chairman's gaze steadily. When Yang was within striking distance of the commander, he suddenly pulled Commander Chu into a bear hug, slapping his back and laughing. The tension in the room immediately evaporated, and the only sounds were the clapping and cheering of the flag officers and Mai Sheng.

"Commander Chu," Yang said, his voice sonorous in the huge room, "as of this moment you are no longer a mere commander. You have proved yourself to me and to your nation. I hereby promote you to the rank of Rear Admiral. Congratulations."

Chu looked over at Lieutenant Mai Sheng, who nodded solemnly at him, her dark eyes shining. Despite his modesty, Chu suddenly felt that victory had just been conceived, and that he was the one who would deliver it to the people in this room.

CHAPTER 2

WESTERN PACIFIC
200 KILOMETERS SOUTH OF TOKYO BAY

Admiral Chu Hua-Feng dozed in the pilot-in-command seat of the Tupolev TU-187 seaplane, his hands crossed over his taut abdominal muscles, leaning far back in the reclined seat, a black blindfold strapped over his eyes. The seaplane rocked gently in the calm sea. The only sound was the slight blowing of the ventilation system, which pulled in the salty, fishy-smelling sea air.

In Chu's dream he was walking with his father in a sepia-tinted image, the deck of his father's destroyer under their feet, the Saturday morning sunshine making stark shadows on the ship's decks. Chu's five-year-old voice was asking one question after another, questions that would seem odd now, but in his little boy mind had seemed vitally important. Questions like, what's a missile launcher, what's a missile do, why do we need missiles? The elder Chu answered each one patiently, steadily, as if being questioned by a government official, except that the answers were filled with endearments, which for his father meant calling him "my little warrior" and "fighter Chu."

But suddenly his father, then Lieutenant Commander Chu Hsueh-Fan, turned to him in the open space between a missile battery and a torpedo launcher, dropping down to one knee, his face so close to young Chu's that he could smell his father's cigarette-smoke-tinged breath and see the bloodshot lines in his eyes.

"Young warrior, there is danger below. You must hurry. You must finish quickly. If you stay too long, they will come for you, and they are strong."

"But, Father, what do you mean?"

"Hurry, my son. Finish quickly. Do not linger."

"But I don't understand," Chu whined.

"There is a satellite update, Admiral," his father said, his face beginning to change in shape, becoming unfocused.

"What?"

"A satellite update, Admiral," the voice said. "Are you awake?"

Chu pulled off his blindfold and blinked several times. The face of the copilot was close in his vision. Chu pushed him back and yanked the lever of the seat, bringing it upright.

"Say that again," Chu said, the dream already gone, with no trace of it left in his memory. He knew he'd seen something he should remember, but it had slipped away.

"We have a satellite update, Admiral. Commander Lo has the data at the console aft."

Chu wrenched himself out of the command seat and hurried aft, his body unsteady from being awakened suddenly, in addition to the rocking of the aircraft floating in the sea.

At the console, Lo Sun sat in the seat inside the wraparound panels. Chu crouched down to look at Lo's display. It was a high-definition still photograph, taken from the air, focused downward on a harbor. Three ships were clearly shown in the center of the deep channel, their wakes white across the darkness of the calm water. The ships looked odd, without pointed bows and square sterns and flat decks. They were cigar shaped, dull gray, in minimal contrast to the surrounding water. The picture was a photograph of his future ship. Soon it would put to sea, and soon after that he would board it and make it his own. Together he and that ship would make history.

The blue laser locked onto the hull steaming slowly in front of them. The heads-up display pointed in the direction of the vessel, the range indicator showing the target only two hundred meters ahead.

Chu throttled up and the submersible accelerated until he felt the shaking of the craft in the wake of the big submarine. The screw, more of a water-jet propulsor, put an incredible amount of turbulence into the water, even at this slow speed. The enormous amount of horsepower required to push eight thousand metric tons of submarine through the ocean stirred and churned up the water for miles astern. Chu was careful to approach the ship from its port rear quadrant rather than directly astern. There a collision could occur from the unpredictability of the wake vortex, an unexpected swirl able to toss his small craft into a rudder and slice open his hull. Still the wake current pushed him downward, then upward, the computer correcting the ship's attitude.

Above Chu's head in the hemispherical view port the blue Pacific waves washed gently across his field of vision. The target ship was still not visible despite the clearness of the water. He had no need for the high-intensity spotlights so close to the surface, but although visibility was up to fifty meters, he still could see only blue haze ahead.

The blue laser range count came steadily down to a hundred meters, then eighty, soon sixty. Chu strained his eyes looking for the stern of the submarine. As his eyes began to water, Chu blinking it away, he thought he saw something, but it was not above, where he'd expected it, but deeper. He swallowed, staring at the sheer size of the hull approaching in the blue fog around him. The hull diameter was much bigger than he'd expected, even though he knew every dimension, every available bit of data in existence about the Rising Sun. But it was one thing to know something intellectually, quite another to experience it in person, especially like this. Chu

swallowed and concentrated, pulling his control yoke upward to ascend closer to the surface.

The heads-up display showed him at ten clicks, jogging
speed, which was a disadvantage if the wake of the propulsor water jet pushed his submersible harder than his
onboard computer could accept. A stray current from
the wake could force him to surface and make him
broach, a potential disaster. Being observed from a periscope was hardly a way to sneak up on a target submarine. And he was so shallow that his speed didn't afford
much control here, where the Bernoulli suction force
from the broad expanse of the hull would compete with
the suction from the surface above. The submersible
could either broach or slam into the submarine hull,
both accidents having the potential to ruin the surprise.

Chu felt like he was walking a tightrope, failure on
either side. The odds were against him, but he had done
this before, a hundred times. He had logged over two
dozen dockings with the practice target submarines,
some deep, some at mast-broach depth, some fast, others
hovering, and over two hundred dockings in the simula-
tor at the Lushun base, and one actual successful approach on the Korean submarine. He could do this, he
promised himself.

He brought the submersible higher, driving forward,
beginning to overtake the slow submarine. The huge ship
wallowed at mast-broach depth, rocking gently from side
to side in the one-meter swells. It was time to put the
Red Dagger in the danger zone, the narrow throat of
water between the sub's top hull deck and the surface.
He felt completely one with the submersible, its onboard
computer an extension of himself. His eyes were wide,
his nostrils flared, his forehead beaded with sweat, his
breathing coming in gasps, an athlete running for the
goal line. The view port showed the gray hull below him,
looking like the top surface of a dolphin, the same coloring and texture. The silvery glint of the waves above him
suddenly changed to a bright white. The dull gray of the
submarine hull showed sharp lines of light shimmering
over its surface, as if Chu were looking at the bottom

of a swimming pool, the bright web of light moving and changing with the sunshine. The sun must have appeared from behind a cloud, Chu thought in the back of his mind.

A rivulet of sweat ran into his eye, forcing him to blink it away. He gritted his teeth, edging the ship deeper as he felt it start to stray toward the waves overhead. Just as he evaded the suction pulling him upward, the suction of the hull pulled him back down. All this depth-control struggle would exhaust the onboard coils if he couldn't complete the rendezvous in a few moments. Again Chu wiped his mind blank—only the waves above, the sub below, and the heads-up display constituting his world. For the first time since putting the submersible between the sub and the surface, he allowed himself to read the digits of the heads-up display. One number of the display read off the range to the aft lip of the sub's fin. The second number showed him the distance to the aft escape trunk hatch just forward of the X-tail.

The display numerals confused Chu for a moment. The distance to the escape hatch was negative—he had gone too far. The fin trailing edge was far ahead, but the escape trunk was behind him. The aft part of the submersible hull would actually be between the surfaces of the X-tail when the docking skirt was over the escape trunk—at least it would be if Mai's data were correct. Chu throttled back, allowing the submarine to surge slightly ahead. With the after escape hatch this close to the X-tail and the suction of the propulsor, the approach was much more difficult than it had been to the Korean ship, where the hatch had been far forward of the screw. At least this ship had a thicker anechoic coating, the dolphin skin, designed to minimize drag and reflected sonar noise. It would provide a rubbery cushion in the event Chu smashed down onto the hull. Perhaps, he thought, it would be better to do that than prolong this energy-wasting dance with the submarine.

The numerals of the display rolled back until the docking skirt was within two meters of the calculated position of the hatch. Chu energized the bottom-scanning video camera at the docking skirt, looking for the hatch, and then released control of the submersible to the onboard computer to allow it to bring the vessel in for the docking. But as Chu released the yoke, the *Red Dagger* began to shake and oscillate, finally heading for the surface, then plunging toward the deck. Chu cursed and grabbed the yoke, frustrated and angry. The computer had failed him, and the dolphin skin surface of the ship was making the location of the hatch impossible to see.

Chu put the submersible close to the fin and again slowed down, this time knowing he would have to approach the hatch on his own. After five exhausting minutes he worked the submersible back to where it had been before, keeping station over the sub's escape hatch. He drove the craft on while searching the video image for the hatch. The more he tried to do it, though, the harder it got to control the submersible. Lo Sun would have to help him.

"Mr. First, quickly, do you have the docking-skirt video up?"

"Yes, Ad—"

"Fine, you talk me into the hatch. I can't maneuver and look for the hatch at the same time. Computer's broken. Hurry!"

"You're at plus two, starboard one point six—"

"Dammit, just tell me how much to come left or right—"

"Back slow, come left, just a hair, good, ahead a half meter, more, more. Now! Down!"

Chu brought the vessel down to the deck of the submarine, the contact light, the surface of the sub rubbery.

"No, now we're too far ahead. Don't pump down yet. Can you back us up? You've got ten centimeters, maybe less."

Chu pulled back on the throttle, the suction from the sub keeping him down, the submersible sliding in increments until Lo called that he was centered over the hatch. Chu flooded the small ballast tank, trimming the vessel heavy so that it would stay down on the slippery hull. A high-pressure air bottle pushed air into the skirt and water out of a slot at the skirt bottom. The pump, at deeper depths, would suck the water overboard and allow the space to be filled with air. Since they were shallow, the air pressure alone pushed the water out.

The heads-up display showed the vacuum established. He should be able to kill the engines, the powerful suction from the docking skirt keeping the two ships together. Chu gently pulled back on the throttle until the engines were idling. He kept waiting for the disaster of the skirt failing or flooding, eliminating the link between the vessels, but the vacuum held. At last Chu cut the motors and toggled off the coil power, unbuckled his harness, and withdrew from the control couch. When he stood, shaking out his cramped limbs, he found he was soaked from head to toe with sweat. He wiped his forehead and accepted a towel and water bottle from one of his men.

Lo waggled his hands to loosen them up after spending the last hour pointing at display panels. Other than Chu and Lo and Wang—the pilot who would shut the hatches after the platoon invaded and then who would take the *Red Dagger* back to the seaplane—the men were all wearing their masks and scuba bottles. The canned air would prevent the men from breathing radioactive dust or steam from the reactor spaces. Once they were in the habitable command compartment forward, they would ditch the masks. Chu and Lo shrugged into their gear.

"Open the hatch," Chu said.

As Lo undogged the hatch, a hiss of compressed air leaked in from the docking skirt. He unlatched the heavy hatch, and the spring force pushed it slowly upward to the open latch. Down below a half meter, inside the wide docking skirt, the rubbery gray skin of the submarine glistened with droplets, a neat circle carved in the hull outlining the hatch. In the center of the circle was the expected hole for insertion of the ISO key. Lo handed the key to Chu like a nurse passing a scalpel.

Chu inserted it and began to spin it clockwise—the opposite direction to a normal valve—and had a bad moment when nothing happened. Could the Japanese have chained and locked the hatch? It would seem to make sense, since this was an entry into a radioactive space with the reactor operating. But if it was locked, the only way in would be with an acetylene torch, which Chu did not have.

Then the hatch budged, just a hair. He looked up at Lo, keeping his expression one of calm and authority.

"Ready, First?"

Lo Sun took a deep breath, put on his mask, and looked over at the other men. "Ready, Admiral. Let's steal a submarine."

"Set event time zero. Insert on my mark," Chu commanded. He donned his own air mask, the men gathering close to the hatch. "Three, two, one, go!"

Chu pulled the hatch fully open, his eyes wide in expectation.

CHAPTER 3

The hatch clicked into the open latch. The hot, stuffy air from down below rose into the clammy cold of the submersible's atmosphere. There was no light coming from the opening, just a dark, gaping maw.

Chu snapped on his vest flashlight button, the beam shining out from his chest. He strapped on a headband light and adjusted it downward. He could feel his heart pounding in his chest and in his ears, his breathing loud in the air mask. He would enter the hatchway first, then Lo Sun, then the other six men. The crew was smaller than on the Korean attack mission. The highly automated Rising Sun submarine required only a few men to operate her, using only one small habitable space. Chu's former crew members were now lending their experience to the other five submersible teams.

The hatch led to the diesel-battery compartment, aft of the reactor compartment, and there was no shielding from the operating reactor here. Unfortunately, they could not make an entry into the forward escape hatch, because the distance between the hatch and the forward edge of the fin was too short—the submersible would not fit without colliding with the fin. They'd have to shut down the reactor since they could not survive the radiation, thereby alerting the Japanese crew. But there was nothing he could do about it. They'd have to run the risk.

An image loomed in his mind of an experiment commissioned by the PLA Navy Medical Command to see what would happen to a man entering an operating reactor space. A video had shown a prisoner from the civil war left at the Wuhan Electrical Generating Station's reactor-compartment door. Motivated by some hidden leverage—family members in prison, promised humane treatment perhaps—the prisoner opened the hatch and entered the containment, where the reactor churned out hot, pressurized water for the power plant as well as a tremendous flux of gamma rays and neutrons and alpha particles. As the prisoner descended the ladder, the hair on top of his head immediately stood on end. At the bottom of the ladder the man's scrawny frame had become chunky, his bony face filling out until his cheeks bulged, the prisoner swelling quickly, liquid rushing to his radiation-damaged tissue while gas pockets grew inside him.

The enlarged prisoner limped as he dismounted the ladder, suddenly stumbling and blind, feeling his way with one grotesquely swollen hand, his other on his eyes. The prisoner's skin steadily changed from a pale to a deep purple shade. The man, becoming nearly spherical from the swelling, sank to his knees, his skin black, his eyes swollen shut, his face toward the lower-level camera. In the next moment he literally exploded, the gases inside him blowing his body apart, blood and organs flying from his abdominal cavity.

Chu lowered himself into the hatch, his boot finding a ladder rung. He descended into the darkness, his head-band light showing a narrow vertical tunnel with only a ladder, some cables and pipes. The tunnel was faired in with sheet metal, polished aluminum from the look of it. The tunnel was still too dark to tell how far down it went.

Chu stopped just below the hatchway, looking for the emergency cutoff switch for the reactor. Intelligence data had indicated that the trip switch would be a large T-handle, although the manual was vague about its exact location. There was also an automatic reactor-kill circuit wired to the hatch itself so that anyone opening it while the reactor was running would trip the reactor. This was only for someone standing on the deck while the ship was at the pier, though. The circuit would typically be disabled at sea—after all, who would expect an outer hatch to be opened when the ship was submerged? And so, for all Chu knew, the reactor had continued to operate as he came in. It would irradiate him with a lethal dose of gamma and neutron radiation until he found the cursed kill switch.

He spun around, one hand on the ladder, the other feeling for a switch. Near the hatch hinge he thought he felt something, and found a rotary switch. Yet in the flashlight beam it looked nothing like the intelligence manual's sketch of the reactor-kill switch. It was most likely the tunnel light switch, and it might set off some kind of alarm or intercom circuit, blowing their surprise.

To his right, Chu's light beam illuminated a computer display panel. There was an electronic eye, several small display screens, a keypad, and a row of variable-function keys. Chu turned away from it. The emergency switch should be located somewhere at the hatch opening. It would be large, with red coloring or yellow and black stripes, not just a computer panel. Unless this hull was different from the intelligence manual, he thought with a surge of dread, with no emergency cutoff lever.

He tilted his head up, the circle of light from above showing Lo's torso leaning down. Chu's eye followed the outside periphery of the hatchway. Finally he found a protruding panel opposite the hinge spring, a T-handle painted bright red with Japanese symbols next to it.

Chu reached for the cutoff lever and tried to turn it. Nothing happened. The switch wouldn't move. He looked at the writing by the switch, forced himself to concentrate, and realized his mistake. The switch had to be pulled far out before being rotated. He pulled and turned it, listening hard for changes to see if he had tripped out the reactor, but nothing seemed different. Maybe the plant had tripped itself off when he first opened the hatch.

But even if it had, he remained in danger. The unshielded reactor would drop only to six percent power even after being tripped. The radiation coming from it would be less intense, but still lethal, as the reactions calmed down in the core. It would take years for a reactor's radiation to reach "safe" levels and in the hours after tripping it, a lethal dose of radiation would be absorbed in just a fraction of an hour. Chu and his team had mere minutes to make it to the forward compartment, on the other side of the radiation shielding.

"Insert! Let's go," Chu yelled into his mask microphone. He put his boots outside the rungs of the ladder and slid down quickly, gripping only the vertical bars of the ladder. The tunnel continued downward two levels, until the lower hatch became visible in a wider spot in the tunnel. He leaned down and spun the chrome wheel in the circular hatch. By the time he opened it, the remainder of his platoon had joined him. When he pulled the hatch up, bright light blasted into the tunnel from the lower level of the diesel-battery compartment, the space painted a stark hospital white. A ladder could be seen leading from the lower tunnel hatch to a catwalk-style deck grating.

Chu lowered himself through the hatch, sliding the remainder of the way down to the deck grating. While he waited for his platoon to follow he reached into his vest pocket for his AK-80, loading an oversize twenty-round clip. The space was cramped and hot, lit up with intense lights—for what reason, Chu could only guess, perhaps so that the room could be examined by cameras to make sure there was no flooding or oil leaks or a hundred other things that could go wrong in a machinery space. Above him were two levels of catwalks, with similar see-through deck grating. The area where he stood, at the centerline hatch stepoff, was sandwiched between the aft curving bulkhead and a large piece of equipment. It was either the emergency diesel engine or the battery housing, Chu thought, but there was no time to sightsee. Next to the hatchway landing was another computer display terminal with another camera eye. Chu glared at it. That had to be a bad sign. For all he knew, there would be a greeting party waiting for him.

The thought spurred him on. "Let's go! Move it!"

Chu waved the platoon to follow him down the catwalk to the starboard side, where the catwalk continued forward. Chu leaned against the weight of his equipment and began sprinting to the forward bulkhead.

The starboard passageway dead-ended at the forward bulkhead of the compartment and continued transversely back to the centerline. Chu rounded the corner and advanced to the passageway's end. There he brought his men to a halt. Before them was a large hatch. This would lead into the reactor compartment, on their way forward. Above the hatch was a large red-lit panel, Japanese script evident, the red light flashing.

"What's the annunciator alarm say?" Chu asked Lo Sun, who understood Japanese. Chu's expertise was Korean and English.

" 'High radiation area,' Admiral."

"Let's go."

"Sir, is it possible the reactor is still operating?" Lo asked, frowning.

"Doesn't matter. There's no shielding at this bulkhead. This space is as radioactive as the reactor compartment. If that reactor is up and running, we're already dead men."

He reached for the hatch-dogging mechanism and spun the chrome wheel rapidly, the hatch dogs slowly rolling back until the wheel stopped. Chu pushed the hatch open into the compartment, stepped over the calf-high coaming and into the reactor compartment.

In comparison to the diesel-battery compartment, the reactor compartment was stiflingly hot and humid. The space was as well lit as the diesel compartment, but the equipment crowded everywhere made it seem dimmer. Bizarre shadows were thrown by the irregularly spaced and sized vessels, pumps, and pipes. Chu stood immediately aft of a large tank, the curving flank of it reaching three decks high. This must be the reactor shield tank, he thought, the tank surrounding the reactor vessel, the vessel itself half the size of the entire inner hull. Chu ducked around it to starboard, but the catwalk ended at the curving line of the hull. He pushed back through a crowd of men entering the hatch, heading to port, where the catwalk passed three huge vertical pieces of equipment—reactor circulation pumps, according to the intel manual—and continued forward. The catwalk grew narrow and serpentine, going around what Chu knew to be the liquid metal surge vessel, then forward between the four steam generator vessels to the forward bulkhead. The forward bulkhead, which would lead to the steam compartment, was crowded with tanks and pipes. Tucked between them was another large hatch. Chu had reached for hatch dog mechanism when a loud snap resounded throughout the compartment.

The snap was followed by several more. Frantically Chu spun the forward hatch mechanism. The loud noises were most likely reactor control rod-drive motors. By now Wang, the submersible pilot, would have shut the lower and upper hatch to the diesel compartment, and the automatic circuit would have cleared of its reactor trip indications. Either the crew was restarting the reactor or the computer system was doing it for them. Chu got the hatch opened and rushed through it, shouting to his men to go. Remembering the video of the dying medical experiment prisoner, Chu raced through the steam compartment, past the heavy equipment—condensers, turbines, piping, pumps. They had to reach the hatch to the command compartment before the reactor came back on-line.

At the forward bulkhead of the steam compartment Chu halted in confusion. In front of him was a hatch, but there was also a ladder leading to the catwalk one level above. And through the grating of the catwalk of the elevated deck Chu could see a second hatch. In spite of the need to get out of there, Chu stopped and forced himself to think. He realized he was breathing like a sprinter, his air bottles probably containing only minutes or seconds of air. He tried to picture the floor plans and maps he had memorized of the ship. None had shown a middle-level hatch.

The lower hatch should open to the lower level of the command compartment, where the electrical panels and the second captain computer modules were housed. The upper hatch must allow entry to the middle level, where the officers' messroom and staterooms were. It would make more sense to enter on the lower level, where the space was most likely unoccupied. Opening the hatch to the middle level, where all the hotel accommodations for the crew were located, would be suicidal.

When he reached out for the hatch-dogging mechanism for the lower hatch and tried to spin it, though, it would not budge. He motioned several of his men over, and together they tried to open the hatch, to no avail. The dogging wheel was hitting a hitch and going nowhere.

Good God, Chu thought. The hatch was locked, obviously to protect the crew in the command compartment. And with the hatch locked, Chu and his platoon were trapped in the engine room of a nuclear submarine with a reactor about to be restarted. Within minutes he and his men would look like that civil war prisoner.

A loud voice, lilting and female sounding but electronically generated, seemed to boom around them, but was muffled by the forward compartment bulkhead. Lo Sun stared at him with wide eyes.

"What did that voice say?" Chu spat.

"Sir, it said, 'The reactor is critical.' "

We're dead, Chu thought, as the hair at the nape of his neck began to stand on end.

Chu stepped back from the doomed operation to open the lower hatch.

The dogging mechanism had obviously been chained and locked from the other side for safety, and there was no way to shoot through or blast through the hatch, at least no way that made any sense. Even if he'd brought hand grenades strong enough to smash through the hatch, with all its lead shielding, it would have been stupid to use them—they'd never be able to restart the reactor and sail the ship with a gaping hole in the nuclear shield.

"Up the ladder," he commanded, dimly aware that his

voice still remained level and authoritative, despite the
mortal fear he felt rising in his throat, turning his stomach. If Lo was correct that the announcement had said
"The reactor is critical," the unit was spewing a tremendous amount of radiation even now. But a critical reactor was not the worst—the reactor power would increase
by a factor of ten thousand, maybe a hundred thousand,
before it was supplying power to the liquid-metal power
loop. He had to get out of there *now*.

He charged up the ladder, the third man up to the
catwalk landing after Lo and Lieutenant Li Xinmin. Lo
grunted with exertion trying to turn the dogging wheel
of this hatch, but it wouldn't budge. Chu bent his back
to the task, his sweaty hands on two spokes of the wheel,
Lo's on two others, and together they heaved. Chu gave
it every ounce of strength he had left, knowing that if
this didn't work, nothing mattered. This would be his
last act on earth. As he heaved against the wheel, he
wondered if he would see scenes from his life, as folklore
reported people did in the final moments before death.
There was no movie show, but as he stared at the un-
moving wheel, he did feel one regret, that he had failed
to connect with Mai Sheng. He abruptly pushed the
thought from his mind and continued straining. Finally
he quit, dropping to the deck.

"It's no good, Admiral. We're trapped," Lo said.

Chu looked at him, too winded to reply.

"Get on the wheel, each man to a spoke, and heave
together when I say," Chu growled into his mask
microphone.

He could feel his breathing becoming labored, his tank
almost out of air. He had pulled himself up from the
deck, glaring at Lo Sun for his expression of hopelessness. He had put six men on the wheel, stepping on
each other, six shoulders crowding together. They were
probably more interfering with each other then helping,
but what else could Chu do?

"Now! Pull together!" he shouted. The men strained,
their breathing loud through their air packs. As Chu

watched, disappointment and fear and frustration mingled into a feeling of pent-up rage. Just as he was ready to scream, two things happened—the men stopped, two of them falling to the catwalk deck, the effort a failure, and Chu's air ran out, the regulator wheezing to a halt, Chu sucking in his face mask.

In anger he pulled off his mask and threw it toward the deck, sweat and spittle flying from it. The mask swung on its air hose, wrapping around his neck and continuing around his head, striking him in the face from the other side. All of a sudden the answer dawned on him, and the answer and the comedy of his mask hitting him in the head combined to make him start to laugh, three quick, choked rasps escaping his throat before he clamped down, his men staring at him.

The answer was simple. Just as he had thrown the mask but couldn't throw it away, the dogging wheel was just as constrained. He'd seen the mechanism up close, and in the panic of the moment he had not registered what he was looking at. But now it was clear. So clear he felt like a fool.

A loud but indistinct voice sounded from the forward bulkhead as Chu made his way to the hatch.

"Was that the ship announcing system?" he asked Lo. "What did it say?"

"Sir," Lo Sun huffed, his own air low, "it said, 'The reactor is in the power range.' We're being fried right now—"

"Get a hold of yourself, First," Chu spat.

At the hatch-dogging mechanism, he leaned far over the chrome wheel, putting his face down to the hub. There a circular chrome ring surrounded the wheel shaft where it entered the hatch bearing—but only from the top did it look like a ring. On the right side a small protrusion extended from it, a small nipple. Chu felt the nipple, moving his fingers slowly around the outside of it. On the other side of the nipple was a set of gear teeth ground into the shaft of the dogging wheel, and pushed into the gear teeth was a single protrusion of metal from the ring. It was a simple mechanical interlock. The hatch wasn't chained and padlocked; it was just interlocked to avoid inadvertent opening from vibrations of the ship. All he had to do was pull up on the nipple and disconnect the key of the ring from the gear teeth of the shaft, and the wheel would be free to rotate. He turned the wheel clockwise, as if to shut the hatch, freed the ring key from the teeth, pulled up the locking-ring nipple, then turned the wheel counterclockwise. The wheel spun rapidly as if oiled that very morning.

The hatch dogs unlatched, the wheel spinning quickly, until the hatch was ready to be opened, outward toward the forward compartment. Suddenly their situation had changed. No longer were they fighting for their survival, running from a nuclear reactor about to cook them like mice in a microwave oven, but were now about to assault and capture a foreign warship. The difference was startling. They were about to change from prey to hunters in an instant.

Chu had to restrain himself from pushing the hatch open and bolting for the safety of the shielded compartment. He had to prepare the men, ready their weapons, and ready himself to attack. It would take only a second, but it was a second he couldn't afford to let slip by. He turned his back to the hatch, and eyed the men steadily while he grabbed his AK-80 and dropped his air bottles. The men, just as panicked as he had been, immediately realized what he was doing. Discarding their air bottles, they put in their earphones to their VHF radios, strapped on their boom microphones. Without saying a word, he looked quickly at each of his men, then turned back around.

He put his hand on the hatch, ready to charge into the middle level. On the other side a half dozen armed officers of the Japanese Maritime Self-Defense Force could be waiting for him. His heart rate climbed, his breathing coming rapidly. There was no turning back now.

CHAPTER 4

Commander Suruki Gama felt a sickness settle in his stomach like a cold rock. What he'd expected to be the most eventful day in his life—the maiden voyage of the Rising Sun-class submarine fleet—was in fact eventful, but in a hideously twisted way.

Perhaps it was the way the day had begun. The phone call that had awakened him at one o'clock in the morning started the day. The Second Captain computer system with its female human voice interface called him to tell him the status of the submarine. "Automatic sequence notification for Captain Gama. Please authenticate." The voice would repeat those words over and over until Gama spoke his rank and name. The call reported that the reactor was critical. It took Gama twenty minutes to fall back asleep. The two o'clock call reported that the reactor was at operating temperature. At three a.m. the steam plant was up and functional. At four the ship was on internal power, being divorced from shore power. At five a.m., with dawn's light seeping into the bedroom from a part in the curtains, the alarm clock buzzed insistently, and Gama, enraged and sick from the sleepless night, picked up the clock and hurled it across the room.

He had arrived at the pier and gone to the plate-glass windows of the concourse pier building overlooking the submarine tied up at the berth below. SS-403 was the hull number of his Rising Sun-class attack submarine. Gama had been given the opportunity to name the ship himself, and in line with the orders of fleet headquarters that the Rising Sun class be named after natural phenomena, Gama had given SS-403 the name *Arctic Storm.* There was something deeply important in christening an oceangoing ship, and this name resonated with Gama, for reasons beyond the grasp of his conscious mind.

The ship was a stubby cylinder, the hull extremely wide compared to conventional nuclear-submarine designs, and relatively short in length. The fin protruded starkly from the hull, its shape rounded and tapered aft, and it jutted impossibly high above the vessel, the fin height roughly equal to the diameter of the hull itself. Aft, the rudder was an X-shape, the surfaces of the X at once rudder and elevator plane. Other than the forward hatch opening and the windows set into the forward edge of the fin, the hull was smooth and unmarked, its skin slick like that of a shark, the material a sonar-evading foam coating over high-tensile steel.

After he had met with his first officer and spoken to the Second Captain computer system, Admiral Tanaka, the fleet commander, had come aboard, greeting Gama warmly, then leaving without saying much. Gama looked after him, knowing that the old man had lost his only son in the American blockade battle. At that point Gama went to the surface control space on top of the fin, and he and his first officer had taken *Arctic Storm* to sea.

A hundred kilometers south, Gama submerged the *Arctic Storm* to a depth of a hundred meters. Five hours later, the ship was taken through her paces, a high-speed, maximum-depth run, including a torpedo-evasion maneuver when the ship was under the control of the Second Captain system. The hull groaned from the pressure of the depth, the deck rolling deeply through the turns. A single tenth of a degree of control surface-angle error potentially could put the ship below crush depth, where the weight of the water above would rupture the hull like a steamroller crushing an egg.

An hour after that the ship had come to mast-broach depth to connect with Yokosuka headquarters for the video conference linking each ship's captain to Admiral Tanaka. It was then that the nightmare had begun.

The reactor had been tripped. Gama had broken his video connection and run to the control room. Strapping himself into the command console's cocoon-like wrap-around panels, he investigated why the ship had lost the reactor. To his back, his chief mechanical officer insisted on starting the emergency diesel, but Gama held him off, equally insistent that they find out what was going on. Finally he traced the problem to the after escape trunk hatch relay, which made no sense. The loss of electrical power from losing the reactor had killed the video surveillance system, and by the time it was back up, the trunk appeared dry, yet the lower hatch had registered being opened and then shut.

Meanwhile the ship began to behave oddly, acting as if the vessel was heavy aft. After three minutes of inter-rogating the Second Captain, the computer finally re-ported a sudden addition of weight near the X-tail rudder minutes before the shutdown. That weight had been added over the exact location of the after escape hatch.

Fumio Sugimota, Gama's first officer, had gone white, saying that it must be a DSRV, a deep-submergence rescue vehicle, that had added the weight. At first Suruki Gama had disagreed with him. The thought of some sort of commando force trying to take the ship was ludicrous. But then the video camera on the steam module middle level revealed what looked like a large group of frogmen assembled at the forward hatch, all of them carrying large machine pistols. In what was seeming like a dream, he found himself giving rapid orders to prepare to fight off an invasion of his submarine.

"Ship Control Officer, take the deck," Gama ordered Lieutenant Jintsu at the ship-control console. Releasing his five-point harness, he tossed his headset to the deck and hurried out of the room.

As Gama dashed aft along the wood-lined passage-way, the Second Captain's voice rang out throughout the compartment, "The reactor is self-sustaining." That meant the chief mechanical officer had recovered the nuclear reactor. Simultaneously the fans came on, their deep bass reverberating overhead, the ducts blowing frosty gusts into Gama's sweat-soaked hair. At least one casualty was over.

Halfway down the passageway toward Gama's stateroom, a few steps from the ladder to the middle level, he saw his stateroom door slam open and his three most senior officers burst from the room. Sugimota was in the lead, carrying an R-35 automatic rifle in each hand, as if he'd known Gama would come. Without a word Sugimota handed over one of the rifles and then followed Gama down the steep staircase to the middle level.

In contrast to the upper level's functionality, the middle level was more lavishly furnished. Bright crystal light fixtures protruding from the bulkheads near the overhead shone down on polished wood grain paneling and carpeting with a vine and leaf pattern on a blue field. The bottom of the stairway emerged into the centerline passageway. On the right, a row of doors opened onto the officers' staterooms. The doors on the left led to the recreational center—the galley and messroom, officers' conference room, and exercise area. The passageway continued aft to the compartment bulkhead, dead-ending at a hatch to the steam compartment. The hatch on this side was covered with wood paneling, disguising its presence.

Gama paused, aware that he was at a severe disadvantage, despite the fact that defending a piece of territory was easier than attacking it. He thought back to his days as a midshipman, his cross-training with the Self-Defense Force, dashing through a forest with a helmet, dark green facial camouflage, an R-35 automatic rifle in his hand. The whole drill had seemed like a childish game of playing soldier. So it felt now, except his stomach was churning with anxiety—anxiety that he would lose his command, the ship he'd been entrusted, the trillion-yen miracle machine for which he held absolute responsibility. That, and fear he was about to get killed.

Gama fought to clear his mind, to flush away such negative thoughts. No matter what, he would conduct himself as a commanding officer, the ship's captain.

His next order was made with a deep voice, hard as steel, without a single tremor. "First, stand by the hatch to the steam module. Navigator, take the doorway of stateroom three. Ops Officer, you take the doorway to the messroom. I'll help Sugimota. When these men come in, all of you shoot low. They'll come in crawling, expecting you to aim high. Everyone clear?"

The others were suddenly reassured. Off they ran to their tasks, unaware of the struggle Gama was fighting inside.

Lieutenant Commander Umigiri, the young navigator, looked at him with narrowed eyes, any fear he was feeling masked. Gama frowned at him, surprised that the youth could exhibit such self-control. "Sir, what if these are our men, sent on an exercise by Admiral Tanaka to test us?"

"Impossible," Gama spat, continuing aft with Sugimota. "I'd have been briefed on it. No more discussion. Everyone, take your safeties to the off position. Here they—"

Chu was about to shove the hatch open when a speaker overhead suddenly blasted out a female Japanese voice.

"The reactor is self-sustaining."

"What did she say?" Chu asked Lo, but in the next moment he already knew. The eerie quiet of the ship was replaced by a booming roar, coming from the overhead. Chu realized the air conditioning was coming back on.

"The reactor is back on-line," Lo said, glancing over.

"Hold it, men," Chu said quietly. Defenders might already be coming, so it would be best to enter the space prepared. "Weapons at ready. Insert on my mark . . . three, two—"

Chu was amazed to discover that he fully expected to die. Never before, not even when he had ejected from the exploding wreck of his Yak over Bo Hai Bay, had he ever thought he was anywhere near death. But now he could feel it, just on the other side of this hatch. Beyond was not some uncaring darkness but an ani-

mated spirit, ready to take him. It was as if a voice had
trumpeted into his skull: *Chu Hua-Feng is a dead man.*

With that thought he became filled with violent fury,
anger at himself, at this fouled-up mission, at the killers
of his father, at the Japanese, and at life itself. The anger
was like a fireball that burned him from the inside. He
sneered viciously, baring his teeth.

A furious scream erupted from his lips the instant before he smashed the hatch open with an explosive thrust.
He surged into the compartment, his weapon lowered,
the silenced rounds bursting from his pistol.

Just before the hatch, Fumio Sugimota lifted his R-35
rifle, his index finger just barely brushing the trigger.
The rifle's safety was off, the clip loaded, a round in
the chamber.

Suddenly the hatch exploded outward at him with a
speed he never thought possible for such a heavy device.
With iron force it smashed him in the forearm and spun
him around. Even before he could register the snap of
his bone breaking, the hatch smacked into the wall of
the passageway, then rebounded from the bulkhead rubber stop and cracked into his face, shattering his nose.

He had the briefest impression of figures standing inside the open hatchway. One of them let loose a rasping,
phlegm-laced war whoop. Just before the hatch swung
back in his face, he tried to raise the weapon to fire it.
He did not hear the thump of the AK-80 firing in automatic mode, the supersonic crack of four 9-mm heavy-
grain rounds.

He didn't feel the bullets as they pierced his chest, his
upper arm, upper back, lower back. It seemed as if he
were pushed, hard, back into the hatch, and then he
had the strangest sensation of floating, his body suddenly
boneless and unable to support his weight. He was falling in slow motion toward the deck, and as he fell he
looked at the intricate pattern set into the carpet, repeating dull-colored interlacing vines and leaves. He'd
never really noticed before, but it suddenly seemed fasci-
nating as he plunged toward it. The pattern expanded

rapidly and vibrated as he bounced once on the deck, then stopped moving.

He kept watching the vines and the leaves, amazed at how interesting the pattern was as a redness became added to it, a sort of paint or liquid spreading over the pattern. At the same time he noticed that he was cold, as if lying outside in the snow. The red then became a sort of grayish black, the dirty green of the vine a shade of light gray. The gray shades, synchronized, began to become darker together, the picture fading as if from a television screen that had lost its power, the view becoming dark black. At first the black was shiny, but then the shimmer began to dim until there was nothing but the dull liquid blackness, and the liquid gave way to vapor, until the blackness was nothing and he was surrounded by nothing and there was nothing.

The door crashed aside, taking much more effort than Chu had expected.

Then he saw that the hatch had spun a Japanese officer against the wall. Still screaming, Chu turned briefly toward the officer, his AK-80 pistol smoothly arcing as well. He squeezed the trigger just for a fraction of a second, enough for the weapon to cough out four rounds at the upper body of the Japanese man. A line of bullet holes popped red dots on his orange coveralls.

Instinctively the arc of the gun swung back to the only other man in the passageway. Chu had a split-second impression of a slender man, also in orange coveralls, with multiple patches and insignia on his uniform, holding an automatic rifle with both hands, the weapon aimed at Chu's knees. Chu's trigger, almost of its own volition, squeezed, firing three rounds. Bright red blood sprayed onto the man's torso. At first he spun a half turn, but then froze. Chu's sense of time had dramatically dilated with the adrenaline, and the man's collapse to the deck took what seemed like an hour. Chu didn't wait, he charged the man, still only a half lungful into his scream of fury. It was Chu's push more than the bullet wounds that dropped the man to the deck.

*   *   *

Suruki Gama looked up and saw his worst nightmare.

The hatch flew open so violently that Gama was sure a hand grenade had gone off, yet the explosion sounded strange, an angry human scream, a shriek straight from the bowels of Hell. The opening hatch pushed aside Sugimota as if he were a doll, slamming him into the bulkhead. A tall, thin phantom, covered from head to toe in black, burst through the opening. His mouth was open, his red tongue stark against his white teeth. A glaringly bright light shone from his thick chest, the glint from it momentarily blinding Gama.

Behind the phantom stood several other men in black, all clutching machine pistols. With that realization Gama raised his R-35 to aim at the invader's chest. Before he could fire, a hot razor sliced into him. Bright red arterial blood spurted from the right side of his chest. Gama watched several droplets of the blood fly up and outward, gliding gracefully toward the bulkhead, where they splattered, and Gama realized his view now was completely filled by the bulkhead. Somehow the entire room, the entire ship, had spun around, and the men from the pantry were gone, leaving him to a blood-splashed wall of wood.

The scream continued, and Gama felt something—a truck perhaps—crash into him. He plummeted to the deck, the feeling of heat deep in his right side insistent. It took quite a while to fall to the deck. As the carpeted deck came up to meet him, the room swiveled until the deck was vertical, turning what had been the deck to a wall. Gama stayed glued to that wall, oddly not sliding toward the pantry.

Sounds now, thumping, boots on carpeting, shaking the deck where his right ear rested. Coughing sounds, whooshing noises—bullets, he thought. Finally the scream from the first invader ended, replaced by short staccato whimpers from other men, one coming from somewhere overhead, the second from behind him. The thumping noises continued. He thought he saw a boot, close in his vision, dull black, no laces . . . he stared at it without blinking.

A hand on his cheek, the fingers blunt, coarse, warm, pulling his face over. The world swirled by, rotating around him. What was once the overhead of the compartment came into view. A black unfocused shape crouched beside him, the shape possessing two eyes, a slash of a mouth.

Loud guttural sounds from the mouth of the shape. Gama could not blink, his eyes frozen looking at the overhead. The hand on his cheek withdrew, and the ship swirled around again, until he saw just the carpeting and the wood in front of him, both beginning to fade in and out.

He felt his tongue fall out of his mouth, the fibers of the carpet irritating it. A copper taste seeped in, the red of his own blood flowing over the carpet and into his mouth. Still unable to blink, he lay like that until it seemed as if he were lying in ice water, the cold coming for him and finding him.

On the outside of his vision a border of darkness grew, forming a tunnel. The tunnel seemed to chase away the colors of the wood and carpet until they were spots of two tones of gray shrinking further to a small dot, the dot not so much winking out as swallowed by the black of the tunnel walls.

There was only dark, and there had only ever been dark, and he felt an acceptance of that. Yes, that was the word, acceptance. It was proper. It was . . . all.

As Chu advanced down the corridor, he looked for the flesh of faces, the black extensions of rifle barrels, the orange of Japanese uniforms. In the second door on the left side he saw all three—a rifle barrel pointed low, a pale face with dark eyes looking in panic up at him, an orange uniform proclaiming his position. Chu's reflexes took over, all the drills, all the simulations, paying off. Four rounds clicked off, puncturing this face, changing it to a red and gray pulp.

A sudden motion from the right. Chu saw another

figure, another wide-eyed face, another rifle barrel. Three rounds in the man's face, and the rifle barrel flew away from the body.

Chu spun around, checking behind him. His men had emerged from the hatch, moving slowly. Lo Sun was kicking open the doors on the right side close to the dead bodies. Chu turned back, continuing on, his eyes wide, his weapon up. There were doors on either side of the passageway. He slammed each open, weapon raised. Nothing in the first two on the left, a fleeting impression of berthing quarters revealed behind each door. The two doors on the right also revealed empty rooms, wider and more open rooms—recreational areas or dining facilities.

At the corridor's end Chu reached a door near a ship's ladder, a narrow, steep metal staircase, one flight leading up and aft, the other leading down and aft. He checked both ladders, then kicked in the door. Inside was a stainless steel and chrome bathroom, with three stalls, two showers, and three sinks. The open area was empty. Chu ran to the right, looking into the stalls, all the doors latched open, the room apparently empty. A door at the wall between sinks captured his attention. He opened it but found only the raw foam-insulated steel of the hull. Several doors on the near and far walls revealed only storage space. Chu turned and left, emerging back into the carpeted corridor.

"Li, below to the computer level. Take Yong. Zhang, secure the computer room. Xhiu, take the radio space. Lo, captain's stateroom. Chen, take the first officer's cabin. I'll go first and secure the control room. Upper-level officers, join me there when your spaces are secure. Report by radio in one minute. Mark!"

Chu grabbed the shining chrome rail to the ladder, spun himself around, and launched himself upward, three steps at a time, the platoon right behind him.

Chu ejected his clip even though it had a half dozen rounds left in it. He wasn't sure of the exact number of bullets remaining in the clip, and he didn't care. He would enter the occupied upper level with a full clip. The half-spent clip clattered to the deck far below, the new one clicking into place as he climbed the final steps of the ladder, emerging on the aft end of the wood-paneled passageway leading forward from the captain's and first officer's staterooms. He turned the corner and sprinted the five meters past the radio room and the computer room to the opening at the end of the passageway, where a heavy plastic curtain was pulled aside and fastened with a restraining strap. He knew the room layout by heart, having read and reread Mai Sheng's intelligence manual so many times he could reproduce it by hand.

The worst problem in hijacking a submarine was taking over the control room itself. Coming in firing could cripple vital equipment, leaving them with scrap metal instead of a warship. Yet coming in without shooting was suicidal. The only reasonable solution was to use surprise as an ally, assassinating the control room crew members before they could react.

He had faced failure and death fully a half dozen times today, but the next meeting with potential failure—and death—he feared. That he had beat the odds so far made this even harder. The submarine was almost in his grasp, and here he was, about to lose it all if just one officer in the control room leveled an automatic rifle at him.

His death would not doom just him, it would doom the mission. Not just the attack on this submarine, but the sea battle he had planned in the East China Sea. If this mission had a glaring flaw, it was that too much expertise was concentrated in Chu's own skull. Dammit, he cursed. One bullet, and Red China would never become the People's Republic of China. His brainchild would be stillborn.

The pessimism rising in him fueled an anger far beyond the moment. That fury ignited him as he roared into the control room with another evil shriek.

When Captain Gama had thrown off his harness and dashed out the door, he had shifted control of the ship to Lieutenant Teshio Jintsu.

Jintsu had trembled as he had strapped himself into the command-console seat, the leather of it still warm from Gama's body. His hands shaking, he had selected the command compartment middle-level video monitor. He had watched while the commandos had burst out of the aft pantry and gunned down all four senior officers. He heard the screaming of the first commando, a tall black-faced vision from a nightmare, the coughing sounds of gunfire, the horrifying liquid thumps of the officers hitting the deck, the forward-looking camera showing the skulls of two officers rupture, spilling blood and brains to the deck. The commandos worked their way forward to the ladder, and Jintsu quickly brought up the camera monitoring the upper-level passageway.

The lead commando ran down the corridor toward control—toward him. With only seconds left, seconds before death, a choked whimper escaped from his lips. Tears of fear and frustration streaked down his cheeks, Jintsu horribly embarrassed that he was disintegrating during the worst crisis of his life. He tried to think, to regain control of himself, but his thoughts spiraled uselessly in panic. Feeling detaching from himself, he watched as he slowly unbuckled the five-point harness and stood from the couch. He hurried around to the far corner of the room, the last seconds of his life counting off.

Teshio Jintsu looked around one last time, then shut his eyes, clamped them shut, and put his hands over his face.

He had a vague impression of a dimly lit space, humming with electronic displays, air blowing coldly into the room, a cocoon-like cockpit in front of him, the tops of the consoles a half-meter higher than his eye level. Two consoles were located farther aft, mostly obscured by the first. There was a console on his immediate left. Far over his right shoulder, two steps led up to the elevated platform to the first console, and behind it in the corner was an odd arrangement that must be the periscope station.

Chu's war cry died in his throat as he found himself in an empty room. In his all-encompassing first glance, his head swiveling from left to right looking for the Japanese, he could see the console on the left, and its seat was empty. What he could see of the aft consoles was likewise empty. He stepped up to the elevated platform, ensuring the first console was deserted. The periscope station was empty. He looked down on the aft consoles to confirm his initial impression—they were deserted.

His AK-80 still at the ready, he slowly crept back down from the elevated deck to the main level. He was walking around the tall equipment console of the first station when he heard something, a muffled wet sniffle.

He spun to his left. Ahead of him was the starboard bulkhead. As he walked toward it, he saw a cramped, unused space between the outboard console of the single forward-facing cockpit and the curve of the bulkhead's equipment panels. Stuffed into the space was a man—no, just a kid—in orange coveralls. His knees were crammed up under his chin, his body curled into a ball, tears streaking his cheeks from shut lids, both hands held up, palms outward imploringly, both hands trembling uncontrollably.

Chu's pistol came down slowly until the barrel was aimed precisely between the youth's eyes. He tensed his finger on the trigger.

"Mother of God," Chu said finally, holstering the pistol. He reached down and pulled the shaking kid to his feet by the front of his coveralls. He towed him out of the control room to the upper-level passageway. He dumped him back on the deck, the young officer still shaking, his eyes still shut, his hands shielding his face. Chu pulled out the AK-80 and put the silencer to the man's forehead.

There was no equipment here that could be damaged. Chu could put an entire clip into the officer and not hurt the ship a bit. The Rising Sun was now his. The men of his platoon had gathered at the forward end of the compartment, and Lo Sun gave him the sign that all was secure. This kid was the last obstacle between Chu and command of this submarine.

There was no way he could let the officer live. The risk was too great. There was simply too much damage to the mission he could do. And there was no time to deal with a hostage. Chu's op order briefing manual had specifically prohibited any commander from sparing a single Japanese officer.

Chu knew it was time to kill the officer. He squeezed his finger on the trigger, but stopped when the boy started to whimper.

The more Chu looked at him, the more he reminded him of Lo Yun, brother of his first officer, the way Lo Yun had looked ten years ago when he had been Chu's Yak-36A backseat weapons officer. Lo Yun had been twenty-three years old when he died, about the same age as this youth.

The whimpering continued. Chu's barrel remained on his forehead. His men looked at him wide-eyed.

Time to kill him. Now. One bullet and the mission continues. It would be quick. Painless. Over in a second. Just one more mess to clean up and the ship was his.

"Oh, fuck," Chu said, hating himself for what he was about to do. He put the silenced pistol barrel in the boy's right eye. He squeezed the trigger slowly.

The bang of the pistol was loud, despite the silencer. The youth's head exploded, leaving brains against the bulkhead behind him and blood on the carpeting, a raw, meaty, liquid mess where an innocent face had been.

"Lieutenant Wong, clean this up." Chu holstered the pistol and walked to the door of his stateroom.

There, in privacy, Admiral Chu Hua-Feng, current commanding officer of the MSDF submarine *Artic Storm* and admiral-in-command of a fleet of the most advanced submarines in history, bent over and vomited.

Five minutes later he sank to the deck, his eyes shut, his fingers pressed to his eye sockets, muttering two words to himself, repeating them over and over—"Good God . . . good God . . ."

*   *   *

Chu went to the control console. He had to loosen the five-point harness for his larger frame. The leather of the seat was comfortable, the arrangement of the consoles well designed. He spent a few moments scanning the panels. All of them displayed Japanese script, even the camera view out the top of the fin, showing the silvery undersides of the waves approaching the ship.

The periscope was down, the instrument's mast lowered sometime during their invasion of the ship. Chu had not yet grasped how to raise the device, nor did he intend to.

But that was the essence of the problem of the moment—and the problems seemed endless—getting the ship to do what Chu wanted it to do. This vessel had very few knobs, control yokes, function keys, or dedicated instrument dials, just a cluster of computer workstations. All were characterized by an arrangement of high-definition flat-panel and holographic displays. This was not a ship that he could treat like the Korean vessel, finding a tersely written procedure in a dog-eared manual, then push some buttons, open an automatic-valve joystick, dial in a depth rate, push a control yoke to change control-surface positions.

No, this ship was completely commanded by the computer system. On the plus side, Chu had managed to raid the ship and take it over without a single bullet entering a computer cabinet. And without the slightest scratch to his crew. On the negative side, the ship continued steaming under the control of the advanced computer system, and the intelligence briefing manuals' details were sketchy about the system. It was either very simple to operate or hopelessly difficult. Continuing adding up the negatives, the ship was at mast-broach depth, shallow enough that a ten-meter-long pole—be it periscope or radio antenna or electronic emission-detection antenna—would poke out of the sea five meters. Which meant the top of the sail was only five or ten meters beneath the surface. Which meant an approaching ship could smash into them and cripple them, maybe even sink them.

So far this ship was blind and deaf. It was an unfamiliar dog without a leash.

Chu knew he had to get the ship deep and steam west, away from the Japanese fleet, now possibly alerted to the fact that their submarines were in the hands of rogue forces. He had to hurry.

Forward, in the computer room, Chu had stationed his computer expert, Lieutenant Zhang Peng. Right now Zhang would be speed-reading the manuals embedded in the computer software, paging through displays, researching the control system. It might take him weeks to understand how to give the simplest order to the computer, or even to become acquainted with how to take manual control of the ship with the computer out of the loop.

Chu ran his hands through his close-cropped hair, staring helplessly at the computer display of the fin camera. He opened his mouth to call out to Zhang, but instead checked his watch. It had been only three minutes since the last time he had demanded an update, and Zhang's reply had been the same one he'd given before that—status unchanged.

"Right one effective degree rudder, change course to one eight five, aye, sir," the Second Captain's odd-sounding female voice responded in Chu's headset. Chu had ordered Zhang to shift the system to English, the language all crew members understood.

Chu had retrieved the cordless headset off the deck near the console. It was a strange mechanism, with one earphone, a boom microphone, and a device that pointed at his right eye as if trying to read where he was looking.

A display in the lower center of Chu's console changed from a readout of tank levels to show computer animation of the submarine ahead. The depiction was strangely real, with waves that caused shimmering patterns on the sub's upper deck. The aft X-tail of the animation blinked, flashing red appearing on the control surfaces. The view suddenly rotated so that the observer looked down on the ship as it began to turn right slowly, from a superimposed line labeled 180, another line five degrees clockwise labeled 185. The numerals 185 blinked for a second as the Second Captain's voice again spoke in his earphone:

"The ship is steady on course one eight five, sir. All control surfaces now at zero effective rudder."

Chu wondered what his script read at this point. Shrugging, he said, "Very good."

"Seems to work, Admiral," from Zhang.

Inside, Chu smiled. The plan was working. It was time to drive the ship deep, then steer westward to the East China Sea and get out of the sea-trials area. The Japanese surface fleet would be coming soon, looking for their missing submarines. Once he'd made some miles east, he would need to communicate with his satellite—to tell the PLA Admiralty the good news—and with the other unit commanders. Then he'd instruct the seaplanes to drop their explosives and cargo of wreckage into the sea. They were loaded with oil tanks, pieces of fabric, scraps of plastic piping, some electrical cables, about a ton of floating detritus each, all designed to buy time, to create the impression to the Japanese navy hierarchy that their subs had all sunk.

More important than that was to learn the ship, how to drive it, how to fight it, and how to make the Second Captain completely functional.

He was bone tired, and there were hours and hours of work to do. But then, so much had gone right. They had done it, they had actually done it.

Chu felt like a proud father watching a son walk his first steps. His plan, his brainchild, was working.

BOOK II

STORM WARNING

CHAPTER 5

SUNDAY
OCTOBER 27

DYNACORP NEW CONSTRUCTION (NEWCON) FACILITY
PEARL HARBOR NAVAL SHIPYARD
PEARL HARBOR, HAWAII

Vice Admiral Michael Pacino lifted his eyes upward, past the flank of the submarine to the structure of the ship's tail towering over his head. The top of the rudder rose over seven stories high relative to the floating drydock's deck. The ship was huge and graceful from this angle, the clean lines of her hull and the sharp edges of her tail section making her seem to lunge forward to the sea, even suspended motionlessly on the dock's blocks. The new ship was beautiful, much of her Pacino's own design. Yet somehow today that thought held no magic for the admiral.

Pacino stood over six feet tall, thin and gaunt in his lightweight khakis and black shipyard boots. His white hardhat was painted with the crossed anchors and eagle of a Navy officer, three stars of his rank posted above, the legend below reading COMMANDER UNIFIED SUBMARINE COMMAND. He wore the three silver stars of flag rank on his collars, with a gold dolphin submariner's pin above his left pocket. He wore a white gold Annapolis ring on his left ring finger, a scratched and worn Rolex diving watch on his wrist. The skin of his arms and face looked tanned, but actually had been damaged from a

frostbite injury during an Arctic mission that had gone
wrong.

His face would have been handsome had he weighed
ten or twenty more pounds. As it was, his cheekbones
seemed overly pronounced, making his large green eyes
seem startling, his lips too full, his nose too straight. His
hair was white, contrasting with his black eyebrows and
dark skin, and his otherwise young appearance. Adding
to the effect were the deep lines around Pacino's eyes,
as if he had spent decades at sea—perhaps on the windblown deck of a square-rigged sailing vessel. When people met him for the first time, they invariably stared at
him, trying to read the conflicting signals of his age. His
tall, wiry frame, the shape of his face, and the tone of
his voice were those of a vigorous man in his late thirties, while his hair and skin brought to mind a fisherman
in his sixties.

Not that it mattered, he thought. He tried to force the
next thought from his mind, but it was impossible. He
was forty-five years old and he felt like he was ninety-
five. Today marked the one-year anniversary since the
phone call. His new bride, Eileen, had been driving up
from Florida to meet him in Virginia Beach. Sometime
after midnight on a deserted section of Interstate 95 in
North Carolina, a drunk heading the wrong direction in
the fast lane had struck Eileen's car at 105 miles an
hour. She had been rushed by helicopter to an emergency room in Rocky Mount, but by the time the chopper landed on the roof she was gone. The phone call
had come ten minutes later, finding Pacino at his desk
at USubCom Headquarters, plowing through his E-mail
so he could take some time off with Eileen. He had
heard the video phone buzzing and had clicked in, assuming that it was her. Instead the concerned face of a
North Carolina state trooper appeared on the other end.
Somehow Pacino knew what had happened the moment
he saw the man's face.

Since then Pacino had been sleepwalking through his
life and through his job. He had been the commander
of the Unified Submarine Force for three years when

the call had come, barely a year after the Japanese blockade. After Eileen's funeral in Boca Raton, Pacino began to spend his days and nights at work, in the office, in meetings, on his commanders' submarines, in training centers, inspecting ships, giving briefings on the new NSSN attack-submarine program, testifying before Congress. But he was conscious of none of it. He would wake up at three in the morning and run on the beach— seven, ten, twelve miles, until his chest was tight and his legs burned with pain. Then he would come back to the Sandbridge beach house and pump weights for two hours, then do a treadmill for an hour. His aide wondered aloud if he was trying to kill himself with exercise, but he waved the idea off.

He had met Eileen when he was in a hospital ship cot, blinded in the sinking of the USS *Reagan.* She had been the nurse aboard the *Mount Whitney,* and had spent her shifts and her off-shifts talking to him, bringing him back. He had been going through the most terrible time in his life to date, after his divorce from Janice and separation from his son, Tony, and he was certain that a relationship was not in his future. Yet he realized he had feelings for her long before he had set eyes on her. She was intelligent, funny, and warm, and he felt like he knew her—she seemed familiar to him after he had talked to her for only a few minutes. Best of all, she seemed to feel the same about him.

They were married at the U.S. Naval Academy chapel under the crossed swords of twelve of his closest friends. Life seemed perfect—he commanded the most advanced submarine force in the world, and he shared it with the great love of his life.

Now that she was gone, he couldn't seem to get on with his life. Eileen was his last thought before going to sleep, on the nights he could sleep, and she was his first thought when he woke in the morning. It felt like he had a case of walking pneumonia or the flu, a case he couldn't shake.

The only solution he could think of to make her fade from his life was to work twelve, fourteen, sixteen hours a day. Today was Sunday. Pacino had spent the entire day at the floating drydock, working, trying not to think.

Pacino looked away from the vessel and over at the walls of the drydock. The floating drydock was normally an open-box structure, with no top or walls on the fore and aft ends, but for this work the shipyard had installed lightweight fiberglass panels on the drydock roof and end walls. The panels did keep out the rain, but they had been installed for one reason only—security. He did not want any pictures taken of this vessel, not by the press, not by photographers in small aircraft, not by spy satellites. This ship was the SSNX, SSN for submersible ship nuclear, X for experimental. The *SSNX* was the first ship of the NSSN-class, in which the N stood for new, the U.S. Navy's uninspired name for both the new attack submarine herself and the multi-trillion-dollar program for several dozen of them that would take the fleet well into the century.

The terms NSSN and SSNX had never been replaced with the name of the class—as previous classes had. Usually the initial ship name would label this family of identical ships, as had the *Seawolf* for the Seawolf class. But this ship would remain simply *SSNX,* as Pacino had insisted, resisting the urgings of his staff and the brass to lend the program a flashy name that would capture the imagination of voters and Congress alike. Pacino had continued to hold out, telling the Navy hierarchy that this ship was too important to rush to a name that was wrong. Names were vital, he argued—just ask the men who had named the *Titanic* or the *Hindenburg.* So, like a baby that went nameless until his parents could look at him, so did the new construction ship remain, as the banners and signs read, simply the USS SSNX.

But even without a real name, *SSNX* was breathtaking, from her smooth bullet nose forward past her sleek, tapered conning tower "sail" aft to the raked-back tail fin with the teardrop-shaped pod on top, the tail fin rising up over the hull as high as the thirty-foot sail. As the ship progressed in her construction Pacino began to feel a longing to take her to sea himself, although command at sea was in his past. He was a fleet commander now. Yet the feeling of wanting to return to the sea was the only positive emotion he had felt in these terrible days.

He checked his watch, not surprised to find that it was nearing eight at night. He had been there since early morning, and with the frantic schedule of Monday meetings, it made no sense for him to stay. But then, given the choice of pacing the dock or lying awake staring at the ceiling, perhaps this was the best option. Slowly Pacino climbed a steep steel staircase to the high wall of the dock and stood at the highest platform to see the ship from above. The shape of the hull seemed comforting, the smooth bullet of the ship seeming to glide through the water even as she lay there, high and dry.

That was another reason he was here at the Pearl Harbor facility, fitting out the *SSNX* rather than completing it on the East Coast. There were too many memories of Eileen in Norfolk and Groton, Connecticut— where the hull of the *SSNX* had been laid down. He had insisted that the ship be completed in Hawaii, and since he was now the bureaucracy's equivalent of an eight-hundred-pound gorilla, the hull had been shifted to the portable floating drydock and towed here for its completion. The hull and mechanical systems were now complete; the remaining work centered around the electronics, the combat control system, and the weapons tubes. Once the latter construction was finished, the ship would be lowered into the water of the harbor, the interior work continuing for the next year. That gave him a year to try to rebuild his life before he would have to return East. Maybe by then he would be strong enough, but for now he would stay and finish this submarine. He told himself that when it was done, commissioned, and turned over to the fleet, he would step down as the admiral-in-command of the submarine force, and turn command over to Rear Admiral David Kane, the former commander of the *Barracuda*.

Looking out over the *SSNX* submarine, he wondered if he really should relinquish command of the fleet.

There was no doubt that Kane could command the
force. Perhaps it was time for Pacino to leave the Navy
altogether and turn his back on this part of his life. But
as he beheld the submarine, he had the undefinable feeling that he would be leaving something undone. It was
a thread to cling to, and though it made no sense, he
would continue on until this undone thing was finished.
Maybe, he thought, finishing it would give him the peace
he sought.

He was barely conscious of returning to the admiral's
quarters and falling asleep, perhaps even less of waking
up and performing all the rituals of showering and donning his tropical white uniform. In his office, he found
himself trying to concentrate on the WritePad computer
display on his oak desk, another meaningless memo de-
scribing a critical problem with the Cyclops command-
and-control system of the *SSNX*.

He swiveled his chair away from the desk and looked
out the window. The shades were partially open, the
glass polarization adjusted so that the bright sunlight
wouldn't cause too much glare to see the computer display. It was just after six in the morning, and the sun
was rising over the Pacific. Another hectic Monday
would soon start. There would be a seven-thirty staff
meeting, an eight-fifteen videoconference with the Norfolk staff, a nine-thirty videoconference with the Pentagon, a ten forty-five shipyard meeting, two meetings
overscheduled at noon, and another five meetings in the
afternoon. There were at least six hours of work Pacino
needed to do himself when the day quieted down, and
his personal assistant had requested the evening off.

The early meetings slipped by routinely. It was as if
this were a slow news day, little going on in the world.
The videoconference with the Pentagon seemed to confirm the torpor of the defense community. The Chief of
Naval Operations, the admiral-in-command of the U.S.
Navy, Dick O'Shaughnessy, glared at the screen, watching wordlessly as Pacino reported. The next admiral
started up, O'Shaughnessy barely nodded, then the next.
The reports were dry and boring. Finally Admiral

O'Shaughnessy, in his baritone voice, closed the meeting, wishing them all the best.

Pacino had been dropped off at the shipyard in front of the DynaCorp New Construction Facility, the NEW-CON building. He went up the elevator and down the hallway to the dock-side conference room, where the shipyard meeting was already in progress. The hull and mechanical engineers were standing to leave, all of them nodding respectfully at Pacino. The shipyard's traditional "crisis football" was placed at the end of the table. It was an old-fashioned leather football with the words CRI-SIS painted on it in white block letters, passed gleefully on by a department solving the problem du jour to the one presently obstructing progress. The ball was being passed from the weapons engineers to the electronic types, the engineers responsible for the Cyclops battle-control system, which so far was a dismal failure.

The DynaCorp vice president of developmental computer systems, Colleen O'Shaughnessy, was absent from the room when the weapons engineers left. As soon as she entered, she saw the ball, pursed her lips, and dumped it unceremoniously into the trash can. O'Shaughnessy was young to be a full vice president, Pacino thought, but that seemed more the rule than the exception with the computer types. She was at most thirty. Her looks were also unusual, in fact startling for the shipyard environment. Her passage routinely stopped conversations and shipyard work, though she seemed oblivious. She had black, shining hair, falling smoothly to her shoulders. Her pronounced cheekbones and arched eyebrows framed large, dark, direct eyes. Though she was of medium height, her legs were long, the muscles toned by workouts. This morning she was dressed in a dark suit with a beige blouse, a simple gold chain at her throat.

Toward Pacino she had at first come off as charming, smiling at him with a set of movie star teeth, shaking his hand firmly and asking after the progress of the *SSNX*. For a moment Pacino felt like he was shaking hands with a senator or a judge. Her manner was so natural

and confident, comfortable around authority. Not sure
who he was dealing with, he had been somewhat curt
with her, waving off the pleasantries and asking her
bluntly what the status of the Cyclops system was. She
had immediately shifted from charming to businesslike,
outlining the problems and the proposed solutions. Her
words were crisp, her thoughts expressed in complete
sentences, her eyes probing his for understanding.

Within five minutes Pacino had known he was in
the presence of a competent professional, and had left
O'Shaughnessy to her work. Occasionally he'd see her
in the hallways of the barge or on the weld-splattered
decks of the submarine. He had worked with her for
several months before the new Chief of Naval Operations had taken command of the Navy from the outgoing
Tony Wadsworth. On Pacino's first report, Admiral
Richard O'Shaughnessy had come up on the videolink.
The handsome older Irishman's features were oddly familiar, and then Pacino realized that his common name
with the DynaCorp vice president was no coincidence.
He had expected Colleen to mention her father, Pacino's
boss, but she had said nothing. Finally, after a shipyard
briefing Pacino asked her, "Are you Dick's daughter?"
She smiled shyly, said yes, and asked him about a shipyard problem, as if the fact had no lingering significance.
After that he had expected some awkwardness in their
relationship, but Colleen O'Shaughnessy was the same
solid professional every day, a reassuring presence in the
face of a computer system that refused to work. Eventually her connection to the Navy brass was forgotten, or
at least pushed to the background.

This morning she breezed into the conference room,
shot him a quick smile and a "Good morning, Admiral,"
nodded at the other shipyard officials, frowned at the
crisis football, swept it into the trash, sat down, and arranged her papers and WritePad on the table, all in one
swift, graceful motion. She scanned her computer display, then looked up at him as she began her briefing.

"The Cyclops hardware and software both failed the

C-1 hull insertion tests. We're at a decision point now," she said, getting right to the point.

The news was so bad that Pacino dropped his jaw.

"I'd never heard it was this serious," he said. "Schedule delays, maybe. Cost overruns, sure. Some loss of function, possibly. Capability restrictions in the first operational year, okay. But failing C-1? With the damned hardware too? What the hell happened?"

"Even I was surprised, Admiral," she said, her voice level, her eyes drilling into his own, unintimidated. "The hardware problems are major, but the correction strategies are straightforward. We're much more worried about software."

"You said you were at a decision point," Pacino prodded.

"Exactly. The decision is between scrapping the entire code and starting fresh or trying to patch it up. That decision is mine. Since we failed C-1, there have been other decisions, made by my management." She looked at him, one eyebrow rising.

"And?"

"I'm no longer a temporarily visiting executive. I'm permanently assigned to *SSNX* until the software commission is done at C-9. I'll be doing the coding myself."

Pacino stared at her, startled. He had thought her a business type, an exec. He'd never thought she'd be one to sit at a display and troubleshoot the equipment, much less write the code herself.

"You'll be coding?"

"Exactly," she said again, her favorite phrase. "I used to own the company that came up with the Cyclops computer system. The system is called Cyclops for a reason—that was my company's name before DynaCorp bought us out. Bought us and brought in their programmers. Now they—I mean, we—are going back to basics."

"How long to get this back on track?"

"Good expression," she said, standing and gathering her papers. "Because that's what this is, a train wreck. Admiral, you'll be the second to know."

"And who'll be first?"

Her smile flashed at him. He found himself looking at her appreciatively in spite of himself.

"I will." She put her bag on her shoulder. "By the way, I won't be attending any more shipyard meetings. No more admiral's briefings, no DynaCorp videoconferences. The only thing I'll be doing is entering code, eating, and sleeping."

"Where can I find you?"

"In the hull," she said, pointing out the window overlooking the dock. "Until Cyclops works, the *SSNX* is home."

As she swept out of the room, the wind of her passage lifted several fliers tacked to a bulletin board near the door.

Pacino drummed his fingers on the table. Then he stood and walked to the trash can. Pulling out the crisis football, he set it on the window ledge. He was gathering his own things when the yeoman came into the room.

"Admiral? Sir? There's an urgent videolink on your WritePad, sir, a Captain White?"

"I'll take it here," Pacino said. "Shut the door."

He clicked into the video connection, wondering what Paully White needed that was so urgent that he couldn't wait till this afternoon's scheduled videolink.

U.S. EAST COAST

The Lincoln staff car was not a car at all, but a huge four-door sport-utility vehicle painted a glossy black. The emblem of the Unified Submarine Command graced the doors and the rear hatch. The logo featured the sail of a surfaced nuclear submarine flying a Jolly Roger pirate flag and, below, three gold stars.

The Lincoln made its way north at one hundred ten miles per hour, hurtling past Monday late-afternoon traffic on I-95 outside of Fredericksburg, Virginia, heading for Bethesda Naval Hospital in the northern suburbs of Washington. The beacons of the Virginia state police cruiser ahead flashed into the cabin through the windshield, and the escort's siren blared intermittently to warn traffic out of the left lane. The windows in the back half of the car were polarized dark black, keeping out the sinking afternoon sun and enabling better visibility for the video screen mounted on the headrest of the right front seat.

Captain Paul "Paully" White sat in the rear. His service dress blues were not blue at all but a dark black. His three rows of ribbons on his left breast pocket were mounted below a gold submariner's dolphin pin, and a gold rope hanging from his left shoulder indicated he was a flag officer's aide, along with four gold braid stripes on his sleeves indicating his rank. His face was set in a dark frown as he watched the video screen, waiting for Admiral Pacino to appear.

Paully White had just turned forty-eight, a subject that grew more sore each year. Despite a chain-smoking habit he had recently gained ten pounds at the belt line, and was not used to seeing a mirror reflection that was other than thin. White had become Pacino's aide in the blockade of Japan by default, when White's position as the submarine operations officer of the aircraft carrier *Reagan* had made him the only fellow submariner aboard. The two of them were on the carrier's bridge when the Japanese torpedoes had hit. The sixth and seventh torpedoes exploded beneath the keel amidships, breaking the back of the giant aircraft carrier, beginning the list to port that would end in the vessel's capsizing. The eighth torpedo had detonated under the control island, slamming Pacino into a bulkhead. Pacino slid down to the deck, leaving a smear of blood on the bulkhead. As the deck began to incline, White lunged for the admiral, and pulled him into his arms.

Without conscious thought, White carried Pacino to the hatch and down four ladders to the main-deck level. Pacino's eighty-five-kilogram frame felt feather light in the wash of the adrenaline coursing through White's veins. He emerged onto the main deck as the carrier listed far to port, and for a horrible moment he was sure he'd lose his footing and slide to the edge and plunge the twenty meters to the sea below, but he steadied up. The noise of helicopter rotors suddenly roared from his rear, and he turned to see a Sea King chopper descend madly for the listing deck. White half ran, half limped to the open doorway, flinging Pacino into the opening as hard as he could, then leaping in himself. As the helicopter lurched sickeningly upward, the deck of the carrier rolled to full vertical. The huge control island splashed into the sea and vanished. In the end nothing but *Reagan*'s hull was visible, a deep crack extending from one side to the other.

The war had come then, Pacino commanding the fleet that eventually prevailed, returning him to the States, to peacetime.

A year later Pacino married Eileen and things had been as smooth as they would ever be at the Unified Submarine Command. Pacino worked constantly trying to get funding for the new attack submarine, the NSSN, and finally the unnamed prototype, the *SSNX,* was approved by Congress. The keel was laid at DynaCorp's Electric Boat yard in Groton, Connecticut, and Pacino was in his glory.

As if he had tempted the gods, his good fortune soon gave way to tragedy. White was one room over from Pacino's office when the awful phone call came late on a Thursday night. That call essentially put an end to the Pacino White had known.

White went with Pacino to the funeral parlor. An hour before the church service, Pacino insisted on seeing Eileen's body. The funeral director took one look at Pacino and without a word lifted the coffin lid. Eileen's body was unrecognizable, her only intact feature her hair. Pacino leaned tenderly over her, giving her remains one last kiss. White held Pacino's right arm as they walked through the rows of tombstones, his young son, Tony, holding his left, and White swore that had Pacino not been physically supported, he would have fallen flat on his face.

The next few months dragged on as Pacino sank deeply within himself. Each day found him worse instead of better, until White suggested a change of scenery. Pacino scoffed at first, but finally set up Admiral Kane as the deputy force commander in Norfolk so that Pacino could take the *SSNX* hull to Pearl Harbor naval Shipyard for its fit-out. White went with him, appointing himself the liaison between Pacino's temporary command post at Pearl and Kane's headquarters in Norfolk. White was the glue that had kept this together, but even with all the shuttling between the two commands, the force was beginning to suffer a lack of leadership. Kane was too loyal to Pacino to fill the gap, and Pacino insisted on spending his time with *SSNX,* refusing to come back to Norfolk and retake his command.

Then the call had come in this morning from Fort Meade, the home of the National Security Agency, one of the remaining intelligence organizations. In the reorganization of intelligence seven years before, the CIA and the Defense Intelligence Agency had been merged into the Combined Intelligence Agency. The National Security Agency had been tasked with eavesdropping of any kind, whether intercepting enemy radio signals or phone calls or computer network E-mails. Their tools were as varied as spy satellites and nuclear submarines sneaked into harbors with thin-wire radio antennae, even starting communications companies overseas. NSA had been targeted to come under the same reorganizational ax, to vanish with its functions subsumed by the CIA, but in the last instant the Director Mason Daniels had called in favors from Capitol Hill, and NSA had survived, even flourished, the budget meaty, the gadgets state-of-the-art. NSA was even considered a watchdog, an independent check, on the CIA. Mason Daniels had stepped down and turned over directorship to the former Chief of Naval Operations, Richard Donchez.

Donchez was the subject of this phone call to Pacino. White had been on the way to the Pentagon for an afternoon meeting when he'd received the call a few minutes ago. Donchez had been found facedown on the carpeting of his office, in a coma. He'd been immediately helicopter-evacuated to Bethesda Naval Hospital. White heard about it before anyone else. His first call was to the Virginia state police barracks, to get the cruiser escort up I-95. His second was to Pearl Harbor Naval Shipyard, to Admiral Pacino, whose closest friend on earth was none other than Richard Donchez.

"Bad news, Admiral," White said to the video image when Pacino's face appeared, the sunshine of the Hawaiian afternoon shining in the windows behind him.

"What, Paully, you heard about the Cyclops system failing C-1?"

White blinked. He hadn't heard, and it was incredibly serious, something that could derail the SSNX program for a year, maybe more.

"No, sir, that isn't it. I'm calling because a few minutes ago I got a call from Fort Meade."

Pacino looked up uncertainly.

"It's Admiral Donchez, sir. He's in a coma. They say it's late-stage lung cancer."

Pacino's jaw clenched. "How much time are they giving him?"

"They ain't sayin'," White said, his Philadelphia accent infecting his speech. "Maybe days. Could be hours. The attending at Bethesda came up when I videoed him. Said any family members should get to the hospital now. He could fade out at any moment."

"Have a car waiting at Andrews Air Force Base. I'll be there by the wee hours."

"But the SS-12 isn't back yet," White said, referring to the supersonic twelve-passenger staff jet. He'd just flown it back from Pearl, and it needed maintenance at Norfolk Naval Air Station before they flew it back.

"I'll grab an F-22 fighter. UAirCom owes me a favor."

Pacino's shoulders seemed to sink, his head to grow heavy. White bit his lip.

"I'll meet you at Andrews myself, sir."

"No, Paully, you stay by Dick Donchez. Tell him I'm on my way. Even if he's unconscious, you tell him."

"Aye-aye, sir."

The video image clicked out, Pacino hanging up on him. White leaned into the front seat. "Why are we going so goddamned slow? Tell the trooper ahead to kick it or we're passing him," he ordered the driver.

"Yessir."

The car, usually whisper quiet, rumbled with the sound of the engine and the road and the wind noise. Paully White sat back, deep in thought.

CHAPTER 6

TUESDAY
OCTOBER 29

Admiral Richard O'Shaughnessy answered the video phone when his aide, Lieutenant Doreen O'Connell, looked up at him and indicated it was the director of the Combined Intelligence Agency.

"Hi, Chris," O'Shaughnessy said, his deep baritone voice commanding yet matter-of-fact.

"Hi, Dick. We need to be on for three o'clock. My DDO has me scheduled later."

O'Shaughnessy looked at his watch. It was quarter to three. Chris Osgood, the DCIA, never gave him less than two hours' notice. And that stuff about the DDO—short for Deputy Director for Operations, Chris' number two at the agency—was their code that the CIA director had something that couldn't wait.

"Where are you calling from?"

"Car. I'm well on the way."

"You're not dressed," O'Shaughnessy said, amusement in his voice, noticing Osgood's pressed shirt collar and striped tie.

"What am I supposed to do, give you a show? And see myself on the evening news strip teasing when some idiot with a microwave interceptor grabs the cell call and peddles it to the evening news?" Osgood smiled over his half-frame reading glasses.

"Three it is," O'Shaughnessy said, clicking off. Standing up he said to his aide, "Doreen, I'm going running early."

O'Shaughnessy was tall, over six feet three inches, yet weighed in at less than eighty-five kilograms. He didn't look thin, but like the decathlon athlete he once was. He was fifty-eight years old, used to being told he looked ten years younger. His hairline was healthy, showing more forehead now than he had a decade ago, but the increased real estate was barely noticeable. His skin was taut, his chin strong, his cheekbones prominent, his eyes dark brown under thick brows. But, of all his features, the most striking were his ears. They protruded impossibly out into space. He had commonly been referred to as "monkey ears" in his days as a midshipman and later as a junior officer, though predictably they were never mentioned now that he was the Big Boss. He had once hired a new aide because, as he had told DeAnna that night, "Know why I hired him? Only one reason. He has big ears. Nothing shows good character like big ears."

He was a natural-born speaker. His voice was fully an octave deeper than most large male voices, the boom of it full and musical. He spoke with his hands, surveying his crowd, his delivery able to set up the most hilarious jokes, his expressions animated yet natural.

But when Dick O'Shaughnessy was the listener, his charm seemed to vanish. Those who had suffered briefing him had described his blank, penetrating stare, always accompanied by extended silences; sometimes lasting so long that grizzled war veterans lost their nerve in front of him. O'Shaughnessy had even become afraid of being lied to by his inner circle, so intimidated were they. He had tried to work on that aspect of himself, trying hard to interject warm words or sounds of encouragement when he listened, but more often than not he was listening too intently to remember to do that.

To lessen the intimidating effect of his stare, he'd taken to wearing half-frame reading glasses. For some reason, peering over the rims of the half-frames gave him a fatherly quality. He didn't use them just as a prop, however, since he genuinely needed the reading glasses now, the WritePad displays having gotten harder and harder to read with each passing year. Yet they illustrated another problem he had. He had difficulty hanging on to the glasses. They managed to disappear every time he needed them. DeAnna found them in all his service jackets, briefcases, lying around the house, yet they were never around when he needed them. Finally, DeAnna had ordered forty-five of them and distributed them to his aides, his personal assistant, his driver, placing five of them at his favorite chair, five in his staff car, three in his briefcase, two in his workout bag, five in his desk, and one in each jacket pocket. And still he mislaid his glasses.

After his aide left the office, O'Shaughnessy quickly undressed, pulling on the worn but comfortable jersey reading NAVY '80 and a pair of Seal running shorts. He made his way to the VIP entrance, then stopped to return to the office to pick up his bar-coded ID—absent-mindedness kicking in again. He had been stretching out for a few minutes when Osgood's black limo pulled up.

Christopher Osgood IV was young for the position of director of the CIA. Osgood was in his late forties, his hair slightly thinning, not enough to detract from his near-perfect good looks. Osgood shared little in common with O'Shaughnessy save his slimness and good nature. Osgood was an Anglo Protestant from Boston, his father prominent in Massachusetts politics.

O'Shaughnessy had met Osgood four years ago at the Marine Corps Marathon, run annually in the city in the springtime. At the time, O'Shaughnessy was one of Donchez's dozens of deputies. Osgood said he was a mid-grade CIA employee. He'd asked O'Shaughnessy to train with him, since he was frequently in the city at lunchtime or after work. O'Shaughnessy had agreed, and on their thrice-weekly runs he'd ask Osgood about work. Osgood would say a few words, mostly shrugging it off. O'Shaughnessy had eventually learned that he worked in intelligence, but had not gotten Osgood to open up about it beyond that. They contented themselves to run, commenting on the weather, letting their friendship grow.

Osgood's and O'Shaughnessy's runs in the last two years had begun to be more than workouts. Since O'Shaughnessy had taken over the Navy and Osgood the CIA, the runs had become intelligence briefings for O'Shaughnessy, and gossip mills for Osgood on Capitol Hill office politics. Occasionally, when something was up, Osgood would schedule a run early, like today. Calling O'Shaughnessy with only fifteen minutes' notice was breaking new ground, though. Something had to be up, O'Shaughnessy thought.

As usual, they started out slowly, picking up the pace only when they crossed the Arlington Memorial Bridge. Once they were past the Lincoln Memorial, no one near them, Osgood started talking.

"Something's brewing in Red China," he said without preamble, talking between deep breaths.

"What?" O'Shaughnessy asked.

"Armies are mobilizing all across the border. Seventy armored divisions, one hundred forty infantry divisions, support units all across the western border of White China. Four million uniformed men, all strung out along the border."

O'Shaughnessy said nothing, not wanting to break the flow of the CIA man's monologue. When Osgood had paused long enough, making it clear he had stopped talking, O'Shaughnessy said, "Sounds like the entire People's Liberation Army."

"It is."

"They calling this an exercise?"

"Nope. Nothing published." Osgood pointed to the right. "Long way? Around the Tidal Basin?"

"Yeah. I've been missing miles. They don't refer to their real exercises as exercises, do they?"

"Nope."

"So maybe it is just an exercise."

"They've pulled the divisions manning the Mongolian frontier. Airlifted most of them."

"Fuel for that must have cost millions."

"Yup. They pulled their divisions off the Indian border too."

"That was gutsy. Nipun in India's not the nicest guy, and he's spoiling to grab territory."

"We found out that all PLA military leaves are canceled."

"How'd you find that out?"

"Leg's cramping," Osgood said, which is what he always said when O'Shaughnessy asked a question that went too far. The Navy man smiled, saying nothing, waiting for the spook to continue. But he didn't.

"All leaves?"

"Every man."

"I hate when it gets cold early," O'Shaughnessy said as two pretty young women came jogging by from the other direction. Osgood smiled at them. They smiled back, then shot quick glances of appreciation at O'Shaughnessy. "Getting dark earlier now." The women were out of earshot behind them. "Every goddamned man?"

"Yup."

"What else?"

"All the airwing fighter aircraft have left the western and central bases. All of the jets have been moved east. All within a few hundred kilometers of the White China frontier."

"Another couple million in fuel. They flying around or staying on the ground?"

"Ground. Under camouflage tarps. In bunkers built within the last few days. In tents. In barns. Wherever they can be hidden."

"And other than that, all's normal?"

"Nope," Osgood said, his Harvard education sometimes undetectable amidst his yups and nopes.

The Thomas Jefferson Memorial loomed ahead, looking gloomy in the fading fall light and the overcast of the day.

"So what else?"

"This is Release 24." Osgood referred to the top-secret classification designating information that could be shared only with the president and cabinet members and a few select agency heads, such as the director of NSA. The only classification higher was Release 12, the president's own classification.

"Okay."

"The Red Chinese leadership has been evacuated from Beijing, lock, stock, and barrel. Beijing, governmentally speaking, is a ghost town."

O'Shaughnessy paused to think this over. The Washington Monument was coming up ahead as the path verged away from the Tidal Basin.

"This is no exercise," O'Shaughnessy finally said.

"Bingo. And you didn't even go to Harvard."

"Fuck you, Osgood."

As another group of runners came toward them, the two men fell silent. When they were alone again, Osgood started in.

"President's been briefed. She'll be calling for Pink's opinion."

Bill Pinkenson, the chairman of the Joint Chiefs, was an Army four-star general, a cavalryman, a tank guy. Pinkenson was of medium height, tanned, good looking in a baby-faced way, an amazingly gregarious officer, quick with a joke. He didn't have the kind of statuesque appearance that O'Shaughnessy had, yet once people met Pinkenson, they never forgot him. He was the consummate politician, and had been maneuvering through the Pentagon for decades, loving every minute of it. He and O'Shaughnessy had been close since the naval officer had first reported to duty in D.C., the Army officer having shaken O'Shaughnessy's hand at their first meeting. He'd insisted that he and DeAnna tailgate with Pinkenson and his wife, Jackie, at the Army-Navy game the next weekend.

"And Pink'll probably want your opinion," Osgood said.

"Mine? Why?"

"Because the Navy's going to have to weigh in on this thing."

"Back up there. You've got the balloon going up in eastern Red China, the Reds preparing to jump over the line and retake White China. Civil War, round two. Except this time they mean to win." The runners turned and headed east, along the mall, the Capitol Building a mile ahead of them. "Doesn't sound like the Navy's got much to do with this. Oh, sure, hopefully President Warner will decide to support the White Chinese, and we may even invade at Shanghai or anywhere else we get a beachhead. My special forces will be involved, the Marine Corps will be saddled up and put on the ground, and we'll start up the ships of the NavForcePacFleet, get the transports fueled up and ready. We'll even escort the Merchant Marine boys into the East China Sea. And of course, the carrier guys will get into this, flying air support for the beach landings. We'll have ourselves a busy time of it, with a war like this. But compared to the Army, the Navy's got an easy day. So why did you mention I'd have to render an opinion?"

"Think again. Something's wrong."

O'Shaughnessy paused, looking over at the Smithsonian as they ran by, the Air and Space Museum coming up on the right.

"Okay, I thought again. I don't see anything wrong."

"How about this? Why would the Reds begin to think they could get away with this? With your fleet and an Army rapid deployment force all ready to go next door in Japan, and the Reds are going to jump across the line and duke it out, force the Whites into the East China Sea? Just like that? What about Uncle Sam? Don't they think we'll do something? We'll bring our fleet up to the White Chinese shoreline, offload a bunch of Marines and Army infantry and cavalry and artillery boys, with our jets pounding the sand with all kinds of smart bombs, and the Reds will be smashed. Why would they waste the effort? And if they didn't see us as a threat, why are they doing this now? They would have done this ages ago. Your western Pacific fleet was all beefed up for this contingency, and the Reds knew that. So why, all of a sudden, is our fleet and RDF no big deal?"

Had Osgood been looking at O'Shaughnessy, he would have seen the admiral's blank, piercing glare. For now, O'Shaughnessy just stared straight ahead at the Reflecting Pool in front of the Capitol.

"Far side?" he asked Osgood, indicating they should either turn back now or continue to the other side of the Capitol block by the Library of Congress and the Supreme Court.

"Yeah."

O'Shaughnessy spoke. "Maybe the Reds believe they would overwhelm us with people—four million men to our half million. Their force is overwhelming."

"You don't believe that, Admiral. We disproved theories like that twenty-five years ago. Look at the war with the UIF—they outnumbered the allies ten to one during the Cha Bahar invasion. But our smart weapons and equipment gave us a force multiplier. Same thing here—"

O'Shaughnessy interrupted. "I know. I know. *I* learned the lesson. I just wondered if the Reds did."

"Sure, they did. That's why they've behaved all this time. Until now."

They ran in silence for a half mile, all the way around the Capitol, passing the Reflecting Pool on the way back, running this time on the north side of the mall.

"Maybe it's a bluff," O'Shaughnessy finally said. "Maybe there's a negotiation going on with the Whites. Maybe they wanted the Whites to see all this maneuvering."

"It's not that visible, Dick. We know about it because we worked like hell to know about it. I guarantee you this, it will be a hell of a surprise to the Whites when the balloon goes up. The Whites haven't mobilized anybody. It might as well be Christmas Day for all the lack of activity in White China. So this is no saber-rattling. And there's another compelling reason they aren't doing this for show."

"Why?"

"The Reds are taking too many risks. They've left their borders unprotected so they can mass on the eastern border. Deserting Mongolia's border maybe. But India's? After all the threats by Nipun? The Reds are blowing it off. Dick, Nipun could strike now and take half of goddamned Red China."

"Which means they're in a hurry, Chris. They'll attack White China and get their land back and execute all the New Kuomintang Chinese, and we'll have a reunited China to deal with. Not a pretty picture. And the Reds will do it fast. They'll take the Whites, or try to, in a week or a month, then get back to business as usual at the Indian frontier."

"You're missing something, Dick. The East China Sea. No way can the Reds dive across the border without you guys pounding them into the pavement. So why are they doing this?"

"Maybe they just think that President Warner won't go to war over this. They're betting that the U.N., the U.S., and Europe don't want to get bloodied in this thing. They'll say, it's a Chinese problem. Too close to Christmas. Too close to the next election. Too much risk."

"After Warner stationed all the ships and troops in Yokosuka? She's got enough troops and equipment over there to win a war, even without resupply from the mainland or Hawaii. I happen to know she's more worried about China than anywhere else, as much today as she was when she stationed the Pacific rapid deployment force there. Plus, Warner saw her only good results in the Japan blockade happen when she stopped delaying and got to business with the Navy. She's convinced now that if there's a Chinese scrape, there won't be any extended decision-making sessions, no encounter groups like before Japan. She's going in shooting with the prewritten contingency plan. She's going in immediately, and she'll fucking hammer Red China."

"I won't ask how you know that," O'Shaughnessy said. "Wouldn't want your leg to cramp or anything." Though he was smiling, he knew Osgood didn't curse like that unless he was at the edge.

"So, Admiral, same question, for the fifth time, to my

slowest pupil. Why do the Reds think they can get away with this?"

"Okay, Mr. Director. I'm stumped. You say President Warner will go ballistic when the Reds jump across the line. I'll believe you. You say she'll immediately commit the forces to help the Whites. I'll believe that. You say the Reds aren't doing a maneuver or a negotiation with the Whites. I'll believe that. And I'm saying the Reds aren't dumb, never have been. They have their problems, but they're goddamned sharp. So here's my answer—I don't know. The Chief of Naval Operations has taken your little quiz today and flunked it. The Department of the Navy gives up here, Chris. What's the damned answer? Why *do* the Reds think they can get away with this?"

In the following long silence they passed the American History Museum, then the Washington Monument.

"Well, Dick, the Combined Intelligence Agency gets the same score you got on that test. We have no goddamned idea why the Reds think this is something they can win."

Suddenly O'Shaughnessy felt tired. "Let's skip the Ellipse run and head back," he puffed.

"I'm with you, Dick. I may even just walk back on the bridge."

As O'Shaughnessy showered in his office suite, all of the details tumbling through his mind, it just didn't make sense. He and Osgood were missing something. Something important.

CHAPTER 7

Pacino hurried to the door of the hospital room and pushed the door slowly open to a dim room with a single bed.

The decor was standard twenty-first-century hospital, a nondescript wallpaper pattern framing a window with shut venetian blinds, the bed against the wall, the man in the bed resting on top of a white sheet. The patient looked small and frail, his coloring not much different from the white of the sheet. The room had enough machinery to be an intensive-care-unit facility, but was located in one of the nameless floors of the cancer ward. A thought came to Pacino that this was where the hopeless, the inoperable, were carted off to die, but he dismissed it from his mind and concentrated on the face of the man in the bed.

The patient had not stirred. For a long moment Pacino squinted through the gloom at the prone man, trying to confirm his identity, then with disappointment realized that he was indeed Richard Donchez. Pacino advanced to the bed and looked down. This close, Donchez's breathing could barely be made out in the quiet of the room, the only other sound a faint beep of a heart monitor. Pacino put his hand on the old man's sleeve, then touched Donchez's hand. The flesh was cold and limp.

"Uncle Dick," Pacino said softly, and when he heard the tremble in his voice, his eyes blurred with moisture. He bit his lip and swore to himself he would not lose control, not where Donchez could see him. He checked behind him, glad that Captain White had remained in the corridor. "It's me. Mikey."

The breathing continued, slow and peaceful. Pacino sniffed, standing over the admiral, his head bent. Pacino stared down, his eyes open but his mind registering nothing. He was lost in the long past he'd had with this man.

Pacino's association with Donchez had started even before Pacino was born. Donchez had been Pacino's father's roommate at the Naval Academy. The two men had progressed through a parallel submarine career, Donchez commanding the old *Piranha* and Anthony Pacino the skipper of the *Stingray*. When the younger Pacino was a plebe at Annapolis, he was called from his room by the main office to see a visiting officer. The visitor was Commander Donchez. Pacino was eighteen years old, his hair shorn, so skinny his ribs protruded, standing at attention in the presence of the commander. His father's friend had a haunted expression, and his voice was gravelly as he croaked out the words: *Mikey, the* Stingray *sank off the Azores in the mid-Atlantic about a week ago. We couldn't confirm it until she was due in. She failed to show up at the pier today. I'm afraid we have to presume your father is dead.* Once Pacino recovered enough to absorb the information, Donchez told him that *Stingray* had gone down as the result of a freak accident. One of her own torpedoes had detonated in the torpedo room and breached the hull. There had been no survivors.

Two decades later, Donchez was commanding the Atlantic Fleet's submarine force when young Commander Michael Pacino rose to command the USS *Devilfish*. It was Donchez who sent Pacino under the polar icecap to find the Russian Republic's Omega–class attack submarine after showing him that the *Stingray* had not perished from an accident, as the cover story had maintained, but had been intentionally taken down by a Soviet Victor III attack sub, whose captain was now the admiral-in-command of the Northern Fleet and aboard the Omega. The loss of the *Devilfish* in that mission remained information so highly classified that only a half dozen men in the upper ranks of the Navy were briefed on it.

After that mission Pacino resigned from the Navy, disappearing to teach engineering at the Naval Academy. There he was vaguely ill at ease, a void having formed in his life. Something vital was missing. He denied it to Janice, his first wife, but what was missing was the feeling of the deck of a nuclear submarine under his feet. He was at his worst when Admiral Donchez appeared in his lab one afternoon and asked him to take command of the USS *Seawolf* for a rescue mission. The submarine *Tampa* had been captured spying in Bo Hai Bay outside Beijing, and Donchez wanted Pacino to bring her out. When Pacino heard that his own academy roommate, Sean Murphy, was being held at gunpoint by the Red Chinese, he went with Donchez to Yokosuka, Japan, climbed into *Seawolf,* and took three Seal commando platoons into the bay to liberate the *Tampa.*

The *Tampa* escaped the piers, but the mission had just begun, for the entire Red Chinese Northern Fleet awaited the subs at the bottleneck mouth of Bo Hai Bay. He'd fired every weapon aboard, and *Seawolf* was almost lost, but eventually after the sinking of several dozen Red Chinese PLA Navy warships, *Tampa* sailed out into international waters. Some thirty Americans had died while under Red Chinese hands, but the remainder fully recovered.

As a reward, Donchez gave Pacino permanent command of the *Seawolf.* He loved every minute of it, until the ship went down in the Labrador Sea in a confrontation with an Islamic supersub. After Pacino recovered, Donchez recommended he be given command of the newly formed Unified Submarine Command, and ever since Donchez had been Pacino's mentor and adviser.

When the blockade around Japan was ordered by President Warner, Donchez counseled Pacino to run the operation from one of his forward-deployed submarines. That had given him the independence he needed to make the operation work.

Without Donchez, Pacino would never have risen to

flag rank. But it had been Donchez the man who was important to Pacino. When young Pacino had heard of his father's death, he had been set adrift in a hostile world. Donchez had stepped in to be Pacino's surrogate father. Hell, Pacino thought, Donchez had *become* his father. Pacino had not thought of him that way at the time, because their relationship had not always been smooth, but that was what proved how close they were— the essence of a father-son relationship was the struggle of the old to educate the young and the young to fight for independence. In hindsight, Pacino saw, Richard Donchez was more his father than Anthony Pacino could ever have been.

Pacino sat there on the bed, remembering, for what seemed like hours. Finally he pulled one of the chairs next to the bed and sat in it, eventually yielding to sleep. In his dreams, he sweated and twitched, the memories rolling by. As he dozed, the man in the bed remained motionless.

Pacino awoke suddenly, in strange surroundings. The only light in the dark room came from a single fluorescent fixture above a hospital bed.

He sat up, his muscles cramped. Rubbing his eyes, he looked at his old Rolex, but the watch's luminescent numeral dashes were no longer visible in darkness. He held it to the light, the timepiece showing a few minutes past four in the morning. He yawned, and when he looked down, he found himself still wearing the Nomex jumpsuit he'd flown in on the F-22 fighter, the suit sweat-stained and stale. At his feet was his flight bag, probably left there for him by Paully White. After a quick glance at Donchez, who still lay motionless, Pacino stood and carted the bag to the room's small bathroom. It took him less than ten minutes to shower and change into his working khaki uniform, then return to Donchez's bed.

The only indication that the old man was still alive were barely discernible sounds of his breathing and the faint beeps of the heart monitor. Pacino sat on the bed to wait.

He must have dozed off, for when he looked again at

Donchez, he was startled to find his eyes open, looking up at him. Pacino said, in a rusty, croaking voice, "Dick, you're awake!"

Donchez didn't respond at first. His dim blue eyes were rimmed with bloodshot lines. His eyebrows—barely discernible dashes of light gray hair—were drawn down over his eyes in a frown. Still, Pacino grabbed his hand and smiled.

"The Reds," Donchez said. Pacino barely heard him, the voice of an old man, all traces of his former vigor gone.

"What? Dick, don't try to talk—"

"You're up against the Reds, Mikey. Get in quick—ohhh," Donchez groaned.

"Dick, please—"

"They're getting subs."

"What? Dick, come on, why don't you—"

"Why don't you listen to me, Admiral?" Donchez said, his old voice returning, a deep strength to it, his bald head beading with drops of sweat.

"Okay, Uncle Dick, I'm listening." Pacino looked down with concern, both of Donchez's hands in his. The old man began coughing, a wet, rattling sound. His eyes shut in pain. When the coughing attack was over, his face had turned beet red. He gasped for breath. "Dick, please take it easy. What is it?"

"Reds . . . have . . . will have . . . nuke subs. Plasma . . . torpedoes. East—" More coughing. Pacino tried to pull the old man up so the fluid would drain out of his lungs. He finally stopped coughing, obviously an effort of great will. The heart monitor in the corner beeped insistently, faster and faster. "Chinasee."

"What, what did you say?"

"East . . . China . . . Sea. Reds. Subs. Get in. Fast."

"Dick, I don't—"

"See . . . see . . . enn . . . oh . . ."

Pacino shook his head helplessly.

"Ohhh . . . shawn . . . ess . . . zee . . . chief . . . naval . . . opera—"

"Chief of Naval Operations? O'Shaughnessy?"

"Yes . . . you . . . talk . . . CNO . . ." Donchez's eyes were shut in the effort to talk, deep lines inscribed around them, tears leaking, streaming down his face. He started to cough, then caught himself. He took a deep breath. "Red subs. Get in . . . fast."

"Dick, try to rest. Try to cough."

Donchez looked up, his eyes no longer even a dull blue but clouded over, milky, so wet Pacino could barely see the irises. "Take care . . . Mikey . . . my . . . son—"

A wet cough, and his body relaxed. He slumped in Pacino's grasp, and he laid his head back on the pillow. The heart monitor was faintly whistling through the room, the beeps gone.

"Uncle Dick. Dick! Dick! Goddamn it, nurse—" Pacino lunged for the call button by the bedside, smashing his fingers against it. Three people, he couldn't tell if they were men or women, rushed into the room. A stethoscope was applied to Donchez's chest, a hand to his wrist, a quick look at a chart at the foot of the bed. After a few moments the doctor stood and backed away from the bed. "What? Aren't you going to try to revive him?"

"Can't, sir. Orders from the patient. No extraordinary means. No CPR, no code blue, no respirator. You can see yourself."

Pacino blindly waved them out. He couldn't tell if they left. He didn't care. He bent over the bed, holding Donchez by his shoulders, saying his name over and over. He was dimly aware that the front of Donchez's hospital gown was now soaked.

He never felt Paully White's strong hands around his arms, pulling him up and away from the corpse.

CHAPTER 8

SATURDAY
NOVEMBER 2

ANNAPOLIS, MARYLAND

The early morning sun was just hitting the copper-roofed buildings of the Naval Academy complex. Admiral Michael Pacino stared unblinkingly across the calm water of the Severn River from the deck of his waterfront house. He'd stood there most of the night, looking across the black, glassy water of the river at the lights of the academy, watching as the rooms lit up one by one in Bancroft Hall, the dorm building, the plebes rising for their Saturday classes. Pacino hadn't seen the inside of this house since he and Janice were married, back when he taught fluid mechanics.

Balanced precariously on the rail of the deck, was a faded photograph in a carved wood frame. In the background was the tall, streamlined sail of a *Piranha*–class nuclear submarine. The sailplanes mounted on the sail gave away how old the ship was, but in the photo it looked brand-new, the paint sleek and black. White letters were painted on the sail, reading DEVILFISH SSN-666. Red, white, and blue bunting decorated white-painted wood handrails erected on the deck. Two men stood in the foreground, both wearing starched high-collar dress whites, black and gold ceremonial swords, both uniforms decorated with ribbons and gold submariner's dolphin pins. On the right was a young Pacino, his hair thick and jet black, his smile untouched by cares, his shoulder boards showing a rank far in the past, the three gold stripes perpendicular to the line of his shoulders. Next to him stood a shorter, bald man, his arm tightly around young Pacino, rumpling the younger man's uniform. Donchez's smile was broad and proud, a Cuban cigar jutting from his mouth. The photo had captured Pacino's change-of-command ceremony when he had taken command of the old *Devilfish* over fifteen years ago.

The dust on the picture had been removed by fingers, the marks still clear on the smudged glass. A half-smoked Cuban cigar, long cold, lay alongside the photo, next to a highball glass, the residue of bourbon stale at the bottom. Pacino wore the blue baseball cap he'd found in his dusty office, the gold scrambled eggs on the brim, a gold dolphin emblem in the center of the cap's patch. The words USS DEVILFISH were written above the dolphins, and the ship's old hull number SSN-666 was embroidered below.

He had buried Dick Donchez the day before. The funeral had been a crowded affair, blurred in his mind. Disconnected images were all he'd retained: the unseasonably green grass of Arlington National Cemetery, the colors of the flag on the black casket, the stiffness of the honor guard folding the flag, the crack of the rifles saluting the admiral, the television cameras, the president and cabinet members, staff members everywhere, aides scurrying around, Secret Service agents trying to look nondescript but standing out anyway. Pacino's friends were all there, flanking him, Paully White, David Kane, C.B. McDonne, Sean Murphy, Jackson Vaughn, Bruce Phillips, a dozen others. His ex-wife, Janice, stood on the other side of the casket wearing a simple black dress, her blond hair cropped short and worn straight, the kinkiness ironed out of it. Young Tony, his son, stood next to him, an awkward teenager in an ill-fitting black suit. As the bugle wailed taps mournfully, Pacino's eyes were downcast. Tony held him up on the right, Paully White on the left.

Afterward, a hand grasped his shoulder. A deep bass voice said in his ear, "We're terribly sorry about your loss, Patch. We knew he was like a father to you. I knew Dick Donchez for years in the Pentagon. Listen, De-Anna and I thought you could come over tomorrow. I've got some stories about Dick I thought you might want to hear. You okay? I'll get with Captain White about it. You'll be okay, Patch. I'll see you tomorrow." The hand clapped his shoulder twice, and Pacino turned to the tall man next to him, connected to the deep voice, O'Shaughnessy. He'd called Pacino by his father's old nickname. He nodded, unable to speak.

The dignitaries and staffers and officers and enlisted men evaporated, slowly at first, then clearing out as the sun drifted toward the horizon, until he sat alone on one of the folding chairs in front of the coffin.

He'd awakened in another strange room, the master bedroom of the Annapolis house. An unease gripped him. He'd dressed quickly, walked through his office on the way to the deck, grabbing the hat and cigar and photograph on the way. The bourbon had come on the second trip, and the third and fourth.

He felt a sudden urge to type a resignation letter. Why not? he thought. Sell the houses, take the sailboat to the Caribbean, be close to the sea, maybe feel closer to the wife and the two fathers and the shipmates he'd lost. The idea started to make sense. Then he swore he heard a voice in his head. A gravelly, cigar-smoke-laden voice, strong and certain and steely, saying only four angry words:

Like hell you will.

OLD TOWN, ALEXANDRIA, VIRGINIA

The house was painted yellow with red shutters. A bronze plaque was hung by the carved wood framing the doorway, pronouncing the house a historical building, erected in 1817. Before it was a wide brick walkway, the cobblestone street beyond winding through Old Town.

The house was tucked in with a row of other houses built the same year, fronting another similar row on the other side of the street. In the door hung an oval white pottery plaque with a single shamrock above green script reading O'SHAUGHNESSY.

The door opened to reveal a smiling woman in her mid-forties, attractive and graceful, her straight blond hair falling to her shoulders in a chin-length bob. She swung her arm around his back, pulling him into the house.

"Admiral Pacino," she said warmly, "it's so good to meet you finally. I'm DeAnna. I've heard so much about you. That article about you in March in the *Washington Post* was just amazing. Did you read it?"

A glass of single malt scotch was pressed into his hand. Then he was swept on a tour of the house, seeing pictures of their children on every shelf, every table. His eyes seemed to find Colleen O'Shaughnessy everywhere. In one picture she was laughing, her black hair was windblown around a close-up of her face, her dark eyes filled with mischief. In another shot she was an awkward pre-teen, her hair permed and cut strangely, her hand up to the camera in protest. He stopped at a prom photo, her gown flowing to the door, the movie star teeth shining. DeAnna remarked lightly, "Colleen is beautiful, isn't she?"

He found himself agreeing, adding that she was extremely intelligent. Admiral Dick O'Shaughnessy came into the room then, wearing a sweater and chinos, seeming imposing, one of the few men Pacino had to look up to, despite his being taller by only an inch. He smiled at Pacino, his hand outstretched, his handshake firm. In his face Pacino saw Colleen's nose and eyebrows. He forced himself to smile back, to engage in the small talk as O'Shaughnessy led him back to a study in back.

The window behind a big cherry desk looked out onto a yard overwhelmed by a single large oak, towering over the houses. Autumn leaves blew aimlessly in the fading daylight. Pacino sat in one of two overstuffed leather seats in front of a fireplace, O'Shaughnessy taking the seat beside him. In the fireplace several logs were snapping. O'Shaughnessy tipped back his scotch, then put it on a cherry lamp stand between the chairs.

"You know, Patch," he said. "I worked for Dick Donchez for years. I was his deputy for special warfare before the Islamic War. You know, he used to talk about you all the time."

Pacino looked into his drink, now empty.

"One time Donchez said you were the best submarine captain ever born, bar none."

Pacino made a sound in his throat, a noise of dismissal.

"He told me about your Arctic mission. I read the entire patrol report, the real one, not the cover story. I also read the patrol report from Bo Hai Bay and the Labrador Sea when the *Seawolf* was lost. I read the debrief from Operation Enlightened Curtain after the Japanese blockade. I couldn't wait to meet this great Michael Pacino, winner of three Navy Crosses, one of which should have been a Medal of Honor, according to Donchez. But there's something bothering me. Maybe you can help me with it."

Pacino looked up.

"The man I've read about, this modern-day Admiral Nelson, maybe you can tell me, Patch. Where the hell is he?"

"Sir?"

O'Shaughnessy stared at Pacino, his brows low over his eyes, the irises black in the dimness of the room.

"A year ago, maybe more, Donchez came to my office. Said he'd been diagnosed with terminal cancer. Said he had only a few weeks to live. Goes to show you what doctor's time lines are worth—he beat the hell out of that estimate. But he asked me if I'd do something for him. He called it one of his last two requests to me, said I'd been a great staffer for him, and needed two last favors. And here I am, I mean, what the hell am I gonna say?" O'Shaughnessy's big hands spread apart in a comical gesture of helplessness. "I ask him what he wants. He looks at me and says, 'Richard, you gotta take care of Mikey Pacino for me.' I bite my tongue and say, 'Look, from what I can see, *that* guy doesn't need *anybody* to take care of him.' He gets pissed off, throws a spaz attack, just like the classic Donchez of old, and just like the days when I used to bring him coffee, I back up and say, 'Okay, okay, yessir.' So then I asked him what he meant, what he wanted me to do, how he wanted me to do it, and Jesus, you know that crusty old bastard Dick Donchez, he just looks at me, fires up a cigar and says, 'O'Shaughnessy, you're a grown-up, a bright SOB, tough-guy Navy Seal, made CNO, four-star admiral, *you* figure it out.' I'm not biting. I mean, what the hell is he talking about?"

O'Shaughnessy got up to poke the fire, threw two more logs on. He went to the desk and poured more scotch from a crystal decanter, gestured at Pacino, who nodded. The Irishman carried the glasses over, handed one to Pacino, and sat back down.

"All he says is, 'Look, Richard, Mikey's not just like my son, he *is* my son. But I'm not gonna be here anymore, so I want you to protect him.' He points the cigar at me, and I say, 'Fine.' He gets up to leave, go back to his NSA headquarters, and I say, 'Listen, you said there were two requests. What's the other?' He stops at the door and hands me an envelope. 'Don't open that till I'm gone,' he says, then slams the door behind him."

"What was it?" Pacino asked.

"I'm getting to that. But before I do, I have to go back to my original question. Where did Patch Pacino go? What happened to him?"

"I'm not sure—"

"Yeah, you do, Patch," O'Shaughnessy said, looking at Pacino with his trademark stare. An uncomfortable silence lingered in the room, the logs popping in the fireplace the only sound.

Finally Pacino grew tired of the look.

"Sir, I don't know what you want. Maybe I should just go," he said, standing.

"Sit the fuck down," O'Shaughnessy said, cold steel in his voice. Pacino sat. O'Shaughnessy continued, "Two years ago, after the blockade was over, President Warner decides to push the SSNX submarine program, you're in charge of it, and it's kicking ass. Now, a year after that, the ship is pulled out of Electric Boat and taken to Hawaii, a zillion miles from the experts, progress is crappy, your reports don't say why, in fact, they don't say anything at all. You've deserted your command, your staff is doing your job for you out in Norfolk, the Unified Submarine Command is a shambles, and the entire Navy, Congress, and the White House want to know why. I want to know why."

"Sir—"

"Shut up, I'm not finished. Now I find out that *SSNX*'s Cyclops computer battle-control system failed its C-1 test. Which, as I understand it, puts the ship a year behind schedule. And I don't find that out from you. I don't find it out from your staff, I don't find it out from the DynaCorp ship superintendent."

"How did you find out?" Colleen, Pacino figured.

O'Shaughnessy reached below the lamp stand and pulled out his WritePad. He clicked the software until the on-line version of the *Washington Post* came up on the screen. He handed the computer to Pacino. The headline read:

SSNX SUPERSUB CALLED 'SCRAPMETAL' BY TRACHEA

Pacino scanned the article. Senator Eve Trachea, the National Party leading member of the Armed Services Committee and Warner's opponent in the coming election, had blown the whistle on the *SSNX,* saying that its computer system was hopelessly fouled up, that the submarine would likely never sail, that the trillion-dollar weapon system was a hopeless failure, indicative of the Warner administration's wasteful and unwise defense spending during a time of peace.

"I don't get it, Pacino. You blow off your command, you decide to work on your new sub program as your only duty, and you screw that up. Hell, from what I've seen, the only thing that's kept you in office is that President Warner liked you. I say that in the past tense, by the way, because she also liked the SSNX program, and it's not exaggerating to say that that submarine may cost her the next election. So I'll ask again, Patch, what's going on with you?"

Pacino looked at him, wondering why he was taking this approach. If he was to be fired, why didn't the admiral just get on with it? Then the older man's voice mellowed.

"Look, Patch, I know about your wife, Eileen. I was at the funeral. And I know you loved her and your life came apart when she passed away. I also know you tried to leave the Navy when she died, and that Donchez wouldn't hear of it. But he's gone now, and honoring his dying request, you're my responsibility now, besides which, I'm your boss. And listen, I know what it's like to lose your wife. Colleen's mother, Mary, passed away when Colleen was just eighteen. It was a horrible time for her. It was a horrible time for me. I never thought I'd shake it. I thought I'd live the rest of my life lonely and hurting." He leaned forward. "And you know something? It still hurts, I'm still not over her. I say her name in my sleep. But you keep living, and one day it gets easier. None of the pain goes away, it doesn't even ease, but you get stronger, you become able to carry a heavier load. And when that happens, you can move on. What I need to know is, for Admiral Pacino, when is that going to be? I can't let an entire fleet rust away while you pick up the pieces, Patch. So, are you going to get out of the Navy or are you going to be in it?"

"Well, sir," Pacino said slowly, "I think I'm leaving. I'll have my resignation on your desk Monday." He stood for the second time.

"Maybe you'd better look at this first," O'Shaughnessy said, a mysterious note in his voice.

"What is it?"

"Damn, I knew I had it here somewhere." O'Shaughnessy cursed under his breath, rifling his briefcase, his desk drawers, the cabinets opposite the fireplace. Pacino stood behind him, embarrassed.

"Hold on. DeAnna? DeAnna! Have you seen that letter?"

"What letter, honey?"

"The one from Donchez, the one he wanted me to save."

"Sir, what letter is this?"

O'Shaughnessy was half out of the door of the study, waiting for his wife. He looked back for an instant and said, "Donchez's second dying wish. DeAnna!"

She came into the office, smiling mischievously at Pacino. "Honestly," she said, going straight to a small side table, in matching cherry to the desk and lamp stand, "Dick, you'd lose your head if I didn't keep an eye on it for you." She shot a look at Pacino, smiling again. In spite of himself, he smiled back. "Here," she said, handing O'Shaughnessy an envelope. "Don't be in here too long, guys. Dinner's almost ready."

The door shut behind her. O'Shaughnessy handed the envelope to Pacino, who sat back down. The letter had been opened neatly along the top by a letter opener. The printing was unmistakable, Donchez's handwriting, cramped and untidy with his age.

> *O'Shaughnessy,*
> *I hope you're watching out for Mikey like you promised me.*
> *This is my second request. I expect you to take care of this, and I don't want to hear about it getting screwed up.*
> *The name for the new SSNX submarine is damned important.*

Pacino looked up at O'Shaughnessy. "I was thinking we could name the SSNX the USS *Richard Donchez,*" he said. "Not that it matters. But I'd still like to see it that way."

"Just read the damned letter." Pacino looked back to the page.

*You do whatever the hell it is you have to do,
O'Shaughnessy. I don't care what it takes, but you give
that submarine the right name, and you make goddamned sure Mikey stays in charge of it.*

The name of the new submarine will be—
Devilfish

Pacino coughed, then looked up at O'Shaughnessy,
handing the letter back.

"Well?" O'Shaughnessy asked.

"Well, what?"

"What do you think?"

Pacino took a deep breath, thinking of an answer for
O'Shaughnessy, then realized he didn't have an answer.
That Donchez would want to name the submarine after
Pacino's first command seemed at first a cheap gimmick,
something Donchez would pull at the last minute, but
then something clicked.

As he pictured the hull of the *SSNX* towering over
him in the floating dock, he imagined that she was christened the USS *Devilfish*. He could see the banners, reading USS *Devilfish*, SSNX-1, he could hear the shipyard
workers talking about "hull X-1, the *Devilfish*," and he
could see the documents, the procedures, one of them
in his mind labeled USS DEVILFISHINST 5510.1B, and he
could see the radio messages reading FROM: COMUSUB-
COM, TO: USS DEVILFISH SSNX-1, SUBJ: OPORDER 13-001 . . .

And as he saw all that, something inside him began
to move, to change shape. It was a feeling he'd had
years ago, the first time he'd read the orders from the
commander of Naval Personnel ordering him to report
for duty and take command of the old *Devilfish*, for the
first time linking his name with the name of that submarine, and for just a moment he could feel again how he
had been back then, long before any of this had happened to him. He had a certain something back then, an
attitude, a self-confidence, a cockiness. That was the
word. Cockiness. And as he imagined the *SSNX* under
the name of his old command, he felt some of that flow
back into him, just a shadow of what he had once pos-

sessed, that old certainty, this time not coming from his genes or his upbringing, but as a gift from Richard Donchez. He felt it fill his chest as he looked at O'Shaughnessy.

"Boss, we'll name the *SSNX* the USS *Devilfish*. And we'll tell Warner that she'll go to sea, one way or the other, on schedule. Trachea will have to eat that goddamned headline. And don't worry about me or the Unified Submarine Command. I'm on the case."

O'Shaughnessy smiled, clapped him on the shoulder, and the two men abandoned the study for the dinner table. The smell of the filet made Pacino hungry for the first time he could remember in almost a year.

But as the staff car drove Pacino back to the Annapolis house, he felt the cockiness leave him again, the emptiness filling him back up. Eileen was gone, Donchez was gone, and now, again, it felt like he himself was gone. Maybe it had been the scotch talking when he'd told O'Shaughnessy he'd stay, he thought. He wondered whether he'd been right the first time, whether he should resign.

He looked down at the gold embroidered ball cap. How would it look if instead of reading USS DEVILFISH SSN-666 it read USS DEVILFISH SSNX-1? Would it change anything in a life that had seen too many changes?

BOOK III

ACROSS THE LINE

CHAPTER 9

MONDAY
NOVEMBER 4

SHANGHAI, WHITE CHINA

It was a few minutes past two in the morning. A few miles out to sea from the shimmering lights of Shanghai, the Shining March cruise missile's onboard computer noted the stars' positions overhead, giving it a stellar fix. It was time to turn back west, in accordance with the mission profile. The fins in the aft part of the ten-ton missile rotated, putting the weapon into a two G-force turn. The onboard gyro rotated through the numerals, the stars spinning overhead. The lights of the city appeared in the nose-cone camera, the reflections glittering on the black water five meters below as the missile sailed west, throttling up to attack velocity. The airframe shuddered momentarily as the unit passed through sonic velocity on the way to Mach 1.2. Over the water, the sonic boom was unnoticed. The city lights grew brighter as Shanghai approached.

The target was within the city center. A palace surrounded by rows of fences, patrols of security troops, and airborne helicopter patrols. The missile was designated as unit number one, its target considered the highest in priority for its mission planners. Along with another three missiles cruising under the detection altitude of the fourteen air-traffic-control radars and the occasional military air-search radar, there was a squadron of MiG–51 Flicker fighters, four of them assigned the same target as missile number one.

The attack would be coordinated. The missiles were arriving from the four points of the compass, missile number one to hit first, the north, west, and south units to come in at 1.5-second intervals afterward. The Flicker squadron aircraft assigned to the palace would come in two waves, the first ten seconds after the last missile, the second thirty seconds after that. In order to accomplish this pinpoint timing, the missile required exact navigation aids. The star fix obtained before was sufficiently imprecise as to mandate another fix on the shoreline.

The coastline approached rapidly. The throttles on the turbojet engine slowed, descending back below sonic velocity. The weapon was slightly ahead of schedule, and the mission profile called for it to fly slowly past its initial navigation aids. A casino building, the Spade Palace, came into view. The edifice was lit up brighter than a lighthouse, lights of every color shining from each facet of the crystal facade, blinking lights outlining the planes of the soaring skyscraper. Chinese and English signs invited gamblers to enter, even at this late—or early—hour. The casino was the first of three way points the missile needed. It aimed south of the building. The shoreline passed beneath the fuselage as the missile headed over dry land.

Within a hundred meters of the Spade Palace, the missile turned north-northeast, speeding up to approach the second way point, a monument erected to General Wong Chen, who had beat back the Red Chinese during the civil war and was a founding father for White China. The Wong Monument was in the form of a giant military sword, anchored at its base and soaring two hundred meters above the seaward approach to the bay. The entire carved blade was illuminated by harsh floodlights, with a single red aircraft-warning strobe bulb flashing at the very tip of the sword. Missile number one flew around the Wong Sword at its base, carving a tight circle around the statute, then throttled up the engines. The mission profile called for a swift approach to the Presidential Palace.

The third way point was the Hilton Hotel, soaring over four hundred meters into the night sky. The grandiose monstrosity had been built in the year after White Chinese independence, another tribute to capitalism. The shining lights of the hotel were visible for dozens of kilometers to sea, the giant English block letters spelling HILTON down the seaward edge of the black cylinder. The missile had been directed to pass three blocks west of the Hilton, sufficiently far that its windows would not shatter from the low-level sonic boom. Reaching Mach 1.2 again, the missile shot toward the Presidential Palace.

As the missile flew over the thirty-meter high whitewashed wall of the palace complex, it was a full twenty-three milliseconds behind schedule. Less than twenty percent fuel remained in the reinforced tanks of the missile's belly, making the missile lighter, and as the throttle valves opened fully, the missile was able to speed up slightly, flying in at Mach 1.24. It sped toward an inner wall. As the missile flashed overhead, several black dogs below barely had time to begin to curl their lips, their heads just beginning to turn upward, the first growl emerging from their throats a tenth of a second later, which would prove to be forty-five milliseconds too late.

The outer ring of buildings flew under the fuselage next, the three rows of office buildings and housing facilities laid out in an ornate geometry. The central row came by next, the buildings dark with the sleeping staff members. Finally the inner ring of buildings slipped past, surrounding a beautiful open courtyard, arranged with several dozen fountains spurting water illuminated by spotlights. Exotic landscaping divided the open space into at least three dozen different conversational areas. Ahead, unlit except by the wash of lights from the courtyard's fountains, the Presidential Palace loomed.

The palace was a mere three stories tall, but was over a kilometer wide. The facade was made of Italian marble with carved pilasters, a columned entrance to a high rotunda leading up steps to ornate bronze carved doors.

In the north wing, on the third floor, the president's living quarters overlooked the greenery of the courtyard and the majesty of the inner palace complex. The living quarters had soaring plate-glass windows, framed by heavy curtains, fronted by a small tiled deck filled with outdoor furniture, potted trees, and a fair-sized swimming pool.

The nose cone of the Shining March missile impacted the thick bulletproof plate glass of the president's bedroom suite. The glass blew outward toward the deck. That was the signal to the fuse software to detonate the explosives. A charged capacitor sent out an intense electrical pulse, lighting the fuse blasting cap. The cap flared into incandescence, setting off the primary explosive train deep in the heart of the warhead.

In a few milliseconds the missile passed all the way into the cavernous bedroom, under the carved marble ceilings almost fifteen meters above the polished hardwood floor. By the time the tail fins—sheared off by the shattering glass of the window—disintegrated, the explosion train was half through detonating. The secondary explosive train temperature rose to that of a bonfire. Three missile lengths into the room, the weapon still five meters from the sleeping president's bed, the tertiary explosive train ignited. Still no trace of the interior heat was visible on the dark skin of the missile, though the tertiary explosives raised the temperature of the high-density molecular explosive to that of the surface of the sun.

At last the skin of the missile vaporized as the detonation blew outward from it. The warhead turned into a fireball of pure plasma energy, the atoms and molecules of what had been solid matter turning to liquid, then to vapor, then to gas. As the temperature rose to thermonuclear range, the atoms' electrons spun off into space, leaving their nuclei in a high-energy glow. The plasma expanded outward, the radiant heat of it turning the flesh of the president immediately to superheated gas, an expanding cloud that blew away from the plasma ball at sonic velocity. His bones liquefied next, then vaporized, joining the plasma front as the volume of energy expanded, now encompassing the entire room. All that had been solid microseconds before had all become glowing photons and spheres of protons and neutrons, electron waves flashing out into the abyss.

In the 1,500 milliseconds before the second missile entered the presidential palace, the plasma expanded outward, the flame front ahead of it blowing the walls and ceiling of the surrounding rooms away, until the upper floor within one hundred meters of the presidential living quarters was completely eliminated, burned cleanly off in a black arc.

Missiles two, three, and four flew in next, their detonators going off more by timing than by impact, and the remainder of the palace grew more insubstantial with each hit. By the time missile four's explosion had become nothing more than an orange mushroom cloud flaming and rising above the courtyard where the palace had once been, the first wave of Flicker fighters streaked overhead. Detaching their bombs, the fighters pulled hard to the right and left to avoid the missile explosions. Twenty Cultural Revolution bombs tumbled into the black and orange fireball of the palace, all of them detonating into white-hot fury in the already hellish conflagration. The initial twenty-five seconds of the Shanghai attack had vaporized the primary target, and the second wave of Flicker fighters pulled up and turned away to their secondary targets.

Two minutes after the first missile's detonation, there was a black carbonized crater, fully thirty meters deep, where the palace, courtyard, and inner circle of palace complex buildings had once proudly stood. The center row of buildings was little more than piles of rubble, bricks and marble and electrical wire, mournful fingers of steel-reinforcement rods sticking into the fiery night, melted glass resolidifying in ugly pools at the bases of the rubble. The outer ring of buildings, the few that were still standing, were in flames, fire pouring from the windows and rooftops. The two circles of walls, built to hold off terrorists and truck bombers, had crumbled but for a few uneven remnants.

In the city, 125 other Shining March cruise missiles had hit their targets. The 100 Flicker fighters sent in as backup had added to the chaos, making the previous century's destruction of Hiroshima, Nagasaki, Dresden, Tehran, and Cairo seem minor by comparison. The Hilton hotel was blown to its foundation, the only thing recognizable the three-meter-tall red block letter H lying on top of what once had been a glass elevator, the glass shattered, half molten and black. Nothing was left of the Sword of Wong except granite dust, lying sn a pile at the site.

Cargo ships were burning in the harbor, and one supertanker laden with crude oil exploded in a kilometer-wide fireball, the shock wave of it blasting through a city where almost five hundred shock waves had already passed.

No building taller than three stories stood. There was not a recognizable car left in the city, all the iron and steel and rubber that wasn't crushed having burned in the city's massive fires. Not a single tree or blade of grass within tens of kilometers was left.

And not a single person within twenty kilometers of the Presidential Palace survived. Those in the circle inside ninety kilometers walked through burning streets, their clothes sooty, their eyes glazed, tears streaming down their cheeks. A father stumbled through the gutted streets, silently crying, carrying two young daughters, their legs as thin as twigs, their pajamas burned off in sections. Both children were dead, the small one's face burned off, the other's intact with her small eyes staring unblinkingly into space. Capturing the scene was the lens of a Satellite News Network camera, the images transmitted to the backpack of the sooty-faced cameraman, from the antenna on the backpack to a transmission van a kilometer away, and from there to the SNN orbiting communications satellite, relayed from there to SNN's network news center in Denver, Colorado, and from there to television and WritePad receivers all over the globe.

Two in the morning on a Monday in Shanghai was two o'clock in the afternoon on Sunday, November 3, on the U.S. East Coast, week ten of the season of the National Football League. The quarterback of the Dallas Cowboys took the snap in the shotgun formation, pulled his arm back, and fired off a bullet-trajectory pass to wide receiver Kevin McConkey in the Redskins' end zone. The football was spiraling through the air when the screen flashed, fading into the face of a reporter. The legend at the bottom of the screen read: BREAKING NEWS—WHITE CHINA FIREBOMBED. The image of the reporter vanished, replaced by the scene of the crying father holding two dead and burned children in a Shanghai street.

"We interrupt this program to bring you breaking news from Shanghai, White China, where only minutes ago an incendiary bomb attack leveled the city. These images, courtesy of the Satellite News Network, show the incredible carnage as—"

In front of the wide-screen television, National Security Adviser Stephen Cogster clanked his beer bottle on the coffee table and pulled his satellite phone from his belt. He punched a single button on it before lifting it to his ear.

"Code seven, NSA for number one. Get her on the phone now. I repeat, code seven."

It took less than ten seconds for her voice to come through the phone. And when it did, the voice of President Jaisal Warner was furious.

CHAPTER 10

She was wearing a black miniskirt, holding the ten-foot handle of a paint roller, her feet bare on the wooden platform of a scaffold. It was Eileen. Her blond hair cascaded down past her shoulders as she dipped the roller in the red paint. She arched her body, rolling the red paint onto a curving wall above her, a few paint drops falling on the dress. Suddenly she looked over at him. Her face was a shattered and bloody pulp. He felt a desire to go to her, to hold her, but somehow knew she was angry. He wondered if she was angry at the loss of her face. She seemed so serious, not like herself, as she painted the curving wall in swift yet careful strokes. Before he could open his mouth, she spoke to him without creating sound, without moving her lips.

Red subs, Mikey. You're up against the Reds.

She started fading into the distance, the curved wall above her becoming a cylinder, a rudder appearing in the foreground, stern planes, a propulsor-turbine shroud. The floating dock around the hull. It was the SSNX, its lower stern section now a gleaming red. Eileen still painted as she drifted farther away. She turned to him and shouted, *Hurry, we've got to go!*

"What?" he said, his voice still a phlegmy croak.

"Hurry, sir, we've got to go!" The voice wasn't Eileen's anymore. It belonged to a man . . .

"Sir, O'Shaughnessy's plane is waiting. They said they'd call you—dammit," Paully White said, picking up the dead phone, tossing it across the room. His voice became high and whining, filling with frustration. "Sir, what are you doing asleep at two-thirty in the damned afternoon? Christ.''

Pacino sat up, looking dazedly at his wrist. His Rolex was gone. He found it on the nightstand. "What are you doing here, Paully? What the hell is going on?"

White had found a remote control and clicked the wide-screen to life. Pacino rubbed his hair as the reporter came up in mid-speech.

". . . armored divisions crossed the White Chinese border at Zhengzhou and occupied the city within an hour. Meanwhile several tank divisions have crossed the northwest border in what seems to be a rush toward the central city of Xuzhou. In the south, several hundred infantry divisions crossed the border at Quangzhou in what appears to be a march toward Hong Kong. In the central regions, a mountain crossing has been accomplished by a dozen armored and infantry divisions in an attempt to cut off the north of the country from the south. The infantry and tank troops have been supported by hundreds of bombers, fighters, and helicopters of the Red Chinese People's Liberation Army. Details from the central campaign are sketchy, but so far White Chinese forces seem to have been completely surprised and overwhelmed, falling back and absorbing tremendous losses as the Reds advance toward the shores of the East China Sea. This is Christie Cronkite reporting for SNN, Tsingtao, White China. Back to you, Bernard.''

"Thank you, Christie. We turn now to Brett Hedley in Hong Kong, which in the last few minutes has come under air attack. Brett, can you tell us what's going on? Brett? Brett? We seem to have lost Brett due to technical difficulties; we'll return to him in a moment. For those of you just tuning in, again, Red China has attacked White China in what looks like the biggest land offensive since the Battle of Iran. We go now to our presidential correspondent outside the president's compound at Teton Village, Wyoming. Diane—"

White clicked off the wide-screen and tossed the remote onto the bed. Pacino stared at the blank screen for a moment, his eyes wide, then looked at Paully White.

"What the hell . . . ?"

"We can watch more of that on O'Shaughnessy's 777." Pacino rose to his feet, walking to the bathroom. "We're due at Andrews Air Force Base in an hour." The water of the shower came on, and Paully called over it. "That gives you about eight minutes to shower and pack."

White found the remote and turned the TV back on, staring at it, barely blinking.

MARYLAND ROUTE 50 / I-595
OUTSIDE BOWIE, MARYLAND

The Lincoln staff car rocketed ahead at 135 miles per hour.

This time the state police had not been notified, because the phones and radios and WritePad links were otherwise occupied. When a Maryland trooper's cruiser came up behind them, beacons flashing, the staff driver ignored him. Eventually the cruiser pulled up alongside the Lincoln, waving to pull over. Paully White, on the satellite phone, pushed a button to make his window clear. The black polarization vanished, and the intense afternoon sunlight streamed into the car. Still barking orders into the phone, he held up a sign, handmade by the aide riding in front, reading ANDREWS AIR FORCE BASE. The sign and the emblem of the Unified Submarine Command on the car's door must have suddenly made sense, for the trooper saluted and sped ahead, turning on his siren.

"You heard me," Paully White said, again blacking out the window. "Defcon one, all Pacific Force submarines. You've got two hours to recall the crews and load up with food. Forget the fresh stuff, canned goods only. Start the reactors now. Divorce them from shore power and get them to sea. Yeah, we'll tell them when they clear restricted waters. Yes, you can guess all day if you want, but the skippers will hear it direct from Admiral Pacino. Got that? See you."

"Atlantic Force?" Pacino asked.

"We can mobilize them, but that would leave the Atlantic uncovered, and it will take three weeks for them to get to China. Look, Admiral, this is a blitz. The Reds will be on the East China Sea in a week, maybe less. Then it'll be over. Warner's gonna have to strike goddamned fast."

"China's a damned big place, Paully. No way they can do this in a week. Even if they were up against minimal resistance, it would take a month to get to the coastline and consolidate. White resistance could blow the Reds back to Beijing. Plus, they weren't able to kill Wong Chen. The general, fortunately, was hanging out with his mistress outside town. And Warner's got the Rapid Deployment Force loaded up into the NavForcePacFleet ships."

"True. The RDF and the NavForcePacFleet is casting off now."

"You're kidding."

"Read the message yourself, sir. The ships are putting to sea, assembling off Shikoku, Japan. The escort in begins in about six hours. They're on their way."

"Sounds like Warner learned her lesson," Pacino said, remembering her vacillation before the Japanese blockade.

"So what do you want with the Atlantic Force?" White asked.

"Defcon one, load up, set sail. Norfolk squadron goes under the polar icecap, Kings Bay squadron through the canal. First ship to the East China Sea wins dinner on me. And we'll see who's right about how long this thing takes."

"Admiral, Captain White?" aide Kathy Cressman called from the front. Pacino's assistant from his Norfolk days, she was now working for his number two man, Admiral Kane. "Warner's on SNN, making a statement. I'll patch it to your screen."

JACKSON HOLE, WYOMING
TETON VILLAGE PRESIDENTIAL COMPOUND

The peaks of the Tetons, the "American Alps" that appeared on all the postcards and prints and oil paintings, were ten miles to the north.

Teton Village was located near the border of Teton National Park, a ski town not unlike Vail or Aspen, with a double mountain marked by bare swaths cut through the fir trees for ski slopes. The supports of the chair-lift cables and tram climbed up the mountain like rungs of a ladder. Skiers crowded the slopes, hundreds of colorful dots on the white field in the bright November sunshine. At the base of the slopes was what once had been a sleepy, quaint town, but three years before, it had been overrun by photographers, newsmen, transmission vans, black limousines, helicopters, Secret Service agents, and tourists who had never strapped on skis and never planned to.

Jaisal Warner's presidential complex, on the south side of the village, was more of a large, rambling log lodge. On the upper story, under a gently sloping, peaked roof a wall of windows looked down on the village to the north; another wall of glass on the other side peered up the mountain. Between the two glass walls were several sitting areas and a dining area, marked by stone fireplaces. On the lower two levels were guest rooms and spas, an enclosed swimming pool, a pub with several pool tables. The Secret Service took up the rooms of the lower level, the press corps and visiting cabinet members the second floor, leaving the president to her master bedroom suite on a level above the peaked roofline, a sort of cabin-above-the-cabin that had a view of most of the valley.

She stepped out of the front entrance of the lodge and walked down the steps hewn from twenty-foot-long logs. She wore ski pants, a sweater, and her fur warm-up boots, her hands ungloved. In her hair she had put her Ray•Bans. Her hair, though golden, had become streaked with gray over the last two years, but the gray was a silvery tone that blended well with the blond. Her skin remained unwrinkled despite her skiing tan, her startlingly blue eyes shining out over her high cheekbones, royal nose, and strong chin. She was tall, her figure slim as a thirty-year old's, though the birthday cake from number thirty had crumbled to dust almost two decades ago. She held the distinction of being the first female American president, having won a surprise landslide that brought her to power from the governorship of California.

The blockade of Japan turned out to be her first international crisis. From a combination of hesitation and bad luck, the U.S. Navy suffered losses so severe that the conflict was almost lost. Late in the game the tide turned, and Warner took control and changed it into a victory. Though three carrier battle groups had been sunk, with thousands lost at sea, it never damaged Warner politically. If anything, the setback rallied the nation around her, the underdog. At the close of the conflict she had the highest approval ratings since George Bush's after the close of the first Persian Gulf war.

Ratings had remained high until Eve Trachea, her National Party opponent in the coming election, spoke up about waste in the Department of War, particularly the trillion-dollar NSSN submarine program. Political cartoons showed Warner in a clown outfit peering through a broken periscope, water leaking in past crooked valve handles. Warner and her staff had come to Wyoming, away from the hassles of the Beltway, to brainstorm a strategy for her reelection. She was walking off the tram at Apres Vous mountain when she'd been waved over by a satellite phone toting staffer.

It was the secretary of war, down in the lodge. As she listened to him, standing there with her skies in one hand, the phone in the other, a thundercloud formed on her face.

The Reds had come over the border into White China, not just killing troops and attacking military installations, but massacering civilians, firebombing the most populated cities with plasma weapons. Tens of millions of people had been killed at the time of the call, which was only minutes into the attack. When she had disconnected, she was asked to take the phone again. This time Stephen Cogster was calling from the White House, her National Security Adviser having stayed after the Donchez funeral to get a few days of work done before returning.

"You wouldn't believe what I just saw," Cogster said in his trademark gentle voice. His easy manner was deceiving. His nickname among his staff was "the Blowtorch" due to his raw E-mails and voice mails to subordinates and peers alike.

Ninety minutes later, the press had assembled around a podium set up for her at the base of the steps to the lodge. The stone foundation and log steps made for an unmistakable background. She stepped up to the podium, gripping it with both ungloved hands.

"Good afternoon, Americans," she said, glaring at the cameras. "Members of Congress, the press. Except that it isn't a good afternoon at all for those who cherish peace and freedom. Less than two hours ago Red China attacked the free and peaceful nation of White China, our friend and ally, brutally killing hundreds of thousands—perhaps millions—of civilians, innocent men, women, and children, in their sleep, with firebomb attacks on thirty-four major cities. The Presidential Palace in Shanghai was obliterated, and we believe that the remaining leadership of White China was murdered in their sleep. In the government we have received reports of death camps being formed"—newsmen gasped, the last fact previously classified top-secret release 24, Warner letting it slip almost casually—"for the rounding up of all political enemies of the Red Chinese. Our estimates are sketchy, but even with conservative estimates we believe that in the last ninety minutes more Asians have died than in all of World War II."

Warner let that sink in for a moment, the only sound

that of camera shutters flickering as photos were taken. She looked at the crowd, her jawline straight, her eyes blue and cold as the snow at her feet. Her fingers formed fists on the clear Plexiglas podium.

"It is clear that the United States cannot and will not sit idly by as our ally is bombed out of existence. Accordingly, I have ordered the Army's Rapid Deployment Force and the Naval Pacific Force Fleet to mobilize to the waters off White China. The RDF, as we speak, has departed and is in the Pacific, well on its way. It is the intention of the United States to counter this cold-blooded invasion with all the might of the U.S. military. Within the hour I will address, by InterTel, a special joint session of Congress, where I will ask for enhanced powers as the commander-in-chief to employ full military force against Red China. In the coming days the ground, air, and sea forces of America will be deployed against the atrocious monsters of Red China in defense of the Whites. To our friends in White China listening to me now, I say, hold on, the cavalry is coming. To those in Red China I say, leave now. Leave White China now or die."

Warner glared into the camera again, then looked from left to right as if she were a professor ensuring each pupil had received the lesson.

"To all Americans I say, with Gods' help, White China and America will prevail. Thank you, ladies and gentlemen, that is all."

All hell broke loose, cameras thrust toward the president, a thousand voices shouting a thousand questions, some barely heard, some phrases echoing out over the snow:

"What about the allies?"

"The European Union president talked to you by—"

"Will you be attacking Beijing—"

"—Russian Prime Minister in London—"

"—air raids—"

"—nuclear weapons?"

"—Madam President, what about Japan—"

"—declaring war?"

"—Madam President!"

Warner ascended the steps of the lodge deliberately, unhurriedly, the slim woman looking almost regal as she walked in the open door.

CHAPTER 11

SUNDAY
NOVEMBER 3

**40 MILES SOUTHEAST OF PITTSBURGH
ALTITUDE: 41,000 FEET**

Pacino stared out the window as the barren scenery slipped below, the aircraft climbing steadily to its cruising altitude.

His thoughts had turned to Dick Donchez, missing him, wondering what he would make of this situation. He shut his eyes, leaning against the window, and thought about Eileen, missing her too, but feeling a guilt that he missed her—was it possible?—less than Donchez. It occurred to him that Dick's death was moving him into the next sphere of his life, where Donchez and Eileen no longer existed. Was that possible? Would the pain of missing them ever not exist . . . ?

Hell, he thought, this was all part of the craziness of losing Uncle Dick. He must still be in a kind of shock. A shock he had to shake off if he was to keep his stars.

A half-remembered dream came back to him, something about Eileen with no face and the *SSNX*. And what Donchez had said about Red subs.

Now that the Reds were attacking, he wondered, could Donchez have been trying to tell him something? Up to now he'd dismissed the rambling speech, assuming it to be part of the old man's delirium. Maybe he should reconsider.

A knock rapped on the door of the office cabin he'd been assigned with Paully White and Kathy Cressman while they waited for O'Shaughnessy to call the staff meeting in the forward cabin. Cressman looked at him, and he nodded. "Come in," she called.

The door smoothly opened, revealing a figure standing in the doorway with a half smile on his face. Pacino stood, thinking the man lost. He looked somewhat familiar, but Pacino was certain he'd never met him. He was as tall as Pacino, but without his gauntness, the man conveying a sense of solidity and certainty, a sort of body confidence, as if he were a professional ballplayer. He seemed to be in his mid-thirties, yet didn't seem young. His hair was long, slicked back from his forehead to his neck. His features were Irish but seemed almost too large, his eyes light green over a protruding nose, his mouth smiling over a strong jaw with an indented chin. He wore a dark sports coat over a linen shirt, the kind that buttoned at the throat like a choker collar, no tie, khaki chinos, and after-ski hiking boots.

Pacino was about to tell the man he was lost, when normally reserved Kathy Cressman leapt to her feet and threw her arms around the big man, squealing, "Jack! Jack Daniels, you son of a bitch! Where have you been?"

"Golfing, mostly," the dry reply came.

Pacino shot a look at Paully, who looked back with a raised eyebrow. Cressman pulled away, smoothing her dress and her hair, her face red.

"Sorry, Admiral. You know Jack Daniels?"

"I need the admiral alone," Daniels muttered to Cressman. Just like that she seemed to disappear into thin air. Daniels looked up, extending his big hand, his smile from before looking like more of a snarl. When he spoke, his voice wasn't friendly. "My name is Daniels. Mason W. Daniels the fourth. Director—temporary director—of the National Security Agency. Everybody just calls me Jack."

Pacino held out his hand tentatively. "What do your friends call you?"

"Frequently," Daniels said, dropping his hand before Pacino gripped it, an edge to his voice. "What the hell, Admiral. I've put in no less than eighteen requests to talk to you on your goddamned WritePad. Dick Donchez says, 'Oh, yeah, you call Mikey, he'll get right with you.' Well, bullshit. Kathy ought to be asking where the hell you've been, Admiral, not me."

"Pleased to meet you too," Pacino said. "It's been wonderful, really, but I'm sure you'll excuse us if—"

"I was trying to reach you for a reason. Then I tried to get you at Dick's funeral. You were a zombie, so I left you alone. Then I rang you at your Annapolis house, where Kathy said you were staying. No answer. I rang it off the hook."

Pacino wasn't surprised. He'd unplugged the main connection to the phone center after the funeral, assuming the calls were coming from reporters. He sat down, waving Daniels to a seat.

"So, what's on your mind?" he said, his voice authoritative but feeling uneasy in the presence of the angry agency head.

"Who's he? Captain White?"

"Meet Paully White, my chief of staff," Pacino said, giving White a conversational promotion. "He's cleared for everything I'm cleared for."

"How the hell do you do. Okay, I'll just get right to it, then, gentlemen. On October 23 six Japanese Rising Sun–class submarines went on sea trials—"

"I know all about that," Pacino said. "I know Tanaka at the MSDF."

"So you know why they sank?"

"What? What are you talking about?"

Daniels sniffed, blowing his nose into a handkerchief. "Sorry, that's why I didn't shake hands. I'm going under to this goddamned cold. Yeah, all six subs were in a videoconference with your man Tanaka when they sank. I've got it all on disk." He put the handkerchief away and tossed a disk at Pacino, who caught it in midair.

A half dozen questions vied for attention in Pacino's mind.

"Why wasn't I briefed on this?" he asked.

"Jesus, why wasn't he briefed on it. Where were *you* on October 24? When Kathy tried to schedule you for that urgent secure videoconference?"

Pacino bit his lip. He'd skipped it, saying he was too busy at the shipyard, taking a meeting with Colleen O'Shaughnessy instead as the Cyclops system bugs grew worse. Fine, he thought to himself angrily. That was then, this is now.

"I'll tell you where you were. You blew it off. Just like you blew off my messages. So what's your next question?"

Pacino shot a glance at White, who shrugged.

"Okay, next is how you got the video disk. Tanaka?"

"No," Daniels said. "We're the NSA, remember? We intercept, record, and decode transmissions? Hello?"

"I read you," Pacino said, wondering when Daniels would drop the attitude.

"Okay, so what happened on the disks?" Paully asked.

"They just disappeared one by one. This was after their sea trials. Dick thought that was significant. They vanished at periscope depth. Dick also thought that was significant. Said I should get with you immediately."

"So why didn't you?"

"Aside from my secure videolink and the eighteen call requests?"

"You could have gotten with David Kane or Paully White, or Kathy, for that matter."

"Could have. Didn't. Donchez was too sick to talk. Don't know if you knew that. I was helping him run the show at the time, and he refused to go to a hospital, refused to leave his office. He kept telling me you'd call us, but you never did, and hell, I was just a *slight* bit busy with this Red Chinese stuff."

"The Reds. Did we have any warning?"

"Sorry. Can't tell you. You're not cleared."

"Donchez would have told me," Pacino offered. Obviously Daniels was struggling with himself, as if following orders he didn't agree with.

"Okay. We had lots of comms. We were breaking

them almost in real time. We knew about the mobilization of troops, moving the aircraft around. Three days before the invasion the PLA pretty much went off-line. They shut up completely. It was scary. Nothing, not even orders back to Beijing for more toilet paper."

"Were you jammed?"

"Nope. There were just no tactical communications. Nothing but entertainment television, computer network transmissions—again, entertainment, all White Chinese— and radio talk shows and rock 'n' roll. Then on Sunday, bang."

"They had a prearranged operational order," Pacino said.

"Exactly, Admiral," Daniels said, a false smile curling across his face. "Donchez said you were smart, but he never said you had a flair for the obvious like this."

Pacino frowned, ready to launch into the agency director when the younger man stood.

"Well, I've done my duty for today. Donchez said you'd need to know this stuff. Now you do. And here's my card." Daniels produced a business card, the electronic scan strip on the back ready for the receiver to insert into his WritePad. "If you need me, just call. I'm sure by the eighteenth or nineteenth message I may call you back."

The door slammed behind him.

"Nice guy," White said.

"Pissed-off guy," Pacino replied. "Get the file on him."

"Already on it," White said, scanning through his WritePad. "Not much here. Mason W. Daniels IV, Princeton grad, class of '01, English major. Harvard Law, Law Review, graduated '04, initial service in the National Security Agency, special deputy to the director."

"Who was the director then?"

"General Mason W. Daniels III." White looked up. "Jesus, he's Mason Daniels' son."

"Wow," Pacino said. General Mason Daniels, Donchez's predecessor, was a legend in the intelligence community, having saved the NSA from the razor of intelligence consolidation, and being credited with numerous intelligence coups, such as the initial warning on the Chinese Civil War.

"Now what, sir?"

"Get Kathy back, and put that disk in."

JACKSON HOLE, WYOMING
TETON VILLAGE PRESIDENTIAL COMPOUND

The eight black Land Rovers crunched through the packed snow at the rear entrance to Warner's ski lodge.

Pacino bit his lip, wondering what the meeting was going to be like. The staff meeting on O'Shaughnessy's 777 had never happened, even though they had been flying in with half the Washington establishment due at Warner's meeting coming up. After Daniels had left the cabin, Pacino had sent Kathy forward to see what was up, but she said the CNO, the Chairman of the Joint Chiefs, and the Army Chief of Staff were closeted behind O'Shaughnessy's door. They didn't emerge until the plane was descending for the airport.

The other Land Rovers ahead of them contained the entourage they'd flown with but hadn't seen. In the front was the truck for Stephen "Blowtorch" Cogster, the National Security Adviser, and his personal staff. Behind him, Freddy Masters, the Secretary of State, his staff members crowded in with him. Then came the Director of Combined Intelligence, Christopher Osgood. Number four drove Mason "Jack" Daniels. Next the Chairman of the Joint Chiefs, Bill Pinkenson, followed by General James Baldini, the Army chief, then Admiral O'Shaughnessy, and finally Pacino and White.

The next minutes were a blur as Secret Service agents and armed Marine Corps guards crowded around them, taking their bags, passing them through metal detectors, hustling them in the double wood doors to the lower level, then taking them to their quarters. Pacino was led down a hall walled by heavy wood logs chinked with beige mortar. Doors lined the corridor, one on the right marked with a sign showing three gold stars on a blue field, the letters below spelling ADM M. PACINO, CMDR. UNIFIED SUB CMD. Looking at it, he felt a vague unease. Why had he been selected to accompany O'Shaughnessy on this errand, when the chief hadn't spent a single minute with him since his coming-to-Jesus talk on Saturday?

His instincts told him O'Shaughnessy liked him and would help him. And Warner obviously had spoken to the chief, asking him to bring Pacino along. But why? This was a ground war going on in White China. Sure, there would be airlift and sealift coming from the Navy, and certainly a Marine invasion with close fighter air cover from the carriers, but all those functions resided with other officers. He was a submarine officer. The only action he'd see in this was detailing the two 688I-class ships to go with the NavForcePacFleet and the Rapid Deployment Force out of Yokosuka. The subs were the *Annapolis,* SSN-760, and the *Santa Fe,* SSN-763, both of them modernized within eighteen months, both admitted to drydocks after the Japanese blockade. They would act as an escort for the carrier battle group into the East China Sea ensuring no cheap diesel boats or robot mines got in the way.

Unless, all that considered, he was here *because* he was a submarine officer. Hadn't Jack Daniels mentioned the loss of the Japanese submarines? Was there some connection he was missing? Was there something Donchez's deathbed soliloquy had meant to tell him?

He cursed under his breath as he was led into the room. An oversize bed was placed against the left wall, flanked by two oak nightstands, and a large window spanned the opposite wall. Pacino glanced out the window at the view of the village below, the busy ski slopes beyond, then dug out his WritePad from his briefcase on the bed. Furiously he clicked through the menus, selecting a chart of the waters off China, ordering the software to display for him water depth.

Just as he'd remembered, the entrance to the East China Sea was guarded by a long arc of islands, the Ryukyu chain. The water there was around a thousand fathoms, but a hundred miles west, the entire East China Sea became shallower than a hundred fathoms—six hundred feet. A true littoral water, where sonar sounds would carry for miles, bouncing off the sandy bottom. For a submarine, that was both good and bad news. Good, in that a sub could hear a surface ship coming hundreds of miles away. Bad, because the sub itself would find it hard to hide out in a thermal layer. It took stealth away from the sub, its best weapon.

If the surface forces were up against subs in the East China Sea, they'd have an easy time of it. The frigates and antisubmarine helicopters would quickly sort out any bad guys.

His thoughts turned to Jack Daniels, who had worked for Donchez at NSA. Daniels had wanted to reach him about the sinking of the Japanese Rising Suns, the information seemingly worth eighteen urgent phone calls, yet anticlimatic when he finally delivered it. Donchez had thought the facts that sea trials were over and that the Rising Suns being at periscope depth was significant.

Jesus, Donchez and his babbling nonsense, talking about Red subs that Pacino would be "up against." What was that all about? Was it possible that the Rising Suns hadn't gone down, that the Red Chinese somehow had gotten their hands on the top-of-the-line advanced-technology vessels? Could Nagasaki Mod II plasma torpedoes in the bows of Rising Sun submarines be aimed at the Rapid Deployment Force? Was that the reason the Reds had chosen now as the time to attack the Whites, because they had a silver bullet in the East China Sea?

Donchez, Pacino thought, had had lung cancer. The Bethesda attending physician had said the cancer had metastasized to Donchez's brain. Pacino had heard about brain cancer, from old Master Chief Gambini, the sonar chief of the *Piranha*. His wife, Maureen, had died of brain cancer, and for the last year of her life had barely recognized her own family, yelling at friends she adored, spitting at her cherished black lab. The brain cancer had turned her inside out. Had Maureen's logical process changed, or just her emotions? And even if she could remember, would that have any bearing on Donchez? Was all this about the Red subs a sign of senility or loss of brain function; a grand fantasy?

And if so, should he give voice to that fantasy when Warner was charged with making a decision? If he told her the East China Sea was potentially unsafe, and she pulled the carriers and troop transports back while his subs scoured the area, what would happen then? Two escort subs would take months to sanitize the East China Sea. And the Pearl Harbor boats would take a week to get there, a week lost, and even with all twelve Pearl ships, it would still take a month to search the operational area. If they delayed by a month, Red China would win. Warner, as Paully had said, needed to strike now. And what of the political damage to her administration? Hadn't she just said, *To our friends in White China, I say, hold on, the cavalry is coming?* What should he tell her?

That the RDF and the NavForcePacFleet was standing into danger, he thought. That some one hundred ten ships stood a good chance of never making it to the beach. So could he really tell her to turn the RDF around?

Warner would have to wonder about him. Yes, he'd got the Navy Cross for *bravery*, but he'd also had two submarines shot right out from under him. Would she think he was gunshy? After all, the ships of the fleet were armed to the goddamned teeth with antisubmarine frigates, antisubmarine destroyers, both carrying depth charges and smart torpedoes. They had variable-depth sonars and towed linear sonar arrays, plus there were Seahawk V antisubmarine helicopters bristling with antisub sonars and more sonobuoys and smart torpedoes of their own. Above all that, the three aircraft carriers had their three squadrons of Blackbeard S-14 slow-flying antisubmarine jets, each with over a thousand sonobuoys, a magnetic-anomaly detector, and a couple sub-killer torpedoes, not to mention the ten P-5 Pegasus patrol planes waiting on the runways in Japan. Each one was bigger than a 757, with more sub detection gear than you could put in a warehouse, and deep-diving antisub torpedoes, eight apiece.

So what had Donchez been worried about? He walked to a table by his couch, picked up the phone, consulted a list done in calligraphy under the seal of the president, searching for Paully White's number, then punched four buttons.

"Captain White."

"Paully, it's me, Get in here."

CHAPTER 12

"Admiral Pacino, the president requests your presence at the meeting," the staffer said, discreetly shutting the door after herself.

"Boss, I'm dying to know what's going on," White said.

"Sorry, Paully, no staff allowed," Pacino said, annoyed. The meeting had been going on for three hours already, well past sunset, and he had not been invited. When he had called the chief of staff's office for word, the secretary had indicated he should stand by until the president needed him.

He and Paully had spent most of the evening looking over the videodisk of the Tanaka videoconference. They'd made some progress, but not much. They had decided to go through it frame by frame, but so far it all looked normal, as normal as it could in Japanese with the NSA translation in captions at the bottom of the screen. During breaks in the examination of the disk, they'd put on the news. The Satellite News Network had the best coverage, but eventually even SNN's reports became stale and repetitive. The Reds were still pushing in the center, consolidating in the north, and attacking Hong Kong by air. The firebombing of Hong Kong had killed SNN correspondent Brett Hedley, a reporter of some notoriety. The video of the fuel-air explosive that had killed him was played several times before SNN decided it was too gruesome to air.

Meanwhile, Pacino had called for his staff aircraft, a supersonic Grumman SS-12, which had been put back together at Norfolk Naval Air Station's maintenance section. The jet was due by half past midnight, and the pilot had been given instructions to stand by at the plane rather than drive out to the village.

"Keep going through the disk, and stay on top of the SS-12. And, Paully, my guess is we'll be getting out of here soon—Warner doesn't seem in the mood to play with this thing. So keep your things packed. If it comes to it, we'll sleep on the plane."

"Aye-aye, sir. Good luck."

Pacino walked down the log-lined hallway to the end, where half-log steps rose to the upper level. The suit-clad staff woman was waiting with her ID tags around her neck and a radio in her hand. She mumbled into it as he approached. She led him up two flights of stairs to the huge main level. Pacino emerged in a large open area, near a window wall overlooking the twinkling lights of the village. Two stone fireplaces were lit in the open area across the way, framing an arrangement of furniture. The fireplace hearths were each big enough to roast a pig in, and the massive logs in them filled the room with warmth. In the center of the sitting area was a coffee table as big as a queen-size bed, cluttered with WritePad computers and printouts, old-fashioned colored paper maps, and coffee cups. Gathered around were four long couches and four deep easy chairs. To the side of the room two pine dining tables had been moved together, their surfaces covered with large note-pad computer displays, charts of the East China Sea, and maps of White China. Tacked to the wall was a huge, twenty-foot-tall colored map of all of White China and the East China Sea.

The first thing Pacino noticed about the men gathered in the room was how casually they were dressed. O'Shaughnessy wore jeans and hiking boots with a ski sweater; James Baldini, the Army chief, looked like he was ready for a cocktail party, wearing a designer sports jacket and gabardine pants; the remainder were wearing ski pants and long-sleeved T-shirts or turtlenecks, after-ski boots. The only exception was Lido Gaz, the Secretary of War, who looked like he was back at the Pentagon, wearing an Armani three-piece suit over a starched white shirt and red-patterned tie. Dressed in service dress blues, Pacino felt like a fish out of water.

"Admiral, make yourself comfortable," Jaisal Warner said. She was standing by the fireplace slim and shapely in her ski pants and boots, her hair tucked behind her ears. She held a steaming mug of coffee in one hand, a small WritePad in the other.

Pacino smiled at her. "Thank you, Madam President." He removed his service dress jacket and placed it on the back of the one empty easy chair, near the window side of the couch arrangement. Warner nodded to the seat, and he sat in it.

To Pacino's right was O'Shaughnessy, James Baldini seated on the couch next to him. On the right corner easy chair was Jack Daniels, and in the couch to his right, facing the window, was Chris Osgood and Stephen Cogster. Warner returned to her easy chair in the midst of all of them. On an opposite couch, between Secretary of State Freddy Masters and Vice President Al Meckstar sat the Secretary of War, Lido Gaz. He was of medium height, slightly thick in the middle, in his late fifties, with silver hair and a craggy, coarse-featured face, and usually the best-dressed man in any room. Gaz would impress people on his initial meetings with his charm and his intelligence, but in the Pentagon E-Ring suite where he held his offices, he was moody, explosive, sarcastic, and bombastic. Pacino was careful around Gaz, and that approach had seemed to pay off. Gaz had always treated him with respect and courtesy.

Between Gaz and Pacino was the chairman of the Joint Chiefs of Staff, General Bill Pinkenson, who shot Pacino a dazzling smile. Pinkenson always seemed like a favorite uncle, telling stories and talking to the troops. Yet when he focused on the task at hand, his judgment was sound and invariably on target.

As Pacino settled into his chair, he found every eye in the room looking at him. A bad taste rose to his mouth, a pool of bile forming in his stomach. This was not the kind of meeting where he would sit in and watch the debate go back and forth. He'd been called to give his opinion. For the tenth time that day, Pacino wondered why he was there, and why O'Shaughnessy had yet to talk to him.

"Admiral Pacino, I want to thank you for coming out with Admiral O'Shaughnessy." President Warner smiled. "I know we've kept you downstairs while we went through some things, but believe me, it was all boring stuff." At that Lido Gaz frowned, as if saying Warner was going overboard. She sat back, gesturing with a laser pointer to the map. "I'm sure you gentlemen will correct me if I mess up this explanation to Admiral Pacino, and forgive me, Admiral, if I get any of this wrong, but here is how I understand this. You can see on the map, the big board, that our Rapid Deployment Force will be going in with the transport ships of the Naval Pacific Force Fleet. The target, and this is release 24, will be Wangpan Yang, the bay south of Shanghai. The generals think we have a good landing zone there. Our forces will fight their way to Shanghai and take this whole area. We've been discussing that for quite some time, so I've spared you about two hours of our deliberations. Once the beachhead is secure, our forces will move farther out to here, while we land more troops by airlift and sealift. Although the RDF will be striking quickly, our main force will be landed over the next weeks and months. Meanwhile we are planning to insert the 82nd Airborne Division here, deeper behind the lines, with the Seals and Green Berets here, the Joint Special Forces Brigade. As you may have suspected, Admiral, the key to this entire operation is the sealift and invasion from the sea. Our question to you centers on the East China Sea."

Pacino swallowed. *Here it comes,* he thought. She'll want to know if they can be assured that the sealift operation would be safe, even though the East China Sea would be an ideal hunting ground for submarines.

"Our three aircraft carriers of the NavForcePacFleet have two escort nuclear submarines, as I'm sure you're aware, Admiral," Warner continued, smiling slightly at him. "They, and the surface force, will be escorting nearly seventy ships, loaded with the Marines and the RDF. Now, you remember the discussion we had before the Japanese blockade, I assume."

"Yes, Madam President," he said, looking her in the eye.

"As I recall during that discussion, you were critical of the employment of our armed forces. And, as I recall, you were completely right." Warner eyed the other men in the room. "Which is one reason you see so many new faces at this meeting that weren't here last time."

She was warning them, Pacino thought. It was no accident that O'Shaughnessy, Baldini, Pinkenson, and Gaz had come to power over the last eighteen months. Now that the pre-Japan crew had been fired, this group was being told that their decisions here had better work, or these men would also be sent packing. He glanced quickly at the four Pentagon leaders, and saw four poker faces.

"And that is one reason you're here, Admiral. Consider yourself my rabbit's foot." The men laughed shallowly, and Pacino shifted in his seat. He was no Pinkenson, able to schmooze with the president and members of Congress, laughing and drinking with people who pushed the buttons on the future of the world. He could never do for a living what Dick O'Shaughnessy did, commanding the Navy on one hand, on the other glad-handing politicians. All he could do was speak his mind, tell his bosses what he thought. Yet here, he was speaking to a commander-in-chief in the face of three levels of his chain of command, any one capable of putting him in charge of paper clips in the Aleutians. He focused on Warner, waiting for her question.

"Since you were so right last time, this time there is one thing I want to know." She looked at him, her blue eyes wide, her smile encouraging. "And that is, will this fleet be safe in the East China Sea? Can your two escort submarines keep them out of trouble? From any Red diesel subs, or mobile mines, or robot mines, or manned minisubs, or any other threats that the Reds may have?

Are we doing the right thing here? If we're putting our force in jeopardy, to hell with what I said to the press, I'll backpedal like crazy if you tell me to. Is the fleet safe? You spoke up last time, and I should have listened. Now, please speak your mind, I guarantee I'll listen."

So will the rest of the room, he thought.

What did Pacino's gut tell him? Daniels had proved to him that six Rising Sun submarines had sunk—say, disappeared. The Reds had jumped over the line into White China. They had done so without fear of reinforcements from the East China Sea. A senile old man had said that Pacino would be up against Red subs. For all Pacino really knew, Donchez might have been telling him he'd be standing against the red anti-barnacle paint of his own *SSNX*. But he was being too cerebral, he told himself. The real question was, *What did his gut say?*

"Madam President," Pacino heard himself saying, his voice miraculously level and deep. "I would never presume to come into this group and think out loud. I would very much like to issue an opinion in two sentences that everyone here nods at, and you send me on my way. But before I give you my opinion, I just want to say a few things first."

He had their complete attention. Daniels had raised an eyebrow. O'Shaughnessy had gone into his zombie stare. Baldini frowned, as did Lido Gaz, lines furrowing into his forehead. Pinkenson smiled encouragingly, though the smile was strained. National Security Adviser Cogster was leaning far back in his couch seat, his hands behind his head, his eyes half shut behind the wire-framed glasses.

"As a submarine admiral, I have some concerns about the East China Sea."

"*Now* you tell us," Gaz spat, only half under his breath.

"Madam President, gentlemen, this invasion was sudden. I know you stationed the RDF over in Yokosuka for just this contingency, Madam President, and I agreed with your decision to do that. I also fully support the speech you gave today. But, gentlemen, we need to recognize the risks. And one thing we're risking is a submarine attack in the East China Sea."

"What?" Cogster sputtered. "What the hell you talking about?"

Baldini joined in, peeved. "Pacino, what is this?"

"Admiral," Lido Gaz said slowly, drawing out the first syllable, "do I understand you to say there are enemy submarines in the East China Sea?"

"I said we are taking risks," Pacino continued, iron in his voice. "I didn't say those risks were unjustified. But I have to tell everyone in this room, I'm worried about something. Number one, eleven days ago six front-line Japanese attack submarines disappeared."

"Sank, you mean," Cogster said.

"Did they?" Pacino shot back. "No emergency buoys, no black-box transmissions?" He was out on a limb, he knew, but Cogster had gotten his blood up.

"Let's ask Chris Osgood what he thinks of that statement," Gaz said in his peculiar lisping manner.

The CIA chief looked up, sitting straight. He shot a look at Pacino, and Pacino was sure there was an almost imperceptible nod behind it. Osgood put on reading glasses, half frames like O'Shaughnessy's, and read through his WritePad. "Admiral Pacino is correct. There were no black-box buoys found at the wreckage sites. And no black-box transmissions recovered at NSA."

"Well, okay," Gaz said slowly, doubtingly, "I guess if you say that, Chris, we'll all just have to accept it."

"Is that true, as far as NSA knows?" Cogster said, shooting a glance at Daniels.

"We didn't get anything from any transmitter at the Pacific wreckage sites," Jack Daniels said, addressing Warner, turning to Osgood and Gaz.

An odd thought occurred to Pacino. "Any salvage vessels at the wreckage sites?"

Osgood nodded, looking down at his WritePad. "Matter of fact, quite a few," he said.

"Anything that can haul up a sub hull?" Pacino asked.

"Only one. Two ships went out there, each one with a surveillance minisub, robot operated. The salvage ship that can haul up floor debris jumped around from site to site. We never saw them bring up anything, but then we weren't watching them carefully. We figured any information on this would come through more official channels. Your contact at the MSDF, Tanaka, did you speak with him, Admiral?"

"Not yet," Pacino said, hating the way his priorities could become crystal clear in hindsight, yet so murky in real time.

"Please," Gaz said in disgust. "Those subs sank. What are you saying, Admiral, that six captains faked their deaths so that they could link up with their revolutionary comrades in the Red PLA? Like my grandmother used to say, 'Maybe so, sonny, but I kinda fuckin' doubt it.' "

"Worry number two," Pacino drove on, fighting for his credibility, "we've never secured the East China Sea, not the first sonar surveillance, not the first SSN patrol."

O'Shaughnessy sat up straight, his face forming into lines of thought, the zombie look dissolving.

"If there is anything there, from whatever source, we'd best get on it now. Get the Seahawks and the Blackbeards and the Pegasus planes out over the water now and get the dipping sonars wet, get some sonobuoys out there. And for God's sake, get the *Annapolis* and the *Santa Fe,* the 688I's attached to the fleet, out ahead of the carriers and scour the lane from Japan to Shanghai, clean it completely up. And one other thing, let's get the fleet on a random antisubmarine warfare zigzag pattern immediately. It's damned hard to shoot at a serpentine target, especially if the zigs come randomly. And let's form the fleet into an antisubmarine formation, destroyers and frigates in front, troop ships spread out, high-value aircraft carrier targets—I mean, ships—coming in three separate task forces, far apart, each carrier surrounded by its close-in-radius destroyers with a roving destroyer-frigate force combing the waters ahead. And finally, if Shanghai is the target, let's set up a feint for someplace else, Tsingtao or Lianyungang, and then zig our way to Shanghai."

Pacino looked at the faces in the room. For a moment

he was about to launch into a speech about Dick Don-chez's premonition, or vision, or hard intelligence, about Red subs, when Gaz asked him straight out:

"Admiral, does your excessive caution here have any-thing, anything at all to do with Dick Donchez?"

Pacino glared at Gaz, trying not to blink. Out of the corner of his eye, he could see O'Shaughnessy's head looking downward, slowly shaking from side to side.

"No," Pacino said. "I hadn't spoken to Dick in weeks, maybe months. When I got to the hospital, he was in a coma. He died within hours." He felt like he'd just be-trayed his own blood, his ear almost waiting to hear a rooster crow three times. Uneasy, he decided to press Gaz in return, to see what was going on. "Why? What's the deal with Dick Donchez? Why did you ask me that, Mr. Secretary?"

Gaz waved the question away, as if it were insignifi-cant, yet he was flustered.

"Admiral, we all know how you felt about Director Donchez," Warner said to him, her face serious, looking him in the eyes. "Toward the end he was saying some odd things, some, well, quite frankly, some very wild things." Pacino shot a look at Daniels, whose eyes were on the rug. "And he was convinced that the Red Chi-nese had plans afoot to obtain submarines." She looked at Pacino even harder.

"Madam President, I appreciate your concern." He was about to mention that he'd only been briefed on the Japanese subs that very day, but decided that, as John Paul Jones had said, discretion was the better part of valor, and said instead, "I don't have anything from Donchez on this. I'd have to ask Director Daniels his opinion on this subject. He was closer to Donchez than anybody here."

The focus of the room immediately turned from Pacino to Daniels, as if in the lions' den he'd thrown a raw T-bone steak at the young NSA director. Warner stood and walked around the back of O'Shaughnessy's and Baldini's couch to Daniel's chair.

"Well, Jack?" she asked. "What's your report?"

"Well, Madam President, at NSA we're running a code-breaking shop, not a naval intelligence task force. We were busy intercepting the Japanese comms coming down on the loss of the Rising Suns and the Red Chinese as they mobilized. I never saw Donchez discuss this or give any evidence. And frankly, Dick was busy himself."

"Doing what?" Warner asked.

"Dying," the outspoken agency chief shot back.

Warner sighed, walking back to the fireplace. "Admiral Pacino, your advice on taking cautions with the fleet is duly noted. And we sincerely appreciate your input. I assume you'll be returning to Norfolk now?"

"No, ma'am, I've got work in Pearl Harbor." He didn't feel like mentioning the *SSNX,* a sore subject with the president.

"Have you got a ride?" she asked, gesturing with her chin toward the window. Snow had begun falling, driven by a slight wind, the flakes large in the gable's spotlights.

"Staff plane's at Jackson Airport," he said, looking at her, standing up and buttoning his service dress blue jacket.

"Well, then, good luck, Admiral. Thanks again." With that she came over to him. He tensed for a moment, unsure of what was going on. Over a head shorter than him, she put her arms around him, hugging him slightly, and gave him a brush on his cheek with her lips, the gesture a sister would give him.

He felt the heat on his face, sure he was blushing, as he turned to the room, nodding to Warner and his Pentagon bosses. "Madam President, Mr. Secretary, Generals, Admiral." He spun on his heel and followed the staff woman quickly down the log stairs, exhaling in relief as he hit the bottom step.

CHAPTER 13

The Land Rover Warner had lent Pacino spun its wheels, finally digging into the fresh, powdered snow and bouncing down the road leading to Route 390.

Pacino had changed into working khakis, wearing an arctic parka over the light uniform. While he had been changing, back in the room, Paully had given him a sardonic look.

"You been kissing the Secret Service girl?"

"What?"

"Your cheek? Lipstick? Honestly, I leave you alone for a half hour, and look what trouble you get into—"

"Shut up," Pacino said, grinning. Wiping off Warner's mark, he felt an odd guilt that he was finding humor in what had been the bleakest period of his life since his divorce. Something came back to him, something one of his submarine skippers, Bruce Phillips, had said to sonarman Gambini, the one who'd lost his wife—he'd said, "don't feel bad about feeling good." A seemingly obvious comment, but perhaps only those who'd lost a close loved one knew how tough it was to do just that. Yet perhaps that was the meaning of the dream he'd had, at least what he could remember of it, that he should do whatever he could to move on, and the past would forgive him for moving on.

It would be just Pacino and White on this flight, Paully having sent Cressman back east with a WritePad full of instructions for Admiral Kane. As the Land Rover arrived at Jackson Airport, the wind was blowing the quarter-sized snowflakes at a gentle angle. The SS-12 could be seen behind the small general aviation building. Pacino directed the driver to pull up to it. The lights inside were a warm gold color, viewed in the darkness. As the Land Rover screeched to a halt, the hatch forward of the swept wing opened, a ladder extending downward to the snow. Pacino ran up and in, greeting the pilot, spinning his finger in a "start-engines" whirl. Paully had barely shut the hatch behind them when the turbines came up in a moan, then a shriek.

"You know the airport's closed, right, sir? The weather's not good enough to take off, Admiral," the pilot called back, He was well versed in the admiral's disregard for most civil aviation weather restrictions.

"Of course it isn't—because we're in a hurry. Now, get this damned thing in the sky before it gets any worse."

"If the FAA comes, it's your ticket."

"Haven't paid those guys yet."

The jet arrived at the end of the runway. The snow had been cleared off an hour before, leaving plenty of time for more snow to accumulate and drift from the wind. The pilot throttled up slowly, allowing the plane to accelerate gently on the slick surface, then, as the midpoint of the runway approached, he gunned it. After a tense moment of bouncing down the snowy runway, the supersonic transport rocketed skyward, engines howling.

Pacino took off his arctic parka and threw it on one of the seats up front, then burrowed into his seat. He turned on his WritePad, deciding to see the latest upload from Satellite News Network on the Chinese Civil War. As he flashed through the magazine-style articles, the unit began to flash—urgent E-mail coming in.

He looked at his Rolex. The last thing he felt like doing after that hairy meeting at the Western White House was work, but he decided he might as well get the E-mail out of the way. After meeting Jack Daniels and getting confronted with his lack of attention to routine administration, Pacino had cleared his entire electronic desk off on O'Shaughnessy's 777, so this would be the only E-mail. As he opened up the system, he saw it was top-secret release 24, the highest Pacino's system would accept. He went through the software, validating his identity, even putting his thumb on the scanning sector so that he could make sure he was Michael A. Pacino before it downloaded.

He read the summary line, listing the date and time of transmission, the classification, the subject, and the sender. He looked at the summary, blinking in astonishment. The line read:

Date	Time	Classification	Subject	Sender
4 Nov	0505Z	TS Release 24	[Classified]	R. Donchez

A message from a dead man? Pacino felt a shiver crawl up his spine.

TETON VILLAGE PRESIDENTIAL COMPOUND

She stood at the window and looked at the black Land Rover that drove Admiral Michael Pacino back to his staff plane. Now her RDF had set sail for White China, and her mind whirled with all the policy meetings she'd had in the week before, as Red China mobilized, and how they had been filled with guessing and unanswered questions, with the wild speculation of NSA Director Donchez before his collapse in his office last week, and with Lido Gaz's exasperation with the idea of Red Chinese submarines in the East China Sea.

In Warner's customary attempt to flush out the opinions of her cabinet, she went around the room. The results were predictable. Al Meckstar, the easygoing VP, voted with Pacino, remembering for the room the devastation last time after the loss of the surface battle fleet to the Japanese. Lido Gaz was disgusted. He insisted the fleet hit the beach after all his work to get it underway fast, and then accused Pacino of failing to finish the SSNX, embarrassing the administration. General Pinkenson, consummate politician, chose a middle ground, suggesting the Japan–based aircraft deploy while the fleet steamed on. O'Shaughnessy voted with Pacino, enraging Gaz, who had to be calmed by Warner. Finally Chris Osgood, CIA director, weighed in, gently disagreeing with O'Shaughnessy and voting for the present timeline. Blowtorch Cogster, the National Security Adviser, attacked Pacino personally, calling his mental clarity into question. Finally she turned to the Secretary of State.

"And so now it comes to you, Secretary Masters."

Masters drew himself up in his seat, puffed out his chest, and stuck his lower lip out.

"Madam, if you want my opinion, you'll just have to hear it in private. I'm not rendering it here."

Warner looked at him, one of the most level-headed, intelligent, and clear-thinking cabinet members she had ever had, but also one of the most pugnacious, far outdoing Gaz on that score. She knew better than to order him to speak—he'd resigned on her too many times for her to do that now. And she needed his opinion. Besides, it was late, far after midnight, and she needed to make a decision.

"We'll recess again," she said to the room. "Secretary Masters, please stay. Everyone else, please leave the room, but don't leave the building and don't fall asleep. I'll reconvene this meeting soon."

The men filed from the room. When they had gone, talking amongst themselves, Masters' expression softened. He joined her at the coffeepot, putting his hand on her shoulder in a fatherly gesture.

"How you holding up, Jaisal? You okay? Anything I can do?"

She put her hand on his, grateful for the support, feeling all the stress and pressure hit her at once. What she wouldn't give for a real skiing vacation, not one of these winter nightmares.

"I'm fine, Freddy. Thanks. Now give it to me straight. What the hell do we do?"

"You mean, what are *you* gonna do? Because after I give you this advice I'll deny I said anything. Seriously, though, you don't have time for all this submarine nonsense. You gotta go straight on till morning. None of this zigzag stuff. Just keep plowing."

"What about the airborne patrols?"

Masters sighed. "If we do all that flying around with antisubmarine planes, those sharp-cookie Pentagon correspondents will shout to the world that we're flapping about enemy subs. It's a loser."

"And what about the fleet formation?"

"We're showing the flag here. Half the reason SNN is onboard the *Webb* is that they're unwittingly campaigning for us. We need a background with cruisers and destroyers and all seventy troop transports. We need to look good out there. You ever think about why they used to have parades, showing the troops? Check out your history. Back in the days when the infantryman was the ultimate weapon, countries thought that if they paraded their soldiers with guns, other countries would count the men and say, whoa, too much, we ain't messing with them. Well, this is a parade, except we're doing it at sea. We need to march across that East China Sea like it's a parade ground. We're the cavalry, so we gotta ride high in the saddle with flags flying, guns blazing."

"But what about the risks Pacino mentioned? And what about the Japanese subs that vanished?"

"Oh, please, they sank, Jaisal. Don't give in to Donchez's senile drama. Let's keep our heads on. There ain't no ghosts and there ain't no Rising Suns flying Red Chinese flags. Now, can I please go to bed? I'm telling you, you and your damned five-hour encounter sessions, I've gotta sit on my fat butt and listen to your political appointees try to find *their* butts with both hands. Christ, what the hell do you think I was doing with my time, planning my investments? No, I'm covering your pretty little rear end and thinking this thing through. The sad thing is, I feel like I'm the only one thinking it through. Everyone else is looking for the political answer, all afraid Iron Jaisal Warner's gonna fire them and send them home like you did the Japan crew."

"Okay, okay, enough, Freddy. That's my style, and

those are my advisers, each of them as hand-picked as you are. They just see reality differently, that's all."

"I think they're blind."

"Freddy, my daddy said something to me I'll always remember. You know the story of the elephant and the blind men? Well, reality is an elephant, and we are all blind. So, Freddy, you want to know reality, you've got to interview every blind man who's touched the elephant."

"Do me a favor, Jaisal? Just don't seat me next to the blind man who tried to find out about the elephant's asshole, okay?"

Warner laughed. "Carol, get the advisers back!"

"What's your decision?"

"Patrol planes from Japan. Escort subs go on ahead to sweep the sea. Otherwise, damn the Red subs, full speed ahead, parade field formation. Let's make it look good, and get the hell to the beach. We'll know by dinnertime tomorrow if it works."

"Attagirl. You explain that to the blind men. I'm going to bed."

BOOK IV

ARCTIC STORM

CHAPTER 14

WESTERN OREGON
ALTITUDE: 53,000 FEET

"Paully," he said dully, "I think you'd better look at this."

"What's up?" White called from aft, where he'd been searching for a Coke.

"And while you're at it, you'd better tell me what the Navy regulations say about a mentally incapacitated commander, how and when he can and should be relieved."

"Okay," White said, frowning, walking forward. "Why, one of your skippers go bananas?"

"No. I'm talking about me," he said thrusting the WritePad at White. The summary line clearly showed the message had been sent two minutes before, and was from Dick Donchez.

White examined it a long time. Then, in gross violation of Pacino's standing orders, he withdrew his cigarette pack with one hand and shoved a Camel into his mouth. His USS *Reagan* lighter brought the cigarette to life, a cloud billowing around him. He looked up through the smoke.

"Is it just me, or did I think I buried this man not two days ago?"

"Three days," Pacino said, still looking dumbly at the WritePad. "It's after midnight."

"Well, I'm Jewish—I don't believe in guys rising from the dead after three days, not even Donchez."

"It's not funny."

"Double-click on it and let's see what he has to say," White said, sinking into a seat.

Pacino clicked into the E-mail software, but there was no written text. There was a video clip, a fairly large one from the listing next to the symbol of the video file. He double-clicked on the video clip, and the WritePad's video software engaged. The screen flashed, the video rolling.

A man in an expensive Armani suit was sitting at a desk, his head bald, a thick ashtray next to the man's hand, a large cigar lying idle. It was Dick Donchez, perfectly healthy, or at least seeming so by comparison with how he'd looked at Bethesda. He looked into the camera.

"Hello, Mikey," he said, his tone gentle, which hadn't often happened. "By the time you see this, I'll be dead, and you'll be fighting the Red Chinese."

He slowly picked up the cigar and puffed it. Diverging from his normal style, he put it back in the ashtray instead of keeping it in his fist.

"They say these things finally are killing me." He laughed. "Have killed me. Listen, Mikey, and please listen hard. I have a deputy director here, his name is Mason Daniels IV. His enemies call him Jack. His friends, his few close friends, call him 'Number Four,' after his three predecessors, who were all in the intelligence game one way or another. I know you've never met him before this, but I had great plans for the two of you. I'd hoped one day you would run the CIA and Number Four would take on NSA. That way you two could sort of," Donchez sniffed, "keep me alive somehow, long after I've gone.

"But that's an old man's dream. Let's get to business, which is this old man's nightmare. First, Mikey, the cancer's in my throat and my lungs, not my brain. I know, the attending physician at Bethesda told you different, the guy with dark hair, big glasses, never shaves? Well, he works for me. If there's any doubt at all, you make your judgment by listening to me here. You think I'm sane, you act on what I'm telling you. You think I'm nuts, you just delete this video and remember our good times.

"You've either found this next bit out from Number Four or from Tanaka at MSDF. Six Rising Sun subs were hijacked. Not lost, stolen. Number Four has given you a video of their meeting when the subs presumably went down. During the conference one of the captains says he will arm the black-box buoy so Tokyo will know what happened. They never found it, did they? In fact, they never found any of the black-box buoys.

"But that's not all. Roll the video to track coordinate 1143. All you'll see on the frame is an open doorway on the *Lightning Bolt* after the ship's captain ran to the control room. This is a photograph of the frame in question."

Donchez held up a grainy photo. In the doorway a blur of black was shown, a hump, a circle, and a vertical protrusion.

"Looks a little fishy, doesn't it? Look at the computer-enhanced version."

Donchez put the first photo down and picked up another. A clear photograph of a man appeared, hunched over in the corridor, wearing a stocking cap, black makeup, black jumpsuit, the vertical protrusion clearly the barrel of an automatic pistol.

"Even more fishy. The man's height, by the way, shows him to be very tall. In fact, he violates the height standards for the MSDF submarine force. He'd never pass the physical. The weapon is also interesting. It's an AK-80. Brand-new, made only in Red China for the PLA. None have ever been exported or obtained by our people, so doubtful the MSDF has any.

"All six Rising Sun subs disappeared just before our Pacific sound-surveillance systems picked up noises. The recordings were poor, but we managed to intercept the recordings the Japanese were passing from the salvage ships to Tokyo. Check this out."

Donchez raised another display board, this one showing six graphs, one atop the other.

"Sound graphs. Shows the explosions as the hulls crushed. Interesting, isn't it? The six initial explosions were all separate. But look here, starting at this line. This second explosion is supposedly the noise of the hull passing through crush depth. The second-explosion noises all came at different intervals from the first explosions, but look at the noise profiles of the second explosions. It's all the exact same noise, the graphs are the same! Here, check it out."

Donchez lifted a fourth display board, this one showing the "second explosion" graph blown up.

"This isn't just the sound profile of the second explosion; this is all six explosion-noise graphs superimposed. I say again, there weren't six hull-implosion noises. There was one, replayed six times, the exact same noise. Isn't physics fun, Mikey?

"Next, video clip of the wreckage at the site. They'd uplinked this to a Galaxy satellite from the salvage lead ship. And yes, we intercepted it and decoded it. Not a bad job, frankly. Now, check out the wreckage."

The video clips of the wreckage rolled, one by one. Donchez's image returned, showing him puffing on the cigar again. "You didn't notice anything out of place, no casual observer would. But guess what. See the floating shoe polish? The enhancement our fancy computers did reveals something interesting about it. The Japanese Maritime Self-Defense Force is relentless about atmospheric contaminants on their submarines. You know, floor wax, cooking grease, cigarette smoke. It all gets into the air ducts, it contaminates the computer systems, eventually it can screw up the ship. The MSDF does not allow any, repeat any shoe polish onboard, of any manufacturer. Oh, I know what you're thinking, someone just brought it aboard unthinkingly. Nope. Back to our enhancement. The shoe polish is made, guess where? You got it, Red China, standard issue for the PLA. Not enough for you? Well, we did the same with the cleaner-fluid bottle floating next to the shoe polish. If they'd used that aboard a Rising Sun–class, they would have killed the DNA processors within hours; it's a nerve toxin to the computer. And no, that's not what sank them, by the way. If you lose the biological part of the computer, it switches to manual, and the lower functions of the Second Captain drive the submarine out of danger, surface it, unless the crew takes manual control. Oh, and guess where the cleaning fluid is made? Can't tell from the video, but the computer enhancement—oh, hell, you've guessed it, Red China once again.

"Still not enough? How about the comms we broke from Red China in the months before this war broke out? We got some quite juicy things out about an Operation *Red Dagger*. I'm not going into the details of that, but suffice it to say, a while back a Korean sub sank with no warning. It sank because it was hijacked, then intentionally scuttled as a demonstration. Number Four has all the details on that, by the way.

"So why didn't I or NSA go to Warner with this, or the CNO, or Gaz? By now you've probably answered your own question. There's a certain knowledge you and I have because we were sub officers, Mikey, and until you've looked at a cruise ship at close range off Club Med, seen it in periscope crosshairs, knowing you could take it down with one shot, with no one knowing it was you, you don't know what being a submariner is. Warner's officials don't know and they don't want to know.

"I tried to tell them about the Rising Suns. Every person I told about it in private mysteriously forgot about it. I spoke to advisers in groups. Same cold shoulder. I went to Warner and Gaz. Now, a lot of the evidence hadn't come in yet, and I was coughing and in a lot of pain, and Gaz heard what I was driving at, and he wouldn't let me finish the briefing. Warner leans on him, and also on a Harvard professor named Masters who thinks he knows everything. If they disagree with you, you are sunk.

"But I didn't want you going in cold, so I asked Number Four to give you some things to think about, but at the same time I didn't want your credibility as damaged as mine is. Maybe that way you can still get something done.

"Now, I asked you to listen to me, and I hope you still are. You probably recommended to Warner that she use caution in using the RDF. You will not see caution from her on this. Push to do anything you can to get those Rising Suns, but realize something—they are good, and the only thing we can hope for is that the Reds can't operate them very well.

"Beyond that, my clairvoyance is at an end. For all I know, the mere threat of using the RDF has sent the Reds scurrying back home and you're on your way to trying to get the *SSNX* ready to go. Or perhaps the worst has happened, and the Reds sank the entire RDF, and we lost White China. I don't know.

"But I do know this. Whatever happens, your instincts will be right. Follow them, Mikey. And use O'Shaughnessy and Number Four. They're good resources, good men. They can help you."

Donchez paused, taking a final puff and putting the cigar out.

"And now, Mikey, if anyone else is watching this with you, please ask them to step away for a moment. I want to talk to you."

Paully White left, reaching for another cigarette in the smoke-filled cabin. Pacino kept watching.

"Listen, goddammit, I know you'll mourn my death. The only thing I regret, the *only* thing, is that I'm not around to help you anymore. You're on your own, Mikey. I don't know what's in store for me, but if I can help you from the great beyond, I'll try to. I've got to tell you, though, I believe that this life is it. After that it's dirt and dust and worms and blackness. Nothing more. But so what? You have to keep living, you have to keep pushing. And even if you lose this thing with the Reds, even if Warner tosses your career down the toilet and you become just some guy going to a job during the day and watching television at night, I want you to know something." Donchez cleared his throat and then blew his nose. "I love you, Mikey. You're my son, more my son than if you had come from me, and I know Tony, your father, would appreciate my saying that. And you've been a wonderful son to me, Mikey. I don't want you having any doubts, any regrets."

The old man's eyes filled with water. He brushed it away with his handkerchief, annoyed.

"Just one more thing, Mikey. You've got to move on, move on from losing me, move on from losing Eileen. You can't do your job if you live in the past. And your job is being yourself. Do your job, Mikey. Be yourself, the one you once were when we were younger and you commanded the *Devilfish.* That's why I renamed the SSNX program, Mikey, so you would remember.

"So remember, my son. Remember." Donchez coughed, drying his eyes and his nose again. "Goodbye." His lip quivered, just for a second, and then the image vanished, the screen reading:

MESSAGE SELF-DELETED

Pacino turned off the WritePad and stared out the window.

CHAPTER 15

"Operation SeaLift is now into its eleventh hour, Bernard," the reporter said.

She stood in front of a massive Sea King helicopter, the block letters reading U.S. NAVY above the door. The rotors were spinning above her head at idle. The reporter was pretty, dark hair and green eyes, long, elegant fingers holding her microphone. A crewman handed her a helmet, the kind that bulged at the ears with a built-in headset.

"We're going on a trip aloft from the deck of the USS *James Webb* to take a look at this huge fleet, the biggest armada ever to go to sea."

The camera view followed the reporter as she went to the far side of the helicopter where there was a large opening.

"Bernard, they're hooking me to a safety line now so I won't fall out this doorway, and from here we should be able to see the entire formation of the fleet."

The noise of the helicopter grew to a roar as the chopper throttled up and took off from the deck. In the lower right side of the television was a small logo that read SNN, for Satellite News Network, a small dual panel below reading 2:10 A.M. EST, a second one reading 2:10 P.M. China Time. On the lower left side was a war logo that SNN had concocted, showing a Red Chinese flag next to a burning White Chinese flag next to an American flag. The words underneath read OPERATION SEALIFT.

The view from the helicopter changed to a gray patch of deck, a section of the sea, and the overcast sky. As the view rotated, the island of the carrier came into view.

The tall structure was a naval architect's dream, a sort of slender pyramid, but with layers on it, each layer bristling with equipment—slanting large, flat panels of phased-array Aegis radars, spheres holding radars, and on top a gigantic flat radar that rotated slowly, majestically above the structure. Flags flew from the island's tall aft mast, the biggest an American flag two stories tall. Painted on each face of the island was the number 80. The chopper continued to rise until the entire carrier came into view. The vessel was streamlined and impressive, the deck one huge expanse of flat gray, angled off to the side. The forward deck rose slightly in a ski-jump arrangement, the bow sharp, a razor cutting into the sea. The wake behind the mighty ship was violent and foaming on a dark blue sea. It could be seen extending far behind the ship, still white and churning in the sea. From afar the carrier seemed to be plowing the sea with purpose and determination.

As surrounding ships came into view, the reporter continued. "Bernard, as you can see, the USS *James Webb* is a huge aircraft carrier, with a displacement of 110,000 tons fully loaded, the biggest ship in the U.S. Navy's arsenal. The number 80 is the hull number. They call this CVN-80, for carrier vessel nuclear. The ship has two nuclear reactors, four turbines, and four screws, and has a crew of five thousand men.

"Coming into view next to the *Webb* are the other two aircraft carriers of the fleet, and as you can see, they are forming a triangle, the lead ships in this mighty armada. On the top of your screen is the USS *Kinnaird McKee*, CVN-81, and at the bottom you should be seeing the third carrier, the USS *Franklin Roosevelt*, CVN-82. Behind the three aircraft carriers, in two rows of five, are the ten Aegis cruisers assigned to the task force. Behind them, Bernard, are three rows of seven ships, the destroyers and frigates."

The chopper climbed even farther, so that the ships behind the carriers came into view. They were beautiful, sharp daggers slicing into the sea, their positions precise in the formation, their wakes ruler straight.

"Behind the warships are six support ships. As you can see, these ships are quite large, the oilers and supply vessels. The ships are sailing in absolutely straight rows and columns. It looks like a parade, except a parade at sea. All the ships are flying giant American flags, and, Bernard, the formation is sailing so precisely that even the radars, the big structures rotating in circles, are synchronized, rotating together. It is just amazing. Then, Bernard, come the troop ships of this convoy. It is absolutely breathtaking seeing so many huge ships. These ships look like toys from up here, arranged in a precise formation of five ships across, fourteen rows of them, a total of seventy troop ships carrying the 375,000 troops of the Rapid Deployment Force."

The helicopter circled back and flew down the row of ships, seeming to stretch all the way to the horizon.

"Bernard, despite the ships steaming five and six across, the convoy is three miles long! It is perhaps the largest show of naval force ever put to sea."

"Christie," an off-camera voice asked, "how will these troop ships get the men ashore? Is it expected that these ships will just dock at a harbor and offload the men?"

While he'd been talking, the lead ship of the convoy, the *Webb,* came back into view. The camera panned in, the ship growing to its true formidable size, taking up the entire on-screen view.

"Well, Bernard, we've been told that of the seventy troop ships, the first twenty are amphibious vessels. By amphibious, we mean that the ships can either half climb up on the shore or have front-loading doors or both, with some of them offloading by opening giant doors in the back and letting off hovercraft and swimming troop transports, even some tanks that come ashore like boats, but that then just keep driving up on the beach and on into the countryside. The amphibious ships all contain the U.S. Marines, and we've been told that the Marines will be landing first. Once the beachhead is secured, the Army troops will follow. The other fifty ships are more like standard cargo carriers, with containers that will be offloaded later in the invasion, Bernard."

The deck of the carrier had come close again, until the view resembled its earlier patch of deck and sea and sky. The chopper bounced on the deck, and then the view became steady. The background noise that the reporter had been shouting over suddenly died, a whooshing sound coming as the rotors wound down.

"Christie, has there been any word on the location of the landing?"

"No, in fact, Bernard," the reporter said as she climbed out of the helicopter. Handing her helmet back, she flashed her dazzling television newscaster smile at the Navy petty officer. "We've been prohibited from going anywhere near the navigation equipment or charts of any kind. In addition, our computers have all been checked to have the satellite-positioning software removed. At this point we can only guess what our position is, but from some of the flyovers done by charter aircraft, and by guessing our speed, we estimate that within the hour we should be crossing the line of the Ryukyu Island chain, which is the border of the East China Sea. From there we'll be heading to our beachhead on the White Chinese coast. Once we get to the beach, the name of this operation will change to Operation White Hope. Back to you, Bernard, this is Christie Cronkite, onboard the USS *James Webb*, somewhere in the Pacific Ocean, reporting for SNN World News."

"Thank you, Christie, and now we pause for these words . . ."

"This is Christie Cronkite, onboard the USS *James Webb* . . ."

"Turn it off," Pacino said.

Since Donchez's last words had deleted themselves from the screen twenty minutes before. Pacino had stared out the window for most of that time. Finally he'd pulled himself together, blinking, his eyes scratchy and swollen. The first thing he'd done was call for Paully to put on SNN, to see what had happened to the Whites. Once he saw how the ships were steaming in a rank-and-file formation, he'd been shocked speechless.

"Warner didn't listen," Pacino said finally.

"I would have thought for sure she would listen to you this time," Paully said. "After all, didn't she say she guaranteed she'd listen?"

"I guess she listened but didn't act," Pacino said between clenched teeth. "I can't believe this. Those ships are sitting ducks. If any of what Donchez said is true, that fleet could be doomed."

"Is there anything we can do about it? You want to talk to O'Shaughnessy? I can patch him in."

"Why? I said my piece. Somehow the word didn't get through. Now, those Rising Suns may be out there. They'll pick off those ships in the convoy like shooting fish in a barrel."

"We've got some work to do, boss. And we don't have any time."

"Okay, how far to Pearl?"

"About three hours."

"Time enough. I'm going to change my mind. Get O'Shaughnessy on the video. While I'm talking to him, you've got to find Tanaka."

"Admiral Tanaka? Can I ask what's on your mind?"

"Tanaka designed the Rising Sun subs practically by himself, we'll need him. Next, get on the horn and find out the status of the Pearl Harbor boats. I want every unit to get out to the East China Sea as soon as possible. Tell them to throttle up to emergency flank."

"Emergency flank? Are you serious? You'll be throwing away twelve nuclear reactors, you know that. You're talking about two hundred million dollars of replacements, with drydock time piling up to a year for each boat. Emergency flank will make every ship radioactive up to the forward bulkhead of the torpedo room."

"Paully. Emergency flank. Now."

"Aye, sir. Your fleet. Your stars."

Exactly, Pacino thought. The stars that he needed to earn once more, and damned quickly. White moved aft to where he'd piled his computer equipment, and began working. Pacino looked out the window. The clouds were all far beneath the plane, and nothing was visible above but the brilliant stars. *The past will forgive you,* Pacino thought. *Follow your instincts, Mikey.*

"Admiral? The CNO is up and on the seat screen."

"Thanks, Paully." Pacino punched the fixed-function key, and a glowering O'Shaughnessy came up, his hair rumpled, wearing a robe. His face was stubbled, his eyes puffy. "What do you want?" he said, his voice flat.

"What happened after I left, Admiral? The fleet's steaming like ducks in a shooting gallery."

"We were overruled. The fleet's making a max-speed run for the coastline. Warner's not in the mood to zigzag. Or to execute a feint. They should hit the beach in a matter of hours, and it'll all be over."

"Admiral, I'm convinced the fleet's standing into danger. They could be targeted any moment."

"Is your conviction the result of new evidence?" he asked, raising an eyebrow.

This was it, Pacino thought. He would have to bring Donchez into it.

"Sir, Director Donchez had gathered quite a bit of new data—"

"We saw all that, Pacino. It's old news. And it may even be tainted. Did you have access to Donchez's 'data' when the meeting with Warner went down?"

"No, sir. I heard later."

"Well, forget it. Anything else?"

"Sir, I'll say it one more time, because no one seems to be hearing me. The fleet's in danger. We have to get them out to the Pacific until my forces can assure them of a safe passage. I've got a dozen 688I subs steaming toward the East China Sea at forty-five knots."

"So now you're not just recommending a zigzag, you want them to withdraw? For what, an entire week?"

"Affirmative, boss. Get the fleet the hell out there. I'm more convinced than ever. Jean-Paul's in deep trouble."

"Noted, Admiral," O'Shaughnessy said, his face a closed book. "Anything else?"

Pacino was amazed. He had hit a brick wall with O'Shaughnessy. His blood rose, and he could feel himself on the edge of control. "Sir, maybe I'm being out of line or tactless, but shouldn't we get back to Warner and tell her she's making a mistake?"

"Pacino, unless I'm forgetting, didn't we cover all this at the briefing?"

"Well, yessir, but she didn't listen. I'm going to ask you, Admiral, straight out. Did you go against my recommendation after I left?"

O'Shaughnessy's face became darker. "You're out of line, Pacino. Now, it's two in the morning and I'm going back to sleep. You have your orders. I suggest you follow them."

"Aye-aye, sir. I apologize for waking you up." What a waste of time, Pacino thought, angry and disappointed. He was about to click off the admiral in disgust when O'Shaughnessy's voice returned:

"Patch? For the record, I backed you up. The fact that you doubted that, I take that as being you not backing *me* up. I suggest in the future you learn to command your tongue better than you're commanding your submarine force."

And then the CNO hung up on Pacino.

"Dammit," he cursed. Putting a wedge between himself and O'Shaughnessy was the last thing he'd wanted. Now the CNO was angry, and worse, he had again mentioned that he thought Pacino was not doing his job.

"Well, that was no help," Paully said.

"Brick walls," Pacino muttered.

"Can you go over his head, to Warner direct?"

"I could, Paully. Believe me, I'm in the mood to try, but I'm keeping in mind one thing."

"What's that?"

"If I push it to the point of getting fired, I can't do anyone any good."

"True. Coffee?"

"Yeah, it'll be one long damned night. Let's keep going. Let's raise the NavPacForceFleet admiral-in-command. Maybe we can make some headway with him."

"Admiral Jean-Paul Henri, the last naval aristocrat?"

"Patch him on."

Henri took some time to come up on the video. A

three-star admiral himself, Henri was a career surface-warfare officer, rising in that sexy portion of the surface navy devoted to antiair warfare. He had commanded an Aegis cruiser, the *Ark Royale,* during the Islamic War. An SNN news crew had been aboard as he shot down more than forty supersonic jet fighters, most of them intent on firing missiles at the landing force that came ashore in southern Iran.

That news crew had made him a household face, on par with the commanding general of the invasion, General Pinkenson. His ship was likewise immortalized, the SNN reporters calling it the "Robocruiser." Henri had never forgotten his taste of the limelight. His offices and sea cabins were decorated with several dozen pictures of him on the bridge of the Robocruiser. He had risen without further media attention, and the loss of it had seemed to sour him. His ambitions seemed fueled by one thing—to get back in front of the television cameras, hopefully as the Chief of Naval Operations.

In addition, for reasons unknown, he'd always been less than cordial to Pacino. He had gone on camera after the Japanese blockade to criticize the way Pacino had handled the submarine war. Pacino had always been convinced that he had found something that would get himself on television, and that he hadn't really meant what he said. Still, Pacino could feel his stomach tensing as Henri's face came up.

He wore large, square, wire-rimmed glasses that made his eyes seem bigger than they were. His puffy face was red from years of drinking, his jaw fleshy, his jowls growing by the year. He was ten years older than Pacino but looked much older. He grimaced as he said:

"Hello, Pacino. I can just guess what you're calling about. I heard all about your wild ideas to make us spend a week getting to the beach when we're seventeen hours away."

Wild, Pacino thought, the same term Warner'd used to describe Donchez.

"You're in deep trouble, Jean-Paul. I thought I'd let

you know. You'd best put your fleet in an ASW formation and get your Blackbeards in the air."

"Yeah, right. Anything else?"

"The 688s. Where did you deploy them?"

"They ran on ahead about five hours ago to scour the East China Sea. They're going about four knots faster than us, so they should be about twenty miles ahead. That should be sufficient to warn us of anything out there, if you've trained those guys right. And so far, no enemy submarines."

"What about the P-5s out of Japan? Are they searching yet?"

"Um, no." Henri's jaw was jutting out pugnaciously.

Pacino imitated him, feeling an uncharacteristic sarcasm surfacing. "Um, why not?"

"Um, because there's no threat, and UAirCom has some problems with them, maintenance and staffing and other nonsense. Now, if you'll excuse me, Pacino, we're on full air-attack alert, and we may be getting paid a visit by a real threat—enemy fighter jets. Flicker fighters, unlike ghost submarines, are somewhat lethal, and they'll be coming in at Mach 1.2, giving us only a few seconds to react. So if it's acceptable to you, I'd like to be getting back to the tactical problem at hand. Oh, and one more thing, Pacino. Don't call me again."

He hung up. Pacino smashed his hand on the darkening screen in frustration, cursing at Henri.

"The Pearl subs? Where are they? Are they up to emergency flank?"

White sighed. "They left within an hour after your call, when we were on the way to Andrews Air Force Base. That's 400 miles down, 4,200 to go."

"Almost four days at max speed."

"The world is damned big. Geography is a killer. Which is why Warner stationed this huge an army in Japan."

"Paully, what's your gut feeling?"

"Sir, I think that's the last conversation you'll ever have with Jean-Paul Henri. I think he and his force are going down. We've done every damned thing we could, and it's not enough."

"There's one thing we haven't done. Get a message out to the *Santa Fe* and the *Annapolis*."

"Careful, sir, that Jean-Paul's turf."

"Hell with him. Send those two subs a message and don't bother copying Jean-Paul. Tell them USubCom suspects the presence of possible Destiny or Rising Sun–type submarines under the control of the Reds. Tell them they could be reverse-engineered copies or copies made from stolen Japanese plans. I don't know, think of something and make it sound credible. And when you're done with that, call ahead to the shipyard. I want to lower the *SSNX*'s floating dock and go waterborne tomorrow. Make sure you tell them to get the *SSNX* out of dock under maximum security. That will mean something to them. I've got a way to sneak it to sea no one will believe."

"How?"

"You'll see. Just tell them. Max security."

"Okay," White said doubtfully. "No problem, I can do that. Uh, can I ask why?"

"You did ask. We're putting the *SSNX* in the water because we're getting the *SSNX* underway. Give me the file on the crew."

White smiled. This was the Admiral Pacino he knew. He clicked through the WritePad until he reached the *SSNX* personnel file, then handed it to Pacino.

Pacino frowned, drumming his fingers on the table, wishing he could figure out what to do next.

NAZE—YAKUSHIMA GAP
USS *JAMES WEBB*, CVN-80

The stateroom of the force commander was cavernous and plush. The bunk was queen-size, the conference table a half acre, the room full of warm, glowing lamps. On the bulkheads were a half dozen pictures of Henri on the bridge of the *Ark Royale*.

Admiral Jean-Paul Henri sat at his conference table, his WritePad computer angled upward so that it could be used as his personal video phone. Pacino's face had just winked out, and the paranoid, grandstanding submarine officer's warning was still ringing in his ears.

Henri sat back and shut his eyes for a moment, thinking. The fleet was almost a third of the way to the beach, and it was damned late to be thinking about antisubmarine warfare. With the press crawling all over the ship, it wouldn't do to be conducting massive air operations, launching aircraft and helicopters. He'd be asked why they were launching the S-14s and the Seahawks, and he'd either have to tell them they were patrolling for submarines or to be potentially caught in a lie, and the latter was no way to ascend to CNO.

In addition, the wind was from the northwest. Turning the ship into the wind for flight ops would mean diverging from the base course, which was straight in to Shanghai. That would lose him time, and according to his orders, time was of the essence. More important, the press was hyper aware of the time. They'd been asking him constantly when they'd be at the beach.

He'd seen something in Pacino's eyes, Henri thought. He touched the screen of the WritePad and played the conversation back. The man, Henri's main competition for the job of chief of Naval Operations, had a haunted look about him. His eyes were hollow. Hollow and frightened. Pacino was scared, Henri thought. If he could believe the reports of some of his old classmates at the academy, it was a rare thing for this guy to be frightened.

Henri reached for a phone. "Officer of the deck, get the captain, the air boss, and the ASW officer to my stateroom ASAP."

"Aye-aye, sir." The phone clicked.

It took all of thirty seconds for the officers to get to his stateroom, all of them looking pumped with adrenaline, spoiling for a fight. Good for them, Henri thought. They had no idea what troubles he was shouldering. If they had any idea of the weight of responsibility of fleet command, they'd run for the hills.

"Gentlemen, I want a squadron of S-14 Blackbeards brought onto the main deck. I want them and their crews ready for launch in one minute or less. Full alert."

"Aye, sir," the captain replied for the men. Henri waved them all out. They knew better than to ask him why, and he'd be damned if he'd tell them.

For a moment he considered calling Kagoshima base, where the P-5 Pegasus patrol planes were on standby, but then reconsidered. That would be going overboard. After all, if Pacino was afraid, maybe that was just because he didn't possess the backbone that Admiral Jean-Paul Henri did.

That had to be it, he insisted to himself.

CHAPTER 16

"The captain's in control," the voice shouted out.

Captain Jonathan George S. Patton IV walked into the control room of the USS *Annapolis* like a gunslinger entering a Western saloon. Patton's carved face was a harsh mask of anger. He stood five foot ten but appeared taller, perhaps because of his thin frame, his sports preference marathon running. His hair was diesel-fuel black, his skin dark, his eyes black and unreadable. His typical expression was a frown, at best a neutral penetrating stare. His smile was seen so rarely that it had been the subject of a shipwide underground newsletter. All captain's smile sightings were logged and recorded. Yet despite his hard shell, he was encouraging to his crews, a sympathetic ear to his junior officers in their struggles to learn the ship and attain qualification. At sea, though, he was crusty, often abrupt, demanding and driven.

Patton was the great-great-grandson of General George S. Patton, the Army general who had flamboyantly whipped hardened Nazi Germany Panzer divisions with a fighting style marked by originality, unconventional and instinctive aggressiveness, and undistilled guts. The younger Patton's appointment to the Naval Academy at Annapolis had come almost without his asking for it, as if the Navy admissions staff were recruiting him as a sort of public relations coup against their bitter rival, the Military Academy at West Point, intending to make him a Navy poster boy.

He'd risen through the nuclear submarine ranks, until at last he was admitted to the school for prospective commanding officers, an unforgiving course of study that flunked one-third of the students, who could then never return to duty on board a sub. One of the requirements was to walk into a control-room mockup in Norfolk, Virginia, command a strange crew, and fight a battle programmed by a supercomputer and an oddball group of war-game nuts, all under the watchful eye of the two-star admiral-in-command of the entire submarine force, Admiral Pacino.

Patton had stood on the conn, the elevated periscope stand, of the control room mockup—so realistic in looks, feel, and even smell that Patton could easily imagine he was at sea. He looked down on the crowd, trying his best to look like he was cool, when in fact he was scared to death. Flunking this scenario would mean cashing in his eighteen-year submarine career, going to Marcy and telling her that he had failed, that their way of life was over. The sonar chief called from the sonar space forward: "Conn, Sonar, new sonar contact, designate sierra one, bearing one eight zero. Contact is putting out a medium signal-to-noise ratio on a single pump-jet propulsor. Contact is classified as submerged warship, classification Russian Severodvinsk–class fast-attack submarine. Conn, Sonar, second new sonar contact, designate sierra two, bearing two six five. Contact putting out a strong signal-to-noise ratio on two four-bladed screws. Contact is classified surface warship, classification Russian Kirov. Conn, Sonar, third new sonar contact—"

By the end the chief reported twenty contacts, ships on every point of the compass, each of them ships from the Russian order of battle, each of them bristling with antisubmarine weapons, each of them lethal. Lesser men would have panicked. Patton, knowing he was doomed, leaned over the railing of the conn and said sardonically, "Well, men, looks like we've got them surrounded."

He prioritized the sonar contacts by their threat level, their distance to him, the submarines first. Within five minutes he pumped out four torpedoes at the submerged contacts, drove away from his launch position, and set up on the surface contacts. Taking a wild forty-degree up-angle trip to periscope depth, he confirmed the range to the Kirov class. The ship was a veritable nuclear battleship, armed to the teeth with torpedoes and antisubmarine rockets. Within the second ten minutes of the scenario, he unloaded two loads of tube banks at the surface ships, sending three to the Kirov, two to a Slava cruiser, two to a Moskva class, one to a Kara cruiser, one to a Kresta II, firing methodically at Udaloy II destroyers, pumping torpedoes out at Sovremenny destroyers, until his torpedo room was out of weapons. Then, with half a fleet of enraged surviving Russians, he turned tail and dived deep, running as fast as he could, zigging occasionally. He found a shallow bank, the depth conveniently below a thermal layer—making him invisible to hunters from the surface. He bottomed the submarine, shut down the reactor and everything that made the slightest noise, and the Russian flotilla sailed overhead, none the wiser. In total, he took down sixteen capital ships and damaged several others. Even better, none of the ships overhead, their active sonars pinging angrily, were able to find him.

Admiral Pacino came into the room laughing, his teeth white in the dim backwash of light from the battle-control-system consoles. He walked up to Patton and extended his hand in a high-five. Patton slapped it and smiled back.

"Excellent job, John," Pacino said. "You have as much aggressiveness as your namesake, maybe more."

Patton smirked in dismissal, knowing the truth, that his heart had been pounding with the fear of failure, and that he'd never thought it would go this well.

"Just one thing, Captain Patton," Pacino said, throwing his arm around the younger captain. "We weren't at war with Russia. The scenario was to find a Destiny II Japanese sub amongst all the clutter of a Russian fleet."

He shook his head, still laughing. "But what the hell, that attack was one for the books. I'll be playing the tape of your battle as required viewing for all prospective commanding officers, and that Destiny II stuff, that'll be our little secret. Just remind me, John, never to give you war-shot torpedoes until I tell you who the enemy is."

Patton blushed, but smiled in pleasure. Pacino took him to dinner, and amazingly enough turned out to be a regular guy. Patton was up half the night telling Marcy about the trip to Norfolk, and how he soon would be named to command a 688I-class submarine. Orders came in to take over the USS *Tucson*. He was tasked as an escort submarine for the carrier battle group out of Pearl Harbor when the Japanese blockade occurred. He went to sea on a moment's notice, screening the carrier *Abraham Lincoln* as the convoy plowed its way northwest to Japan. The Japanese submarines attacked when *Lincoln* was barely an hour out of port. Patton and *Tucson* had just heard a bare sniff of the first Destiny attacker when the Nagasaki torpedoes were launched. Patton drove at flank toward the firing submarine, unloading a tube bank into it. It sank without ever knowing Patton was there. The same happened with the second Destiny III and the third. By then the Nimitz–class carrier *Abraham Lincoln* was bow down, only her massive brass screws showing above the water. When Patton found the fourth Destiny III attacker, he had only one torpedo left, and fired it at the final submarine, expecting this one to shoot back.

One torpedo was not enough. The Destiny came to the surface, wounded. Patton watched through the crosshairs of his periscope, waiting for a hatch to open, crewmen to come out, but there was no sign of life. More curious than angry, he ordered *Tucson* to surface, and he and a landing party of his officers boarded the Japanese submarine, packing 9mm automatics and MAC-11 machine pistols. With an acetylene torch Patton carved his way into the vessel. On the *Tucson*, one of his officers filmed the boarding from the periscope video camera. He went down a ladder to an empty submarine. The entire forward compartment was tiny, holding only three decks of computer consoles. It turned out the ship was unmanned, computer-driven. Patton returned to *Tucson*, took the Japanese sub in tow, picked up survivors of the *Lincoln* task force, and sailed to meet an oceangoing tug.

On the way back to Pearl, the tug reported seeing flames coming from the open fin hatchway of the Japanese sub. When it stopped, it found that the computer onboard had executed a self-destruct sequence. The contents of the forward computer cabinets had burned to ashes. After all that trouble, the Pearl naval experts learned nothing about the computer system.

The periscope video film was released by the Navy to the media. The film replayed on every television screen, and soon pictures of John Patton forcing his way into the Japanese submarine made the covers of every newspaper and magazine, paper and electronic. Patton became an instant icon, his name synonymous with dagger-in-teeth courage. Only John Patton himself knew the truth. He had been burning with curiosity and just wanted to meet face-to-face the men who'd downed his task force.

When the *Tucson* went into a drydock modernization program, Pacino pulled Patton off, sparing him the dull reality of the shipyard. He was handed command of his second submarine, the USS *Annapolis*. The chance of a second sub to command was extremely rare in Pacino's navy, and this was the ultimate compliment.

Now here he was, in the center of it all, once again guarding a surface task force, this one so huge as to dwarf the *Lincoln* carrier group. The *Annapolis* was steaming at flank, making forty-one knots on the improved hydrodynamic seven-bladed screw. There was one major problem with this, though.

Searching for an enemy submarine required that the searching platform be quiet. And steaming at all-ahead flank was anything but quiet, making sonar reception much more difficult. True, the *Annapolis* was as close to a brand-new submarine as any captain could ask. The ship had been completely gutted on its shipyard overhaul, and was now fitted with a new quiet screw and

new whisper-quiet electric drive. The clanking reduction
gear and geared propulsion turbines had been ripped
out, replaced by electrical propulsion turbines powering
a massive but quiet AC motor driving the screw's shaft.
The reactor had likewise been removed and replaced by
a DynaCorp S10D 200 megawatt thermal nuclear power
unit, increasing shaft horsepower from 35,000 to a whop-
ping 70,000, raising the ship's top speed to 41 knots, a
speed previously attainable only by the venerable but
prohibitively expensive Seawolf–class. In addition *Annapolis* had also had its battle-control system—sonar and
fire-control—ripped out and replaced with an ultramod-
ern BSY-4 system previously available only on the Sea-
wolfs. An additional ship-wide computer network had
been installed, complete with video systems, giving Patton instant information in his stateroom about the status
all over the ship.

Patton had just completed a tour of the vessel, timed
to coincide with an hour before watch change. He'd gone
back as far as the shaft seals in the aft compartment
forward to the chief's quarters. The ship was amazing,
her 6,900 submerged tons, 362 feet of hull packing
twenty-six Mark 52 Hullcracker torpedoes, ten Mark 80
SLAAM submarine-launched antiair missiles, and ten
vertically launched land-attack and ship-attack Javelin
cruise missiles in the vertical tubes in the bow. The ship
had the latest radar-invisible periscopes, the latest communication suite and antennae, and the most modern
electronic detection systems ever installed on a submarine, as modern as the last remaining Seawolf hull. The
ship was sleek and clean and combat ready.

But that was not enough to succeed in this situation.
He was doing an antisubmarine sweep at forty-one
knots, and the ocean sound acoustics were terrible at
that speed. The ideal speed, fifteen knots, would give
him an acoustic-detection range against another 688I
hull at approximately ten nautical miles, twenty thousand yards. But a search at forty-one knots meant the
water noise around the hull was dramatically increased.
The massive reactor circulation pumps were running fast,

four of the two thousand horsepower monsters pouring their noise into the sea. Plus the screw—although hydrodynamic, was still loud at flank speed, putting out high decibels aft. At forty-one knots, the same target hull would not be detected until a distance of two nautical miles, only four thousand yards, a degradation of seventy-five percent.

There was worse news still. The most likely candidate for an intruder submarine was a diesel boat. True, it would be tough for a diesel boat to get in the proper position in front of them, but a boat lurking directly ahead in their path would be dead silent, no rotating machinery at all to make any noise in the water, just a quiet screw and main motor. The only thing they'd hear would be the launch of torpedoes. An old nuke boat was louder, but if it was cruising slowly, it would put out much less noise than *Annapolis*. Again, the only way to detect it might be its launched torpedo.

That made the *Annapolis* something of a sacrificial lamb. They were now thirty nautical miles ahead of the convoy. Astern of them by ten miles was the USS *Santa Fe,* commanded by young Chris Carnage. If a hostile submarine was waiting for them, the *Annapolis* and *Santa Fe* would draw their fire. His operation order required him to make an emergency transmission to the carrier in the event he came under attack. That meant he'd have to come to periscope depth and shoot at the same time, a truly impossible tactical burden.

There had been no excuse for Admiral Henri not sending them out days ahead of the task force, to sanitize the western Pacific and the East China Sea. Hell, it wouldn't have cost him anything. They could have sailed ahead while Henri loaded troops and equipment. They could have done an initial East China Sea search at twenty knots and a second at a slower fifteen, with *Santa Fe* escorting in the convoy a mile ahead while *Annapolis* drove ahead. Between the S-14 Blackbeards and the P-5 Pegasus patrol planes out of Japan, the East China Sea could have been cleaned of every single marine mammal, much less offensive submarines. But now all the two U.S. subs were amounting to was a security blanket for Henri, perhaps at best a lightning rod for any attack that would be aimed at the convoy.

Patton looked up at the officer of the deck while the youth gave him a status report. No sonar contacts, ship was at best detection depth, sound channel good at seven hundred feet, ship rigged for patrol quiet, as best as they would do while at flank. He nodded, checking his watch and frowning, when the offgoing engineer officer of the watch came in. Patton got his report, nodded curtly, and walked into the sonar room, forward and starboard of the control room.

At the second console sat Senior Chief Byron De-Meers, his acerbic sonar expert. They had served together since his days on the *Providence,* because Patton had taken him on his two command tours. He and De-Meers meshed well. Their words were minimal but each was attuned to the moods and thoughts of the other. DeMeers had formerly been plump, with a bald pate, penetrating eyes and a dark, full mustache, but two years before he had discovered a fitness center, and now he was a poster boy for chiseled abs and pumped-up pecs. For the first time in two decades he was considered attractive by the opposite sex. And he was single, his wife having filed for divorce after his first submarine tour. He now had several aggressive women calling the boat every time he was in port, but for the most part he stayed on the ship, tending to his equipment and the sonar system's software programming.

The chief sonar billet on the *Annapolis* was perhaps the number two slot in the entire fleet, and working with Patton seemed to agree with him. He wasn't too enthusiastic about this mission, though, having said to Patton in private that it was a fool's errand, a waste of time, that they were being employed by an admiral who didn't know how to spell submarine. Patton, again keeping his mouth shut, had thought that it was damned hard to disagree.

"Tell me again about your search plan," Patton said to DeMeers.

"If I do, it'll be the twelfth time this run." DeMeers sighed. "But okay." He turned the half-empty Coke bottle upside down, draining it. "The search plan is in four parts.

"Part one—diesel boat search. We're looking for a diesel on the battery, looking for low-frequency mainmotor or screw noise. Not much chance of finding her, so processing time would normally be low since we don't want to waste time, but on the other hand, 'Diesel Boat Eddy' is more likely to be found out here than the other threats, so we've upped the processor time.

"Part two—snorkeling diesel boat search. We're trying to find a low- and medium-frequency ocean noise from a diesel engine, like we'd hear from a diesel boat snorkeling at periscope depth, recharging the batteries. Not much probability on this one, because anyone trying to attack the fleet would sure as hell want to keep it quiet.

"Part three—nuke boat. We've got it tuned for three nuke profiles. The first an older 688 boat, like the kind we sold to the third world. Low probability on those. Second profile is an updated Han–class, like the Reds used to have, but which should have rusted to dust twenty years ago. Who knows? Maybe someone kept an old vintage boat and sent it to sea. Also low probability. And damned loud if it is out there—I'd hear it with my naked ear. Third profile is a French Rubis–class, the sub they sold on the market for ten years. It's tiny, it's loud, and it has only eighteen weapons. This is also low probability.

"Part four—all sub classes. This is the transient classification system. We're looking for any of about four hundred transient noises, all of which are guaranteed to be man-made. Hatch slams, pump start-ups, check-valve slams, dropped wrenches—"

"Torpedo tube doors coming open," Patton added.

"Oh, yeah. Torpedo gyro start-ups, torpedo propulsor start-ups, and a bunch more. None of which can come from whales or shrimp. The processor module is brandnew, and we're not sure how well it's going to work. You'd better prepare yourself for some false alarms. We could hear a hatch slam and it might just be a whale fart."

"And that's it?"

"That's it, Skipper."

"What about that alert that came from USubCom, the one about possible variants of Japanese Destiny or Rising Sun ships being used by the Red Chinese?" Patton had read the skeletal message from Admiral Pacino, with veiled references to the Reds possibly having some Japanese–type submarines, but it had sounded strange.

"USubCom thinks the Reds stole the technology, reverse-engineered a nuke platform based on the Destiny or the Rising Sun. Yeah, I saw it. Trouble is, a reverse-engineered carbon copy of a Destiny won't sound like a Destiny. The sound signature would be nothing like the copied boat."

"So, why would USubCom put us on alert for a Destiny or Rising Sun?"

"Especially when our intelligence would come up with any carbon copy the Reds had been building or testing out in Bo Hai Bay? You got me, Skipper. I'm lost."

"Doesn't add up. But what if they somehow got the Japanese to do something for them? Japanese could still be upset with us after the blockade. . . ."

"Come on, Captain. That makes zero sense. They put the Rising Suns to sea with American permission."

"Yeah, and then they all sank."

"Who knows? Maybe the USubCom engineering guys sabotaged the Rising Suns. Maybe the Japanese subs were considered too much of a threat," DeMeers said, his active imagination firing up. Patton glanced at the dogeared science fiction novel on the side console, DeMeers' passion. He wondered if the sonarman's reading preference was affecting his on-watch thinking.

"I highly doubt it. And it just seems like it's off the wall. Destinys? Rising Suns? What next, a Severodvinsk–class Russian?"

"No more whacky than a Rubis or a Han or an old Los Angeles."

"True. What if we put some processing time on a Rising Sun?"

"I'd be happy to, Skipper. Just one problem. We don't know what the hell they sound like."

The old search paradox had returned, Patton thought. They couldn't very well search for a sub unless they knew its "sound signature," the pure tones that it emitted from its rotating machinery. It was usually discovered only by shadowing a new submarine, lead ship of the class, with a U.S. sub, recording the sounds heard as it submerged the first time out of the shipyard. But absent that acoustic intelligence, it would be difficult at best to find an intruder submarine. Perhaps only the transient noises would give it away.

"So, here we are, steaming ahead of the convoy, going max out at forty-one knots, half deaf because of our own speed, half blind because we have no idea what we're searching for, with cryptic messages that there might be an advanced-technology Japanese sub or mirror image out here, and we're supposed to keep the whole East China Sea clean with all that?"

"That's it, Skipper. That's why you get that command pay."

"Yeah, all forty bucks a week," Patton said. "You got an old Destiny III search plan?"

"Sure. It's covered with dust, but yeah, I could find it for you."

"Do me a favor. Load it in. It's as realistic as a Rubis or a Han."

"No problem, coming right up. Anything else? Fries with your Destiny III? A Coke?"

"Just an open seaway. That's all I want. Last thing I need is to have the convoy attacked on my watch."

"We lost the *Lincoln* together, sir. I'm not all that interested in losing a second task force." Uncharacteristically, DeMeers' voice was dead serious.

Irritated, John Patton returned to the control room, frowning and thinking.

CHAPTER 17

Even after almost two weeks, the command console took some getting used to, Admiral Chu Hua-Feng thought, busy scanning the screens.

For two weeks Chu had put the crew on a crash course to learn the ship. The training sessions had taken hours, with the Second Captain both driving the ship while simulating combat-screen readouts for the control-room watchstanders. The Second Captain had proved one of the keys to the operation's success—up till now. The Second Captain ran everything aboard, including the galley ovens, and fortunately they had managed to convince it that they were the legitimate crew members. Had that gone wrong, the mission would have been scrubbed.

After the Second Captain had listened to and obeyed Chu's first order, he'd put up an antenna, and using the computers they'd hauled aboard from the submersible just before cutting it loose, Chu had communicated with each of the other Rising Sun submarines. He'd been pleasantly surprised to find that not one of his unit commanders had had trouble taking over their vessels. In fact, of the six, only *Arctic Storm* had given the invading Chinese a struggle. The other five crews had walked aboard, fired a few shots, and calmly taken over. That he alone had had to fight his way aboard seemed odd, an inconsistency. Perhaps it had something to do with this vessel, this very ship, he'd thought, wondering for the merest moment if the machine could have a soul, but he'd shaken off the superstition immediately and gone on to the next of the endless number of tasks required to train the crew and the flotilla.

At times over the last days he had thought the task impossible, the men not understanding, fatigue setting in, the stress and the lack of fresh air and sufficient sleep and customary food beginning to make his men lose their edge. But finally, after one of his acidic speeches, the mood had changed, and like a soccer team roaring onto the field after being shouted at by the coach at halftime, the ship had begun to function, and the team solidified. The last exercises had been dramatically different, the ship the winner of each. After a day of crew rest, they were here, positioned at the Naze-Yakushima Gap, waiting for the fleet of Americans.

The Satellite News Network had proved amazingly useful, broadcasting the positions and intentions of the Americans, leaving out only their eventual landing site. It was such pinpoint intelligence that Chu had wondered if it was disinformation, but the confirming Chinese satellite photos of the incoming flotilla had shown the ships' positions exactly where the news reports claimed.

So far the plans for the attack had been going well, with the briefing of the crews being done in parallel with Chu training his own ship's men on the assault. A debate had raged about how the attack should be conducted, and Chu's plan had been called into question by his own men, chief among them the engineering officer, Lieutenant Li Xinmin, who insisted that the American 688 submarines be attacked prior to the surface force, while Chu planned to simply allow the 688s to drive blindly by. When the debate rose to a crescendo, Chu retreated to his stateroom and programmed a simulation, playing it that evening to the men in the messroom. In the first simulation scenario, Chu programmed them shooting first at the 688 subs. In response to word that the submarine screen had sunk, the ships of the incoming American fleet broke up and retreated, making torpedo targeting nearly impossible, with only ten percent of the ships sinking. In Chu's second scenario, with the surface ships coming under attack, the entire force was demolished, without exception. Chu had thought that would end the debate, but then the men had begun to worry about the effect of the 688s and their revenge, with a wave of land-based patrol aircraft screaming in to sink the Rising Suns.

That was not Chu's private worry. Each ship had 24 weapon tubes; each tube had two weapons, a loaded weapon and a magazine weapon. That was 48 torpedoes per ship, a total of 288 large-bore antiship weapons. With one torpedo expended per target, his forces had 288 chances to sink surface vessels. With one fleet of 170 ships, the 288 torpedoes should hold out, provided they didn't have duplicate targets. The only question in Chu's mind was what would happen when the second force from the American side came, as they eventually would. Surface ships hunting them unsuccessfully would soon yield to submarines. The first might be more 688I's, the antiques. But in time others would come, more capable units. They would begin to hunt down his force, and his ships had only so many weapons. The key had to be a rapid demoralizing strike, something so devastating that they wouldn't come back for more. Whether he could achieve that, no one knew.

With that thought Chu decided to turn to the task at hand and stop thinking about eventualities. He was a dark soul, as he'd known for years, and men like him did not drink in the champagne of victory, they waited for the pain of failure. And so, in Chu's mind, the time for debate had ended. He resumed the mantle of the commander and made the orders that had brought them here, where his force was set up to kill the invading surface fleet.

Chu reclined in his control couch at the intricate command console, looking over its marvels. The displays could be configured in any of a thousand modes. The screens could read out computer machine language, sonar curves, sonar raw data, weapons presets, camera video displays, virtually anything. He'd read through some of the manuals, even had some of the Japanese captain's notes translated to English, and by now he was becoming confident. The ship would function, and he would lead it and the men to victory.

He looked at the center screen, the god's-eye view of the sea, showing his *Arctic Storm* in the center. There were no sonar contacts, but he had instructed the Second Captain to show for him the approximate position of the other Rising Sun submarines. Twenty kilometers to the northeast was the *Lightning Bolt*, twenty kilometers to the southeast the *Thundercloud*, the three subs forming a triangle, but which was actually a bottle, with Chu's ship the bottom of the bottle, the other two the sides. Much farther to the east, in the Pacific Ocean, were the subs that would act as the bottle cork. The *Earthquake*, *Volcano*, and *Tsunami*. Chu's *Arctic Storm* was positioned directly in the path of the approaching American Rapid Deployment Force convoy. If the landing was to be Shanghai, as he was hoping, the convoy would drive right toward him. However, if Tsingtao was their course, it would bring them within two kilometers of the *Lightning Bolt*, and his *Arctic Storm* would be south of their track by about twelve kilometers. Similarly, if Hong Kong was their destination, the *Thundercloud* would be close and he would be off track by twelve kilometers. Either way, his three subs would still manage to bottle up the incoming fleet. He hoped central White China was the target, so he could shoot down their throats. Sinking three aircraft carriers of the massive Webb class would be glorious.

With his computer link to the radio gear, Chu had ordered the other subs to their coordinates using an ingenious encryption system—music. He had broadcast old, scratchy American and English rock 'n' roll songs, each one referred to in a code book. The Rolling Stones was the address for the *Thundercloud*, the Beatles selected for the *Volcano*, and so on, with individual songs keyed to different preplanned codebook positions. All the while he'd brought no suspicion upon himself from the listening American fleet. And that was for his initial positions.

If he needed to maneuver the fleet as the Americans

approached, he would use VHF bridge-to-bridge radios, having his Korean–speaking first officer come up on the radio as if he were a fishing boat captain speaking to other fishermen, telling them to get out of the way of the convoy, which would risk collision, scare the fish, and possibly dump them in their huge wake waves. Chu's trawlers currently filled the East China Sea.

"Admiral," Chen Zhu, the operations officer at the weapons console said, "is it time?"

"Yes," Chu said, his eye on the chart, then on his watch. If he acted too soon, he'd have to turn off the torpedo gyros to keep them from overheating, but if he warmed up the weapons too late, he'd lose vital seconds in the attack sequence. He decided to take the risk. "Open all twenty-four outer doors. Apply power to all torpedoes."

Chen spoke into his boom mike to the Second Captain, which then reported back to Chu:

"All doors coming open, sir, all torpedoes indicate power applied. All gyros are coming up to full revolutions now."

"Very good."

A tense moment of silence filled the room, only the electronic hum of the consoles and the deep bass roar of the air handlers audible. Then Lieutenant Commander Xhiu Liu, the navigator who stood watch as the sensor-console operator, reported:

"Admiral, I have a strong detect on a muffled seven-bladed screw showing up on low-frequency analysis, with high broadband noise from multiple pumps, with high flow noise and several flow-induced resonances. Sir, it's a 688I-class submerged warship, making way at high speed, headed directly toward us!"

USS *ANNAPOLIS*, SSN-760

Captain John Patton leaned over the port chart table aft of the periscope stand and frowned.

The deck trembled with the power of the main propulsion turbines. At flank speed, the screw turbulence caused the trembling to be transmitted to the huge thrust bearing and to the main motor, from there to the motor foundation to the hull. A couple more hours of shaking like this and the crew would experience severe fatigue. Doing a sonar sweep at forty-one knots was like searching for a contact lens on a superhighway at eighty miles per. Every instinct he had screamed at him to slow down and clear the ship's baffles.

Except that Admiral Henri's op order prohibited him even from coming to periscope depth, since that would dramatically slow him down. And the restriction on periscope-depth maneuvers meant that he was driving blind, having no idea what was going on topside. Patton walked his dividers across the big chart display, the electronic points measured to twenty nautical miles. They were now officially in the East China Sea. If USubCom's odd message had any validity at all, anyone waiting for them would be here, inside the protection of the Ryukyu Island chain. Why? Because everyone with a satellite television set knew where the American task force was. No one knew where it would go, but it had to make the turn at the southern island of Japan, south of Yakushima Island, and head on in. This would be the place to find anyone set up for an ambush.

He had to slow. But he also had to "sweep the sea" for the safety of the task force.

"Fuck this," Patton said out loud, raising the eyebrow of tall, skinny Lieutenant Karl Horburg, the young officer of the deck standing on the conn, "Off'sa'deck, slow to ten knots and turn off reactor recirc pumps. Notify Sonar that we're doing a baffle-clear maneuver. I want a good hard search at ten knots until I say to speed up again."

Horburg held up the standing order message from the fleet commander, not saying a word.

"Yeah, I know," Patton said, grimacing. "Baffle clear, OOD! Let's go!"

Horburg in turn barked to his subordinate. "Helm, all ahead one-third, turns for ten knots, maneuvering stop all reactor recirc pumps! Sonar, Conn, slowing to ten knots, baffle clear!"

"One-third, Helm, aye, turns for ten, downshift recirc pumps to stop, maneuvering answers, one-third, turns for ten. Recirc pumps will be downshifted as reactor power permits."

"Very well, Helm." Horburg plucked a microphone from the overhead, the mike suspended by a coiled cord. "Sonar, Conn, supervisor to control."

"Conn, Sonar, aye," a voice from the overhead speaker announced.

The helmsman called over his shoulder from his aircraft-style console, "Maneuvering reports all reactor circulation pumps at stop, all pumps coasting down, reactor in natural circulation."

"Very well, Helm," Horburg called.

Senior Chief Byron DeMeers appeared behind Horburg on the conn, a bemused expression on his face.

"You notice the speed indicator?" Patton said, nodding to the ship-control panel.

"Yeah! This is great," DeMeers said, a rare smile cracking his features. The chief paused to take a swig of his omnipresent Coke bottle. "A real sonar search. How many minutes are you giving me when we steady on course? And where you turning first?"

"Take two minutes heading north, then two south," Patton said in his don't-argue-with-me voice.

"Come on, Skipper, give me three minutes each leg," DeMeers said. "Who knows? It could be the difference between finding someone and getting a medal or finding a torpedo in our hull and getting a posthumous medal."

"Screw you, Senior Chief. Three minutes. No more. Now, get back in your hole and find me a bad guy." Patton's voice sounded irritated, but Horburg smiled, knowing the captain always sounded like that when he was amused.

The *Annapolis* coasted slowly down from forty-one knots to ten. She turned to the north, her BSY-4 sonar system straining to pick up a submerged contact. The nose-cone sonar spherical array, the wide-aperture hull array, and the thin-wire towed narrowband array were all tuned to the slightest noise of the ocean. These in turn fed the onboard supercomputer, the processors displaying, filtering, and analyzing the massive data gathered by the arrays, searching for the man-made noise—the needle in the haystack of nature's acoustical background.

For 180 seconds, Byron DeMeers added his own ears to the search, listening to each narrowband tonal bearing. One was a group of clicking shrimp, the other a lonely whale, one a trawler in the distance, a fourth a fishing boat even farther away. The screen glowed brightly to the east, where one hundred ten ships of the convoy were bearing down on them at thirty-five knots. They were putting so much noise in the water that the entire screen from bearing 085 to 095 was blued out with high-intensity broadband noise from the thrashing screws and plowing hulls.

At the clicking of the third minute on DeMeers' stopwatch, he spoke into his microphone. "Conn, Sonar, ready for leg two." Dumping his processor buckets in the narrowband sector, he waited for the ship to come around, concentrating on the broadband contacts as the ship turned. His noises remained constant at their bearings, the approaching convoy, if possible, getting even louder as they approached.

"Sonar, Conn, steady course south."

"Conn, Sonar, aye."

Another three minutes, another search.

On 155 hertz, the spike of a narrowband frequency tonal kept growing. The bell tonal could only be man-made, a frequency put into the water by rotating machinery. It was a turbine generator perhaps, spinning like a top blown by high-pressure steam, converting thermal energy to mechanical and mechanical to electrical, the high note as pure as an opera singer's final note.

"Sonar, Captain, you ready to resume speed and base course?"

"Captain, Sonar, no," DeMeers said calmly into the

microphone, dropping the bombshell. "Conn, Sonar, new narrowband contact, designate sierra two four, 155 hertz bearing zero seven five or two five five, low signal-to-noise ratio, possible submerged warship."

CHAPTER 18

"Sir." Xhiu's voice from the sensor panel grew more urgent. "The enemy submarine contact is inbound at eighty clicks, distance unknown, but the bearing rate is steady. He's barreling in at us, sir, distance to track is zero!"

Chu knew the tone for the entire battle would be determined by his initial response—would he put the crew on edge or reassure them?

"Very good, Navigator. Continue to track contact, tag number ST-1, and report speed, solution, and distance to track." ST-1 stood for submarine target number one, Chu's shorthand in case several contacts cropped up. "Ship Control Officer, bring us around to the left, left ten effective degrees rudder, course north, speed twenty-two clicks, depth three hundred meters, and keep the angle gentle."

"Aye sir, left ten degrees rudder, course zero zero zero, speed increasing to twenty-two clicks, diving to three hundred meters, flat angle."

"Very good. Nav, get a Second Captain target solution." Chu was driving off the track of the target, getting a parallax computer solution to the target using only listening sonar, as the Second Captain's on-line tactical manual recommended.

"Aye, sir, solution is crude but shows target ST-1 inbound, seventy-seven clicks, distance thirty-five kilometers. Our distance to track is six hundred meters and opening very slowly. He's going to pass very close, sir."

"Very good, Nav. Ship Control, slow to five clicks."

"Five clicks, aye, Admiral."

"But, sir," Xhiu said, "he'll be coming just a few ship lengths from us. We need to open distance."

Be cool, Chu thought. "No, ship silence is more important than distance," he said.

"Sir, are you still committed to letting the American submarines go? We never thought they'd come this close. This one may detect us. Maybe we should shoot at him now."

"No," Chu said. "We'll let them both go. Otherwise the torpedo noise and explosions will alert the fleet. Now, listen up in the control room. Target ST-1 is coming at us like a freight train going full out, and he's making just as much noise. I sincerely doubt he'll ever look up to take notice of us. Everyone calm the hell down. Be alert for the second 688I. The fleet's order of battle showed two escort subs. Also, watch the first one for any sign of a counter-detection." *Please let me know,* he thought, *if the 688 hears me.*

For the next few minutes Chu waited. His lower left panel remained tuned to the face of Lieutenant Commander Xhiu Liu, the sensor-panel operator's face as much an instrument as any Second Captain display. The excitable navigator's eyes grew wide, one hand to his headset earphone, alarm growing on his face. Chu waited for what seemed an eternity for the man to speak.

"Nav, what is it?"

"Admiral, contact ST-1 signal is suddenly growing dim. He's slowing down. Coasting down, screw turn count coming way down. Sir, I don't—I don't know what he's doing. He's—" The navigator had begun to sputter. Odd, he had such a cool head when doing commando operations, but put a nuclear submarine under him with orders to fight and he grew as fidgety as a six-year-old. Perhaps it was his frustration level—during a commando raid a man had control, but up against an enemy sub, only the captain had control.

"Just watch him," Chu said calmly, trying to reassure Xhiu.

"Yessir, still slowing, still slowing."

Seconds clicked by like molasses. Chu watched the raw sonar data appearing on the upper right console. The processed data—crowded curves and graphs and broadband waterfalls—were crammed into the center right display. He found the 688I, where a pulsing computer cursor outlined it, the narrowband three-dimensional graphs surrounded by thin lines of boxes as the computer outlined the noise to process, looking outward, seeking transients, nailing down the bearing to the vessel. The central god's-eye view showed his own ship in the center, a blinking diamond symbol marking the estimated position of the enemy submarine.

"He's much slower now, sir. The bearing rate is high left—he's turning. Another sonar contact coming up also, sir. Contact WT-1, multiple contacts, surface warships, bearing 088, bearings very diffuse, a whole range of bearings to the east. On my mother's blood, they're everywhere. I'm tracking, must be, no, sir, over a hundred ships! I can't—"

"Congratulations, you found the convoy, but what is ST-1 doing?"

"Um, he's slowing and turning, steady on his new course."

"Turn-count speed?"

"Eighteen clicks."

He's looking for us, Chu thought. *Maybe he sniffed something at high speed, and he's slowed down to get a better picture.* "Men," he said, "the 688I's turn is most probably a routine sonar calibration maneuver. Everyone relax." He smirked—he never thought he'd say those two words in the heat of this operation.

More time clicked off.

"ST-1 is turning again, sir, straight toward us, coming around. Could be moving into attack position, Admiral." Xhiu was losing his cool, Chu thought. He glanced significantly at Lo Sun, as if to say, *Get over there and calm him the hell down.* Lo walked quietly around the command console to stand behind the sensor console.

"Steady, Navigator. Weapons Officer, program tubes

ten and eleven for target ST-1. Nagasaki II torpedoes, weapon ten programmed for ultraquiet swimout. Weapon eleven for high-thrust gas-generator ejection with high-speed ship-to-target transit. Gentlemen, your attention, please. Prepare to attack submerged contact ST-1."

USS *ANNAPOLIS*, SSN-760

"Sonar, Captain, classify sierra two four *now*!"

There was no arguing with John George Patton when he had his blood up. Contrary to the intent of the U.S. Navy regulations, he maintained an easygoing, almost casual relationship with DeMeers. The expert sonarman had been a frequent guest at Patton's Sandbridge Beach house, where they ate grilled burgers and talked about how the Navy was going to hell, or at least they had until the new admiral had shown up to kick everyone's ass in gear, as DeMeers put it. But when there was trouble, Patton's formerly easy manner vanished with so little a trace that an observer would never have guessed that the two men had put away several dozen cases together. At this moment it was strictly military discipline, officer to enlisted, the rank of O-6 to E-8.

Patton had the words on his lips, prepared to say, "Snapshot tube one." Within ten seconds that would flood the number one tube, open the outer door, and launch down the bearing line to the intruder submarine. Yet he couldn't open the door until he had a definite hostile target for practical reasons—having an open door caused a flow-induced resonance at high speed, like blowing over a bottle mouth. The whistle would scream out into the sea and announce their presence. Patton didn't intend to open a tube door unless he was ready to shoot to kill, which he was, his knuckles going white on the stainless steel handrail of the conn platform.

The officer of the deck, Lieutenant Horburg, half stood, half kneeled on the leather seat at the second console of the BSY-4 row of computers, the row called the attack center. Furiously he dialed in a stack of dots, trying to use their two maneuvers to see what distance and speed of the target fit the data. He also needed to gauge where they'd be in the near future, say, five minutes, when a torpedo would be programmed to launch. The solution was crude, but was coming in, showing the target 24,000 yards to the northeast, just outside the sector of sonar clutter from the surface task force.

Patton concentrated on the BSY panel, position two, waiting to see what fell out of Horburg's computer game. So far it looked like the target was zooming up to them at over 35 knots. Patton frowned, knowing that couldn't be a lurking diesel boat, not with that speed. It had to be nuclear, but if it was hostile, why didn't it slow down to be quiet and shoot at them when they didn't suspect? Only one reason, Patton thought. It wasn't an enemy at all. It had to be the *Santa Fe,* the other escort submarine.

"Captain, Sonar aye, sierra two four is a submerged contact, distant, low signal-to-noise ratio, making forty knots on one seven-bladed screw, classified 688 class improved."

"Captain, aye," Patton called. "Designate sierra two four the USS *Santa Fe.*"

"Conn, Sonar, aye."

"Supervisor to control."

DeMeers walked in, his shoulders slumping, a fresh bottle of Coke whooshing open as he unscrewed the cap. "Don't suppose we ought to be shooting Chrissy Carnage," he said. "Bad for the fitness report."

"Yeah," Patton said. "And the *Santa Fe* wives' club would tend to frown on that."

"Damned shame. It looked like it would be a good watch. Get rid of some of those old torpedoes."

"Anything else out there?"

"Cap'n, the sea is as clean as a hound's tooth. It's just us, Chrissy, and about a gross of big, fat surface ships."

"Yeah, well, while we sit here and chat, those surface ships are gonna go screaming overhead, and they'll think *we're* the bad guy."

"I guess it's back to fucking flank, then," DeMeers

said, his disgust not completely feigned. "Hell, it's like trying to listen to a distant voice with your head in the dryer. While it's going."

"Tell it to Admiral Jean-Paul Henri," Patton said in a mock French accent. He snapped at Horburg, his tone acid, as it always was when he gave his orders. "OOD, let's kick it. Course west at flank."

"Flank it west, aye, sir," Horburg said. Stepping up to the conn, he lifted another coiled-cord mike to his mouth, looking like a yuppie trucker with a CB radio. "Maneuvering, Conn, shift the reactor to forced circulation."

A speaker rasped from the overhead, "Shift the reactor to forced circulation, Conn, maneuvering, aye. Commencing fast insertion."

"Sonar, Conn, increasing speed to flank, turning to course west. Helm, right full rudder, all ahead flank, steady course west!" Horburg barked at the helmsman, who turned the control yoke and reached to the panel and rotated a knob, called the engine order telegraph, to FLANK. A needle on the telegraph panel rotated from the position marked ⅓ to FLANK. On the helm-display animation of the stern of the submarine, the rudder moved to the right to the thirty-degree position.

"Sir, my rudder's right full, maneuvering answers all-ahead flank," the helmsman called.

Horburg slurred his "Very well, Helm" response, saying, "Vrewlm."

"Conn, Sonar, aye," from DeMeers on the overhead speaker.

"Conn, maneuvering," the speaker blared, "Reactor's in forced circ, reactor recirc pumps one, two, three, and four running in fast speed, answering all-ahead flank."

Horburg hit the mike button, his response slurred to a single word: "Maneuvering, Conn, aye."

The deck began to tremble again as the speed-indicator needle climbed from ten knots past fifteen, sailing through the twenties and thirties, slowly approaching forty, finally settling out at forty-one knots.

"Sir, passing course two six zero to the right, ten degrees from ordered course."

"Very well, Helm."

"Sir, steady course west!" the helmsman called.

"Very well, Helm." Despite his obvious compliance to Patton's orders, Horburg turned formally to the captain. "Captain, ship is at flank speed heading west."

"Into the sunset," Patton said, half to himself. He had one eye on the chart display, the other on the sonar display mounted on the overhead at the attack center.

Strange, he thought. He'd completed his slow sonar search, yet he didn't feel any better. When they'd come through the Naze-Yakushima Gap, he'd had the oddest feeling, that there was something out there. But then when he'd slowed down, turned the pumps off, and coasted down to best listening speed, he'd found nothing there. Of course, he only gave it seven minutes and was still going ten knots. Who knows what he would have seen if he'd gone two knots, bare steerageway, and given it a good hour for the narrowband processors to integrate all the major frequency buckets at all points of the compass? Dammit, he almost answered aloud, if he'd done that, the convoy would have overrun him, all their screws cavitating and thrashing the water upstairs into a sonar sound nightmare. No, that was the best he could do, and it had cost him dearly. Counting the coast-down and acceleration time, he'd lost a full eleven minutes at forty-one knots, slipping behind his previous position by 15,000 yards, a full 7.5 nautical miles, so now he was only some three miles ahead of Chris Carnage's *Santa Fe,* twenty-three miles west of the convoy instead of his previous thirty. His orders were explicit, to get as far ahead of the convoy as possible. It was just too bad, Patton thought, that to follow the spirit of Jean-Paul's orders he had to violate the letter of them.

Patton stared at the chart, but his eyes were focused into infinity. It just didn't seem right. He had that irritating feeling he experienced when he knew he was forgetting something.

He walked into DeMeers' realm. The blue overhead

lights of the sonar room cast a sickening glow over the large consoles of the BSY-4 displays. Two of DeMeers' four console seats were empty. Only DeMeers and his operator, a third-class petty officer, had on their headphones. The senior chief took one earpiece off, a look of mischief on his face.

"Something's not right," Patton said.

"True, I haven't seen a woman in a week," De-Meers said.

"I'm serious. There's something out there."

DeMeers' face immediately changed to a frowning look of worry. He looked at Patton for a long moment. "I don't know if I've ever told you this, Skipper, but you've never been wrong when you've said that in the past."

A shiver crawled up Patton's spine. This was almost the same eerie conversation they'd had two years ago, a half hour before the *Abraham Lincoln* took its first torpedo.

"Senior, I'd give anything to be wrong right now."

"Want to take a console?" DeMeers asked, holding up a headset.

"Nah. I'll go back to control. Just keep a weather eye out."

"Yessir."

Patton absentmindedly wandered out of sonar, finding himself back at the chart table without remembering going into the control room. There was no shaking the feeling.

There was something out there.

Xhiu's question hung in the air. Chu ignored it for a second to scan his console displays.

"No," he finally said, "I'm not going to shoot him."

"But, Admiral, he's gone right past us and sped back up. He didn't hear us."

"Exactly, Nav. He's not a threat. Not right now. And shooting him will just put a big ball of noise in the ocean, and the surface force will hear it, even over the noise of their own screws."

"But the second submarine is nearing closest point of approach. What about him?"

Chu smiled at his console, knowing his face was being displayed at the sensor-control console where Xhiu Liu was strapped in. "You know what I'm going to say to that, don't you, Nav?" Xhiu cracked his first smile of the watch. "Let him go."

"Aye, Admiral."

"Now, are we set up on the convoy?"

"They're coming in at sixty-five clicks, distance thirty-five kilometers."

"It's time to come up to mast-broach depth. Target ST-2, the second submarine. Is he opening distance now?"

"Past closest point of approach and opening," Xhiu said.

"Very good. Ship Control Officer, slow to fifteen clicks, mast-broach depth, twenty-two meters, up-angle thirty degrees. Mr. First, take the command console."

As the deck tilted upward, Chu's seat leaned down toward his aft-facing console. With some difficulty he unbuckled his harness. Pulling himself up with hand-holds placed at the top and sides of the console, he stood on a deck that was slanted at a thirty-degree angle. Lo Sun squeezed into the narrow gap between the cocoon-like console and the reclining seat, strapping himself into the harness. In the meantime Chu pulled himself to the circular platform of the periscope stand in the corner. He hit a mushroom button, and the periscope seat unfolded and lowered, the arrangement a sort of motorcycle without wheels. Chu straddled the seat, his hands on the scope grips, his eyes to the binocular eyepieces. Because the periscope mast was retracted, the display in the binoculars was dark and dead. Chu trained the seat until it was pointing exactly forward, the way he liked to start a periscope search.

"Second Captain, control room lights on dim," he said to his boom microphone. The room lights dimmed till he was in twilight, to eliminate glare from the room interfering with his view out the instrument.

"Nav, range to the convoy?"

"Sir, twenty-four kilometers."

"Admiral, ship's depth is passing through one hundred meters," Yong Wong reported from the ship control console.

"Bring her up," Chu ordered. "Second Captain, raise the periscope mast."

He returned to the periscope, and as it rose from its haven in the fin, the darkness in Chu's eyepieces lightened just a bit. He rotated his left grip down, training the view to angle toward the surface high above. With his right index finger he pulled a trigger on the right grip, and the motorcycle seat slowly rotated clockwise, as did Chu's view out the rotating periscope mast. He could see sunbeams streaming downward from a lighter portion of the sea directly above, but otherwise it was a blur. Chu kept rotating the instrument slowly, his view trained upward.

"Thirty meters, sir. Taking ship's angle flat."

"Very good."

As the deck angle began to become level, Chu was able to sense the deck rocking almost imperceptibly, rolling to starboard just a little, then back to port. The waves overhead came into focus, their underside an odd silvery color. The sea was not as calm as he'd expected, but with small waves. Now that he could see the surface, he sped up the platform rotational speed.

"No hulls, nothing close," he said into his boom mike.

Finally the lens of the fiberoptic transmitter mast, the periscope, broke the surface. Water blurred the lens for a moment as Chu rotated the platform, still looking for ships passing too close to their position. Nothing was visible as the film of water cleared from the lens. The horizon came sharply into view, the world above composed of only two elements—white overcast sky and dark blue water—and the line of the horizon was ruler sharp. Chu slowed his rotational speed, searching in low power for surface ships.

"Nav, latest bearing to the convoy."

"Sir, zero nine four."

Chu trained the scope to the east. He increased the optic power to medium, and the horizon seemed to grow closer. Yet there was nothing coming. He snapped his right grip again, increasing the power to high, with 24X magnification. The sea jumped slightly in the view, making it harder to see clearly, since the slightest movement of the ship made the scene outside jump. But even in 24X the horizon was clean.

"Second Captain," he muttered, "superimpose geographic plot on top of reticle."

The computer god's-eye view came up in a sort of heads-up display, superimposed on top of the view outside. The plot showed up as the direction he was looking, and at the other end of the bearing line at twelve o'clock were several dozen hostile-contact diamond symbols. The distance to the convoy was shown as being nineteen kilometers. He bit his lip—he should be able to see the tall masts of the aircraft carriers by now, or at least the lead vessel.

"Ship Control, change depth to twenty-one meters keel depth." That would stick the periscope mast skyward by nine meters, a telephone pole sticking up above the sea. His new "height of eye" should make a difference. As his view moved farther from the waves, the ship coming shallower, the horizon changed. What once before had been a sharp line between sky and sea now blurred slightly.

And now visible were three black spots on the horizon. Chu focused high power on the spots, finding them to be just portions of the tall islands, the massive hulls of the ships still hidden by the curvature of the earth. He then applied double-high power with a trigger on the right grip, increasing power from 24X to 48X, but the first spot on the horizon jumped around, tough to keep it in sight. Even in the bouncing image, though, Chu could see that it was the island of an aircraft carrier.

"Three surface contacts, gentlemen. Bearing zero nine five to the center target. Contacts are hull down but approaching rapidly." Chu cleared his throat, enjoying the moment. "Designate the central carrier target number WT-1. Target to the left is WT-2, target to the right is WT-3. Prepare for torpedo attack, tube assignments to follow. Ops Officer, all weapons nominal?"

Chen Zhu, at the weapon console in the opposite corner of the room, piped up. "All twenty-four primary torpedoes nominal, Admiral."

"Very well, all tubes and all weapons shall be set to ultraquiet swimout, all speed settings to ultraquiet slow speed, shallow-draft approach, immediate enable. If we are detected or if we need to hurry, we'll switch to impulse mode on the gas generators and go to high-speed transit. Now, tube assignments . . . Target WT-1, central aircraft carrier, assign tubes one and two. Target WT-2, left carrier, assign tubes three and four. Target WT-3, five and six."

"Aye, sir," Chen said. "Tube assignments set and coming up on your heads-up display now."

The tube assignments flashed up for a moment, the geographic plot vanishing. The three carriers were closing, their islands becoming more focused, the ships grayish blue in the haze. Soon a row of other ships became visible, just the mastheads. And then the hulls of the carriers came into view, the center one first, then the ones flanking it.

"Status, weps?"

"Tubes one through six ready for launch, targets locked in on visual and sonar. Did you want to confirm range with the laser?"

"No, it could give us away. Five seconds, gentlemen," Chu said. The three carriers were now easily made out at 24X. "Ship Control, take us down to depth twenty-six meters."

"Twenty-six meters, aye."

"Three, two, one . . . tube one swimout!"

"Tube one enabled in swimout mode, sir, and tube one is clear. Bow camera indicates weapon one away."

"Tube two swimout."

"Two enabled, swimout mode, camera indicates weapon away."

The launch sequence continued until the first six Nagasaki II torpedoes quietly left the ship, two en route to each aircraft carrier.

A kilometer from the *Arctic Storm,* several torpedoes slowly made their way to the aircraft carriers coming toward them, their passively listening sonars guiding them in. Over forty kilometers farther west, the two escort submarines cruised on at top speed, their sonars hearing nothing suspicious.

CHAPTER 19

Weapon number one, the first launched from the bow of the *Arctic Storm,* plowed through the sea toward the approaching convoy. Its onboard computer—small and simple, yet of vastly superior power compared to the original Nagasaki design—computed the distance to the target and the target's heading and speed. The weapon was driving toward a point in space where its speed would cause its track to intersect the carrier's. It was guided in mid-flight by a nose-cone sonar array, the front of the weapon a flat-panel cover over the transducer. Initially the weapon sonar was programmed to be passive listen-only, in receive mode. Pinging was rarely to be allowed, only if the unit lost its target in passive mode, but the target was so loud ahead that losing it would be impossible. The four massive screws of the target aircraft carrier thrashed loudly in the sea, coming from exactly the same bearing the weapon expected to hear it.

According to the computer model of launching platform, ocean, and target position, the weapon calculated that it was halfway to the target. It had been set by the launching tube to "immediate enable" mode, meaning it was allowed to detonate at any time after leaving the tube rather than being required to count out a distance from the firing ship. Fully armed, the warhead was warmed up, awaiting only for the initial low-explosive charge to detonate.

Aft of the nose-cone-mounted sonar transducer electronic package but forward of the onboard computer hardware was a ring around the torpedo skin linked to several redundant electronic modules making up the hull-proximity sensors. One sensor was magnetic, feeling the lines of the earth's magnetic force, which were evenly spaced through the sea, but tremendously focused by the huge iron mass of a ship, a target. The magnetic sensors saw the distant spacing of the magnetic lines of force as white light and the gathering together of many lines of force, focused by the ship mass, as darkness on a white field. When the electronic module saw a dark spot of increased magnetism, they fed a positive signal to the computer's warhead-detonation software. The second sensor was a wideband optical sensor, looking outward to the sea and able to sense the darkness below and the light above from the surface; a dark surface ship's hull caused a positive signal to the detonator. The third sensor was a blue laser, shining outward in all directions to the sea, able to sense the presence of something that was not water or surface reflection. To it a hull stood out in stark contrast to the rest of the environment.

For the surface-ship-target mode, the torpedo had enabled the magnetic proximity sensor and the blue laser, with confirmation coming from the less reliable visual sensor. The software wanted to see a "hard detect" on magnetic or a definite laser sighting, confirmed by optics if possible. The optics could be fooled by a sudden cloud obstructing the sun, and were fooled at night by the phosphorescence of a ship's wake. A laser detect absent a magnetic detection would be a valid detonation signal, since the weapon would assume that either the magnetic sensor had failed, or that an antimagnetic anomaly device was in use. This was a new torpedo countermeasure employed by warships to alter the magnetic field surrounding the ship, a device that was only modestly successful.

The weapon sped on at low-approach speed, 60 clicks, putting out its 186 hertz tonal into the water and emitting broadband white noise at 83 decibels relative to the ocean's background noise, in the 50-decibel range. A broadband white-noise receiver would have picked out the weapon from a distance of ten kilometers. The 186 tonal sound-pressure level was emitted at 78 decibels, and would appear on the typical narrowband receiver at a distance of 30 kilometers. But the nearest broadband receiver was in the sonar dome of the destroyers behind the row of cruisers. The three aircraft carriers had no sonar systems, leaving that equipment to the cruiser, destroyer, and frigate hulls. The second row of warships, the Aegis cruisers, had bow-mounted sonar domes configured for active pinging sonar rather than passive listening, and were capable of streaming a DynaCorp T-65 and T-148 towed sonar arrays, but the towed arrays were fragile and required clear sea miles astern, making the array unusable while steaming in a tight formation. The cruisers also were not using their active sonar domes, since the active sonar would interfere with the passive sonar searches of the 688I submarines ahead. In the third row behind the cruisers were the Aegis destroyers, which carried bow-mounted active sonars, all disengaged, and towed sonar arrays including the T-65, T-148, and T-22, all of which had been retracted and stowed for later use outside the battle formation. In addition, the destroyers carried a Seahawk V patrol helicopter with a dipping sonar transducer capable of active or passive sonar. The frigates behind the destroyers were similarly equipped, though the towed array systems varied.

The only passive sonars engaged by the convoy were onboard the 688I submarines, because a surface-ship sonar would hear so much broadband noise from the waves, hull flow, and screw that it would never hear an intruder submarine until it was within a fraction of a kilometer away. The surface ships counted on active pinging, when it was authorized, and a deep-running towed array that could dip far below the surface thermal layer, which kept noise from the surface channeled back to the surface and noise from the deep focused back deep. At the moment, though, these were uselessly stowed on large cable reels waiting for the ships to move to open water.

The passive-searching 688Is, far over the horizon on

the other side of the *Arctic Storm,* were crippled by their distance from the torpedoes going the opposite direction and by the fact that they were facing west and the noise was due east. Their bow sonar spheres and wide-aperture hull arrays were not positioned to hear astern, and the propulsion noise from the reactor and turbine systems as well as the screw noise made detection of astern noises impossible in any case. Both 688I's were equipped with rear-looking sonar systems in a towed teardrop array, but that rearview system was more of a self-defense mechanism, a last-resort warning of torpedo attack, rather than a sophisticated fleet defense sonar.

As the result of the poor deployment of the escort fleet's antisubmarine-warfare equipment, six Mod II torpedoes sailed eastward undetected toward the hulls of the aircraft carriers.

The first-launched weapon sailed under the bow of the center aircraft carrier. Its proximity sensors, tuned to the most sensitive mode, detected the hull magnetic-force anomaly almost immediately. The optic module saw darkness above. The blue laser easily saw the hull, so close that it was less than a half torpedo-length away. The three hull-proximity detectors faithfully sent their signals to the weapon computer software, where a series of hard and soft interlocks monitored and controlled the arming and ignition train of the explosives. The weapon computer followed its programmed logic, which directed it not to wait—there was no delay built in for this weapon as there was for the second unit. That way the first would detonate under the bow of the target and the second would detonate under the aft hull. A software "soft" contact closed, sending power to a physical contact that completed the battery circuit to the two low-explosive ignition canisters, one forward in the warhead zone and one aft. The canisters, receiving the spark of electricity, blew up, thereby igniting the secondary explosives, which were less sensitive but more powerful, located at the torpedo centerline at the forward and aft parts of the plasma warhead. The secondary explosive then detonated the forward and aft high-explosive, shaped charges. The explosion front expanded from the forward shaped charge heading aft and from the aft shaped charge heading forward; the two explosions compressed the warhead material in the center to several hundred atmospheres. The elevating temperatures and pressures of the explosion zones started the reaction required for plasma formation, a complex series of chemical containers vaporizing and adding components to the recipe at different timed stages of the detonation. The temperature and pressures soared as the explosion compression continued, bringing four masses of plasma igniter together into one critical mass. The plasma igniter exploded ratcheting the temperature and pressure even higher, though the skin of the torpedo remained intact at this point, the weapon still moving through the sea as its internals became a ball of flame.

As the weapon internals reached tertiary ignition temperature, the components of the plasma fuel detonated, and plasma ignition commenced, almost instantaneously converting the mass energy of the warhead molecules into thermal energy. The central mass became a plasma, an ultradense molecular structure sending all molecules' electrons into space in a single concentrated wave; then wave after wave of photons flashed outward as the plasma mass glowed. The ignition continued, the plasma volume increasing from mere cubic centimeters to a cubic meter, finally the plasma front erupted from the skin of the torpedo and consumed it in the growing plasma volume. The water around the torpedo was added to the plasma volume, growing from a cubic meter to over twenty cubic meters, the volume fed by the igniter material until it was completely consumed. The volume was now reaching hundreds of millions of degrees, hotter than the surface of the sun. The thermal energy was greater than the detonation of a half dozen old-fashioned hydrogen bombs.

The plasma volume reached outward and upward, reaching the first molecules forming the hull of the aircraft carrier above. First the epoxy resin of the outer layer of paint, then the urethane intermediate coating, and the inorganic zinc primer, all those chemicals disassociated from their complex molecular structure and dissolved into atomic nuclei and electrons. The plasma front reached the next layer, the steel formed of carbon and iron atoms in a matrix called a solid phase, with an elongated grain structure formed by the rolling of the steel plates in the mill at a place called Bethlehem. The steel plate grains melted together from the intense heat of the approaching plasma, the iron and carbon swimming together in a volume of high-temperature suspension. The rising temperature excited the molecules to the point that they too joined the plasma.

The plasma's growth soon stopped, the intensely high temperatures unable to be sustained for more than a few microseconds. The cooler temperatures of the surrounding world drew the heat away by radiation, convection, and conduction until the hundreds of millions of degrees had become mere millions. The plasma volume—once at the boundary of the steel hull above, having eaten its way a meter and a half into the ship—collapsed. Though not hot enough to be a plasma, the remaining high temperature was still intensely hot, hotter than all phenomena except a fission-bomb explosion. The thermal energy of the former plasma boiled the water within a hundred meters into an intense volume of high-pressure steam. The shock wave from the steam and vaporized iron slammed upward into the hull. The incredibly high temperatures reached the hull remainder next, hot enough to change the steel to iron vapor. The molecules wanted to fly out into space from their incredibly high kinetic energy, but having nowhere to go because of the surrounding matrix of steel, this caused a soaring pressure wave that blasted through the ship.

The heat, pressure, and blast effect propagated upward through higher-level decks of the ship's hull, the solid metal continuing to vaporize and add to the pressure wave. The hull continued to disintegrate, the structural steel vaporizing as well as the steel of heavy equipment—catapult machinery, the anchors with all their chains and winch machinery. In addition to metal, there were other atoms in the advancing fireball—electrical cables, plastic insulation, more paint, vinyl flooring tiles, life jacket material, paper, computers, and flesh, the flesh of human beings who had been warehoused in the forward third of the hull in places called called berthing compartments. Row after row, columns and columns, of bunks housed men and women sleeping in the afternoon after having stood their watches through the night. Some of the people were sitting at tables, playing cards, studying technical manuals, writing letters to wives and husbands and children who slept on the other side of the hemisphere.

The people in the berthing compartments never became aware of the blast of the fireball reaching them. Their molecular structure was burned and vaporized long before their nerves had time to transmit sensations. Their brain matter disintegrated into basic elements in the next microseconds, with no time to record or react to the physical phenomenon of the high-temperature fireball.

As the blast wave reached the upper deck, it no longer had the thermal energy to vaporize the molecules it encountered to their gaseous state. It had enough energy, however, to melt the metal atoms it encountered, and was still transforming water molecules to high-pressure, roaring steam. The temperature was still hundreds of thousands of degrees hotter than the blast wave of conventional explosives. The shock continued upward and aft, consuming the ship, the iron atoms melting from solid to liquid, now at a temperature that the iron and carbon combusted in the presence of the oxygen atoms of the air, the ship literally burning like the tip of a struck match. The blast moved on, reaching the upper deck of the ship and violently blowing the deck surface structure high into the sky. Some resolidified iron chunks tumbled end over end two kilometers in the air. The blast roared over the three dozen jets that had been tied down in a ready position, half of them F-22 DynaCorp fighter jets being prepared for the assault on the Asian continent to the west, the other half S-14 Blackbeard twin-engine antisubmarine aircraft readied to take flight in the event of a submarine alert. In a flash these advanced jet planes became molten and burned aluminum and carbon fiber and burned plastic, their structure likewise blown thousands of meters skyward.

The blast peeled the deck back and up. The ship just forward of the island vanished into what visually appeared to be an orange ball of intensely hot flames. The explosion age was now twenty milliseconds. Twenty thousand microseconds before, the ball of thermal energy had been contained in the body of a weapon called a Nagasaki II. Now the miraculous thundering sphere of white and orange heat blew farther aft toward the island, the forward surface of the tower above the formerly flat deck burning and disintegrating.

The ship that had been christened the USS *James Webb* was now only half a ship. The forward section had been either consumed by the plasma, vaporized by the plasma after effect into a gas, melted by the intense heat of the post-plasma blast, burned into flames by the continuing fireball, or sent hurtling outward and upward. The place where there had been a ship's bow, was now a spherical ball of high-temperature molecules of steam and condensing iron vapor and combustion products from the burned steel. The sphere was two hundred meters in diameter, and was cooling as it expanded, now turning from orange to a reddish glow, some of its periphery darkening into black smoke. The sphere was beginning to change shape, the physics of hot air rising and cool falling causing it to press upward and collapse below. As it did, the sphere began to rise from the hull waterline.

The sphere, rising above the deck, started an effect called thermal radiation. The intensely high temperatures emitted infrared energy at an enormous rate, and the traveling waves of heat melted the glass of the island that had looked down at the deck, then moved farther aft and set the bodies of forty-three crewmen on fire, burning their flesh rapidly down to the bone, igniting their lungs and cooking their brains, though not nearly as quickly as the bodies in the bow. The radiation wave reached the aircraft anchored on the aft deck and ignited them all to balls of burning carbon fiber and jet fuel. The deck surface was now engulfed in an orange volume of flames.

The radiation waves continued in a shock wave. The air surrounding the surface of the earth acted as a drum, the explosion as a drum beat. A double shock wave traveled outward from the sphere, smashing into the island, where the 117 men inside had already been busy dying from the radiation and blast effects. The wave blasted over the flaming ruins of the aft deck aircraft to the two other aircraft carriers—still untouched—smashing every glass window in their islands and blowing them inward. The shock wave weakened as it progressed outward, breaking only a third of the glass windows of the Aegis cruisers' bridges.

The bow fireball, now a hundred milliseconds after having breached the deck, rose over the island, transforming from a sphere to a mushroom cap, leaving below it a thick stem of rising black and brown smoke and orange flames, feeding the rising orange and red ball continuing to rise into the sky, the buoyancy of the atmosphere bringing it higher. As it rose to a level five hundred meters above the deck, the ship seemed suddenly to take notice of the fact that it no longer had its front half. The ship had been going thirty-five knots, or sixty-five kilometers per hour, some eighteen meters per second. Since the explosion the hull had continued moving almost two meters, the effect of the blast slowing the ship slightly, but as the first full second moved into the second, the half hull moved another two meters forward into water that had flooded into the crater of steam.

Where there had once been a steel structure that kept seawater out, only a ragged, blasted, burning edge where the ship ended and the sea began still existed. Water flowed remorselessly into the hull, submerging ruined equipment and dead, broken bodies, invading aft where there had once been watertight bulkheads and now were ruined and ruptured pieces of steel. The ship's forward part, at the front half of the island, listed slightly into the water as the event passed into its third second. The aft deck began to tilt upward, the still rotating screws beginning to emerge from the water.

In the fourth second the ship pitched forward as the water rushed in and filled the hulk of the vessel. The screws came completely out of the water aft, still turning, water droplets cascading everywhere. The burning airplanes on the deck—those that hadn't been blown overboard—began to slip forward, sliding down the deckplates toward the sea. As the first flaming jet was about to hit the water, five seconds after the torpedo detonation, the second Nagasaki II torpedo detonated under the aft hull.

Ten seconds after that torpedo detonation there was nothing left of the 110,000-ton ship bigger than a few meters across. Some of the debris began to rain down on the sea, which was now white boiling foam two kilometers in diameter. Other debris was already sinking rapidly to the ocean floor, including the two reactor cores, each the size of a house and made of high-tensile alloys, mostly intact while they sank, boiling the seawater that had flooded their coolant passages. Some of the debris floated on the water, mostly from the island, which had taken the least damage, since it was in the middle of the ship and high above the water. Included in the flotsam on the foam were chunks of wood conference tables, a few rubber hoods that had shrouded the radar scopes, pieces of paper, several foam mattresses from the amidships berthing spaces, and twenty or so bodies in various states of dismemberment. The naked torso, arms, and head of one man bobbed in the gentle waves, one of his hands gone, the other missing fingers. The body was lit up by the lights of the exploding plasma fireballs to the east as the carriers *Roosevelt* and *Kinnaird McKee* began their cycles of death. The man's face was slightly charred, the flesh of his face partly red from blood, partly black from the flames, and his right eye was punctured, leaving behind a misshapen hole and running flesh, but still he was quite recognizable. His clothes were burned away, leaving no trace of the three silver stars he had worn on his collar or the fleet command pin he'd worn beneath a surface warfare insignia—crossed swords in front of the bow of a destroyer. There was also no sign of the name pin that he had worn over his right pocket, which had read VICE ADM. JEAN-PAUL HENRI.

CHAPTER 20

Captain Eddie Maddox threw his binoculars to the deck and lunged behind the helm console, blinded by the first flash.

As his husky frame turned and began to fall to the deckplates, the shock wave hit the slanted glass of the bridge. Twenty panes of silicon matrix glass exploded into the room, the shards of glass more lethal than hand-grenade shrapnel. The first shards ripped into his left arm and opened his flesh. Just a moment before, he had raised the binoculars to his eyes, for some reason sensing something wrong at the position of the lead carrier, the *Webb*. He had begun his twisting lunge with most of his body already shielded by the console, only his left shoulder and arm above the level of the top of the panel.

As Maddox fell, the second blast sounded from the direction of the *Webb,* and the hull of the John Paul Jones–class Aegis destroyer USS *John Glenn* below him trembled in the pressure wave of the explosion. Above him, the helmsman took a thousand shards of glass full in the face and chest. The enlisted man, still on his feet, was already dead as his body began to collapse, over twenty pieces of glass embedded in his now nonfunctioning brain. Maddox fell below the helmsman's belt, a third detonation sounded from west northwest, the bearing to the carrier *McKee*. The light in the bridge deck flashed and flickered from the fireballs ahead, while a fourth detonation sounded, again from the *McKee,* then immediately afterward an explosion to the left, where the *Roosevelt* had been steaming.

The helmsman's knees began to buckle as the dead youth tumbled to the deck. His hand was still gripping the gas turbine engine combined throttle, and as he fell, he pulled the throttle lever fully back to its STOP detent.

Four more explosions followed, two so close that they could have been a single detonation, as Maddox's frame hit the deckplates, smashing the side of his skull into the hard vinyl-covered metal. His body bounced, and as it flew upward an inch, another explosion sounded and the helmsman was tilted backward, his knees fully folded, his torso nearly horizontal, the glass still flying over his head and into the aft bulkhead of the bridge. Maddox hit the deck a second time, his eyes clamping shut in fear and pain. Glass ricocheted from the aft bulkhead and rained down on him, but the horizontal torso of the helmsman partially shielded him. Maddox came to rest on the deck while Ray Hargraves, the helmsman, fell toward him, his back sailing toward Maddox's bleeding arm and shoulder. Two more explosions ripped into the bridge, these detonations closer, from ahead.

As the *John Glenn* slowed, Maddox drifted into a state suspended between consciousness and coma. Images from the past flashed in and out of view almost faster than he could register them. His father's face two decades ago. His own face in the mirror that morning, shaving a cheek in a face that looked hauntingly like his dad's. Mom's casket, covered with flowers, the bottle of whiskey later that day. Annapolis graduation, hats slowly sailing toward the clouds, then coming down just as slowly. His wife Amanda's kiss at the altar, her mouth promising yet evasive, mischief in her eyes. The cry of what was supposed to be a baby boy but had turned out to be a girl, the expression of incredulity suspended on his face, turning to a father's smile of relief and thanksgiving. His daughter Doloris pedaling her bicycle for the first time, the fall after ten feet of clear navigation. His son Richie lobbing the basketball to the net. Admiral Chambers' quarters, the beer cold on his lips, the tough

admiral asking him to command a new John Paul Jones–
class Aegis destroyer. Amanda's tears, her voice
trembling at yet another West Pacific deployment. The
loneliness of the *John Glenn* captain's cabin when he
read Amanda's E-mail requesting a separation, the next
E-mail in the queue from Chambers congratulating him
on an excellent job. Dad's funeral service, another black
casket, this time Maddox lingering on graveside, unable
to leave. The convoy, his own voice complaining of
steaming in a tight formation. The Seahawk V helicopter
pilot, a young lieutenant who reminded him of Richie,
his son, saying they should be flying ahead and looking
for submarines, Maddox's own voice again, this time saying that violated fleet orders, yet inside agreeing with
the chopper pilot. And the flash in the binoculars, the
carrier *Webb* there one second, replaced with a piece of
the sun the next.

As he drifted slowly in the images, the shock waves
and explosions punctuated the lucid dreams racing
through his mind. The intrusive present kept coming and
going in disconnected bursts.

The coldness of the deck, its hard surface.

The hard deck against his cheek, punctuated by ten
pieces of glass, one beneath his cheek.

Explosions, still coming, the deck shaking with each
one.

The heaviness of the body lying on top of him, sharp
pain from glass shards between the body and his side.

The feeling of bleeding from his left arm, and the loss
of feeling from his left hand.

A voice, no, two, maybe three, but no words, just
groans, cries of pain, liquid coughing and sputtering.

One of the groans his own voice.

"Captain!" from behind him, where the aft bulkhead
should be, the voice unrecognizable, maybe his father,
maybe his navigator.

A wailing sound, a shipboard alarm, shrieking and
falling.

Another voice, hard and authoritative, but laced with
fear just this side of panic, screaming, "This is the navi-

gator, I have the deck and the conn. The captain's down, I have control of the rudder and engine order." The voice was greeted by only gasps and coughs.

A foot pushing his body backward. The vibrations from the deckplates as the gas turbines spooled up and the shaft began rotating again, the screw aft boiling up a wake.

The deck tilting far to starboard, so far that the body on top of Maddox rolled off, then flattening.

Roaring all around. Explosions, still coming, now astern and distant.

SS403 *ARCTIC STORM*

Thirty weapons fired, thirty hits.

Not all the torpedoes had gone to their designated targets. One weapon slated for a cruiser behind WT-3, the carrier on the right, had gone farther into the convoy and struck a destroyer behind the cruiser rows, sparing the cruiser. Chu had closed distance by quite a few kilometers by then, and launched a new weapon at the cruiser.

The plasma explosions would normally be flashes bright enough to blind a man, but the periscope had a built-in filter that limited the amount of light admitted to the eyepieces, momentarily clouding the view when a flash went off. It was a well-designed system, and for the first time Chu wondered if there were any more Rising Suns in drydocks or shipyards that might counter his force, the only threat that had much credibility against his six submarines.

The attack from his *Arctic Storm*, out in front of the convoy, had taken out a good fraction of the warships. The thirty torpedoes had taken down the carriers, the two rows of cruisers, perhaps half of the destroyers and frigates, even some of the support ships. Chu had advanced slowly on the convoy, and initially the ships had continued westward toward him. He had underestimated the power of the torpedoes. He'd known from his read-

ing that they were plasma weapons, but he was not prepared for their destructive power. He could have saved
three weapons had he not double-targeted the aircraft
carriers, since one weapon alone would have been more
than enough to put a carrier down. As the carriers exploded and sank, the cruiser row had taken their hits,
exposing the destroyer ranks. By then the destroyers and
frigates were under attack by the *Lighting Bolt* to the
north and the *Thundercloud* to the south, as were the
amphibious assault ships and the troop carriers.

In Chu's periscope view there were no longer any visible contacts, just some smoking wreckage and an oil-
slick fire in the west southwest, one of the oilers' load
now burning on the surface of the sea.

"Navigator, any contacts on sonar?"

"No, sir," Xhiu Liu said from the sensor console. "It
is possible there are a few surviving surface ships, maybe
even dozens, that are masked by the noise of the sink-
ings, though, Admiral. We have a broadband sonar blueout all across the eastern bearings, and it's so loud it's
blocking most tonal-frequency intervals. We're deaf,
sir."

"Well, if there are any survivors, you can bet they're
heading east. We'll let the *Volcano* take care of them."

"I agree, Captain. I'll keep watching."

"Second Captain, lower the periscope," he said into
his boom microphone. He stood, his back cracking, and
stretched. The long hour of leaning over, peering into
the eyepiece, had made his muscles ache. But it was a
good ache, like the kind he'd had playing sports on the
fields of the aviation academy so long ago.

"Ship Control Officer, take her down to three hundred meters, steep angle, increase speed to twenty-five
clicks, and take us west. We should be encountering the
688I's fairly soon. Even as deaf as they are, the noise
we put up killing the task force will wake them up. I
expect them to arrive around bearing two six five to two
seven five. Navigator, I know we've been up here shooting for a while and everyone is tired, but I want your

maximum attention to the submarine threat. They'll be coming soon."

"Aye, sir."

"Mr. First, I'll take the command console."

Chu strapped back in, reconfigured his panels, and shut his eyes for a moment. They had eighteen torpedoes left. Once the 688Is were on the bottom, he would probably have fifteen or sixteen. That would be enough to hold off part of a second landing force, but then he would be powerless. It wouldn't be good enough to call out a second force's position to coordinate an air strike—the American battle formation was too expert at fighting off air attacks. They had to be attacked from the sea, and without torpedoes and a delivery platform they would own the East China Sea.

So it was a matter of time. Eventually his six ships would run out of weapons, and there was no resupply. He had put down the initial force, and a second landing convoy would need to come out of Hawaii or California, which would be at least seven to fourteen days' travel time even at fast transit speed.

He had bought his generals a week, maybe two. How close could they come in a week? he asked himself. They would need to overrun the Whites in a week or risk being pushed back.

While he waited for the 688Is to return in search of him, he dictated several messages into the Second Captain, one a report to the Admiralty, one a message of congratulation to his ship commanders, one a warning about the 688Is, and one a redeployment plan for a force coming out of Hawaii, the East China Sea entrance to be more to the south. Once the messages were edited, he settled back to wait.

USS *JOHN GLENN*, DDG-85

"Rudder to left full, throttling up to ahead flank. There are burning ships ahead and aft. I'm steering around the wreck of the *John Paul Jones,* the cruisers are gone, and the other destroyers ahead are burning and sinking."

The babbling voice of the navigator. Who was he talking to? Captain Eddie Maddox wondered.

"Navigator," Maddox's voice called. "What are you—" His strength had seemed to sink away from him.

"Sir, are you okay?"

"What happened? I can't see."

"Hold on, Captain. The fleet's been attacked. I'm steering us out of the column, I'm breaking formation."

"Get the hell away from it," Maddox said. "Break to the south if you can, get away from the formation, and head east. Get us back to the Pacific if you can, but be alert for survivors, I want to get anyone we can see. Find some lookouts. And see if you can get Robinson up in the Seahawk"

"Aye, sir, but I'm by myself up here, and the battle circuits aren't working."

"Just do what you can. You don't have to do it in ten seconds." Maddox groaned. "Was it an air attack? There was no warning."

"Don't know, sir. The carriers went up in huge mushroom clouds."

"Radars?"

"Can't tell, sir, I'm steering around four ships that are sinking."

"How many ships down?"

"Sir, you'd better ask, how many ships are still afloat."

"What?" Maddox tried to move his left arm, but it wouldn't move and he had no sensation from it. His right seemed to work, but is bulk was on it. He pushed himself half up, shoving away the dead body and fallen glass, and reached up to the console handhold. Grasping it and pulling as hard as he could, his body a mass of aches, he managed to stand, then tried to open his eyes, but there was nothing but blackness. He was blind.

"I can't see," he said flatly.

A new voice.

"Nav? What the hell?" The young officer fresh from surface warfare officer school, Ensign Boyd.

"Boyd, take the helm," the navigator, Lieutenant Commander Bosco, ordered.

"Yessir."

"Course south, ahead flank."

"Relieve you, sir."

"Stand relieved, Captain, I'm checking on the radar." Footsteps. A door opening, being pushed, a scraping noise. Maddox felt dizzy and weak.

"Nav," he said, "Where's the navigator?"

"Back, sir."

"Where can I sit?"

"Here." An arm on his right side. "Gotta get the doc to look at that arm, Captain. Let me get the glass off. Okay, here's the captain's chair. You look pale, sir."

"I don't doubt it," Maddox said. "Do we have radars?"

"All gone, Captain. Phased-array panels are blown apart from the shock waves. Electronics are fried. The rotating structures are blown off, and the masts are gone. Sir, anything exposed to the weather is damaged and scorched."

"What about the Seahawk?"

"It was stowed. It could be okay."

"Find Robinson. Get him up. I want a full report on the fleet. Meanwhile, keep steaming east to the Pacific. Get us the hell out of here."

"Aye, sir."

Lieutenant Brandon Robinson had been in his stateroom in a deep sleep after being up all night standing watch on the bridge, trying to cross-qualify in surface warfare. Completing surface quals wasn't a requirement, but it filled the time, and it could pay off if he stayed in the Navy. The midwatch had gone from midnight to six in the morning, and he was beat. He could remember the exact moment he had gone from sleeping to stark consciousness, that first booming explosion. He hadn't waited for the crew to call battle stations; he had run aft and down to get to his, at the Seahawk, the onboard light antisubmarine-warfare helicopter, his chopper. He ran to the helodeck, the ship taking one shock wave after another. When he finally arrived, in the darkness, he had had to manually open the helodeck door. The power returned, allowing him to get the heavy roll-type door open. And out the aft-facing doorway he had watched as the fleet disappeared, the first flashes of detonations knives in his eyes. He had to turn away, flashing lights swimming in his vision, the merciless noise of the ships exploding rocking his eardrums.

The ship's engines suddenly throttled up to maximum revolutions, and the deck rolled hard to starboard, then leveled, then rolled again to starboard, finally leveling again. Whoever was on the bridge had taken matters into his own hands, Robinson thought, and was maneuvering them out of the convoy formation, as the op order allowed if the formation came under attack. He waited by the Seahawk, stowed in the helodeck and cabled down, chancing the occasional look out the aft door. The sea was empty astern except for smoke and foam on the surface, now far in the distance, the destroyer's wake white and boiling behind them. They were alone.

The navigator burst into the room, a look of determination on his face.

"Battle comm circuits are out," he puffed. "Launch the Seahawk, Robinson. Cap'n wants a patrol and then an ASW look ahead."

Robinson's airman had not shown up after the explosions. The navigator helped him get the chopper rolled out and preflighted. Within ten minutes, Robinson was at idle, Bosco saluting him as he lifted off the deck.

It didn't take long to survey the situation. Robinson flew west for a few miles, seeing nothing left of the fleet except patches of foam, one or two smoking wrecks, and the flame from a burning oil slick. There was nothing else. One hundred ten ships, all gone except for his.

And what were the chances of that? He wondered, feeling oddly like the sole survivor of a holocaust. He snapped off the images of the dead sea with his digital camera. His orders were to transmit the images directly to the ComStar Navy communications satellite, to get the information back to the Pentagon with a forward marked OPREP 3 PINNACLE, the code for an emergency message that needed to go immediately to the president. The photo survey done, he turned and flew back ahead of the *Glenn,* which was far east of the convoy's position when it had met its fate.

He prepared to lower the sonar dome, pessimistic that he would achieve results. The radios were out, making communications between his chopper and the *Glenn* impossible, but the captain evidently wanted to know what was ahead. If Robinson found anything he could classify as hostile, he could shoot it, but what of the 688s? He presumed they were much farther west, and by now the *Glenn* was tens of miles from the sinking position of the fleet. Any threats ahead of the ship would have to be hostile. Robinson had two torpedoes, and he was authorized to use them.

He flew on, passing the *Glenn,* then five miles ahead hovered and deployed the AN/SQS-69 dipping sonar transducer, a sphere of hydrophones that he lowered into the water on a strong cable reel, the assembly capable of penetrating the surface thermal layer a couple hundred feet below. He streamed the dipper, the ball sinking steadily into the sea while he hovered fifty feet above the surface. He had to lean over to scan the display panel that his airman would normally have been searching. In passive listen-only mode, the display showed nothing visible. It was time to ping.

He punched in the keystrokes to tell the system what he wanted, and when he was ready, the dipping sonar pinged hard. A high-power burst of sound reverberated through the sea, spreading out at sonic speed, trying to find anything to bounce off. The ocean bottom gave one return at the same frequency, the same note, as the transmission, but the dipper was listening for a higher or lower note, as would be returned by a moving object, for instance, a hostile sub.

There was nothing. Robinson shrugged, knowing it was rare to catch a fish on the first cast. He pinged a few more times. Then he pulled in the dipper and flew

234   *Michael DiMercurio*

ahead, another two miles, sank the ball, and hovered again.

Robinson thought about the pilots he'd known on the ships of the convoy and about his friends on the *John Glenn,* and he wondered how many of them were now dead. He forced the thought from his mind, concentrating on the display, but the thoughts persisted. Would he and the *Glenn* survive to escape this mess? And if they did, what next?

It didn't matter, he harshly told himself. Find the sub in the water ahead, or better yet, find no sub, and let the *Glenn* escape. Please let the *Glenn* escape, his thought becoming a prayer.

CHAPTER 21

SS-405 *EARTHQUAKE*

Commander Ko Tsu watched his sonar panel with one eye and his navigator's face on the display next to it with the other.

"Looks like we have one that escaped, sir," his navigator, Jin Lu, reported from the sensor console.

"What have you got?"

"Dual six-bladed screws, high-frequency tonals from one or more gas turbines, coming in from the west, bearing two seven two. This ship is a destroyer. Captain, John Paul Jones–class."

"Ship Control, take her up to twenty-five meters." The deck tilted at a steep twenty-degree angle, forcing Ko back against his seat harness. "Mr. First, would you like to make a periscope approach?"

Ko's first officer, Lieutenant Commander Jinan Hsu, smiled, revealing buck teeth. "Yes, Captain, very much."

"Take the scope, then. I'll watch from here."

The *Earthquake* had expended twenty-four torpedoes from the aft sector of the westward-bound convoy. Unlike the *Arctic Storm*, the *Lightning Bolt*, and the *Thundercloud*, which could all see their targets, his own position was to the east, and though he had had visual contact when the shooting began, by the time his first eight weapons were away he had been shooting blind, just putting torpedoes out the bearing line and hoping they connected to ship hulls. At first he directed the crew to count explosions, but his count, his navigator's count, and the Second Captain's count had come out different, all between one hundred and one hundred twenty explosions, but not enough to determine if they'd killed all the ships of the convoy.

"Nav, any other ships?" he called. He had to watch his weapon load, perhaps even be ready to withdraw to the south and let *Volcano* and *Tsunami* take on the other escapers.

"No, sir, just this one—wait, sir, higher-priority target, active-dipping sonar, correlates to a Seahawk antisub helicopter, bearing 280. I've got one, now two pings. Also very faint rotor noises. Sir, looks like he may be leap-frogging ahead of the destroyer contact."

"Designate the surface ship target WT-25, the chopper target number AT-1."

"Yessir."

"Captain, passing through one hundred meters, ship's angle going to up ten."

"Very good. Mr. First, get ready on the scope. Ship Control, throttle to stop, come to ten clicks. Attention in control, men. I'll be launching the Nagasaki in tube 25 down the bearing line, keeping the weapon in tube 26 warm and ready to go in case weapon 25 has a problem. Then we'll shoot the chopper."

"Ten clicks, sir, ship's depth fifty meters, angle up ten going up to five."

"Very good." Ko looked at his panel, noting the ship was slowing to fifteen clicks. That was slow enough that his first officer could raise the periscope without fear of shearing it off. "Mr. First, raise your scope."

"Aye, sir," he said, then told the Second Captain to raise the mast. With a stroke on the panel Ko brought up the view out the periscope, on the main display on the right column.

"Twenty-five meters, Captain, ship's angle flat."

"Very good, Ship Control. Weapons," Ko called, "Apply power to tubes 25 and 26, and open bowcap doors."

"Aye, sir, 25 and 26 warming up now."

"Open bowcaps 25 and 26."

"Opening now."

"Enable number one and two Darkwing missile tubes for low-altitude, low-speed target."

"Aye, sir," from the weapons officer. Ko would target the chopper as soon as the number 25 torpedo was away, but he wanted the Darkwings ready in case the chopper detected him.

"Weapons Officer, program 25 for ultraquiet swimout mode, low-speed transit."

"Aye, sir, programming now, bowcaps now open, 25 and 26."

"Very good."

The navigator spoke again, one hand on his headset. "Sir, new ping, bearing 287, target AT-1."

"Darkwings enabled, sir, missiles one and two," the weapons officer called.

"First, do you have an air search going? Train to 287."

"Yessir, on 287—"

"Anything in high power?"

"Not yet."

"Try high and ultrahigh power. Find that chopper. Weps, status of 25?"

"Torpedo 25 is ready in all respects, sir, target bearing loaded in."

"Shoot 25."

"Second," the weapons officer said, "shoot 25. Sir, tube 25 indicates weapon has cleared the tube in swimout mode."

"Captain, bow camera indicates weapon 25 away," the navigator said.

"Very good. First, the chopper?"

"I've got something, Captain. Very distant, just a jumping speck in ultrahigh power."

"Keep on him. I want to try a laser-missile guide-in. Weps, program the Darkwing missile for a laser visual guide-in to the chopper."

"Aye, sir."

"Nav, torpedo 25 status?"

"Captain, 25 is running normal at bearing 274, on bearing to target WT-25."

"Keep on it," Ko said. Calmly he reached down to the

side of his seat and withdrew a thermos of tea. Pouring it into an insulated cup, he replaced the thermos and took a sip of the steaming brew.

"Chopper's coming, sir," Jinan Hsu reported from the periscope. The periscope display on Ko's command console showed an image of a helicopter, the aircraft so distant that the power magnification caused it to jump around. Hadn't these Japanese engineers figured out a way to stabilize that? Ko thought, annoyed.

"Very good, First. Keep on him until we launch the Darkwing. We'll monitor the surface target WT-25 on sonar."

"Sir, the chopper is in range," Jinan said. "I recommend we shoot it now, then confirm the hit on the Jones-class destroyer."

"No, wait. If we shoot the Darkwing now, we can't laser-guide it in. Just keep cool, First, he's not going to hear us."

"Aye, sir."

"Torpedo running time, Weps?"

"Eight minutes, sir."

"Nav, still have both the weapon and WT-25?"

"Yes, Captain."

"Nothing to do now but wait, gentlemen."

Ko sipped his tea, watching his displays.

Robinson picked up the dipper and flew on another mile and a half. So far he'd detected nothing.

He was unaware that as the dipper sphere came out of the water, a Nagasaki torpedo had sailed into detection range. He flew within a half mile of it as he progressed farther east, sanitizing the area for the USS *John Glenn*.

Once he had put the dipper in, the screen immediately read something bearing west, behind him. He scanned the panel, disturbed, again missing his airman. Hurriedly he withdrew the dipper and flew back west toward the *Glenn*. He scanned the panel again, seeing that the frequency correlated to a high-speed water jet. It had to be a torpedo. The *Glenn* was under attack. He had to tell them, and the only way he could communicate with them was to fly close to the blown-out bridge and signal them to take evasive action.

The *Glenn* was about five miles astern, still plowing through the waves heading east. It took only three minutes to close the distance to the destroyer, and when he was only halfway there, the officer on the bridge got the message. He put the rudder over hard to the left, the ship turning hard, rolling far to starboard. The ship steadied on course north, hoping to confuse the incoming torpedo. The warning to the *Glenn* complete, Robinson turned back to the east to try to find where the torpedo had come from. The enemy sub must be far away, he thought, or else he would have heard it on the dipper.

He was a mile from the *Glenn* when he heard an explosion. The shock wave tossed the helicopter as though it were a toy. Robinson fought for control, a sinking feeling grabbing his gut, and he almost didn't want to look back.

The chopper came around, and in the sea a mile west, a ball of flame rose over what had once been the destroyer *John Glenn*. A white and orange and black mushroom cloud ascended slowly, flaming and burning. He could still see the wake of the ship leading north to the blast zone, but the ship was completely gone. The flames rose higher, blown eastward by the prevailing winds, and all Robinson could do was watch, dumbfounded, as his ship burned. The mushroom cloud rose high above him, at a thousand feet mostly dark smoke blowing up into the atmosphere.

Angry and frightened, Robinson checked his fuel gauge. Onboard were two torpedoes, and if he could find the enemy sub, he could shoot it and put it down before he ran out of fuel. He had two full tanks of JP-5. That should keep him up the few hours it would take to find this murdering bastard. He turned the chopper slowly to the east and flew on to a spot a mile beyond where he'd been. There he set up to hover and dropped the sphere.

. SS-405 *EARTHQUAKE*

"Captain, I think we should consider shooting AT-1. He's coming back around and heading east. I think he's mad."

"Let him come a little closer. I want you to have a clear view on low power."

"Low power, sir? He could get a shot off."

"Weps, we enabled in laser guide-in mode, Darkwings one and two?"

"Yessir," the weapons officer barked.

"Wait, Mr. First."

The seconds clicked off, until the chopper stopped to hover, only a few kilometers away, and lowered his dipping sonar. The pulse of it was so loud that Ko Tsu could hear it with his naked ear. He smiled.

"Mr. First, that's close enough for me," he said. "Weps, shoot Darkwing one. First, enable the laser and guide it in."

Driven by the steam gas generator at the base, the missile erupted from the fin-mounted missile tube pointed at the waves above.

Still enclosed in its protective bubble of steam generated by the rocket motor inside the fin, the nose cone of the missile penetrated the surface. The two-meter-long missile burst into midair. Gravity momentarily took over from the impulse of the steam force, and the missile was starting to fall back toward the water when the low-G contact clicked in and the solid rocket fuel ignited in a full-thrust rush.

The missile zoomed skyward, accelerating to three hundred clicks as it soared up to a height of a kilometer. As the weapon finished its ascent and turned downward, it found a laser signal from the periscope mast of the submarine. Then, much fainter, it received the laser signal bouncing off the target, which coincided with the heat from the target's engine exhaust. The missile dived toward the target, accelerating to four hundred clicks, then five hundred as the target grew large in its seeker window. The exhaust nozzle was white-hot, and the missile arrowed straight for it. When the windshield of the target was within a meter of the missile nose cone, it detonated.

Within milliseconds the missile metamorphosed into a growing white-hot fireball and blast shock wave. The explosion expanded until it enveloped the target, the vaporized helicopter joining the fireball.

Robinson had just stopped to hover and drop the dipper, sensing somehow that he was getting closer.

Just then a white exhaust trail of a missile climbed a thousand yards into the sky. Robinson watched it dumbly, slowly registering that the missile had come from nowhere, from a patch of featureless blue sea no different than the rest of the ocean. It rose so high that for a moment it was invisible, above the limit of his windshield view. Then he realized that it would be descending for him. He had to try to get away.

He moved his hands on the collective and hit the rudder pedal. His finger stabbed the switch on the cyclic grip that would ditch the sonar dipper and free him to fly away. In the fraction of a second it took to do that, the white flame trail of the missile became visible again. The missile grew huge in his windshield.

He never even felt the blast.

As the fireball grew, encompassing the target in the orange flames, pieces of helicopter flew off into space and fell toward the sea.

Among the parts were the high-speed rotors, which detached from the hub and hurtled horizontally away from the wreck. The tail had been sheared off, and it fell end over end to the sea, just fifty feet below, splashing into the white foam and sinking. Most of the rest of the helicopter was unrecognizable molten or flaming chunks of aircraft.

One of the chunks falling to the sea was a scorched flight helmet reading LT. B. ROBINSON USS JOHN GLENN. Inside the helmet was a black mass, burned and crusty, beige bone showing through burned flesh. The helmet tumbled until it hit the water. It splashed and floated at the surface for a few seconds, then sank to the sea floor 850 fathoms below.

"Helicopter AT-1 is down, Captain," the first officer said.

"Anything at the bearing to the surface contact, WT-25?"

"Yes, Captain, a column of smoke, maybe two kilometers high."

"Nav, any sonar detect at the previous bearing to WT-25?"

"No, sir, the destroyer is gone. We're alone again."

"Very good. Everyone, relax. We'll wait here at battle stations for any more surface contacts and the 688s. If we don't have anything in an hour, we'll secure. Mr. First, what did you think?"

"Fantastic, Captain. This ship is simply amazing."

If only it had more torpedoes, Ko Tsu thought.

"That it is, Mr. First," was all he said.

CHAPTER 22

The first explosion was so loud in DeMeers' headset that he was certain his eardrums had ruptured. He hurled the headset to the deck, clapping both his hands to his ears. Water was running furiously in his eyes and down his nose.

He shook his head to clear it, his ears ringing and useless. His main display he turned to broadband water-fall, which showed reverberations throughout the bearings of the sea. He pulled up "the onion," the broadband receiver towed from a mile-long cable coming out of the starboard towed-array tube mounted on the top of the starboard sternplane vertical stabilizer. The BSY-4-ON41B stern-facing sonar set was designed to give them a warning of a torpedo inbound from directly astern, in their cone of deafness, the baffles. The onion was named because of its teardrop shape, the aft half of it hemispherical.

The onion display flashed up, the aft bearings turning into a loud sonar blueout, which meant there was so much broadband noise that nothing could be heard through it. For a half second DeMeers wondered where Captain Patton was until he realized that for some time he had been standing right behind DeMeers' shoulder, looking at the displays.

DeMeers' voice was unrecognizable and almost inaudible when he tried to speak to the captain. "Trouble at the convoy."

Patton said something DeMeers didn't catch and vanished.

In the control room, Patton rushed up the steps to the elevated periscope stand and grabbed the stainless steel handrail. He took a quick look around. Then orders poured from his mouth to the officer of the deck, Kurt Horburg.

"Off'sa'deck, man battle stations. I have the conn. Helm, left one degree rudder, steady course east. Sonar, Captain, coming around to the east. Quartermaster, log that the captain suspects the convoy has come under attack and is returning east to investigate and, if possible, counterattack. OOD, flood tubes one through four and warm up weapons one through four."

The deck tilted far to the right, then back to the left as the ship went through its flank-run snap roll, reversing course. There was a flurry of acknowledgments, except from sonar. Patton shook his head. DeMeers had hurt his ears, and who knew how much that would paralyze them?

"OOD, mark range to the convoy."

"Captain, leading aircraft carrier generated-solution range is twenty-four nautical miles. Our ETA is thirty-five minutes from now, sir."

"Sir, passing course one zero zero, ten degrees from ordered course," the helmsman barked.

"Very well."

The battle-stations crew flooded into the room's forward door, taking over from the afternoon watch crew. Forward, to the left of the entrance door, was the ship-control station, a sort of airplane cockpit arrangement. Two pilot seats flanked a console and a vertical instrument panel was stuffed with computer-driven displays. The panel extended into the overhead and slanted back over the two pilots' heads to a seat aft of the center console. To the left of the arrangement an L-shaped wraparound panel surrounded a swivel seat. The four men of the ship-control team were the helmsman in the right pilot seat, who held the airplane-style yoke that controlled the rudder and the bow planes. The planes man in the left seat had control of the stern planes and the ship's angle. The chief of the watch sat at the left L-shaped ballast-control panel, which controlled the ship's physical trim and dive systems, the tanks and pumps and hydraulics, and the masts of the sail high above them. Finally, the diving officer, behind the two pilot seats, supervised the other three.

Aft of the ship-control station was the rectangular periscope stand, the "conn," where the captain and officer of the deck stood their watches, although they were free to roam the room. The conn was surrounded by gleaming handrails and was packed with equipment in the overheads—sonar repeater displays, television monitors, microphones on coiled cords for various battle-announcing circuits, several phones, a folding command seat, and two stowed type-21 periscopes mounted side by side on stainless steel poles extending into the overhead.

On the port side of the conn aft of the ballast-control panel was a tightly packed row of navigation consoles, where the satellite receivers and inertial nav equipment were set up. On the starboard side of the room was the attack center, a row of BSY-4 battle-control consoles set up to allow tracking of multiple targets. Four officers manned these computer screens. The aft station of the attack center was the weapon-control console, set up to program the torpedoes in the torpedo room one deck below.

Aft of the periscope stand were two navigation-plotting tables, one devoted to the navigation electronic chart, the second to tracking the main enemy contact.

The entire room would easily fit into most family rooms with room to spare. Not one cubic centimeter of volume was unused, every reachable space from the deck to the overhead packed with equipment, panels, consoles, displays, intercoms, phones, cables, valves, piping, alarm boxes, seats, or plotting tables. At battle stations, when twenty men would stand watch in the room, the chief of the watch was required to quadruple the air conditioning to the space, not so much for the people as the electronic equipment.

Lieutenant Horburg was relieved at the conn by the battle-stations OOD, a slightly older lieutenant named Dietz. Patton's executive officer arrived as well, his face marked by the lines of his bedspread. Commander Henry Vale was taller than Patton, with light skin and dark eyes and hair, his body slight, wearing wire-rimmed glasses that gave him an academic's look.

Patton pulled on his headset. Horburg took his battle station at the second battle-control console of the BSY-4, position two, the master target-solving station. Four other officers manned positions one, three, and four, the weapons officer taking a station at the aft panel, the weapons console. The navigator manned the aft plot table with a ring of men around him, plotting the manual solution to the master target. Meanwhile the ship-control team was replaced by the battle-stations crew, and several phonetalkers stationed themselves around key watchstanders.

Patton blew into his boom mike, testing it, then called to Vale, who at battle stations would be the fire-control coordinator, in charge of the men finding the solution to the master target.

"Coordinator, Captain, test."

"Cap'n, Coordinator, aye," Vale replied.

"Sonar, Captain, test."

"Conn, Sonar, aye," came the reply. It wasn't De-Meers but his first-class petty officer, O'Connor. Patton raised a finger to Vale, telling him to hold down the fort. Patton left the room through the forward starboard door leading to sonar.

"How's the hearing?" Patton asked DeMeers, who had been joined by four sonarmen sitting in the consoles. The senior chief was standing behind them, looking over their shoulders.

DeMeers shook his head, pointing at his ears.

"Dammit," Patton said. "O'Connor, you got the bubble?"

"Yessir," the sonarman said. "Senior's backing me up, Cap'n."

"What's going on out there?"

"Blueout across the eastern bearings. One loud explosion after another. The convoy is taking hits, sir. And I'm worried." O'Connor turned to look up at Patton. "I'm not sure we'll hear the bad guy. Or bad guys. This is damned loud, Captain. It's deafened the senior chief, and we're getting up to 140 decibels from out here, peak, from detonations, and we're over twenty miles away. God knows how loud it'll be when we get in close. Plus, I don't know what I'm looking for. The search plan has us all over the frequency map."

"What are you saying, O'Connor?" Patton asked harshly.

"I'm saying I'm not sure I can hear an attacking submarine over all this, and even if the sea was quiet, I might not see him first. I need to know what I'm up against—diesel boat, Destiny II, Rising Sun, older 688. I can't search for all of them at once, it would take a week! So if we go in, we go in half deaf." O'Connor pointed at DeMeers.

Patton looked at the senior chief, making his next question loud and lip-readable, "You agree, Senior?"

"Yessir." DeMeers' voice was still distorted, a deaf man. "We're putting our head into a lion's mouth."

Patton glared at them, feeling bile flood his stomach. He jammed his hands in his pockets—after all, he hardly needed the crew to think he was frightened, although he certainly was. O'Connor was dead right. Heading into an op area with no confirmed search plan was worse than looking for a needle in a haystack. What frequency tonal? How loud? Did low frequencies show up first? Where should the processors be set? Wide bands or narrow? The sonarmen knew they were putting their necks on a chopping block and so did Patton, but he had to show them confidence, because that was all they had at this point—just the captain's instincts and his guts.

"Listen, goddammit," Patton finally said, his nostrils flared, his black eyes flashing. "I'm going in and I'm going in shooting. You guys find me a fucking target, I don't care how hard it is. You got that?"

O'Conner nodded, looking as if he'd just been asked to drive a car at one hundred mph at midnight with no headlights.

As Patton returned to the control room he wondered how he was going to explain all this to fleet command. He'd missed the intruder submarines, he wouldn't hear them when he returned to attack them, and his sonarmen wanted to just go home. When this mission was over, he would probably lose his ship, his command pin, his shoulder boards, and probably his dolphins, because losing a convoy he was charged with protecting was not the way to promotion. Of course, that assumed he walked away from this operation instead of becoming fish food at the bottom of the East China Sea.

Vale was staring at him. "What?" Patton said, irritated.

"What's going on, Captain?"

"I'll tell the men," Patton said. "Attention in the fire-control team." A dozen whispered conversations—all of them business—halted. "Starting a few minutes ago, we heard multiple explosions from the bearings of the convoy. We've turned around and are heading back to the convoy's position at flank speed. Meanwhile sonar reports a blueout across all eastern bearings, with explosions continuing. The convoy is probably under attack. What we don't know is whether the attack is coming from an intruder submarine or submarines or whether it was an air attack. My intention is to make maximum speed toward the convoy, and when we're closer, slow down, rig for ultraquiet, and commence a slow-speed sonar search for any possible submarines. Carry on."

"Conn, Sonar, aye," came through Patton's headset.

So now, here I am, Patton thought, *flanking it into a war zone like a fool, with no idea who the enemy is or what he sounds like. I might as well just wear a sign that says, "Shoot me."*

PACIFIC OCEAN
ALTITUDE: 51,000 FEET

There was a big difference between sleeping on an airplane and trying to sleep on an airplane.

Pacino was alternately too hot and too cold, trying to get comfortable in a seat that reclined all the way back. At the moment he was sweating, his head throbbing, sleep eluding him despite the bone-tired ache in his limbs and back. He tried to force himself down deeper, to let go of the world. Still half awake, he saw a stream of lucid visions, one of them the SSNX painted red, the hull being lowered into a sea of blood.

A sound came to him from a long way away. He could hear snatches of a voice, a television, tuned to SNN, Paully having forgotten to turn it off. "In other financial news today, the European Union stock market lost over twenty points on fears that the renewed hostilities in White China— We interrupt the World Financial Report for breaking news from the East China Sea. Operation SeaLift has apparently met with disaster. Reporting from the Penatagon is our war correspondent—"

Pacino sat up abruptly, reaching for Paully White's shoulder.

"Paully, wake up, quick."

Both men watched, eyes wide with incredulity. The report was only half done when the pilot called back on the intercom:

"Admiral, we're getting a secure voice radio call from Air Force One. The president wants to talk to you."

SS-403 *ARCTIC STORM*

Admiral Chu Hua-Feng had reclined the command-console seat. His headset had grown uncomfortable, so he had pulled it off. His eyes shut, he was breathing deeply, listening to the electronic hum of the computer and display systems. A high-pitched, distant whine sounded from the inertial-navigation rotating element, a small titanium sphere that spun at over 10,000 rpm. Below the whine purred the deep bass of cool air blowing in through the control-room ducts.

The seat of the console was relaxing to the extreme, and Chu was beginning to believe he would be able to spend days in this seat if he had to. In a pocket below the cushion was an endurance package, with several candy bars, two bottles of water, and a waste bag. On discovering, it, the navigator had been jubilant, talking about stocking his bag with tea, magazines, cookies. His assistant, the operations officer, had joked that if he had one of those decadent Western blow-up dolls, he could stay in the seat for months. Chu had glared at his officers and told them to knock off the joking, but privately he had chuckled over it.

He was lying there, reclined far back, nearly flat, when he thought he heard a buzz in the earpiece hanging around his neck.

"Admiral, new contact, we have a seven-bladed screw."

Xhiu Liu, the navigator at the sensor console, had snagged something. Chu sat the seat up and pulled on the headset simultaneously.

"Designate contact ST-3," Xhiu said, his voice back in focus as Chu strapped on his earpiece. "Submerged warship, American 688-class improved, bearing two six four. Contact is extremely distant but is making way rapidly. Admiral, we have a broadband trace on him from his equipment, maybe some kind of pump. In addition, we've got an intermittent rattle."

"Very good. Next tube, Chen?" Chu asked Chen Zhu, the operations officer, standing at the weapons-control console.

"Number eight, sir."

"Warm up weapons eight and nine. Flood both tubes. Wait on the bowcap doors; let's keep them shut for now. Program eight as the ultraquiet unit and nine as the impulse unit." The weapon in tube eight would be set up to swim out quietly at slow speed, while tube nine would be reserved for trouble. In that case a solid rocket motor would blow the weapon out into the sea, the torpedo preset for a high-speed transit.

Chen acknowledged, but Chu was already on his next stream of nearly instinctive orders. "Ship Control, right five effective degrees rudder, throttle up to thirty clicks, steady course north."

"Five degrees, thirty clicks north, aye, Admiral."

"Navigator, set up to get a leg on target ST-3. Three minutes north, then three minutes south. Something tells me he's way out there."

"Sir."

Chu waited, watching data as valuable as gold roll onto the displays. He was feeling fully alert, the way an athlete feels at the start of the second half of a game. The ship's pulse was there in front of him, and after the first thirty torpedoes had been fired, he was getting used to the rhythm of the ship. He was almost comfortable with the odd blind-console stupid-Second Captain Japanese design. It was working out so well that he could believe that this was how he would design a submarine.

And yet, had the system really had its shakedown cruise? Certainly they had taken the ship through combat. He had fired thirty torpedoes and made thirty confirmed hits, and twenty-seven ships with tens of thousands of men had gone to the bottom or vaporized in plasma explosions from his targeting and tactical skill, but then, that was the nature of a submarine—an assassin that was invisible, its stealth its main weapon. But how would it perform against another submarine? Hadn't the Japanese scheduled the *Rising Sun* sea trials as a submarine-*versus*-submarine exercise? Was there some weakness in the vessels that would make them do poorly against another sub, even ones as unsophisticated as a 688-class? The only answer to that question would come with the first undersea challenge, and by all appearances that was happening right now.

"Leg complete, sir. Recommend maneuver to the south, Lo Sun said from Chu's right shoulder at the auxiliary command panel.

"Nav, any change in turn count or speed of ST-3?"

"No, Admiral. Still inbound."

"No sign of change in his heading? Does he hear us?"

"Doubt it, sir. He's as loud as a train wreck." Xhiu's face was amazingly calm, his voice steady and deep. Could it be that his fidgety navigator was getting some confidence?

"Very well, Nav," he said, giving the next orders to turn the ship to the south to get a parallax distance to the incoming American.

USS *ANNAPOLIS*, SSN-760

"Sonar, Captain, you have any detect of the *Santa Fe*?"

"Captain, Sonar, no." The reply left Patton profoundly dissatisfied. Chris Carnage and *Santa Fe* were out there somewhere, and if he came on a submerged target, it would be nice to know it was a genuine enemy.

And the worst of it was that there was no contingency plan for this. The more normal ASW sweep plans were bristling with contingencies—what to do if the other sub is attacked, what to do if both the companion sub and the convoy are attacked, but nowhere was there a contingency for the convoy being completely wiped out while the sweeping subs were tens of miles out. He was risking the ship, perhaps foolishly, by going into a hot zone, unsanitized and unsafe, with no idea of what he was looking for.

He had thought of one idea. He could lay a field of passively circling Mark 52 torpedoes in the area where the convoy used to be. If they detected anything they'd run for the sound, perhaps get a target. Yet that would expend his whole torpedo load for perhaps one hit, and if he did it properly, he'd run the risk one of his own torpedoes turning back around to come and get him. In the end, the idea was a loser.

He looked down at the chart table from the conn. It was time.

"Helm, all stop!" he barked, the helmsman answering

up. "OOD, rig for ultraquiet with the port side of the engine room shut down."

The ship would coast down from forty-one to five knots, and Patton was rigging the ship for quiet the old-fashioned way. Shutting down half the plant was potentially a suicidal move. The sonar girls loved it, but the officers hated it, because valuable minutes were needed to be able to return to power in the event they needed to turn tail and run.

At five knots though, he would be able to hear all the way to Tokyo. And if he was fifteen miles from where the convoy had gone down—and they had been targeted from over the horizon—he could be overrunning the attackers even now.

"Sonar, Captain, slowing."

"Captain, Sonar, aye."

"Supervisor to control," Patton said, waiting. De-Meers and O'Connor soon came out, both frowning. "Well, gentlemen, here's where you earn your medals," Patton said.

"I'd rather earn my way home," DeMeers said, his voice only slightly distorted.

"Good, you can hear me," Patton said. "So get in there and find the bad guys. Go on, shoo." He waved them away.

"Sir, ship's speed is four knots," Lieutenant Dietz said from the other side of the conn.

"Helm, all ahead one-third," Patton called. "Sonar, Captain, report all contacts."

"Captain, Sonar, aye, no contacts."

"Heads up," Patton said, his tone confident, his jaw set. He had to act as if he were entering a battle he could win, despite feeling he couldn't.

CHAPTER 23

"Admiral O'Shaughnessy is here with me."

President Jaisal Warner's voice was projecting from a speaker phone. On Pacino's end, he had an old-fashioned UHF radio handset, taken from the flight deck. He was sitting on the cramped jumpseat behind the copilot, and he could see the stars shining above the Pacific through the wind screen.

He clicked the button on the phone to speak. "Hello, sir. I heard the news."

"What do you recommend?" Warner asked without preamble.

It was just like her to do that, he thought in frustration. She had all the facts, and all he had was a news broadcast.

"Depends, ma'am," Pacino said firmly. "We lost the whole RDF. Is there anything else we can throw at the Reds?"

O'Shaughnessy's voice came on, his tone so neutral it could have come from a computer. "Patch, we've embarked the backup rapid deployment force out of Pearl Harbor. If the RDF was big, the BU-RDF is gigantic. President Warner feels that we are at a crossroads, and with the world watching, she is unwilling to—"

"Admiral," Warner interrupted, obviously unhappy to have the CNO give her opinions for her. "Forget the politics I'm up against for a second. We have—"

Feeling emboldened by O'Shaughnessy's use of Pacino's father's old nickname, Pacino said, "Madam President, hold on. I will not forget the politics, because one thing I've learned, one thing *you* taught me, is that it's *all* about politics. I can't fight a war if you don't have time to let me win." He wished they were on a videoconference call, so he could see her face, gauge her reaction. He had to get through to her this time.

"Believe me, Admiral Pacino, I remember Japan. I'll give you time."

Here go my stars, he thought. *Stars that she got for me after Japan.*

"Ma'am, please forgive me, but god *damn* it, you didn't listen to me. If we'd done what I recommended last night in Jackson, your fleet would be on its way. Late but intact! Now we've lost, what, a half million troops? Once again you don't give me time, time to scour the East China Sea, and now you call me and say 'forget the politics.' "

Jaisal Warner's laugh came though the circuit. "Admiral, that's the second time tonight I've been spoken to with that kind of bald candor. I have to tell you, it hurts, but I appreciate it."

Pacino wondered momentarily who the other person had been, then replied. "Thank you, ma'am. I think."

"So, what now, Admiral? The backup force is embarking now, and we'll have the ships convoying in from Hawaii."

"How many ships?"

"Two hundred," the CNO said. Pacino lifted his eyebrows. "This time we have 430,000 troops embarked, not as tightly packed as before, but they'll be on the way very soon."

"But what about all the urgency? It'll take four days to get them there, more if the weather goes against us."

"We have other things going on," O'Shaughnessy said. "Don't worry about it. General Baldini will hold off the Reds with some troops he's airlifting and parachuting into White China. We'll be putting some Stealth bombers to work with a lot of fuel-air explosives and plasma anti-troop weapons. And we're not stopping there. White China's given us unlimited permission to use WMD's in the Red-occupied zones." WMD's were weapons of mass destruction. Warner was pulling out the stops, authorizing chemical weapons, dispersion glue weapons, incendiary devices, even large-scale plasma bombs. This was heating up into a hell of a ground war, he thought. "We think we can freeze the Reds where they are, or at least slow them down, for about seven to fifteen days. That's enough time to get the backup force into the East China Sea."

So why the hell didn't she authorize his suggestions yesterday? Pacino thought. *Then we'd have 375,000 troops and a fleet.* But that was hindsight. Now she was asking for his revised opinion.

"Okay," he said.

"So, Admiral," Warner said, "now that you know the gloves are off, we all have a slight problem, even greater than the fact that Congress wants to pass an order of impeachment against me."

"Impeachment?"

"Haven't you been listening to the news? They want my neck for the loss of an entire army. Can't say I blame them." Pacino thought he heard a slight sniffle. "Three hundred seventy-five thousand troops lost. Every one of them has a family, that's millions of votes, and if you believe the news, I've lost eighteen points in the last twenty-four hours. I figure I've got about two weeks before I'm Jaisal Warner, private citizen. That's four days to get the backup force to the East China Sea, and a week to win a ground war. What do you think, Admiral?"

I think you'd better take a good look at the balance in your blind trust, Pacino thought.

"Sounds like we're in the huddle, with the quarterback saying, 'Same play, on one.' The backup force could get attacked just like the first RDF. I think we stand a good chance of getting our butts kicked."

"Do you think they will sink us before we get to the East China Sea?"

Pacino thought, the circuit silent for a moment.

"Hello?" Warner said.

Well, would they? He thought. What would he do, fresh from the killing of an entire convoy?

"Madam President, before I answer, I want to think this through. Can I have an hour?"

"Twenty minutes."

"We'll be landing soon," Pácino said. "Can you video into my quarters?" That would be perfect, he thought. He'd be able to see her face and, even better, he could get Paully's opinion, even call up Number Four, Jack Daniels, and see if he had any hard intelligence about the men who had managed to steal a submarine force.

Red subs, Mikey. You're up against the Reds.

So be it, he thought. Red Rising Sun submarines, the most advanced in the world.

"We'll video you in, what, half an hour?"

"Perfect, ma'am."

Warner and O'Shaughnessy clicked off without warning. Pacino walked back to the cabin, deep in thought. Paully White was there, concentrating on the widescreen.

"What'd she say?"

"You probably know more than I do," Pacino said, sinking into the seat next to Paully.

"Warner has another rapid deployment force," White whined. "Now there's suddenly time to get a Hawaiian convoy to the East China Sea. Where was that plan yesterday?"

"Paully, never mind. I need you, now. We've got a war to plan."

"I'm ready. What's on the list?"

"Get Number Four Daniels on the horn. Ask what he has on the Rising Sun, and see if you can get him on the case to track down Admiral Tanaka. We're going to need him. Then we'll need to put Bruce Phillips from the *Piranha* on a video conference."

"Bruce will be well on the way to the East China Sea by now."

"That's okay. But before you do anything else, we need to get *Santa Fe* and *Annapolis* the hell out of the zone."

"But aren't they going in to see if they can find—"

"I don't care, Paully. They can't win against a half

dozen Rising Suns who know they're coming. Tell them to get the hell out of the op area right now. When we go in, we'll go in coordinated—Pegasus patrol planes, Blackbeards, Seahawks, the 688's, Bruce's *Piranha*, the works. And we'll sanitize that damned zone but good."

"ELF call signs, emergency periscope depth?"

"Yeah, and tell them to withdraw at emergency flank. And don't give me any backtalk about ruining reactors, Paully."

"Hell, no, Admiral. I'd tell them emergency flank even if you were quiet about it. Those boys are standing into danger."

"Hop to it, Paully. Bring 'em out."

EAST CHINA SEA
USS *ANNAPOLIS*, SSN-760

"Conn, Radio, we've got the first letter of our ELF call sign."

ELF, Patton thought in frustration, extremely low-frequency radio waves, transmitted out of Lualualei Naval Radio Station off Maili, Oahu. Transmitting the ELF radio waves required tremendous power. An entire nuclear plant big enough to light up Baltimore had been built on-site at Lualualei just to power the massive antennae. The radio waves, unlike the higher frequencies, were able to penetrate the upper layers of the ocean and the earth's crust. Unfortunately, the data rate was so slow, it would take ten minutes just to receive two alphabetical letters. Admiral Pacino had ordered that subs change their call signs to a single alphanumeric encrypted character, with a second letter thrown in as a confirmation, because he didn't want to wait ten minutes to drag a submarine to periscope depth in an emergency.

Patton had not been thrilled with the new system. The office of submarine captain was one of the last existing dictatorships in the world. At sea he was accountable almost to no one, receiving radio messages rarely, transmitting almost never. But with an ELF call sign, the brass could call him to periscope depth at any time of the day or night. It might take them twenty minutes to get the radio computer's attention, but at that point they were required to come up and see what the Navy Com-Star satellite had to say.

An emergency ELF call could mean a declaration of war, retasking, new rules of engagement, new orders, anything. Though Patton was sorely tempted to wait until the second or even third ELF call, buying himself time to try to detect an enemy submarine, he knew he had to come up. For all he knew, the convoy had been hit by an air attack instead of a sub assault, and there was a new mission waiting for him on the ComStar's broadcast.

"OOD, clear baffles and take her up," he ordered.

Five minutes later, he watched the television screen in the overhead. In the periscope view that Lieutenant Dietz was rotating in the hot-optics module, there was nothing there but sea and sky and a stark, ruler-straight horizon. There were no seagulls, no clouds, no aircraft, and no convoy ships.

And there was Patton, hanging out at periscope depth like a sitting duck. An insistent nagging feeling entered him—he needed to continue the search, and quickly.

"We have him slowing from seventy-seven clicks to ten, Admiral."

"Very good, Nav."

Chu waited, staring at his panels and yawning.

"Well, sir? Aren't you going to shoot him?"

Could it be that they had been detected? Chu was torn—he wanted desperately to know if they could hear his ship, and if so, at what range. That would be a price-less piece of information. Yet the mission was too impor-tant to risk his vessel during the very first encounter with the Americans. It would eviscerate his command structure—since he did not have a real replacement—and it would discourage his force.

If he sank the 688, it would be over for the American effort. They would know they were defeated then, wouldn't they? They would back away from Red China and let the Whites fall, and his plan—and it was Mai Sheng's plan also, he admitted to himself, her idea to get the Rising Suns—would succeed. He could return home, marry Mai, perhaps have children, and rebuild the PLA Navy once its coastline was again part of the one unified China. He needed to get on the SNN World Report that he had not only sunk the American surface force but had killed their escort submarines too.

Unbidden, the dream of his father returned to him. *You must hurry, young warrior, for they are coming, and they are strong.* That had to be the meaning of the dream, he thought. He had to strike hard and fast, and deter the West from coming in for a rematch.

Because one thing was certain—he could continue to win only if his tubes were full of weapons. He was down thirty weapons, only eighteen left, and he didn't know how the other subs had fared; they could be even lower. The far east cork force, the *Volcano* and the *Tsunami,* should be fully loaded out, he knew, but the *Lightning Bolt* and the *Thundercloud* could be out of torpedoes, for all he knew. And if the West came back with another deployment of ships and equipment, he would sink only a fraction of them, and eventually he would be defeated.

It had to be now. Detection-distance question be damned, he thought.

"Open the bow door to tube eight," Chu said to Chen Zhu on the weapons panel. "Lock in target parameters to weapon eight."

"Door coming open, sir. Target parameters set. Weapon is ready."

"Shoot eight in swimout mode in three, two, one, mark."

"Eight is away," Chen said.,

"Bow camera confirms unit eight swimout," Xhiu reported.

"Very good. Watch it, Nav."

"Aye, Admiral," Xhiu said crisply. Chu stared at the display showing his face, smiling to himself at the navigator's improvement. Xhiu seemed to be getting his sea legs, Chu thought.

Now they had only to wait.

The radioman came running into the room with Patton's WritePad computer. Patton had no sooner slipped on his reading glasses than his jaw dropped open.

```
041811ZNOV13
FLASH FLASH FLASH FLASH FLASH FLASH FLASH FLASH FLASH
FM    COMUSUBCOM
TO    USS ANNAPOLIS SSN-760
SUBJ  URGENT MISSION RETASKING
SECRET SECRET SECRET SECRET SECRET SECRET SECRET SECRET
//BT//
```
1. (S) IMMEDIATE REPEAT IMMEDIATE EXECUTE.
2. (S) ABSOLUTE URGENT YOU CLEAR DATUM OP AREA ASAP ASAP ASAP.
3. (S) DISENGAGE ALL SEARCHES, ALL ENGAGEMENTS, NO EXCEPTIONS.
4. (S) CLEAR DATUM AT EMERGENCY FLANK REPEAT EMER-GENCY FLANK, ESCAPE VECTOR SOUTHEAST IF POSSIBLE, SECONDARY ESCAPE VECTOR NORTHEAST.
5. (S) RENDEZVOUS POINT BRAVO HOLD POSITION NORTH LAT 30DEG00MIN00SECONDS EAST LONG 135DEG00MIN00SECONDS, SOUTH OF OSAKA, JAPAN. RENDEZVOUS TIME COORDINATE 071200ZNOV13 OR EARLIER.
6. (S) UPON EXIT OP AREA SEND SITREP VIA SLOT BUOY EVEN IF NO NEWS.
7. (U) ADMIRAL M. PACINO SENDS.
```
//BT//
```

The words were out of his mouth even before he reached paragraph five: "Emergency deep! Emergency deep! All ahead full! Right full rudder, steady course one two zero! Dive, make your depth eight hundred feet, steep angle!"

All hell broke loose. Dietz snapped the periscope grips to the up position and lowered the scope with the hydraulic control ring. The helmsman dialed in FULL on the engine-order telegraph. The planesman put his stern planes on full dive until the ship took on a ten-degree down angle. The ship-wide circuit one PA system blared out, "Emergency deep! Emergency deep!" all through the ship. The engine-order telegraph answering bell rang as the answer needle climbed to FULL speed. The deck tilted dramatically downward, and the depth indicator on the ship-control console began to spin—60 feet, 80, 100, 120, then deeper.

"Increase the angle, Dive," Patton commanded.

"Twenty-degree down angle on the ship, Stern-planesman," the diving officer said.

"More!"

"Down thirty-five degrees!"

The deck became a steep ramp, the ship hanging by its tail, the forward part of the control room almost fifteen feet lower than the aft part. The depth indicator kept spinning—200 feet, 250, 300, the numbers rolling faster as the ship picked up speed. The speed indicator climbed through 15 knots, on to 20, then 25. Soon the depth read 750 feet, and the deck began to level off as the diving officer pulled them out of the plummeting dive.

"Sir, steering course one two zero," the helmsman barked. "Answering all ahead full."

"All ahead flank," Patton commanded. Stepping up to the conn, he found the coiled cord to the microphone that announced in the nuclear control room, called maneuvering. "Maneuvering, Captain, all ahead emergency flank!"

Emergency flank meant they would be burning out their brand-new reactor, taking a ten-million-dollar plant to two hundred percent power and frying the aft spaces with high radiation. The crew would be ordered out of the reactor compartment tunnel and aft compartment unless absolutely necessary for ship safety. At emergency flank he'd be able to make speed in the high forties, maybe even fifty knots. He watched the speed indicator as it climbed to forty-one knots, normal for a flank bell at 100 percent reactor-rated power.

"Captain, Maneuvering, all ahead emergency flank, aye, resetting battle-short switch and resetting reactor-protection limits."

"Conn, aye," he replied. Now that things were calming down in control, the crisis was switched to the nuclear-control room. For the next five minutes eight men would be sweating, trying to bring the reactor to a state as close to meltdown as it could achieve. Throughout the ship high-radiation alarms would start to go off, since the nuclear shielding was not designed to handle such a level. The deck began to tremble with the power of the emergency flank bell. Every ounce of shaft horsepower went to the screw. The speed indicator climbed slowly from 41 knots to 43, 45, 46, finally settling at 49.5 knots. He'd doubled horsepower, and had added only nine lousy knots. That was because the drag of the water outside the skin of the ship had quadrupled. And in fact, the power to the main turbines hadn't really doubled, since some of the power intake was lost to heat leaks and thermal inefficiencies. Still, to trash a ten-million-dollar power unit to make nine extra knots seemed extreme.

Absolute urgent you clear datum op area asap asap asap.

The term "clear datum" was submarine-speak for "get the hell out of there as fast as you can." It was the equivalent to "retreat" for the Marine Corps, rarely used, and if it was, it meant there was ship-threatening trouble out there. Pacino was damned serious.

Patton leaned over the chart, watching the ship's position dot as his vessel ran for the Ryukyu Island chain, the entrance to the Pacific. It had been a hell of a day.

The violent explosion caught him completely by surprise.

The sonarmen of the submarine *Annapolis* never heard the Mod II Nagasaki torpedo trying to catch up to them.

The Nagasaki had been approaching the *Annapolis* when the ship was at periscope depth, and when the ship went deep and sped up, the Nagasaki had found itself in a tail chase. The onboard computer automatically up-shifted the propulsor speed to fast, accelerating the unit to maximum attack velocity of eighty-five clicks, all of five clicks slower than the *Annapolis*. The weapon had closed to within a half kilometer, but as the target sped up, the distance began to open. The torpedo fell behind six hundred meters, then seven hundred, growing to a kilometer.

Minute after minute clicked off. At two kilometers' distance the weapon's onboard computer's calculations showed that the unit would run out of fuel within thirty seconds, and when it did, the target would escape.

A software interlock clicked in at the low-low fuel tank level. The gas turbine's combustion chambers flickered off as the fuel went dry. Before the slowing turbine could drain the coil, changing from a generator to a motor, the software interlock took the turbine out of the circuit, and the torpedo plowed on with only the superconducting coil spinning the AC motor-driven shaft. But the coil had already been running low, which had brought on the gas turbine, and now with the electricity voltage dropping, the torpedo knew it was seconds from shutting down.

In tactical attacks, the weapon programming instructed it to self-destruct rather than just sink. The odds were that a close torpedo detonating could inflict as much damage as a direct hit, especially when the torpedo was a plasma weapon.

With only ten seconds of onboard power left, the low explosives forward and aft of the warhead detonated, starting the complex chain leading to plasma ignition, and within milliseconds the torpedo ceased to exist, a high-energy plasma taking its place.

There was no target ship in the vicinity to vaporize, just endless depths of ocean water. The target was distant at that point, some 2.2 kilometers away, but close enough that the explosion force would likely still sink it.

The shock wave traveled through the sea at sonic velocity, taking only a second and a fraction to reach the hull of what was, for a brief moment, still a submarine.

When the violence of the Nagasaki plasma detonation was over, the ship no longer met the definition of a ship, a vessel that kept water out and people in for a sea voyage, for the water had come in to join the people.

CHAPTER 24

Dante didn't know dick about the inferno, thought Captain Jonathon George S. Patton IV.

While he had been contemplating the universe at the plot table not ten seconds ago, things had comparatively been fine. But in the next second the fabric of his entire world had been ripped apart.

One moment he was surrounded by his nuclear submarine, steaming at emergency flank, deep, almost at test depth, following orders to clear datum, to get the hell out of the East China Sea and rendezvous at the Point Bravo Hold Position.

Except that now the *Annapolis* would never make it to Point Bravo.

From what Patton could understand, an explosion had happened aft in the engine room. He still couldn't tell if the problem had been caused by the nuclear reactor or came from outside, from a torpedo or depth charge. Both reactor-plant troubles were equally nasty—the reactor going supercritical and exploding in a blast of steam and radioactivity was not a pretty sight, nor was a double-ended shear of a twenty-four-inch steam header, blasting high-energy steam into the compartment so fast that the crew would be roasted lobsters in less than thirty seconds. And if a torpedo or depth charge had hit them, who knew if the ship could survive?

It was as if he had been suddenly awakened, like the time when a senior in high school when he had been struck broadside by a driver speeding through a red light. One moment he'd been behind the wheel, not a care in the world. The next, after the loud, resounding bang, passed in a whirlwind of impressions: being tossed across the seat, fighting a spinning steering wheel, tires shrieking, engine racing, until he had hit a tree, the horn sounding, engine dead, the silence until the siren sounded far in the distance. This was an identical feeling, down to the banging noise, the tremendous energy of the explosion deafening him, throwing him into a bulkhead aft of the starboard periscope, the deck careening sideways.

He felt his feet swept out from under him. On pure instinct he screamed, *"Emergency blow both groups! Blow!"* He smashed into the deck on his chest, his arm folded under him, breaking his fall but bruising his forearm. The world spun around him, black at the very edges, the blackness growing until Patton saw the world through a tunnel of light that grew dimmer every second. He blinked, struggling to hold on to consciousness. He vaguely heard a clunking noise and a grunt, then a tremendous roar surrounding him, a white fog enveloping him. For a split second he thought he was floating in clouds, but then realized with gratefulness that the fog was the condensation boiling off the ice-cold high-pressure air piping behind the ballast-control panel. The ultrahigh-pressure air banks would pressurize the ballast tanks—if they still existed—to try to drive out the water and give them buoyancy to get to the surface.

"We going up?" he asked to no one in particular. When there was no answer, just the tremendous roar continuing, he shouted it. "Hey! Chief! OOD! Anybody—we going up?" He struggled to get to his feet, but the room was crazy, fog everywhere, the surface beneath him hard and solid, but was it a deck, a bulkhead?

A second explosion followed, an eruption from a deck below. The ship lurched from the force, and then the roar increased. Just then Patton smelled smoke, and the lights flickered out, every one of them. In the darkness a hot, rolling, heavy cloud of a horrible chemical smell swarmed over him, the first taste of it souring Patton's mouth, crawling down his throat and grabbing his lungs.

He felt himself begin to convulse, vomit spurting from his mouth.

It was as if a rocket had ignited under him. He fairly sailed to his feet, his hands instinctively reaching into the overhead. He missed the first time, missed the second time, the third time grasping a box nestled in with the other equipment. The latch of the metal box snapped open, and his hand scattered a dozen breathing masks down to the deck.

The hot black chemical smell was overwhelming him. With his arm he tried to lift a mask, but a shooting pain exploded in the forearm. Dimly he remembered hitting the deck with the arm cushioning him. The thought was instantly discarded as his other arm reached for the mask and put it on his forehead, down to his chin, then cinched up the straps. Yet there was no air. His eyes bulged and his lungs were bursting. *Chemicals! fire! no air! dying!*

Desperately he struggled for control against the surge of panic. With his right hand he found the hose from the mask's regulator, touched along to its end, the hose connection a cone of metal. By feel he reached up to the manifold, a series of pipe stations six rows across, each row a place to plug in a mask. He'd done this a thousand times in drills, blindfolded, feeling his way, but in those drills there had been one element missing—raw animal fear. Finally the hose connection clicked into the manifold, and he sucked in a huge, whooshing breath of air. His rib cage expanded to three times normal size, like some kind of cartoon character, and he breathed out his lungful of chemical smoke, the smell of it rank in the mask. He sucked in a second breath. With the air came mental clarity, his faculties returning.

He realized that he was standing in a dark room, full of noxious smoke, with a dying crew, a sinking submarine, and he had no idea what was going on. With his good arm he reached into the overhead and found a battle lantern. It was supposed to click on automatically but hadn't. With a flick of a switch a beam of light came on, yet the smoke in the room was so thick, the beam penetrated only halfway to the deck. He then located a portable flashlight in its cradle and shined it until he found the ship-control panel. There two unconscious men lay half out of their seats. He was peering through the smoke when the deck seemed to throw him forward, into the panel this time. He shook his head feeling dizzy.

That sense of being thrown hadn't been his equilibrium, but the deck suddenly coming level, he realized. The depth gauge on the ship-control panel read 33, and Patton could feel the deck moving beneath his feet, rocking gently. The ship was on the surface. The chief must have heard his order and hit the "chicken switches" that had activated the emergency ballast-tank-blow system. For a second Patton searched for the chief who'd followed his orders, thinking that the ship had emergency-blown from damned near test depth, and now they were safe on the surface.

The third explosion in sixty seconds disrupted his fleeting sense of safety. His thoughts shifted to the smoke and what could be causing it. An oxygen fire? Burning torpedo self-oxydizing fuel? A battery fire, hydrogen lighting off in the compartment? Or was it chlorine gas generated by seawater flooding into the battery well? Or even the cyanide gas that would come from burning rocket fuel from the Vortex Mod Charlie missiles? Or was it all of them? Did he and his ship have mere seconds left?

A fourth explosion went off, the roar of it not dying down but continuing. The darkened room was lit by glaring flames climbing up the aft door to the room. Its light diffused by the heavy smoke, the flames spread onto the overhead, making their way toward him, eating the insulation of the hull, creating more black smoke. Patton shook himself. He'd been staring transfixed into the flames, not moving.

Only seventy seconds had passed since the first explosion, but already he knew his ship and his crew were doomed. The flames kept growing, until the aft half of the room was engulfed in the roaring violence. No longer thinking, Patton took five steps forward to the lower bridge tunnel hatch. The tunnel led to the sail high above. Furiously he spun the hatch wheel, undogging the hatchway. With just one arm the hatch took forever to open. He pushed hard, and the hatch lifted into the darkness of the tunnel and latched open.

His crew—he had to find anyone alive and get them out the hatch. He pulled the helmsman out of his seat, but the lad slumped to the deck, unconscious. Patton could have reached into the overhead to get him an air mask, but he knew that would take precious seconds that he didn't have. Frantically he tried to find anyone moving. The officer of the deck lay sprawled on the conn, his forehead cracked open, blood spurting out of a neck wound. Patton moved to the attack center, where he found young Karl Horburg's head smashed into the glass of the display, his forehead buried in the television tube. By now the flames were roaring in the overhead above them, and Patton had to retreat. He tried to shout through the mask, but there was no one to hear him. The heat of the space was growing unbearable. Flames were blazing overhead, scorching his hair. Patton disconnected his air hose, ran forward to the sonar space, found another air manifold, and plugged in. Thank God, DeMeers was still alive, lying on the deck.

There was no time to rig an air mask. Patton needed to get up into the bridge trunk, where twenty feet above the upper hatch led to fresh air, where there was no fire, no smoke, no chemicals. Patton was reaching for DeMeers, struggling against the constraining hose, when the next explosion came. Patton was hurled into the sonar consoles, and the deck listed, a tilt barely perceptible at first, then more and more noticeable. They were tilting aft, and there could be only one possible reason. The stern was sinking.

The ship must be flooding from the engine room. In a burst of anger and frustration, with every ounce of strength he had left, he threw off the mask, grabbed DeMeers' shoulders, and hauled him up. Groggily the sonar chief lurched to his feet.

"Go!" Patton screamed, shoving DeMeers toward the black opening of the bridge tunnel, illuminated only by the flames from the burning hell of the control room. The next explosion blew glass and plastic at the two of them. Flames bloomed from control into the sonar room. Patton could feel his uniform coveralls catch fire, but he kept going, shoving DeMeers—now awake, panicking—up the tunnel. The flames whooshed up the hatchway, then up Patton's legs. Frantically he unlatched the hatch and pushed hard to close it. As it clicked, the ring of flames was choked off.

"Go on, up!" he yelled at DeMeers, who slowly started ascending the ladder. Patton stopped to pat out the flames on his coveralls, which were flame-retardant but had finally given into the heat and the fire. It took some time before the flames went out, leaving Patton's hands red and stinging. He looked up, the tilting tunnel black. He reached for the battle lantern and hit the switch. The light of it shone through the smoke, not as thick here. He put the handle of it in his teeth, and with his good arm he hauled himself up the ladder as fast as he could. DeMeers had reached the upper hatch.

"Open it! Can you open it?"

DeMeers had managed to get the hatch open, but it wasn't enough. The heavy clamshells above the bridge cockpit that faired in the sail, making it hydrodynamic, would need to be pulled down. While DeMeers fought to open the clamshells, Patton pulled a package out of a cubbyhole, a sort of backpack. Suddenly the bright light of day shone down into the slanting tunnel, just for a second, before water started rushing in.

"We're sinking!" DeMeers shouted.

"Get out!" Patton ordered.

"Come on!" DeMeers' voice was faint in the roar of water hitting Patton in the face, washing over his ears. Its coldness was shocking after the broiling temperatures in the dying submarine.

"Get out—take the survival pack," Patton yelled. "Go on!" The flowing water was blasting into his nostrils and mouth and ears, like having a fire hose full force in the face. He felt himself start to lose his grip. This was it. He had watched his ship smashed with a torpedo or depth charge, and within seconds she was flooding and burning. He had tried to get her to the surface, where he could save his men, but it was not to be. Now his best friend was about to die in a futile effort to save him, and he couldn't allow that.

"Get out!" he screamed one last time.

What happened next was nothing short of a miracle. Byron DeMeers grabbed Patton's coveralls with one hand, the sail handhold with the other, and in one heaving motion rocketed Patton out of the sinking submarine free of the hatch, completely flooded with water. The light of day came back—waves were washing over his head, and he was spitting and retching, the deep convulsions gripping into his stomach, the water he'd swallowed spurting out of him. Finally Byron's bald head popped out of the water, and Patton could breathe again. DeMeers shook his head, blinked, and said, "Look." In his hand was the survival pack.

In three motions of DeMeers' hands a hunk of limp rubber appeared on the waves with them. DeMeers pulled the CO_2 bottle and the life raft inflated. Patton was exhausted, giving in to shock. He barely remembered being pulled into the raft by the senior chief. Then he was lying on his back, his left forearm throbbing and swelling, nausea threatening but nothing but dry heaves shaking his body.

"Is it just me," he croaked, "or were we, just four minutes ago, aboard the *Annapolis* steaming southeast at emergency flank?"

"We were, Skipper. And now we're all that's left." DeMeers' face took on a grim look. He frowned deeper as he pulled the pin on the emergency satellite radio, a device resembling a grenade, that would broadcast their distress signal to the overhead ComStar satellite.

"There were 134 men aboard, Senior. One hundred thirty-two of them just died. And so did my ship. What the hell happened?"

"Had to be a torpedo," DeMeers said.

"Well, hello," Patton said, sitting bolt upright. He'd noticed a periscope close enough to swim to in ten strokes. "I think you're right, Byron. Look."

DeMeers' eyes bulged out, his face turning red.

Patton glared at the periscope, the design of it strange-looking, and without thinking, he flipped it his middle finger. "Fuck you," he muttered.

As quickly as it had come, the periscope vanished, sinking vertically into the water.

"Did I imagine that?" he said, dizziness starting to overtake him.

"No, sir. I saw it too. I'd like to kill that murdering bastard with my own two hands."

Patton didn't hear him. Darkness had come to claim him at last.

The crew of the American submarine named *Santa Fe* heard the torpedo coming and turned to run. The ship's superior speed slowly opened the distance, but the vessel was unable to overcome the effects of the plasma detonation within five kilometers, and the ship's hull ruptured. The *Santa Fe*'s men, all 138 of them, died not from fires or smoke inhalation, but from a hull fracture that opened up the entire forward compartment at test depth. The water poured in with such force that it separated flesh from bone, turning muscle and organs to liquid that mixed instantly with the seawater, and they were no more.

The hull of the *Santa Fe* came to rest eleven kilometers from the position of what had once been the *Annapolis,* and when it did, what had once been the most powerful naval force in the history of the planet ceased to exist with barely a sign left on the surface of its passing.

Not far from the ocean bottom that had become a field of debris, Admiral Chu Hua-Feng, PLA Navy, climbed out of his cramped command-console cockpit and limped to his bunk in the captain's stateroom. His muscles were aching and tired as he lay down to sleep.

When he closed his eyes, the faces of the doomed men in the life raft were staring back at him, the angry black-haired man raising his middle finger again and again.

BOOK V

SSNX

CHAPTER 25

MONDAY
NOVEMBER 4

BARBERS POINT NAVAL AIR STATION
OAHU, HAWAII

The SS-12 cabin was heavily soundproofed, yet the sounds of the flaps and slats could be heard whining as their mechanisms lowered them into the slipstream of the airflow around the supersonic jet, making its final approach to runway zero four, illuminated by bright white lights in the predawn darkness. None of this registered with the admiral, sunk in deep concentration.

"Time's our enemy," Pacino said. "If the backup rapid deployment force leaves now, it'll take them five days and six hours to get to the East China Sea. That's dawn on Sunday the tenth, local time. The Pacific Submarine Force we sent yesterday, at emergency flank, arrives late Friday the eighth. That leaves thirty hours to try to scour the East China Sea before the BU-RDF arrives. It's not enough."

"We've got to think long and hard about the 688s," White said. "Still no word."

"How long has it been since the second ELF call to periscope depth?"

"Ninety minutes, sir. We should have heard an hour ago one way or the other. I think we may have to presume the *Annapolis* and the *Santa Fe* are unable to hear our radio call."

Pacino felt a black feeling. He knew that the 688's radio receivers or transmitters weren't the problem. He wasn't sure how he knew, but he did. *Annapolis* and *Santa Fe* were gone. And with them at the bottom of the ocean were his two handpicked, personally trained commanding officers, Chris Carnage and John Patton. He bit his lip. The war had suddenly become personal.

With those officers almost three hundred highly trained crewmen of Pacino's Unified Submarine Command were gone. He felt an anger rise in him like none he'd experienced in years, perhaps exceeded only by the day Dick Donchez had told him his father had been murdered. And now these men, his sons, had died at the hands of a rogue submarine commander, and that commander and his men were still lurking in the East China Sea, mocking him.

The airplane landed on the runway with a hard jolt, the engines screaming in reverse, the jet down at the naval air station two miles from Pearl Harbor.

"Paully, *Annapolis* and *Santa Fe* are gone, they're down. And I have to assume that any other 688s we send in will get attacked before they can react."

"I don't know, Admiral. The *Annapolis* and *Santa Fe* were operating under the late Jean-Paul's orders, out ahead and flanking it, loud as train wrecks compared to these Rising Suns. Is it possible that if they were doing a proper sonar search, they'd have detected them?"

"Maybe. I'll think about it. Meanwhile, we've got a videoconference with Warner in fifteen minutes. We owe her an answer about whether the rogue subs will be coming out of the East China Sea to meet the task force of the backup RDF in the mid-Pacific."

"I'd say it depends on what goes out on the news, sir."

"What do you mean?"

"I mean, with all the news transmitted instantly to the world from Satellite News Network and all the other wannabes, this rogue force is cut into our plans. President Warner announces to the world that we're coming, they embark news reporters on the *Webb,* and they take a chopper up to look down at the goddamned formation.

What better tactical data could this rogue commander have?"

"Stop calling him a rogue. It makes him sound like a good guy. Let's call these subs the Red Squadron and the flotilla commander Red One."

"Fine, Red goddamned One. Anyway, this dude gets his intelligence beamed right to his television widescreens, and SNN transmits Warner's every mood."

"Quiet, let me think," Pacino said. "Maybe there's something I can do."

"About the media? Are you kidding?"

"Sshh." Pacino rubbed his eyes, an idea beginning to surface.

When he opened his eyes, the jet had taxied to Pacino's hangar, the lights overhead flickering as the engines died. Pacino and White stood, gathering their things as the door came open.

Pacino walked out into the warmth of the Hawaiian night. A breeze was coming off the sea, and the smell of it was comforting, the hot air welcome after the chill of the Tetons. At the bottom of the stairs Joanna Stoddard waited, his administrative assistant, there at four-thirty in the morning to meet him and Paully. She was in her thirties, pretty in a suppressed librarian manner, married to a surfer. When she was younger she had worked for Pacino as a lieutenant, one of his junior aides. She had left the Navy to get married, then immediately asked him to hire her as a civilian, and had been with him ever since.

"Joanna, good to see—"

She interrupted him. "The reporters have been after me. Everyone wants to know what you're going to do next. Including Warner and the CNO. The president and Admiral O'Shaughnessy are waiting for your video-conference once we get there. And there are four visitors in your office now, a Japanese man claiming to be Akagi Tanaka."

Pacino and White shared a look. "Who else?"

"Colleen O'Shaughnessy and Emmitt Stephens from

the shipyard. Admiral Dick Livingston from Naval Personnel."

"How's the *SSNX*?"

"I canceled the christening ceremony so Stephens could get it lowered into the water. You better bet the press were mad about that—"

"Christening ceremony?"

"Yessir. To name it, remember? Admiral O'Shaughnessy's orders came over on your WritePad? Naming the *SSNX* the USS *Devilfish*?"

"Oh, yeah." Donchez again, Pacino thought, feeling an ambivalence to the ship's name, the memories of the first submarine by that name too painful. "So is it in the water? And loaded out with Mod Charlies and Mark 52s?"

"Captain Stephens called and said something about the SSNX security provisions being complete. Beyond that, he wouldn't answer my questions."

The two officers and Joanna walked to an idling staff car. The big black Lincoln utility truck lacked the usual fender flags, and the decals of the Unified Submarine Command had been removed, evidently to avoid the SNN and network news crews. Pacino got in the back right-side seat, Paully in the back left, Joanna riding shotgun.

"And Colleen O'Shaughnessy? What's she doing in my office at oh-dark-thirty?"

"Wouldn't say. You know her, if she doesn't want to answer, she just stares you down with those huge brown eyes of hers." Stoddard sounded almost catty, he thought.

"I think she got that from her old man."

The Lincoln pulled away from the hangar and sped out Coral Sea Road to the west gate, not the normal way of getting to Pearl Harbor. They came in the Ewa Beach gate to the Pearl Harbor Naval Reservation, the driver waving and roaring past the gate that opened just in time, then closed behind them. The Lincoln raced to a pier where a waiting boat was tied up. As White and Pacino boarded the boat, the diesel exhaust brought back memories from his youth, at the academy when they'd driven the yard-patrol diesels. Two sailors brought their bags and briefcases and joined Joanna as the boat engine throttled up. The boat sailed out of the West Loch past the Waipio Peninsula to Pearl City Peninsula, where the new Unified Submarine Command West Headquarters building was located.

"Roundabout way to get to the office," Pacino remarked to Joanna.

"You're the man of the hour, Admiral," she said, looking at him strangely. "They all want to know what your submarines are going to do to keep the backup RDF out of the drink."

Pacino grimaced at her. "So do I. Come on, let's get to work."

A jeep at the peninsula pier took them the half mile to the USubCom building. The white three-story edifice looked like it had been built in the Hawaii of 1905, complete with columns and small windows, yet inside it was equipped with the latest technology. Pacino's office had the only large window, looking out over the East Loch toward the submarine piers, now empty. The office had a feeling of tropical airiness, and on the light, knotty pine plank walls were framed photographs of nuclear submarines, old friends standing next to the sails of their subs, a picture of Pacino the day he took command of the *Seawolf,* a picture of Donchez standing by his ancient *Piranha,* and a photo yellow with age, of Anthony Pacino and his young son standing next to the sail of the *Stingray.*

Facing the window was a huge desk made of the timbers of the USS *Bonhomme Richard,* John Paul Jones' ship from over two centuries before. The desk had two lamps and a dozen photographs of young Tony Pacino. On one side of the desk was a black glass conference table used for videoconferences and meetings. On the other side was Pacino's oak library table, where he did most of his work.

He threw his hat on the library table and sank into the chair, already thinking.

"Chart display," he said, snapping his fingers. Paully White found the large electronic chart computer display and put it on the empty table. Pacino punched into the large menu and configured the display to show the East China Sea, then the sea between Hawaii and Japan. He studied it for some time, then looked up at Paully.

"I'm ready. Joanna, get the videoconference set up, then get with Emmitt Stephens and Colleen O'Shaughnessy. Tell them they'll be on next in about ten minutes. Then when we're done with them, get Dick Livingston in here."

Paully White and Pacino sat at the glass videoconference table and waited for the screen to come up.

"What are you going to do, boss?" White asked quietly as the presidential seal flashed on the large video wide-screen.

"Just watch," Pacino hissed. Warner's face appeared, her eyes glazed and tired, her hair—for the first time in Pacino's memory—not perfectly coiffed. Next to her was an equally tired-looking Dick O'Shaughnessy.

"Admiral," Warner said, smiling. "Let's get to it. Have you thought about what we're going to do with your submarines? And how to escort in the backup RDF? And will these Red submarines be penetrating the deep Pacific to get the RDF? And when will we be able to come ashore in White China?"

She still didn't understand, Pacino thought. If he was going to win this submarine war, he would need to control it all, including the timing, the surface force, the media, and the president herself.

"I've thought about all that, ma'am. And the answer is good. Madam President, I have a plan to clear the East China Sea of these Red submarines and get the backup RDF to shore with no losses. We can win this thing, ma'am. And I can make that happen for you."

"Okay," Warner said, one eyebrow lifted. "And exactly how do you plan to do that?"

"Believe me, Madam President, Admiral O'Shaughnessy, the plan is solid. I'm sure you'll find out just how solid when General Baldini comes ashore with every single man of the force behind him."

Warner scowled, unused to having her questions evaded.

"Admiral Pacino, what is your plan?"

"My plan is to take full command of the U.S. Naval Force Pacific, including all elements—the Unified Naval Air Command, the Unified Surface Naval Command, the NavForcePacFleet, including the backup Rapid Deployment Force. All force commanders will report to me, and I will have absolute authority over the entire operation. General Baldini will be my subordinate until we reach a point twenty miles from the beach, at which point he will take tactical command from me with the exception of the submarine assets of the USubCom and the ships of the NavForcePacFleet, which will remain under my operational command.

"During the RDF's transit to Chinese waters, all elements of the press will be ejected from the ships of the RDF and flown back to Hawaii. The press will be absolutely in the dark about the operation, and in fact Admiral Copenflager of the task force will have orders to send F-22 fighters aloft to intercept any aircraft of any nationality trying to see what the task force is doing, including aircraft chartered by the press. All such planes will be jammed and escorted to Hickam Air Force Base, where they will be impounded and the reporters detained until the end of the operation. If press planes fail to turn back, they will be fired upon."

"Hold on right there, Admiral!" Warner was furious. "What the hell are you talking about, firing on reporters, are you crazy?"

"Madam President, that's my plan. I want orders in writing from you and Admiral O'Shaughnessy making me supreme commander-in-chief U.S. Pacific Military Forces, and I want it in twenty minutes. Then don't plan on hearing anything for a while, a week, ten days. The next thing you'll hear is a call from the Red Chinese ambassador begging your forgiveness."

"Pacino!" O'Shaughnessy began to shout, but Warner put her hand on his gold-striped sleeve.

"Admiral, this is impossible, I don't know what you're talking about. I want to know your plan for your subs, and I want it *now*."

"No," Pacino said.

"What?" A look of disbelief crossed her features.

"I said no," he said calmly, sensing Paully White staring at him. "Either I'm Supreme Commander Pacific or I quit."

"Admiral, there's no way! You aren't running anything except your subs. Now, get this idea out of your head and tell me right now what the subs are going to do to keep the force safe. I have a press conference in forty minutes."

"Madam President?"

He had her complete attention, a look of understanding and even fear dawning on her face.

"Yes, Admiral?"

"I quit. Good-bye." He hit the kill switch on the video console, and the wide-screen winked out.

"Um, sir, what the hell did you just do?"

"You sound like Warner, Paully."

"Admiral? Captain Stephens and Ms. O'Shaughnessy are ready," Joanna said.

"Send them in. Ah, Emmit, Colleen."

The two shipyard officials walked in. Pacino smiled and pointed at the table.

CENTRAL OHIO
AIR FORCE ONE
ALTITUDE: 38,000 FEET

"Has he gone completely nuts?"

Admiral Richard O'Shaughnessy was still staring at the dark wide-screen. He turned to face a president so angry as to be on the verge of losing control.

"No, ma'am," he said slowly in his deep baritone voice. "I think I know what he's concerned about." He picked up a remote control and flicked the satellite-receiver console to life.

". . . task force on the way to the East China Sea, where we've asked Commander Fred Duke to explain how the antisubmarine-warfare units of the task force work. Commander, you indicated that this task force has helicopters that can attack submarines. Will they be able to do the job against what would seem to be—"

O'Shaughnessy killed the tube.

"Pacino's right. Whoever was out there in the East China Sea knew we were coming and what our tactical deployment was. He blew us away so easily because he knew exactly when and where we were coming. He knew the very mood of the task force commander, may he rest in peace."

"What are you saying, Admiral? That the television news lost us the battle?"

"Not quite, Madam President. I think what I'm saying is that not listening to Admiral Pacino lost us the battle. If we'd done what he wanted to do, we'd be ashore in White China now, or tomorrow, or Wednesday, with only the embarrassment of waiting."

"Okay, and what would I have told the press?"

"That's Pacino's point, ma'am." O'Shaughnessy laughed, the president shooting a look of fury at him. "You, Madam President, are a security risk."

"What? Choose your words carefully, Admiral."

"That's just it, Madam President, you don't. Your words go around the world. To White China, we say hold on, the cavalry's coming. To Red China we say, get out, get out or die. Did I capture that accurately? And then two hundred news crews on the USS *Webb* tell the world what we're doing out there. We should be ashamed of ourselves. And how many press conferences did we give, or that you gave, where you let various military cats out of their bags? Pacino's right. The only way he can clean up the East China Sea is sneak in there while the Reds are kept guessing. Look over here a minute." O'Shaughnessy walked to a world globe placed on a small table. "Hawaii's here, and White China's here.

The East China Sea is the front yard to White China. Now look at the great circle route between Pearl Harbor and Shanghai, or Tsingtao or Hong Kong. They all pass through the Ryukyu Island chain about here, give or take a few miles. For the Red forces, they don't need to know exactly where we're going, they just need to know when we'll get there.

"Admiral Pacino has suggested a way to stop the information flow. You're a politician, you've proved yourself to him, and he's volunteered to take this off your shoulders. He did a great job in Japan. Trust him now. He'll do this right, ma'am, if you'll just let him."

For a long time Warner didn't look at him, just kept her back to him. Finally she spoke, and when she did, her voice trembled.

"Admiral? You're fired. Get out of my conference room."

CHAPTER 26

Colleen O'Shaughnessy walked into his office as if she owned it.

It was just after five in the morning, and the sun had yet to rise above the shimmering water of the East Loch. She wore jeans and a simple white blouse under a black blazer, her shoes fashionable black combat-style boots. Around her throat was a thin gold chain. Her jet black, gleaming hair fell just below her shoulders, her bangs cut just at eyebrow level, bringing out her eyes, which were the biggest Pacino could ever remember seeing.

She sat opposite him with her back to the video screen. On her right sat Emmitt Stephens, the man responsible for the construction of the SSNX. He found Stephens looking at him oddly, then realized Stephens had asked him a question and he hadn't heard it because he was still staring at Colleen.

"What?"

"I said the news is good and bad. Good news first." Stephens went through the notes he'd written on his WritePad computer. "SSNX hull and mechanical systems are ready for sea trials. The reactor is certified, all tests complete with the exception of initial criticality and pier-side steaming. All weapons are loaded, but what you wanted with war-shot torpedoes and Vortex Mod Charlies, well, I don't want to know. Now for the bad news. I'll leave that to Colleen. If you'll excuse me, Admiral, I've got a lot to do."

"Listen, Emmitt, I want you to do something. Start the reactor and bring it to the power range, then bring steam into the engine room and put the electric plant in a normal full-power lineup."

"Sir, Admiral, are you . . . sir, you can't just do that. This isn't an operational ship. The initial criticality is monitored by the Naval Reactors people. And it'll take weeks to get a new reactor even close to the power range. It's not safe."

"Emmitt. Reactor. Critical. Now."

Pacino and Stephens had worked together for years, and the engineering duty officer had never been comfortable with Pacino's insistent pushing. He had gotten *Seawolf* out of the dock in four days when the work should have taken three weeks, then done it again for the Seawolf–class ship *Piranha* when it had had the Mod Bravo Vortex missiles attached. When Pacino wanted a ship, Stephens had always jumped, but it was unheard of to treat initial criticality like a normal start-up. The reactor could come screaming out of the nonvisible range with enough reactivity that they wouldn't be able to control it. A Russian submarine in Vladivostok shipyard had suffered such an incident on a restart after a core replacement, and if not for the Russian-designed double hull, the entire city of Vladivostok would have had to be evacuated.

Pacino looked imploringly into Stephens' eyes, his hands out in an unconscious imitation of Admiral O'Shaughnessy. "Emmitt, you're the only one who can do this. The SSNX is your baby, you built it with your own two hands. Don't let it be a white elephant, useless in its moment of need. There are about a billion men, women, and children in White China counting on you right now. If we delay a single minute, that's another minute that the Reds hold the East China Sea. Can you do this, can you get it going?"

Emmitt Stephens stood, knowing that Pacino was pulling his old trick, giving him a pep talk that could fire him up, make him work around the clock, coax from him the impossible, and he smiled suddenly, knowing that once again it had worked.

"Aye, sir. I'll do my best."

"Good man. See you pier-side."

Pacino waved at him, then turned to Colleen O'Shaughnessy. She looked back at him, and he found himself somehow drawn to her. She started talking about the Cyclops battle-control system and how it was still nonfunctional.

". . . failure modes have revealed almost nothing, and the decision was made early this morning to scrap the DynaCorp code and return to an earlier version before the acquisition and restart all code entries at that point."

"Okay, I admit it, I'm lost. What's all that mean?"

"Well, Admiral Pacino, it means your onboard computer has just had a lobotomy and has the brain of a newborn."

"So what now?"

"So now I recode it, writing it so it'll work."

"Just you?"

"That's right. Just me." Her voice was deep, throaty, yet refined and certain, the voice of a woman unused to being questioned.

"How long?"

"About a month to get to the C-1 test, maybe a week after that to get to C-9. And just so you know, that's the optimistic schedule. If I'm honest with myself, this could take three months all told."

"Today is Monday, right? You've got until Thursday. By then we'll be in the East China Sea. And you'd better go get some sensible clothes. You can't dress like that at sea."

"Excuse me? What are you talking about?"

"The SSNX is leaving, Colleen, and you're going with it. You'll have to do your coding on the way. We leave in sixty minutes. See you at the pier."

Her air of confidence cracked, just a little. "I'm not reading you here. I—"

"You're getting underway on the *Devilfish*, Colleen. The SSNX is deploying to the East China Sea operation area—for those of us in the know, the 'op area'—and you are the battle-control system."

"But—"

"Joanna, can you help Ms. O'Shaughnessy pack? Get

her to her house and down to the pier by zero six hundred. Yes?"

Paully White poked his head into the room.

"You'd better see this," he said, switching the wide-screen on. A reporter was standing on the tarmac in the noon sunshine in front of Air Force One. The stairway led to an open door, and the airplane was flanked by Secret Service agents and newsmen.

". . . an announcement concerning the war in White China and the deployment of the U.S. backup Rapid Deployment Force. And here she comes now."

Jaisal Warner walked down the ramp, wearing a dark suit that emphasized her slimness, smiling and waving at reporters. Behind her was Admiral O'Shaughnessy in his service dress blues, his stripes gleaming gold and climbing high up his sleeves. Colleen O'Shaughnessy froze, having moved behind Pacino's shoulder at his seat at the conference table. Pacino could faintly smell her perfume, and he turned to look up at her. Her features had become soft while she watched her father walk down the steps behind the president.

Warner walked up to a podium, looking determined. "Good afternoon, Americans," she began. "Effective immediately, I am appointing Admiral Michael Pacino, U.S. Navy, the supreme commander-in-chief of Pacific U.S. Military Forces. As such, Admiral Pacino will lead the invasion and liberation of White China. All force commanders will, as of this moment, immediately report to him. And, per the special request of Admiral Pacino, also effective immediately, the U.S. military and all branches of the federal government are commencing a total news blackout of the conduct of this conflict against the Red Chinese." A small uproar broke out among the reporters. Warner held up one hand. "Please, ladies and gentlemen, bear with me. After a detailed study into the loss of the first Rapid Deployment Force, and under the direction of Admiral Pacino, I am ordering the press removed from all U.S. military establishments, starting with the aircraft carriers of the task force of the backup RDF. In addition, any aircraft of any nationality which attempts to approach anywhere within a thousand miles of the task force will be intercepted by the Navy fighter jets of the force and escorted away. In the event any aircraft does not heed the orders of the fighters, that aircraft will be shot down." Warner paused for effect, greeted with pin-drop silence. "Thank you, ladies and gentlemen of the press, for your cooperation. And for all Americans, I ask for your prayers for the men of the Rapid Deployment Force, and for Admiral Pacino. That is all."

As Warner walked away, bedlam broke out, shouted questions flying at her from all directions. Paully White clicked the wide-screen off. The silence in the room was only momentary, though, for a dozen phones suddenly began ringing in the outer office.

Colleen O'Shaughnessy looked at him in astonishment.

"You'd better hurry, Colleen," Pacino said, putting his feet on the desk and his hands behind his head. "The supreme commander has spoken."

"Good to see this hasn't gone to your head, Admiral," Colleen said, crinkling her nose at him. Then she swept out the door.

"You knew," White said in awe. "You knew she'd do that."

"Of course," Pacino said. "What the hell else was she going to do? Fire me and Dick O'Shaughnessy? And have the second RDF put on the bottom by the Reds? I don't think so."

"Yeah, well, when this is over, you'll be retired. Your paycheck stops the day they hit the beach."

"Paully, if we can do this, I'll be happy to retire. Let's just worry about coming out of this with a task force that reaches the beach instead of the bottom of the ocean."

"You ready for Tanaka?"

"Listen, I want to talk to him, but I need to talk to Dick Livingston, then to Bruce Phillips on the *Piranha,* and we've both got to pack. Get out to the SSNX and meet me aboard. And get Tanaka out there—"

"He's going with us?"

"Yes, so get him some clothes and set him up in a stateroom. Settle Colleen into one of the other staterooms—in fact, give her the executive officer's stateroom, so she doesn't have to share the bathroom with anyone but the captain."

"Sir? Um, who is the captain?"

"Don't know yet. That's what Admiral Livingston is here for. Now shove off, and I'll see you at the SSNX."

"Maybe you should start calling it by its real name. *Devilfish*."

"I don't know if I can. It's just a little too weird."

"Sir," Joanna interrupted.

"I thought you were taking Colleen down to the pier."

"She said she didn't need my help," Joanna said, glaring at Pacino. "Anyway, sir, SNN has some good news."

"The only good news that could come right now is no news," Pacino grumbled.

But when the wide-screen came up, there was John Patton, wearing orange search and rescue coveralls. The voiceover said, ". . . survivor of the sinking of the submarine USS *Annapolis*. Captain Patton, who didn't go down with the ship, was plucked from the sea by a helicopter of the Japanese *Kaijo Hoancho*, or coast guard. After arriving at Yokosuka, Captain Patton and an unidentified second survivor had no comment for our news cameras. Meanwhile, Admiral Pacino, the newly announced supreme commander of the Pacific forces, has made no statement and has been unavailable for comment. Meanwhile, at the Pentagon, inside sources revealed today that—"

Pacino switched it off, feeling an exhilaration he hadn't since he'd married Eileen. With a stab of guilt he realized that in his moment of happiness, her memory had been swept aside.

"Did you see that, Admiral?" White asked, incredulous.

"Looks like the SSNX has her captain," Pacino said, unable to suppress his smile. "Joanna, get on the horn to NavForcePac Admin in Yokosuka. Get Patton down here on a supersonic jet—an F-22 maybe, or an F-14, but get him back here fast."

"You're putting him in command of the *Devilfish*? After he lost *Annapolis*?"

"Damned right I am. He's probably pretty angry at the Reds by now. Let's put him in the saddle. He'll do fine. Now get me Admiral Livingston. We've got to get a crew for the SSNX—I mean *Devilfish*."

"Yessir," White said, smiling back.

Suddenly Pacino had a good feeling about the operation. It wouldn't be easy, but then, at least if it failed, it would be his fault, not some politicians' or the news media's. He smiled at Livingston, ushered him to a seat, and began to speak.

PACIFIC OCEAN
300 NAUTICAL MILES WEST-NORTHWEST OF OAHU
AIRCRAFT CARRIER USS *DOUGLAS MACARTHUR,*
CVN-85

Rear Admiral Gregory Copenflager sat up straight in his seat before the videoconference camera.

"Yes, *sir*," he said, receiving an order he would be glad to follow.

"One other thing," Admiral Pacino said from his Pearl Harbor office, "even before you redeploy into the ASW formation. You may have seen this on the news. I want all reporters rounded up and transported to Pearl Harbor. I want their gear—suitcases, underwear, cameras, tape recorders, computers, all of it—sent on a separate airplane. And before you bring them up on deck, blindfold them. I know it sounds paranoid, but I don't want them reporting anything except how poorly they were treated. No ship formations, order of battle information, attitude of the troops, nothing. We'll see to their reception on this end. And don't worry about them smearing your career. You just blame the whole thing on me. Is that completely clear?"

"Yes, Admiral. We'll get on it immediately."

"And, Greg, you should expect to be at the Point Delta Hold Position for some time. I want you to make the best time you can, with your random zigzag pattern, for Point Delta, but don't expect to go in as soon as you get there. You're not crossing the line until you hear from me personally, and that word won't come until I know the East China Sea is clear."

"Aye-aye, sir," Copenflager said, his jaw muscles clenching.

"Good luck, Greg. And watch yourself."

"Same to you, Admiral. Good hunting."

Copenflager, the admiral-in-command of the backup Rapid Deployment Force Fleet, clicked off and looked over at his staff and the captain of the *MacArthur*. "Round up the press, put them in the ready rooms, and confiscate their gear, then blindfold them. Get five Hawkeyes ready to airlift them back to Pearl, and put their gear on the sixth. No more ship announcements until they are all off. Once they're gone, execute the maximum-dispersion order, cargo vessels no closer than two miles from each other, random distribution, ASW ships in a large-area screen. It's zero five forty-five now. In one hour's time I want the reporters off and the formation redeployed. Questions? Very well, gentlemen. Execute."

The staff rose and vanished. Copenflager stood up, relived. Maybe with Pacino in command, things would be different. They'd better be, he thought, looking out the window at the formation, or else for him it would be a very short war.

UNIFIED SUBMARINE COMMAND HEADQUARTERS WEST PEARL HARBOR, HAWAII

The president was glaring at him. Pacino couldn't remember her ever looking at him like that, even after he got kicked out of the Oval Office before the Japan blockade.

"I'd still like to know what you're doing. I've heard rumors about the SSNX."

"I'd like to know where you're getting rumors like that," Pacino said to the camera, hoping his voice sounded sufficiently hard.

In the background Admiral O'Shaughnessy's face, as usual, was unreadable, yet Pacino thought he detected just a slight smile. Pacino felt a certainty he hadn't had in a long time. A single word was running through his mind: *Devilfish*. He knew it was silly and superstitious, but somehow that name was making a difference to him. Donchez must have known that the name would bring back other things from that time to him. His old cockiness seemed to be returning, the self that had been lost now beginning to resurface.

"Like I told you, I'll be damned if the Red force commander learns anything about this mission from the news. And the reason I want to know where you got those rumors is because my plan may be starting to work. Madam President, the absence of news is not enough against this guy. We need to get things into the news that are misleading, some completely false, some edged with enough truth to confuse him. If you'll just lay low until this operation is over, ma'am, you won't be embarrassed by anything you say that turns out to be my disinformation."

Jaisal Warner was not happy. "So I'm just supposed to trust you, and three weeks from now you'll call up and say you're at the beach?"

"Not quite like that, ma'am."

"You're the supreme commander, Admiral. I'll give you your autonomy. And you'd better win this thing. If anything goes wrong, I'll consider today's developments evidence of your insubordination, and the only thing you'll command is your Annapolis sailboat."

Just a few months ago, a statement like that from the president would have upset him. Maybe it was his new-found—or rediscovered—confidence, but instead of just acknowledging the president, he narrowed his eyes at her, stared her down O'Shaughnessy-style, and said: "What do I get if I win?"

Warner tried to look serious, but she was too much an open book. She flashed the smile that had gotten her on the front pages during her campaign. "I'll prepare something for you that I'm sure you'll appreciate, Admiral."

"No, I want to know," Pacino said, feeling suddenly that he had to get Warner convinced on a gut level that the operation would succeed, even if he himself had his doubts. "Because you're going to have to deliver."

"Don't you have a war to win, Admiral?" she asked, shaking her head.

"This is good-bye for a while, ma'am. Remember, don't believe the rumors." He clicked off, turning to face Paully White, who looked at him in astonishment.

"What was all that about disinformation, boss? We didn't do any of that. We didn't put out any rumors about the SSNX."

"I know, but I want Warner off balance about that. If she thinks I'm using the SSNX, then the media will find out, and then our Red force friend finds out."

"So how will you sneak the sub out of Pearl?"

"Emmitt Stephens and I had a talk about that a few months ago. Emmitt put something together to get SSNX to sea in broad daylight with no one the wiser. I think you'll like it."

"What now?"

"Lets shift over to the SSNX. We'll have to do this so we avoid the telephoto lenses of our media comrades. Get Joanna, she seems pretty good at this sort of thing."

It took a half hour to get to the pier at Ford Island on the south side, where Emmitt Stephens had berthed the SSNX. When Paul White saw it, he stared, whistled, then laughed.

CHAPTER 27

Bruce Phillips was more hungover than at any time in his adult life. Truth be told, he was probably still drunk.

He lay deep in his rack, in the captain's stateroom, buried under the covers, wearing boxer shorts and a T-shirt. The air conditioning in the room was turned up to full blast, practically cold enough to make his breath visible. It was early in the morning on a Monday. The ship had been shifted over from Hawaii time to the East China Sea time zone, eighteen hours ahead, resetting the ship's clocks to just before midnight. Which meant he could get away with sleeping in the bunk even though he'd been in it for hours, trying to sleep off the alcohol.

It had all started Saturday night, when Abby O'Neal had told him their relationship was over. She'd flown into Honolulu for a week's vacation from her Washington, D.C., job, where she was a senior partner at Donnelly & Houston, a firm of maritime attorneys and lobbyists. They were slated to get married in a year's time, but the *Piranha,* Phillips' command, had been moved four months before from Norfolk to Pearl Harbor as a permanent change in home port. It hadn't bothered Phillips, since he knew he'd be giving up command of the ship in the next year. It was a long time to be away from his fiancée, but then they were engaged, and he had thought that had meaning to her.

A future in the Navy didn't hold any great promise

for him. After all, what good was commanding a desk after commanding the last remaining Seawolf–class nuclear fast-attack submarine? He had made plans to resign his commission and try a new career. Abby knew of his plans, and she had fully agreed to the temporary separation.

Yet as the weeks apart grew into months, her calls started coming less frequently. More and more she mentioned the managing partner, Albert Donnelly, son of her firm's founding partner, who had recruited her to the D.C. company and advanced her career beyond her wildest dreams. He learned that Bert had gotten a nasty divorce a year before, becoming one of Washington's most eligible bachelors. He was interested in her despite her engagement, but she'd held him off. By the fifth month of their separation, she seemed distracted, almost cold. Phillips had shrugged it off, knowing she was susceptible to fairly strong mood swings. On impulse he had invited her to Hawaii for a week to be with him, to grab some fall sunshine, get her tan back before Thanksgiving.

When he met her at the airport, he had dressed in his best tropical suit, armed with a dozen red roses. When Abby appeared, Phillips smiled at her, his arms outstretched. As she drew closer, though, he saw that something was seriously wrong.

Despite fresh makeup she looked like she'd been crying. She couldn't look him in the eye when she came up. Her hands were clasped together, and she seemed somehow small. Her hair was different too, the sleek black gone, now done in soft, brassy red curls, the length far shorter. Her eyes were different too, the brown gone, replaced by the odd blueness of colored contact lenses.

"Abby, what is it?" he asked her, his voice sounding strange in his own ears.

"I came to tell you in person, Bruce. It's over." She pulled her diamond ring off and handed it to him. "I'll start with the part you know and work my way to what you don't. I love you, I've loved you since I first saw you. But, honey, I can't take the separation, and it's even more than that. You love that ship and your Navy life more than me. I asked you what your plans were, and I'd hoped you'd leave the *Piranha* when your rotation came up, but you made a special trip to talk to the admiral and begged for a back-to-back command tour, and he gave it to you. Another three years on the damned *Piranha*. Well, Bruce, you want her, you can have her. That fucking ship is all yours. And I'm giving you my orders now. This is your honorable discharge, Captain. I'm leaving on the next flight back, and I don't want to talk anymore. Good-bye, Bruce."

He'd stood stupidly dumbstruck, his tongue useless in his mouth, watching her walk away, disappearing into a ladies' room. For a full five minutes he stood there with his mouth open, trying to understand, and starting to understand all too well. He found himself walking into the ladies' room. He ignored the annoyed shouts, banging on the stall door he thought was Abby's, only to find it was someone else. Finally a security guard had come and dragged him out.

He'd found a bar on Ward Avenue and had lined up shot glasses of Wild Turkey for the rest of the night. Finally he was ejected as being too drunk to stay. Somehow he had told a cab driver to take him to his ship rather than his quarters, and he had fallen flat on his face at the pier where the gangway went over to the hull topside. The sentries had carried him aboard and put him into his rack.

The time since then had passed in a blur. He had alternately slept, vomited, was put in the corner as the stewards changed his sheets and mattress, then slept again, vomited again. He had been shaken awake by the duty officer, the executive officer behind him. They'd told him that the ship had emergency orders to get under way. Phillips had waved them off, not caring, angry at the ship that had lost him the only person that had really mattered to him, Abigail Patricia O'Neal. He had rolled over in disgust and gone back to sleep.

Had it been up to him, he would have slept for weeks, but his mouth got so dry and he was so empty that he struggled to his feet, his head spinning, and walked to the sink in the corner of the stateroom. He pulled down the stainless steel sink and clicked on the lights on either side of the mirror. The fluorescents flickered, then caught, revealing a gray-skinned face that he didn't want to see this morning.

He would have resigned his commission after he'd sobered up, but now the ship was at sea. Even if he had a mind to do that, his second-in-command was a lieutenant commander in the Royal Navy, who was there on an American–British exchange program, and who, by U.S. Navy regulations, could take command of the *Piranha* only if Phillips became physically or mentally incapacitated, and getting dumped by a girlfriend didn't qualify, no matter how debilitating it was in reality.

Bruce Phillips had a narrow face, strong chin, a flattened boxer's nose, with several days' growth of beard. His hairline was so far in retreat that he wore a tight crewcut. As a quirky consolation prize, he had a nicely shaped head, or so Abby had always maintained, back in the past that seemed like another life. Phillips was short, barely breaking five feet, but muscular, his deep chest and narrow waist somehow compensating for his lack of vertical stature.

Phillips splashed water on his face, wondering if it made any sense to shave, then decided not to. He went into the head between his stateroom and Roger Whatney's, his executive officer, where he stepped into the shower, letting the heat of it on his shoulders bring him back to life. *To an empty life,* he thought.

Through the rush of the water he could hear Whatney's south-of-London accent: "Skippah, we've got an urgent call to periscope depth. Seems the admiral wants a little chat with us." He paused. "Captain, are you okay? Sir?"

"I'm okay, Roger," Phillips said, shutting his eyes, feeling a headache starting behind his eyes. "I'll shave and dress and meet you in my stateroom in three minutes."

"Aye, sir, I'll set up the video."

FORD ISLAND
PEARL HARBOR NAVAL STATION
PIER 5

"I don't think I believe this," Captain Paul White said as he looked at the thousand-foot-long garbage barge. Trash was piled up forty feet high the full length of the barge, tied to an oceangoing tug by several thick lines. "It looks like garbage. It smells like garbage. It has sea-gulls all over it, like garbage."

"It is garbage," Pacino said. I told you I could sneak the SSNX out of here right under the cameras of the newshounds."

"You're telling me that—thing—is a security cloak for the sub?"

"Grab your bag and follow me," Pacino said, stepping on the gunwale of the huge barge. A few feet into the garbage pile Pacino reached for a sheet of waste ply-wood—which came open on a hidden hinge like a door. He disappeared inside, his voice calling for Paully to follow him. A tunnel fabricated of plywood and sheet plastic extended deep under the garbage pile, lit by light bulbs hung from the overhead. The tunnel ended in a tall doghouse over the circle of a hatch. A sentry came to rigid attention and saluted Pacino. Turning to the con-trol panel against the plywood wall of the doghouse, the sentry punched a mushroom button. The hatch, pro-pelled by hydraulics, opened, the circle of it shining in a warm yellow light. Pacino yelled, "Down ladder!" and tossed his bag down, then lowered himself out of sight into the submarine.

"I don't believe it," White said.

PACIFIC OCEAN
578 MILES EAST OF TOKYO, JAPAN
ALTITUDE: 47,000 FEET

"Didn't anyone say what this was all about?" Captain John Patton asked, his voice distorted by the oxygen mask and the acoustics of the intercom.

"Sorry, sir," the pilot said from the forward seat of the swept-wing F-22 supersonic Navy fighter. "They just told me to get you to Pearl Harbor ASAP."

"So who gave you those orders?"

"Air Boss."

"Did he say where he got them?"

"SuperCinC-Pac, sir."

"Excuse me?"

"The Supreme Commander-in-Chief Pacific, the admiral in charge of the entire U.S. military in the Pacific and the invasion force on the way to White China. The second force, anyway."

"Sorry to sound stupid, but I've been out of it for a while. I was socked away in a bare room with no TV, and goddamn it, I have no idea what's going on. Who is this admiral?"

"You ought to know, sir. He's one of you bubble-head submarine guys, Pacino."

"Pacino's the supreme commander?"

"Yessir."

And he wanted to see Patton badly enough to fly him out on a supersonic fighter, Patton thought with a sinking feeling. How would he explain the loss of the *Annapolis*?

Pacino and White had set themselves up in the VIP stateroom aft of the executive officer's stateroom.

The room was multipurpose. The aft wall was taken up with two large bunks that went into the bulkhead like Pullman compartment sleepers, with a pull-down door that covered up the clutter of them. On the opposite end was a double desk. The center of the room was taken up with a table surrounded by six leather seats, and on the wall opposite the door was a full-width video-conference console. The wide-screen television was on, the sound muted, the channel selected to Satellite News Network, which showed a reporter in a studio reading news.

Pacino had commandeered the large leather seat directly opposite the videoconference console, his papers, chart displays, and WritePad computer laid out on the table surface. He was studying the charts, dictating quietly into the WritePad, writing messages to the fleet, occasionally glancing up at the video wide-screen. Paully White moved about the room, barking into a phone, bringing in fruit and Cokes, talking to people in the passageway outside the room while Pacino worked. The tactical problems revolved through his mind, over and over again. From this a plan was starting to evolve.

Paully White's voice intruded finally, the captain having to yell to get through Pacino's deep concentration.

"What is it, Paully?"

"Emmitt Stephens, sir."

"Bring him in."

Pacino checked his watch. It was 0600 local time, and he had wanted to set sail by now, but gathering the crew on such short notice had been a problem. It was one of Pacino's tactical problems: how late the SSNX could leave and still manage to arrive in the op area of the East China Sea at the same time as the *Piranha*, the second half of the pincers he intended to clamp around the Red Force.

Pacino stood to greet Stephens. With his gray hair hanging over his ears, he looked sweaty and exhausted.

"I wanted to give you the news in person, Admiral," he puffed. "The reactor's critical, and we're heating up now, emergency rates. We should be bringing steam into the engine room in an hour."

"Excellent, Emmitt." Pacino clapped the older man on the shoulder, and Stephens smiled slightly. "How was it?"

"Goddamned hairy, sir."

"Well, let's start the engines of the tug, order them revved up. I want them loud, because once their engines are on, I want you to start the emergency diesel. Warm it up slow, but get it on-line using the DC electrical end. When it's warm, put it on the DC bus and divorce the SSNX from shore power. We'll finish the reactor start-up on the diesel in the Pacific."

Pacino expected the usual protest at the gross violation of fleet procedures, but Stephens just nodded and repeated back the instructions.

"And, Emmitt, did I mention that you'll be going with us as chief engineer?"

"Gee, Admiral, that must have slipped your mind."

"Hope you have a spare set of underwear."

"Admiral, you're getting predictable in your old age. I packed a bag."

Pacino smiled. "Start the diesel, Eng."

As the stateroom door shut behind Stephens, Pacino found Paully staring at him. "What?"

"You're really enjoying this, aren't you? You're in your element." It almost sounded like an accusation. Or maybe that was just Pacino's take, because it was true, he felt alive again. The flurry of orders was coming naturally into his mind and out of his mouth, his men and machines moving to the beat of his conductor's baton. Paully was dead right, he did love it. He'd had a brief taste of this during the Japanese blockade, and it had seemed to define him. For the first time in years he realized that he no longer missed commanding a submarine, that he no longer felt the emptiness inside him since *Seawolf* had gone down. The void of submarine command had been filled by fleet command, and he couldn't—didn't even want to—go back. But if he was wrapped up in the intricacy of commanding a fleet, he also couldn't escape feeling guilt. Guilt at feeling good, when he had no right, no right at all, Eileen still quiet in her grave on the other side of the world, leaving a jagged and bloody hole in his life that would never be filled.

Yet a half million American lives and a billion Chinese lives depended on his next decisions, and it occurred to him that he owed it to those people to release the grief, to get on with his life, even if that meant saying good-bye to Eileen's memory. He felt her for just a fleeting moment, and what he sensed was not anger at him but a sort of encouragement.

Pacino narrowed his eyes at White. "I love it, Paully,

every second of it. Now, where's Tanaka? I still need to talk to him."

"Joanna?" White called into the passageway. "Hold on, sir." He vanished for a moment, then came back with an odd look on his face. He was holding a bulky envelope in his hands. "Joanna said he's gone. He left this."

"Get her in here," Pacino said slowly, a pang of anxiety running through his gut. He opened the envelope and found a note and a pile of data disks.

"Sir?" Joanna said.

"Tanaka?"

"He gave me that envelope on the pier and said he had to go."

"Did you explain this isn't really a garbage barge?"

"Yessir," Joanna said in annoyance. "He just said it wasn't right. He was really upset—he made it all the way to the hatch and got all teary. I think he was embarrassed that a woman saw him that way."

Pacino read the note. Paully waited, an eyebrow cocked.

"Says he can't go," Pacino said, reading. Tanaka had written that he couldn't go to sea and put his own submarine fleet on the bottom, even if it had fallen into the hands of an enemy. The last lines said it all: he had dedicated the Rising Sun class to the memory of his dead son, who had gone down under fire from one of the USS *Piranha*'s Vortex missiles. Shooting down a Rising Sun would be like having his son die all over again. Suddenly Pacino had a new window into death and grieving, and he felt for the older admiral with the dead son. Pacino folded the letter, putting it slowly into his breast pocket. As he glanced at the disks, he noticed a second note taped to them. That note was more official:

Admiral Pacino-san, here you will find all the data I have been able to accumulate on the class of the Rising Sun. Regrettably the noise signature is a mystery even to me, as the sea trials tests were designed to find out exactly how detectable the Rising Suns are,

but with this data you will at least know what you are
up against. Best luck to you, Admiral, and with full
wishes of your quick prevailing, I remain your servant,
Akagi Tanaka.

"Paully, put the data disks of the Rising Sun into the
computer. I want to assign one of our officers to analyze
it. But it would be nice if we had that decided by now.
We need to go over the crew manifest." Pacino checked
his watch. "What's taking the diesel so long?"

"Emmit will get it going. Besides, aren't you waiting
for Captain Patton?"

"Hell, no. I'll put him on a speed cruiser to catch up
to us."

"Wouldn't a helicopter be better?" Paully asked. "He
could grab a Sea King chopper right from Hickam Air
Force Base and be here in a half hour."

"No. Don't forget we're a garbage scow. Someone
lowered to a trash barge from a chopper would raise
news reporter eyebrows."

"I keep forgetting."

Just then the ship's emergency diesel roared to life,
loud even though it was located a hundred feet aft, two
compartments away.

"I'd rather breath diesel fumes than this garbage
stink," Pacino said. "Let's see what's going on with
Bruce Phillips."

"I'll call the *Piranha* to periscope depth."

From the files that Admiral Livingston had downloaded to his WritePad computer, Pacino went over the
list of officers for the prospective crew. There was Lieutenant Commander Christopher Porter, academy grad,
top of his nuke school and sub school classes, Navy
diver, sport sky diver, single, ex-sonar officer of the *Barracuda* when Pacino had been aboard during the blockade, now at shore duty in San Diego, in Honolulu on
vacation, put under arrest a half hour before, the young
girl in the hotel room left to wonder what was going on,
but security too tight to tell her what was up. Porter
would make a good officer, and he knew sonar. Pacino

made his decision—Porter would be the ship's navigator and operations officer. He'd also be charged with studying the Rising Sun and determining how to attack it.

Next on the list, Commander Walt Hornick, ex-chief engineer of Bruce Phillips' USS *Piranha,* assigned in the normal course of duty rotation to teach at the nuclear-power school in Groton when the Reds had begun mobilizing, he'd been given temporary orders to attend an urgent training class. The school at the Pearl Harbor Training Facility was a sham, of course, and he'd been awakened at four in the morning on Saturday and taken to the SSNX. He'd gotten the hull lowered into the water and placed under the garbage-carrying barge. Hornick now waited in the wardroom with the others, mystified that he'd been shanghaied for the purpose of getting out of its dock a new construction sub that had never been to sea. Pacino dictated the words "executive officer" to the computer, and the words appeared below Hornick's photograph.

The chief engineer slot was occupied by Emmitt Stephens, even though he wasn't an officer of the line. That left the junior officers. The file opened up to a dozen photos, all of the officers waiting down below. It occurred to him that this was a job for the ship's executive officer, and he buzzed the wardroom. A tentative voice answered.

"Send Commander Hornick to the VIP stateroom," Pacino said.

Paully came in just then. "*Piranha*'s up on the video-conference, Admiral. Are you ready?"

No, Pacino thought, *but I'll fake it. After all, that's what fleet command is all about—faking it and making it look planned.*

CHAPTER 28

He felt better with fresh coveralls on, a steaming cup of coffee in front of him on the conference table, the state-room tidied up by his steward while he was in the shower.

Captain Bruce Phillips sipped from a mug with the emblem of the *Piranha,* a scaly, snarling sharp-toothed fish staring out, the hull of the Seawolf–class submarine behind it. The legend above read USS PIRANHA SSN-23, and the ship's motto below, DEEP—SILENT—FAST—DEADLY. On his starched collars were two silver eagle pins, the emblems of his rank. Above his left breast pocket his gold dolphin pin gleamed in the spotlights rigged for the videoconference.

Seated next to Phillips was Roger Whatney. His British executive officer was wearing an olive drab sweater with soft shoulder boards on his epaulets, the boards showing two broad gold stripes with a narrow stripe between them, one of the stripes making a loop-the-loop. The XO had short hair and a fuzzy mustache, not to mention a dry sense of humor and a mind like a razor blade.

"Good morning, Admiral," Phillips said crisply.

"Bruce, it's good to talk to you," Pacino said. "You too, Commander Whatney. I know you're both in a hurry to get to the operation area, so I'll get right to it. Geography lesson first. On the left half of your screen you should be seeing a chart display of the East China Sea. To the east you'll see the eastern border of the East

China Sea, the Ryukyu Island chain. To the north in the chain is the island of Yakushima, just off Kagoshima, Japan. There's a substantial gap in the islands from there south to the island of Naze. To the east of the Naze-Yakushima Gap is the Point Delta Hold Position, which is on the great circle route to Shanghai from Honolulu. Southwest by a hundred miles is the Point Echo Hold Position, which is our destination. Farther south by fifty nautical miles is the Point Foxtrot Hold Position.

"I have the surface force making a serpentine course toward the Point Delta Hold Position at the north end of the island chain. They will orbit there until the East China Sea is clear. Once we've cleaned up the op area, the fleet goes in, straight shot to the Shanghai beach.

"Next, how we clean up the op area. Zero hour is midnight Friday evening Beijing time, four days from now. I'm proposing you come into the op area northwest from Point Echo. That's just on the south part of the Naze-Yakushima Gap, just a little south of where the initial RDF task force went down. I'm not sure if you've briefed your crew on the Red force, but we have reason to believe it consists of six Japanese Rising Sun–class subs, all of them hijacked at sea by some kind of fast submersible. Which means I want you to rig for non-penetration, Bruce. Put chains and locks around your escape-trunk upper and lower hatches. I don't want you guys being hijacked like the Rising Suns were.

"Anyway, you'll penetrate at Point Echo and search for the Rising Suns. The 688s will be entering far to the south, from Point Foxtrot, heading north. This is the tough part of the plan, Bruce, because we have reason to believe the 688s are at a severe disadvantage. So I have something special in mind for them."

Pacino continued for another fifteen minutes, then called for questions. When there were none, he closed, saying that he'd transmit the official hard copy of the orders, and that they would soon be back in touch as he and the SSNX got closer to the op area. Then, without fanfare, he clicked off.

Phillips hoisted a phone to his ear and ordered the

ship to return to base depth, course, and speed. As he hung up the phone, he shot Whatney a look.

"Roger, what the hell is going on? East China Sea? Rising Suns? Locking the escape hatches? The god-damned SSNX?"

Whatney had the grace not to smile. "You missed a lot, Skipper. I took the liberty of compiling some hard copies of messages and a video disk of the news reports for you to brief yourself on. You've been pretty sick, sir. Maybe you'd better go back to bed."

"The hell," Phillips said, now intrigued, and glad to have something that would take his mind off Abby. "I'm going to curl up with this for an hour. Then meet me in here and let's go over this."

Whatney left, and Phillips began to read. On the bulk-head clicked the second hand of an old-fashioned brass chronometer. He'd been reading for twenty minutes when he noticed that his headache was gone.

"Sir, the ship is divorced from shore power. The diesel is carrying all ship's loads." At the door to the VIP stateroom, Walt Hornick was holding his hat in both hands looking like a supplicant.

"Ship's company embarked?" Pacino asked.

"No, sir, we're missing the captain and the DynaCorp Cyclops system representative."

"O'Shaughnessy?"

"Yessir."

"Well, what are you doing about it?"

"Sir, we were going to send a car for her, but—"

"Oh, stop worrying, you two," a sultry female voice said from the passageway. The door opened and Colleen O'Shaughnessy appeared. She wore a set of perfectly fitting, creased and starched ship's coveralls, complete with American flag and the ship's emblem patches, her name embroidered over one of the pockets. The built-in belt narrowed at her slim waist, the material generous at her curving hips and at her ample chest. Her dark, shining hair was pulled back in a ponytail, her sleeves rolled up two turns, revealing thin forearms and a large man's watch strapped to her left wrist. Pacino knew he was staring at her, but couldn't help himself. The uniform was hardly something that should look good on a woman, yet Colleen looked stunning in it, and he completely forgot what he was going to say.

Fortunately, Paully broke the spell. "That just leaves Captain Patton. I guess we should be shoving off now, Admiral."

"Right, right," Pacino said, finding his voice, blinking at Paully. "Colleen, did you get your stateroom?"

"Yes, Admiral, I'm hanging out in the exec's stateroom. Where are you putting him?"

"Everybody moves down a slot except the captain," Pacino said, the strangest tight feeling invading his chest. We're undermanned, so it won't cause any crowding."

"I'll be below in the computer spaces," O'Shaughnessy said, looking around the room. "Nice digs. I don't have much time to waste. But even though we're on a stinking garbage scow, don't forget to call me for dinner."

She turned on her sneaker-clad heel and disappeared. Pacino found Paully White, for perhaps the tenth time that day, watching him.

"What the hell was that all about?" White stammered.

"What do you mean?"

"I mean you two staring at each other like that. I feel like I'm watching a couple sixteen-year-olds."

"Excuse me? What the hell are you talking about?"

White sighed. "Nothing, sir. I'm going to the control room. I think your boy Hornick needs help getting this thing to sea. He comes off as somewhat by-the-book."

"Good idea," Pacino said, returning to his charts.

"You know, Admiral, maybe it's time you moved on. You know, saw some women socially, dated."

"Paully!"

"Sorry." The door shut, leaving Pacino alone and confused.

EAST CHINA SEA
50 KILOMETERS WEST OF THE
NAZE-YAKUSHIMA GAP
SS-403 *ARCTIC STORM*

Admiral Chu Hua-Feng sat in the end seat of the officers' messroom table and watched the wide-screen television with his officers. Cigarette smoke wafted to the ceiling from several ashtrays.

". . . the first full day of the news blackout. Since her announcement at noon eastern time the president has been unavailable for comment. Our Pentagon correspondent, Diane Shaw, has this report from the War Department. Diane?"

"Roland, the War Department seems to have issued some incredibly strict gag orders to virtually every officer, enlisted man, and civilian employee here, as the press has been unable to get statements from anyone. We have seen quite a bit of coming and going as the chairman of the Joint Chiefs and the Chief of Naval Operations, along with the Secretary of War, have left for the White House and then returned, although within the last hour they have left again. But despite all this shuttling back and forth, there remains no word. Back to you, Roland. This is Diane Shaw, reporting for SNN World News."

"Thank you, Diane. Back in our Denver news center we've got Annette Spalding, the senior SNN war correspondent who was embarked onboard the USS *Douglas MacArthur* just after it sailed from Hawaii. Annette, what can you tell us about the forcible ejection of the press corps from the backup RDF task force?"

"Well, Roland, it was quite arbitrary and almost chilling the way we were treated, marched up to the deck in blindfolds, our cameras confiscated. Then we were literally thrown into the inside of a Navy plane with blacked-out windows. The—"

Chu shut the wide-screen off. "It's been like this for hours, gentlemen," he said. "Mr. First, what do you make of it?"

"Not much, sir. I think our main source of intelligence has just dried up."

"We still have the spy-satellite photographs. We'll be able to track the second-wave task force with those."

Lo Sun shrugged. "Photos don't show intentions. We couldn't have had it any better in the past. But with this blackout, who knows what's going on? And it's not just the task force, sir. Our information about the conduct of the war on the mainland has died out too. It's not like our people broadcast anything except propaganda. I know, it's incorrect of me to say that, but if you want truth, you watch SNN."

"No need to apologize, Mr. First. I agree with you. At least time is on our side. It will take the task force some time to get here."

Chu stared at the muted television screen, wondering when and from where the task force was coming. How should he deploy the fleet? What if they came in from the south? And how long could he hold this force off? They were down on their torpedoes, and if one of the low-load subs was caught, how long could it fight?

For the first time in the operation he felt a wave of anxiety. He left the messroom and walked slowly up the steep stairs to his stateroom, remembering once again the dream about his father. He crashed into his bunk for a nap, to contemplate this new turn of events.

HICKAM AIR FORCE BASE
OAHU, HAWAII

The runway seemed to approach slowly. Almost imperceptibly the wheels of the landing gear made contact with the concrete surface of the runway. The jet coasted down the strip, the pilot gently applying reverse thrust, then braking until the blur of the runway became focused. The pilot taxied off the strip, throttling up to take the heavy jet over to the hangars on the military side of the airport.

Patton checked his watch: a few minutes past eight in

the morning. It felt like they'd been flying all night. Inside the hangar, the canopy lifted slowly, and the moist Hawaiian air filled the cockpit. Patton climbed out, his muscles aching. At the sound of another jet landing off to the east, he looked up and watched as another Navy F-22 left the runway and taxied toward them. As he stood there, his helmet under his arm, a ladder was wheeled to the opening canopy of the other jet's cockpit. The backseater stood and lowered himself down the ladder and removed his helmet. Patton blinked—it was Byron DeMeers.

"What are you doing here?" Patton asked.

"What are *we* doing here?"

"Sirs, the staff car is waiting," Patton's pilot said. He thanked the young lieutenant, handed back the flight helmet, and climbed into the car. Soon they were speeding along an empty road. They passed several guarded checkpoints to a small pier head, where the car screeched to a halt.

A female civilian was waiting for them and she pointed to the boat tied up at the small pier.

"Where are we going?" Patton asked. The woman just looked at him, motioning to the boat. He shook his head and climbed in after DeMeers.

The boat bounced over the water in the East Lock, past Ford Island, out to the main channel and into the Pacific. Patton raised an eyebrow at DeMeers, who just shrugged.

The boat ride seemed to last forever, but was perhaps only an hour long. By the time the coxswain throttled down, Patton's back was aching from the pounding of the waves. He stood, joining the coxswain on the helm platform, and looked out over the water.

"I don't believe this," he mumbled. As DeMeers joined him on the helm platform, his jaw dropped, too.

A few hundred yards ahead was an oceangoing tug pulling a huge garbage barge, piled forty feet high with trash, drawing a mob of circling seagulls. The rotting garbage stank, the horrible smell of it rolling across the water and invading Patton's nostrils.

"So this is our punishment," DeMeers said. "Driving a garbage tug."

"It's worse," Patton said. "They're not pulling up to the tug. They're bringing us to the barge itself."

"I knew I should have listened to Mother," DeMeers said. "She wanted me to stay on the farm."

"What the . . ." Patton said.

Where the coxswain had tossed over his line to the barge, a piece of scrap plywood moved aside and a man in coveralls stepped out. He grabbed Patton by the arm and pulled him inside. Rapidly he returned for DeMeers.

But stranger than the barge, the man coming from nowhere, the tunnel under the garbage, was what the man in coveralls said when he reached the hatch. The man found a microphone, clicked the speak button, and said, "*Devilfish*, arriving!" That was the announcement made when a ship's captain crossed the gangway to the ship. Mystified, Patton looked down the hatch. The ladder led to a deck some fifteen feet below, and the smell coming from within was unmistakable. That odd combination of diesel fuel, lubricating oil, ozone, cooking grease, sweat, amines, and non-contaminating floor wax was unique to one vessel—a nuclear submarine.

Patton looked over at DeMeers, then back down the hatch, then at the man in coveralls.

"Go on, sir," the man said. "And welcome aboard the *Devilfish*, Captain."

"Why did you call me that?" Patton asked.

"Well, sir, because I always call the commanding officer 'captain.' Is there a problem, sir?" The man seemed genuine, not understanding Patton's confusion.

"Of course not," Patton said, glancing at DeMeers. "I always walk onto garbage barges and take command of the submarine underneath. Down ladder!" he said, lowering himself down, DeMeers following him.

Once they were down, the sentry started laughing until his belly hurt. They'd had a lottery to see who'd get to admit the captain. It had been worth every second.

* * *

At the bottom of the ladder, Patton found a crowd, officers and chiefs lining an immaculate wood-paneled passageway, all at attention, a chief blowing a bosun's whistle, something out of a square-rigger navy movie.

Patton looked at the men in their khaki uniforms, his head spinning. Then he heard a familiar voice, the voice of the man who had made his career:

"Welcome aboard the USS *Devilfish,* Captain Patton. Are you ready to take command of the first ship of the SSNX–class?"

Slowly Patton pivoted to look at the tanned, white-haired admiral. A smile came to his lips as his heels snapped together, his body becoming upright, the salute stiff at his forehead. Pacino waved a return salute, then reached out to shake his hand. The admiral's grip was fierce and tight, and Patton returned it.

"Admiral. Sir. It's good to see you."

"Blood and Guts John Patton," Pacino said, his smile growing even wider. "It's damned good to see you again. We here, all of us, cheered when the news came in that you'd survived. Are you hurt, are you okay?"

"I'm fine, sir, physically anyway. But I lost—"

"Don't worry about that, John," Pacino said quickly. "Not now. We're here for the change-of-command ceremony. Gentlemen, attention to orders." Pacino pulled out a single sheet from his coverall pocket and handed it to Patton. "Captain, you may read your orders."

Patton squinted at the page and began to read. "From, Chief of Naval Personnel, to, Captain Jonathan George S. Patton IV, U.S. Navy, subject, permanent change of duty, reference, U.S. Navy regulations, et cetera. Paragraph 1, Captain Patton hereby ordered to report to and take command of USS *Devilfish,* SSNX-1, en route a classified-operation area in the Pacific Theater. Paragraph 2, Captain Patton shall report to the Supreme Commander-in-Chief, U.S. Pacific Military Forces, Admiral M. Pacino, for duty until specifically detached by said commander. Paragraph 3, these orders effective immediately as of today, 4 November." Patton looked up at the row of officers, and the group broke into applause. He swallowed hard, the lump in his throat as big as a fist.

The captain's stateroom was cavernous compared to the old 688-class cubbyhole. It had a bunk that could sleep two, with a full instrument readout and phone station accessible from the bunk. It could be folded up by day, and the space transformed into a high-tech office. Nearby was a desk with a high-backed leather swivel chair. At a large conference table, the captain's place faced a soffit above the stateroom door entrance where a row of wide-screen televisions was placed. Above the central wide-screen was a camera for videoconferencing.

Pacino noted, "We had the lockers stocked with uniforms in your size. We'll go to control in a few minutes. Before we do, why don't you have a seat, John?"

Patton sank into the swivel chair at the head of the table. A sense of unreality flooded him as the deck rolled beneath his feet. Ocean waves were rocking the boat, a submarine that he'd just been given command of. A ship that he didn't know the first thing about, and here was the admiral-in-command of the entire Pacific military forces sitting him down at his conference table to ask him the question of the hour, which was, what the hell happened out there?

"So, John, are you sure you're okay? No burns, bruises, cuts, concussions?"

"They checked me out at Yokosuka, sir. I had some burns to my shins and knees and hands, but it's about as serious as sun poisoning. Byron and I—Senior Chief Byron DeMeers, my sonar chief—were dehydrated and suffering from exposure, but nothing a bottle of spring water and a cheeseburger wouldn't solve."

Pacino grinned at Paully White, shaking his head. "So, what happened? Did you ever detect the Rising Sun? Or the torpedo?"

"Neither one, Admiral. I'd slowed down to about five knots, I was in the zone where the surface group went down, and we were doing a max-scan sonar search. Senior Chief DeMeers can tell you more about the search plan, but we were at battle stations and maximum sensitivity on the wide-aperature array, hitting broadband spherical hard, and streaming both towed arrays with the onion out, and we heard exactly nothing. Zero point zero. The next thing we knew, an explosion blew us to hell. I was tossed off my feet, and I ordered an EMBT blow. Someone lived long enough to hit the chicken switches, and up we went. Next thing I knew, there were flames and smoke everywhere. By the time I could get to the officers to see if they were alive, the flames had engulfed the room. I ran forward to see if Byron was alive, and when I found him, I pulled him up to the bridge tunnel. By then the entire upper level was on fire, and we went up the tunnel, and the ship began sinking. Byron saved my life—he pulled me out of the ship and put me on the raft—and the rest is history. The first I knew that I'd been attacked by a sub and not by some reactor casualty was when we were floating on the raft and a periscope popped up, and it was no American or European Union technology. It just looked at us for a few seconds."

"What did you do?" Paully White asked.

"What could I do? I flipped it off."

Patton looked in astonishment as the officers laughed, exchanging looks and shaking their heads.

"What's so funny?" Patton asked. "A hundred and thirty men died on my ship, it was my responsibility, and now it's gone and so are the men."

Pacino instantly sobered up. "Sorry, John, you're right. We didn't mean any disrespect. It's just that you did what all of us here wished we could have done— give the bird to the Red force commander. Anyway, let's continue the tour. Maybe by the time we're aft, Captain Stephens will have the reactor in the power range."

Patton followed the admiral out of the stateroom thinking that somehow he had just passed one more test, this one as important as the first had been, back in Norfolk so many years ago.

CHAPTER 29

Patton stood in the control room, trying not to rubberneck.

It was absolutely huge. Huge and beautiful and open, designed by a master craftsman and submariner. In the center of the room was a raised periscope stand not entirely different from the one on the *Annapolis*, except that it was twice the size. In fact, the room could house four 688-sized control rooms, it was that big. At the aft end of the periscope stand was the captain's command station, a console covered with displays, phones, cameras, and keypads. Aft of the console were the two side-by-side navigation plotter tables, but there all resemblance to his 688-class ended. On the port forward control-room corner was a ship-control station, but instead of a cockpit panel with four men, there was a deep leather seat where one man alone drove the ship, the console surrounding him with displays, a joystick between his knees, a throttle lever at his left.

Next to the ship controller, more toward the centerline, was a console for the ship systems, taking the place of the old ballast-control panel. On the port wall were a series of consoles, navigation aft, radio equipment just forward of that, then the repeater equipment for electronic countermeasures, then a sonar panel, then the weapons-control panel leading up to the ship control station.

The starboard bulkhead was the strangest part. Lined along it were five stations unlike any Patton had seen on a nuclear submarine before. They were five-foot-diameter eggs that one stepped into, and the canopy overhead was made of a black substance that formed a hemisphere above the person's head. A leather-lined structure was inside, not truly a seat but a sort of padded rail to lean against. On the rail were a helmet and gloves.

"What are these stations?" Patton asked the admiral.

"Battle-control stations," Pacino said. "You'll get inside one—the forward one is VR zero, which is yours. Once you're in, you lean against the rail and put on the helmet and gloves. The canopy comes down around your head. What you'll see is a three-dimensional environment surrounding you, with a spatial relationship to your contacts. When we come to periscope depth, the computer makes your world look like your head is above water and the ships are all around you. This models the universe around the ship, and is linked to a computer called the Cyclops, a new DynaCorp wonder subsidiary. The VP of Cyclops is aboard now. I'll introduce you to her."

"Her?"

"Right, Colleen O'Shaughnessy."

"O'Shaughnessy—any relation to Big Boss?"

"The old man's daughter. Sharp cookie too."

"Can you show me this battle-control system in action?"

"No. It doesn't work, not even in demonstration mode."

Patton's breath caught. He didn't want to sound stupid in front of the admiral, but he was astounded that the ship was on an operational mission without a fire-control system.

"Excuse me, sir? It doesn't work? How are we going to fight these subs?"

"We don't, not until Colleen finishes her coding. The system is down hard until she does."

"Okay," Patton said doubtfully.

Pacino had already shown him the aft spaces of the forward compartment middle level, the staterooms of officers' country and the wardroom. They had started in the upper level, where the crew's berthing spaces were, and the galley. The control room had been the first tactical space Patton had seen. Pacino took him forward into sonar, on the starboard forward exit to control, where five seats were placed behind an L-shaped line of consoles. The room was empty of watchstanders.

"Shouldn't there be someone here?" Patton asked.

"They will be."

"Let me guess, sir. Sonar doesn't work."

"Correct, it's tied into Cyclops. If the Cyclops computer is down, so is sonar."

On the other side of a central passageway were radio and electronic countermeasures. Located forward, the computer room spanned the full width of the ship, a bite taken from the port side by the stairway and the electronic-countermeasures room. Sitting at a console with a deep seat and a number of displays was a crewman typing furiously into the keyboard. He paused to look at it, then cursed, then more typing, another look, another curse. The crewman had normal underway coveralls on, but a long black-haired ponytail.

"Colleen? We have a visitor," Pacino said.

A woman stood from the console, not a tall woman, but beautiful and very well built. She stood, an annoyed look on her face, and extended her hand to Patton.

"Captain Patton, I assume," she said with a quick smile, her voice unexpectedly deep.

"Colleen, I've heard you're working on the Cyclops. Any prediction on when you'll be done?"

O'Shaughnessy turned to Pacino, smiling at him. "He's worse than you said he'd be Admiral. Not only did he get the 'when'll it be fixed' question out in the first minute, but it was his first question. Jesus, did they separate you two at birth, Captain? Admiral Pacino comes in here no less than once an hour to ask that same question. Now, please forgive my rudeness, but this sub is a hunk of scrap metal unless I can get this working. Now scram!"

"Don't say scram," Pacino said. "That means 'shut down the reactor' in sub talk."

Patton watched as Colleen mimicked the words as they came out of Pacino's mouth. Mimicking a three-star admiral. Then he looked at Pacino, and realized that something was going on between the two of them, something more than just business. Patton turned to leave behind the admiral.

"Good luck, Ms. O'Shaughnessy," he called.

"Colleen, please." She was already lost again deep in her world.

"She's a beauty," Patton said, "isn't she?"

"I hadn't noticed," Pacino said.

On the lower level was a machinery space aft, a middle area with a central passageway, a stores room to port, more berthing spaces to starboard, and the torpedo room forward. This room put the one on the *Annapolis* to shame. There were weapons crammed in everywhere on hydraulic rams, the room barely allowing him to get forward to the torpedo console.

"Two 21-inch tubes on the bottom, two 36-inchers on the top. The room holds forty-eight 21-inch weapons or thirty-four of the 36-inch large-bore missiles. Our load-out this run is mostly 36-inch Vortex Mod Charlie missiles, with two tube-loaded Mark 52 21-inch Hullcracker torpedoes and two room-stored Mark 52s."

"Vortex missiles?" Patton asked. "Why haven't I heard of them?"

"Because they're classified secret, of course. I'll tell you more about them later, but they're a small version of the solid-rocket-fueled mod bravo we employed in the Japanese blockade. The weapon does a swimout on an oxidized-fuel propulsion module, then at fifty knots the control fins pop out and the solid fuel ignites, and the missile travels to its target at three hundred knots. It doesn't have the range of the old mod bravo, but if we're in close, we can get a kill."

"For the SSNX, what's close?"

"On your 688 the most distant sonar contact you could hear, a submerged target, came at what, twenty to forty miles?"

"Yessir."

"For the SSNX, that's close. We can detect a submerged contact eighty or ninety miles away."

"How? What did you do?"

"Sonar's completely different on this ship. We don't have a wide-aperture array or a spherical array, not since the redesign. We use a system called ADI, for Acoustic Daylight Imaging."

The two men climbed the aft ladder back to the middle level, and walked back to the control room.

"How does it work?"

"Easy to explain, hard to engineer it and implement it, even harder to connect it to a computer and make the readout meaningful. In the past we used broadband sonar, just listening to the ocean, all frequencies, all the white noise. Worked great on surface ships, since they're so loud you hear them a hundred miles away. And it worked great on the first- and second-generation Soviet subs too, because they were clanking train wrecks. But once the third-generation Soviets came out, we switched to a combination of broadband sonar and narrowband, using towed hydrophones on long cables, and the hydrophone array was a couple hundred feet long, capable of hearing very selected frequencies a long way away, as long as it was connected to a damned good computer. The limiting factor was the computer."

They were back in control, and Pacino leaned against the elevated periscope-stand handrails. Patton sat down in the command seat on the port aft part of the periscope stand.

"As the computer got better, detection range didn't. Then the Destiny–class Japanese subs came out, and they were too silent to pick out at a distance with our narrowband processors. The Seawolf–class ships did pick them up, because they were much quieter and had better narrowband towed arrays. But with ships out there like the Rising Sun, narrowband is proving to be old technology. And we suspect that the next generation of enemy sub may employ an active quieting system, deliberately putting out noise that exactly matches a sub's machinery, but phase-shifted so that it cancels out the machinery noise. John, we're ten years away from enemy subs being so quiet that they match or beat the Seawolf or SSNX classes, and with active quieting they will actually be more silent than the ocean around them. Invisible."

"So what next, Admiral?"

"ADI, acoustic daylight imaging. It's a quantum leap in sonar, John. We're changing the way we think about sonar as a sensor. In the past we tried to listen with it. We tried to listen for very specific noises, but that's not good enough. Now we don't listen anymore, we see. Sonar is no longer an ear, it's an eyeball. It works like this. The ocean is full of background noise. Waves. Fish. Shrimp. Whales groaning. Wind. Storms. The occasional lava from an underwater volcano. But it's everywhere. Up till now we've tried to ignore the background noise and pick the needle out of the haystack. Not anymore. Now we're using the background noise just like your eyeball uses background light to see. The background noise of the ocean 'shines' all around us, and when it hits an object, the object reflects the sound or blocks the sound or focuses the sound, just as an object reflects and changes light waves so that your eye can interpret the reflected light waves as the representation of a spacial object.

"Same thing here. The ocean's background noise hits an object, say, a target submarine. The object changes the way the background noise hits our receiver, just as an object you see changes the light that hits it so your retina senses the change. Even if a target submarine is floating with no machinery on, its density difference from the water causes the background noise to go around it, be blocked by it, or be focused. It creates a sound 'image' that our computers interpret and represent in three dimensions. Let me tell you, it's a computer hog. It takes more data processing than any computer in history has ever tried to deal with, and the challenge is getting it to go fast enough to represent the real world. Then it has to distinguish between long range and close range and represent it to you so you can comprehend it, there on the virtual-reality stations in the control room.

"Once Colleen gets it going, I'll show you. You can 'see' a dolphin swimming by a half mile away. A supertanker on the surface looks like a big blob of a super-tanker. A target submarine image looks like a sub-marine. John, there's no more waterfall displays or graphs of frequency against time, no more frequency-bucket integration, no more putting tea leaves at the bottom of the sonar chief's teacup. Now you can see the enemy just like a fighter pilot can see the other plane in a dogfight. Of course, most of the time they'll be so distant that you'll just see a dot, but if they were to get close, the contact would look like a sub."

"I can't believe this. Is this for real? Seeing the enemy?"

"We've been working on this for decades, and only now are the computers capable enough to manage it. Of course, Cyclops isn't really capable yet, but it will be soon."

"When?"

"By the time we're in the East China Sea."

"How do you know?"

"I just do. Don't worry about it, and never ask Colleen questions that start with the word 'when.' But don't forget, what's motivating her is that she's going into the op area with us. I think she wants that system up as much as we do."

"Conn, Maneuvering, the electric plant is in a normal full-power lineup," the speaker in the overhead announced. "Propulsion shifted to the propulsion-turbine generators supplying the AC main motor. Ready to answer all bells."

"I haven't seen the engineering spaces yet," Patton said, glancing up at a television display showing maneuvering, the nuclear-control room.

"All that's new too," Pacino said. "I'll get you aft once we're down. Right now we've got a ship to submerge."

"How's this going to work with the garbage barge overhead?"

"Just pull the plug like you normally would. The barge has a sub-shaped hole in it. Once we go down, the barge will flood and sink, putting enough garbage in the Pacific

to warrant a major clean-up operation. It'll make the
headlines, I'm sure, and they won't be hauling garbage
to the Midway Island incinerator for a while. So give me
bad marks for the environment, but we're the only ones
who know the SSNX is at sea."

*With a dead computer, a revolutionary sonar system, a
man-machine interface that is untested, and a bunch of
unknowns for a crew, all under the command of a captain
fresh from the sinking of his last submarine,* Patton
thought, a sudden pang of insecurity flashing through
him. He looked at Pacino, who seemed so sure of himself, so rock-solid certain, and smiled.

"Helm," Patton called to the lieutenant at the ship-
control station, "submerge the ship to two hundred
feet."

"Two hundred feet, aye, Captain," the young officer
acknowledged from across the cavernous room. "Opening forward main ballast-tank vents. No periscope cameras or sail camera on this submergence, sir. Forward
vents indicate open. Taking the throttle to all ahead two-
thirds, two degrees down on the bow planes."

The deck took on a slight angle, just barely perceptible, and the depth readout on Patton's command-area
console began to click off a few feet deeper.

"The trick on this is to get deep fast enough to clear
the barge as it sinks," Pacino said. "You should try to
get deep and then go twenty knots off your present
course, evade to the south."

"Aye, Admiral."

"Sorry, didn't mean to give you rudder orders, John.
It's just that we thought this out when we built the
barge."

Patton nodded.

"Opening aft main ballast vents," the diving officer
called. "Depth eighty feet. Down angle on the ship,
down two degrees. Speed five knots, increasing to eight.
Depth one hundred, one twenty, down angle five
degrees."

"Officer of the Deck, take her to three hundred feet
at ahead standard, clear datum to the south."

"Aye, sir," a lieutenant standing behind the ship-control station said.

For the next few minutes Patton watched as the ship departed the surface and sailed away from the barge. He decided to take the ship back to periscope depth to observe the barge sinking. Taking the scope, he ordered the ship back up, in time to see the barge, most of it submerged, sinking slowly stern down, the tug frantically disconnecting the tow line. Patton felt himself tapped on the shoulder.

"John, we're late, we need to get to Point Echo now."

"Lowering number two scope," Patton called. "Helm, make your depth 850 feet, steep angle, all ahead flank."

"Emergency flank, John."

Patton squinted at the admiral, starting to feel less a king on a throne than an errand boy.

"Helm, emergency flank."

The deck took a steep down angle, the hull groaning and creaking from the increased pressure of the deep. The deck began to vibrate, slightly at first, then more violently as the ship sped up. Patton craned his neck to look at the speed indicator. Sixty-six knots, over seventy-six miles per hour. He'd never gone this speed in a submarine before, and it was exhilarating. He walked to the chart display, using the electronic dividers, and calculated the time to Point Echo. It came out to two days, eighteen hours. He looked at his watch, then called to the officer of the deck.

"Off'sa'deck, change ship's time to Beijing time. That makes it zero five hundred Tuesday, November 5."

That meant their ETA was 2300 Thursday evening, November 7. And Pacino had said that he'd given the DynaCorp VP until Thursday to get the computer system up and running. Suddenly Patton felt dead tired.

"Off'sa'deck, proceed on course to Point Echo. I'm going to my stateroom. Don't wake me, I'm getting an equalizer battery charge."

"Aye, Captain. PD time, sir?" The young lieutenant wanted to know when to slow and pop up to periscope depth to get their radio messages from the orbiting satellite.

"Don't come up. We'll be running straight in." A safe bet, he thought, since the supreme commander-in-chief was aboard. Who else would be sending them radio messages?

Patton waved to Pacino, who was leaning over the chart display, and walked into the door to his stateroom from the aft bulkhead of the control room. At his table he found Byron DeMeers drinking a Coke and brooding.

"Byron. What do you think?"

"Skipper, my head hurts. I feel like I've been sent back to school, and I don't know anything. This Acoustic Daylight Imaging system, it's more complicated than you can shake a stick at."

"The only thing I want to know about it is, will it work?"

"Who knows?" DeMeers said. "We'll be in deep trouble if it doesn't."

"What do you think of the ship otherwise?"

"I'll tell you what I think. It's a piece of shit without an operational sonar system. The only thing this tub does is haul around my ears, and if I can't use them, this thing is just a big 377-foot-long target."

"Oh, quit crying, you goddamned sonar girl," Patton said. "And get out of here, I want some rack. You'd better sleep too, you've been up around the clock."

"No time. I've got to learn the Cyclops sonar system, or else you are going to be hurting."

CHAPTER 30

WEDNESDAY
NOVEMBER 6

"I think it'll work," Colleen O'Shaughnessy said, staring at her panel in the computer room.

"It has to be more than just a thought," Pacino said. "This system can't crash once we penetrate the op area and start looking for the Red force."

Colleen's eyes flashed in anger. She looked up at him, taking a breath, her voice acid as she said, "If you want a guarantee, then give me two weeks to do the C-1 and C-9 tests. Otherwise, I guess you'll have to live with the system as is, just like the rest of us. Besides, if the system has problems, I'll be here to debug."

"Not good enough, Colleen. I need you to do whatever you have to do to get that system to be reliable. Our lives and the mission are depending on it. When it's time to launch a torpedo, we can't just call you up and ask you to fix it."

Colleen O'Shaughnessy looked up at the tall admiral. She had been up for three nights without sleep, ever since the ship left Hawaii underneath a garbage barge.

"Looks like that's your only choice."

"I'm telling you, it's not good enough. It has to be

absolutely bulletproof, Colleen. And it has to be that way by 1800 local tomorrow. You've got twenty hours."

"Why 1800? We don't get to the op area until eleven p.m."

"*We* don't get to the op area. *I* get to the op area, *ship's company* gets to the op area. *You* get off at 1800. That's when the personnel transfer goes down."

"*What?*"

"You'll be donning scuba gear and locking out of the forward escape trunk when we're at periscope depth. We'll dive, and you'll be picked up by an old tanker that will happen to be in the area at the time. I hate to make you leave the ship like that, but we can't risk surfacing or even broaching the sail."

"Admiral, I'm coming on this operation. Scrub this personnel transfer or whatever you call it. I need to stay with the Cyclops. You and your country-bumpkin computer operators can't do this without me."

"Colleen, I don't have your father's permission to take you into a hot operation area. Are you willing to get it from him in writing that you can penetrate the op area? And enter a war zone?"

O'Shaughnessy's voice rose a full three octaves as she made her attack. "What is this, Pacino? I'm an adult, I speak for myself. What are you doing, talking about my father? Are you just trying to cover for yourself because he's your boss?"

"Get a hold of yourself, Colleen," Pacino said, his voice iron. "You're a civilian and you're not authorized in the op area. Furthermore, I have to go to your father, because he's the only man in the Navy who outranks me right now. And I'll tell you one more thing. If you were my daughter, I'd shoot any man who put your life in danger. You signed on to design the computer for this submarine, not fight it in combat."

"I'll be goddamned if I'm going to—"

"Tomorrow. Eighteen hundred. You've got twenty hours. I suggest you use them."

O'Shaughnessy cursed at him, a word he never

thought would come out of that pretty mouth. He shut the door and found himself looking at Paully White.

"Can she deliver?" White asked.

"All I can tell you, Paully, is what I think. And you know what? It doesn't matter what I think. It matters what she thinks."

"Chilling thought," White muttered, rolling his eyes.

"Shut up, Captain," Pacino said harshly. As he walked past him down the passageway to control and aft to their stateroom, White was left staring after him.

"Listen up, scumbags," Lieutenant Commander Christopher Porter commanded, standing up in front of the crowd in the officers' wardroom. "Sorry, Admiral, Captain, Captain White, Ms. O'Shaughnessy, I meant them," Porter amended, suddenly realizing that his favorite way to start a briefing might not be appropriate with the brass.

Porter's position was the ship's navigator, the new title a return to the old days, when the navigator was the lead tactical officer. The other officers were all gathered for a training session. A black, curving screen had lowered around them, an expansion of the eggshaped bubbles in the control room. The officers in the room had donned helmets, the eyepieces clear, but each one containing a filter to cause the image of the wall of the surface to seem three-dimensional. The lights lowered, and the screen shimmered with a yellowish light, the appearance of the acoustic daylight. A red form grew close on the yellow background, the form appearing three-dimensional in the glasses of Pacino's helmet.

"Identify," Porter called.

One of the junior officers spoke up. "Fish!"

"Correct." The picture changed as the fish went by, a more distant bluish blob floating into view. "Identify."

"Submarine contact," another voice said.

"Correct. Friend or foe?"

The crowd watched for some time.

"Bad guy, Nav. Rising Sun class."

332   *Michael DiMercurio*

"Wrong," Porter said, seeming to enjoy the hapless supply officer's confusion. "Anyone else?"

"688-class American," Patton spat out.

"You cheated, Cap'n," Porter said, smiling.

"The hell."

"That's okay, sir. Shows motivation."

"Let's wrap, Navigator. The weapons brief is next, then the war plan brief. Anyone needing a cup of coffee, get it now. I don't want anyone racking in here."

"Aye, sir." The lights flashed back on, and the dark screen retracted into the overhead. Porter tapped a remote, and the wood doors covering a wide-screen panel opened. "Gentlemen, weapons briefing." Porter flashed the remote at the screen, and a profile view of the submarine came up, black lines on a white field, a naval architect's plans. "Lead weapon in the attack is the Vortex Mod Charlie swimout missile. Speed of attack is three hundred knots, warhead is plasma, guidance is blue laser. The weapon is a thirty-six-incher, for tubes four or three. Range is forty to fifty miles. At max range, that's a time of flight of ten minutes. There's no evading this baby; it has a wide blue-laser search cone with a reattack mode. Questions on the Vortex?"

Porter paused and scanned the room. When his eyes lingered on Colleen O'Shaughnessy, a pang of annoyance unexpectedly flashed through Pacino's chest. He shot a look at Colleen, whose expression was a blank mask. He felt a moment of discomfort, realizing that he was jealous, which was absurd. After all, he was in his forties and Colleen was not even thirty yet. And even that meant nothing, because he was still trying to make sense of life after having lost Eileen.

Yet he was honest with himself, he had to admit that he admired Colleen, liked her, found her attractive. And what sense did that make? What would she want with a dinosaur like him? What business did he have getting involved with a combat-systems vendor representative, who coincidentally just happened to be the daughter of the number one admiral in the Navy and Pacino's boss?

He glanced at Colleen one last time before concentrat-

ing again on the briefing. She seemed to sense him looking at her, and she turned with her large eyes on his,
her expression a smoldering anger, still mad at him that
he was kicking her off the ship before the battle came.
But just before she turned back to look at Porter, he
could swear the corners of her eyes lifted, that she'd
broken his gaze to avoid smiling at him. Guilt settled on
him again, and he looked at his left finger where his
Annapolis ring was. A year ago he'd removed Eileen's
wedding band, the inscription reading *I'll love you forever,* and placed it on a ribbon around a photograph of
her he kept by the bed of his Pearl Harbor headquarters
bedroom, then switched the academy ring from his right
finger to his left. An odd impulse took hold of him, and
he suddenly pulled the class ring off the left finger and
put it on his right. He looked up and saw Colleen had
seen him make the switch. He tried to return his attention to Porter.

". . . Mark 52 range at eight to forty miles depending
on transit speed and depth. Okay, now on to sensors.

"We've been over sonar in depth. Let's review the
OTH sensors. We have two over-the-horizon targeting
sensors, the Mark 12 'Yo-Yo' and the Mark 4 'Sharkeye.'
The Mark 12 Yo-Yo is dropped by a P-5 Pegasus patrol
plane, is about ten feet in diameter, and pops out a small
buoy that stays on the surface while the main body of it
sinks to eight hundred to one thousand feet, whatever
best listening depth is. The Yo-Yo pod is a sonar receiver much like our acoustic-daylight-imaging sphere in
the nose cone, and anything detected is relayed up a
cable to the buoy, which transmits the data by tactical
datalink to the overhead ComStar satellite, then down
to us at periscope depth. Using the Yo-Yo remote over-
the-horizon targeting pod, we can receive sonar signals
from fifteen hundred miles away. The Yo-Yo range is
less than our own sphere, but it's not bad. Detection on
a submarine might be up to one hundred miles, but
we're counting on fifty.

"Now, the Sharkeye Mark 4. In the event the Yo-Yo
isn't available, such as when there are no P-5 Pegasus

patrol aircraft available, we can use our own Mark 4 Sharkeyes. The Sharkeye is a pod like the Yo-Yo, except contained in the upper section of a Javelin cruise-missile body, replacing the warhead. On this run the ship is loaded with only two plasma Javelin cruise missiles. The other ten missiles in the vertical-launch tubes are rockets to launch the Mark 4 Sharkeye remote sonar pods. The Sharkeye has a detection range of about twenty-four to forty-eight miles, with the confidence interval set at thirty miles. We're hoping we can use the bigger, higher-definition Yo-Yos, but if something goes wrong, we'll have our Sharkeyes.

"So that's everything. Anyone need a break?"

"Let's take five," Patton said, "then get back here for Admiral Pacino's war briefing."

"Gentlemen, we're reconvened," Porter said, bringing the afternoon training session to order.

"Nav, the doors locked?" executive officer Walt Hornick asked.

"Yes, XO."

"Everyone cleared for this? Only gold dolphin wearers in here?"

Pacino looked around the room. Colleen O'Shaughnessy was absent, and he felt relief, then annoyance. He had to stop this. His feelings for her might jeopardize their working relationship. Plus, he had to keep his mind on the mission's business.

"Admiral, we're ready," Patton said.

Glancing at the chart display, Pacino stood and addressed the officers.

"Good afternoon, gentlemen." He always began formally, an old habit. "This is the East China Sea. Marked in red is the position of the sinking of the initial RDF convoy, in the gap between Naze Island and Yakushima. The Naze-Yakushima Gap is directly on the great circle route from Oahu to Shanghai. Gentlemen, my theory is that the Rising Suns are lurking up here, in the gap.

"Now, that's not how I would defend the East China Sea against a convoy or against an attacking squadron of submarines. I'd spread out. But here is what the enemy is thinking—I'll wait here at the doorway, and the convoy will come in there, since they're in a big hurry to get to the mainland. Since my speed is faster than the convoy's, and since I have a spy satellite overhead taking pictures of the surface ships, I know where they're headed. Plus, Shanghai is the trouble spot, because the Red thrust objective is to split White China in two. So Shanghai is the key to the defense of the Whites. It's top secret, but any dummy could guess that. Everyone with me so far?

"Okay, so our Red force is clustered at the gap. Aren't they afraid of us? Afraid a U.S. sub detachment will come to get them? Captain Patton, what do you think?"

"I don't think they're losing a minute of sleep over it," Patton said in a ringing voice.

"Why, John?"

"Because they put us on the bottom before we even knew we had company. Men, I was going five knots, dead slow, trying damn hard to hear a Rising Sun class that I knew was out there. Next thing I know, I'm on the deck and the ship is on fire, and my coveralls are flaming, and my sonar chief drags me out of the hatch and throws me on a raft and I'm looking at a fucking periscope. Does everyone understand this? These Rising Suns are badasses. They kicked the shit out of us, and they think they can do it again."

"Well put, Captain." Pacino smiled. "We're not a threat to these guys. The 688s are toys."

"What about the *Piranha*, the Seawolf class?" Chris Porter asked.

"Good point, Navigator. Any theories? No? Here's mine. The SSN-23 is in just as much trouble as the 688s, because he's using the old narrowband-broadband detection methods against a target whose tonals we don't know. If the *Piranha* knew what it was looking for, life would be simple. Just set the frequency gate to pick up a 237 hertz tonal and wait for it to fall into your lap. But we don't know what tonals these guys put out."

Pacino took a drink of water, looking into the eyes of the men around him, an old trick to gauge his audience.

"So my plan is to use acoustic-daylight sonar to the maximum extent we can. At zero hour ten P-5 Pegasus patrol planes will fly out of Kagashima to drop the first load of twenty Yo-Yo remote-sonar sensors. We'll be hanging out at periscope depth to receive the signals. We'll spend a lot of our time at PD this run, guys. With the Yo-Yos out there, we'll use our intelligence of the location of the six Rising Suns to call in torpedo strikes. I'm putting the twelve 688s of the Pacific Fleet here at Point Echo with us. Yes, they're loud and relatively vulnerable, but I brought them out here for their torpedo rooms. With twelve subs, each carrying 26 Mark 52 torpedoes, I've got 312 torpedoes I can vector into the target locations. That will be like a bunch of bees buzzing around them.

"Now, the Rising Suns have good torpedo countermeasures, according to the tapes we've gotten from the Maritime Self-Defense Force. They have four pods that detach from the X-tail aft that sound just like a Rising Sun, just louder. Each pod inflates a foil balloon that acts as a sonar reflector. Guaranteed to confuse a torpedo. But like I said, they have only four apiece, so we run the bastards out of decoys. Then they have a ventriloquist sonar, an active system in the tail that puts out fake sonar returns to the incoming torpedo, throws it off. They can evade one weapon, maybe two at once, but not a dozen.

"Now, even though I'll be putting out torpedoes from our vintage 688s, the main weapon will be *Piranha*'s Vortex Mod Bravo battery, ten weapons, all long-range. If it's a good day, Bruce Phillips aboard the *Piranha* fires six Bravos and this war is over. If it's a bad day, some or all of us take plasma torpedoes on the chin. No guarantees. Next resort after *Piranha* are the Vortex Mod Charlies we carry, the smaller, shorter-range Vortex, or Vortex-Lite, if you will. We've got more of them than the *Piranha* has Mod Bravos, but with their shorter range, we'll have to go in deeper in the op area to get them on target.

"In general, gentlemen, I'm optimistic, but here is my list of worries. One, the Rising Suns have anti-air missiles. If they detect the P-5 Pegasus patrol planes, they might shoot them down, and with them, our Yo-Yo remote OTH sensors. If that happens, I'll blow the wad on the Mark 4 Sharkeyes, but if I only detect some of the Rising Suns, we'll be in trouble. I'll have to send in *Piranha* to shoot what we see, and risk that it may be shot at by the Rising Suns we don't see.

"Next worry, that we look out here and don't find any Rising Suns. If I missed my guess, the boats are dispersed. If that's the case, we'll deploy and redeploy Yo-Yos until we see them. At some point we may need to draw their fire. Not a popular option, and the only way to do it is with the *Devilfish*, because everyone else is blind. If they take us down when we do that, the operation is over and the convoy goes in without us."

"What? The convoy goes in anyway?" Porter asked.

"Exactly. The Rising Sun weapon loadout is 48 weapons per sub, total of 288 units. We lost a total of 110 ships. Say that's about 120 weapons. That means they have about 148 or so torpedoes left. We would draw their fire with a convoy until there are no more torpedoes."

"But they have enough to take down the lion's share of the second convoy," Porter protested.

"Look, I didn't suggest this. It's just what General Baldini will do. I know that guy. He's bullheaded, and he's been known to do frontal attacks on brick walls. Maybe he'll gamble that the Red force spent more than 120 weapons on 110 kills, and that he can at least get half his men in. Half of a 400,000 man force is better than none, or so Bull Baldini thinks.

"There is one consolation here," Pacino continued. "According to the Japanese, the maximum speed of the Mod II Nagasaki torpedo is only 46 knots. A 688 can outrun a torpedo in a tail chase, which I suspect is what happened to the *Annapolis*. But you can't run from a torpedo you didn't detect, so our sonar system is key.

"And the last worry on the list is that this mission falls on its face if Cyclops fails. We'd better hope the computer works and doesn't crash on us."

"If it works anything as well as Miss O'Shaughnessy looks, it'll do *great*," a young voice said from the other side of the room.

"That's enough," Pacino said, suddenly furious, biting his lip. "Any questions? Captain, please dismiss your men and come see me in the VIP stateroom."

Pacino left the wardroom and crossed the hall to the stateroom, his heart still thumping in anger. No doubt about it, he'd feel better when Colleen was off the ship.

CHAPTER 31

THURSDAY
NOVEMBER 7

"Tanker in sight, bearing mark! Range, mark! Three divisions in low power, angle on the bow starboard five. Off'sa'deck, take the scope," Patton called, releasing the grips and turning away.

"Where's O'Shaughnessy?"

"She's not at the escape trunk, sir," the helm officer said, putting down his phone.

Patton and Pacino exchanged a look. "I'll go for her," Pacino said. He walked out of the control room, past the door to sonar, and down the forward centerline passageway all the way to the end at the door to the computer room. He tapped in the combination to the button-type lock, the alphanumerics set to "S-S-N-X," clicked the latch, and walked in. Colleen O'Shaughnessy sat at her console, typing away, as if there were no personnel transfer waiting for her.

"You're late," Pacino said, trying to keep his voice level. "We need to get you going. Wrap up there and get into the suit and tanks." He pointed at the wet suit on the deck, the scuba bottle lying next to it.

She just kept typing, ignoring him.

"Colleen, let's go." He reached for her upper arm, and she shrugged him off, continuing to type.

"What's the matter with you?" he cried, his anger rising.

"I'll tell you what's the matter with me," she said, her voice low, quiet, and furious. "You're treating me like a child. Now, cut it out and leave me alone. I've got two terabytes of code to fix."

"Colleen, we'll manage. Turn it over to Commander Porter. We need to get you off the ship."

"Why?"

"Because your life is in danger."

"No, it isn't, yours is. Especially if you kick me off the ship. Admiral, the code's corrupt. It has maybe an hour at a time to run before it collapses, and I have to cold-start it." She kept typing while she spoke.

"Fine, we'll cold-start it when it shuts down. Now let's—"

"You don't understand. Each time it shuts down, I have to process and fix the error message. It's how the debug-system module works. We might even lose the system fifty times in an hour if there are fifty lines of code incorrect. And your Mr. Porter won't be able to do that. So it's not whether my life or your life is in danger, it's the mission that's in trouble. This mission goes exactly nowhere without Cyclops. You said it yourself, Admiral, I *am* the battle-control system." She stopped typing, dropped her hands into her lap, and looked up at him. "I'll tell you the real reason you want me off the ship. It's because of your feelings for me."

Pacino dropped his jaw, looking down at her. The ponytail was gone. She had combed out her hair, and it looked freshly washed, shining in the light of the overheads. Her skin was as healthy as if she'd been outside in the sun, her eyes shining.

"My feelings for you?"

"Exactly. And it's okay, Michael. I have feelings for you too. I have since the first time I saw you 137 days ago at the DynaCorp shipyard meeting."

"I never knew," Pacino sputtered, his chest so tight

he could barely speak. "Why didn't you say something, or do something? Something to tell me?"

"You weren't ready. You're still not. Besides, I did do something. I'm here, aren't I?"

Pacino struggled to think. "But, Colleen, your life is in danger. We're headed for a combat zone. You can't be here."

"Why not?"

"Navy regulations, for one thing—"

"Screw them. Next?"

"Okay, your father."

"If I were a guy, that wouldn't matter, would it?"

Pacino pushed against his mental haze. "You're right. Maybe it wouldn't. But you're still leaving. I'm not putting you at risk any more than I already have. It was wrong to bring you here."

"Look at it this way, Admiral. If this were 1912 and I were on the *Titanic,* would you evacuate me?"

"Yes."

"Now, if I were on the *Titanic* because I alone had the information to prevent it from hitting that iceberg, and that were my purpose, then would you evacuate me?"

"Dammit, yes."

"And have a thousand deaths on your conscience? I doubt it. You'd let me stay to try to save the ship. Because, Admiral, without me *this* ship is the *Titanic.*"

Pacino looked her in the eye for a long moment. "You're right, I do have feelings for you," he admitted waiting for the pang of guilt to set in, but it was late.

Colleen smiled. "I want three kids."

Pacino laughed, his mouth open to reply, when the door lock clicked, then the latch, and the door opened against the jamb. It was Patton, one eyebrow raised.

"Loss of battle control!" a speaker in the overhead boomed.

"Back to work," O'Shaughnessy sighed, turning back to her panel. Pacino waved at her and left the room, pulling Patton after him.

"Shove off the personnel-transfer tanker," Pacino said. "She's staying with us."

"Is she nuts? We're going to be—"

"We're going to be without a battle-control system unless she's onboard to fix it."

Patton sighed, walking back to control. When Pacino arrived there, Patton had already ordered the ship to return deep at emergency flank. He looked at Pacino strangely.

"You got a second, Admiral?"

Patton waved him into his captain's cabin. On the table was a package wrapped in brown paper, with an envelope taped to it. The envelope said, PERSONAL FOR COMMANDING OFFICER.

"I've already read the note," Patton said. "It said to give the package to you when we were close to the operation area." He looked at Pacino, curious.

Pacino opened the package. The brown paper was wrapped around a folded black cloth, the material coarse and heavy. As he unfolded it all the way, Patton whistled. It was a Jolly Roger pirate flag, the skull and crossbones white on the black field. The flag was large, the size of a bedsheet. Above the grinning skull was the legend in uneven white letters, USS DEVILFISH, and below the crossbones the legend read, YOU AIN'T CHEATIN, YOU AIN'T TRYIN. Pacino looked at it, startled.

The flag had flown on the bridge of the first *Devilfish,* and it was one of two things Pacino had pulled out of the captain's stateroom before he had abandoned ship. The second had been a photograph of his father standing in front of his submarine, the doomed *Stingray.* Back in Norfolk, Pacino had taken the flag and the photo to the *Stingray* monument, a black marble obelisk dedicated to the men who had died in the sinking of the submarine, Pacino's father's name engraved first on the list. Reverently Pacino had bent to leave the flag and photograph, and had limped on his crutches away, never expecting to see the flag again.

He had heard reports about it, though. Someone reported that on a visit to see Admiral Donchez at his

Commander Submarines Atlantic Headquarters, the Jolly Roger flew over the building next to the American flag. Pacino had shrugged it off as a false rumor. But here the flag was, yet another reminder of Donchez.

"Let me see the note," Pacino said. The note simply said, *Give this to Admiral Pacino when the ship is close to the operation area.* It was in Dick Donchez's handwriting. Pacino swallowed hard.

"Hang it in the control room," he said to Patton.

POINT ECHO HOLD POSITION
40 MILES EAST OF THE NAZE-YAKUSHIMA GAP
USS *DEVILFISH*, SSNX-1

Pacino checked his Rolex. Thirty minutes to zero hour. He had been pacing the ship for the last few hours, circling between the computer room, control, sonar, and Patton's stateroom.

Now Paully White, Patton, and Pacino were sitting at Patton's conference table, looking at the chart display of the East China Sea. Pacino felt his stomach tense, his pulse racing, the pre-game jitters thrumming through him. He struggled to find something useful he could do. He had already brought the *Piranha* up to periscope depth and briefed Bruce Phillips on the final details of the war plan. There was nothing to do now but wait.

What if he was wrong? he thought. What if the subs were hundreds of miles south, or dispersed throughout the sea? What would he do then? He could do nothing until the aircraft dropped their Yo-Yo remote sensors into the Naze-Yakushima Gap, and then the battle would begin or he would be forced to switch to Plan B.

For a moment he thought about Colleen, but that was like poking his hand into a hornet's nest, feelings overwhelmingly strong on the other side of that mental wall. All he would allow himself to feel was concern for Colleen and hope that nothing happened to her. Or him, he thought.

When the clock reached 2255 local time, Pacino stood.

"Let's man up," he said, walking forward into the control room. He ducked out through the forward door to the passageway to its end and into the computer room.

"Man . . . battle stations!" the overhead speaker boomed, repeating the message.

"Well, this is it," he said.

As Colleen looked up at him, her face was a mask of worry. Her eyes rotated between him and her computer screen. "Good luck, Michael," she said, and Pacino thought it sounded so strange to hear that from her lips, yet so good.

"You too, honey," he said, hating himself for the weird way it sounded and made him feel.

Her face relaxed for just a second, a serenity coming over her, and then the curtain fell, the frown returning, her fingers typing on the keyboard, a curse under her breath at the computer. He stepped to the door and looked back at her, wanting to remember her like this.

BOOK VI

YO-YO

CHAPTER 32

THURSDAY
NOVEMBER 7

The P-5 Pegasus Antisubmarine-warfare patrol plane idled at the end of runway one eight. The strip pointed due south toward the dark water of the East China Sea. The only light in the cockpit came from the backwash of the instrument panel and the lights of the runway. The flashing numerals of the digital chronometer, synchronized with the overhead satellite atomic clock, flashed *53 . . . 54 . . . 55 . . .*

Commander David Toscano's Nomex-gloved hand was already poised on the throttles to the four fan-jet transit engines mounted in pairs on the high wings of the ungainly aircraft, and when the numerals 55 flashed, he moved the levers forward to the detents at the instrument panel. The jets howled far behind him, making the plane shake with the power. Toscano's feet remained planted on the toe brakes, watching as the needles climbed on the electronic analog-mimic instruments—oil pressure, fuel flow rate, revolutions per minute. The jets were coming up normally to full thrust. The heavy bird would need every ounce of power the DynaCorp engines could deliver because the day's load was heavy, featuring fat war-shot Mark 79 torpedoes, each weighing twenty tons, plus two Yo-Yo Mark 12 over-the-horizon remote-sonar-sensor pods, a massive two tons each.

Toscano looked over at his copilot, who nodded behind his visor. The clock ticked, *58 . . . 59 . . . 00.* At zero zero exactly Toscano released the toe brakes. For the first second the P-5, shuddering under several dozens of tons of thrust, did exactly nothing, sitting immobile on the runway. Toscano's fingers tensed on the control yoke, toes poised on the rudder pedals. The P-5 finally budged, accelerating in the first few seconds to a walking speed, even as the jets aft screeched at full power. Toscano shot a look at the panel—all nominal—then back at the runway. At fifteen seconds they were at a jogging speed. Another five seconds clicked off, and the airspeed needle showed them at twenty knots, only about fifty feet of runway behind them, almost two miles of concrete ahead.

The big bird slowly gained speed until the ground was rushing by beneath them, highway speed, the aircraft bouncing slightly. To a hundred knots the airspeed climbed, then 120, 140, half the runway gone, the plane shaking insistently. At the three-quarter point the jet had made it to safe takeoff velocity, 175 knots, but Toscano held it down, the wings bouncing behind them. To 180, 190, 200 knots—the concrete's end could be seen ahead. Toscano gently pulled back on the control yoke and the nose came up, only darkness in the windows ahead, the shaking airframe instantly calming, the P-5 airborne over the water of the East China Sea. The needle of the radar altimeter climbed as the jet fought for altitude. As they passed through a thousand feet, Toscano throttled back and put the yoke forward.

"Gear up," he said. The copilot hit the lever with the round handle, and the P-5's wheels retracted into the fuselage. "Flaps up," and the whine behind him indicated the wings fairing in the flap surfaces. The Pegasus was fully airborne.

Toscano dialed in the navigation chart to the forward display. As the number one Yo-Yo drop zone began flashing, the coastline of the Home Islands faded to the north of the blinking dot representing their aircraft. Transit time to the drop zone at jet speed was about fifteen minutes. Toscano concentrated on his navigation and his instruments, the P-5 known to be temperamental.

At the drop time, Toscano broke his silence. "Start the turboprops." His copilot hit the auto-start button on the starboard turboprop, the engine with its huge diameter prop feathered during takeoff. The prop windmilled in the airstream, and the engine came up to speed, the copilot monitoring as fuel injection began and the prop came up to idling revs.

"Number one turboprop is up." He started the port prop and soon reported it running at idle.

Toscano pulled back on the jet throttles, their howl dying to a whimper. Quieter than the jets, the grinding turboprops would keep the massive jet hanging above the water at ultraslow speed. Toscano descended to the water. He checked the nav display. They were one mile from the drop of the number one Mark 12 Yo-Yo.

"Mark 12 forward door open," he commanded on his boom mike. The copilot hit the lever, and the fuselage opened up beneath them.

"Eight hundred yards to drop number one," Toscano said. "Arm the drop mechanism, Yo-Yo unit one power on."

"Power on, unit one and engaged, drop mechanism enabled. Ready for Mark 12 release."

"Four hundred yards, stand by."

SS-403 *ARCTIC STORM*

Chu looked out the periscope and commanded, "Darkwing unit two liftoff in three, two, one, mark! And laser guidance, I have the aircraft in the crosshairs."

"Darkwing missile two away, sir," Lo Sun said from the command console. The huge maritime patrol plane was dipping so close to the water that the bomb-bay doors were almost skimming the waves. Chu had gotten the ship to periscope depth, manning battle stations, just seconds before. It was as if the airplane knew where they were. He hadn't circled or done a search; he'd come right in from nowhere. The Second Captain had given them only about seven seconds' warning of the aircraft, but in that time Chu had bolted from his stateroom table, shouted at the ship-control officer to take the vessel up, and grabbed the periscope.

He felt a sudden chill. The Americans were coming for him. This was something he hadn't anticipated, that the Japanese would have cooperated and told the Americans about the Rising Suns.

His thoughts were interrupted as the trail of the missile flashed into his view in the periscope.

Toscano watched the navigation display with one eye, the instruments with the other. It was time.

"Drop unit one."

The copilot pulled up on the console Yo-Yo drop lever, and the plane lifted slightly as the two-ton weight left the plane.

There was a brief flash of light from something out the window of the cockpit before the airplane exploded. The airframe disintegrated. Toscano's body was ripped in half at the seat belt, the father of two dead before he even realized he'd been hit.

Tens of thousands of pieces of debris rained down on the water. A jet engine, nearly intact, splashed into the water not far from the Yo-Yo as the unit sank into the water of the East China Sea, its surface transmitter being barely missed by several pieces of what had been the plane's tail section.

Deep underwater, the Yo-Yo unit began transmitting up the cable line to the surface transmitter, seeing the deep water around it with the acoustic daylight imaging. The sea around it was full of medium-sized chunks of debris sinking on their way to the bottom. What was left of the cockpit sailed by a few minutes after. Soon the sea calmed, and there was only the ocean and the solitary shape of the submarine, lurking above at periscope depth, some twelve hundred yards away.

Five P-5 Pegasus patrol planes had taken off from Kagoshima. Five of them took missile hits as they flew near or over the *Arctic Storm*'s position. Five of them disintegrated and hit the water, their crews all dead.

The first Yo-Yo made it into the water, but the others blew up with their aircraft.

No other P-5s were operational at Kagoshima, and if there had been, it didn't matter, since all the Yo-Yo remote pods were expended. There were no spares.

Five aircraft down, Admiral Chu Hua-Feng pulled off his sweaty headset, there at the periscope station, and wiped his forehead.

Though he did not know it, he had won the first round.

POINT ECHO HOLD POSITION
USS *DEVILFISH*, SSNX-1

"The AWACs radar plane over Kagoshima reported it lost all five P-5 aircraft," Paully White reported from the radio repeater console.

"What do you mean, lost them?" Patton asked.

"They dropped off the radar. The AWACs watch the aircraft with a look-down radar, since the P-5s fly too low for land-based radar to see them, and they reported that all five Pegasus planes hit the drink."

"I'm getting a Yo-Yo display," Porter said from battle-control position one. "And a confirmed target, designate submerged warship."

Pacino bolted upright from his leaning position at the plot table. This was serious. The P-5s most likely had come under attack from the Rising Sun's sub-to-air heat-seeking missiles. Pacino blinked, then looked over at Patton. The Yo-Yos were scrubbed. The damned Rising Sun commander had blown Pacino's patrol aircraft out of the sky, and now he was forced into Plan B. Fortunately, he'd seen the need to put the Sharkeye remote sensors aboard Javelin cruise-missile airframes. Without them this mission would already be over.

"Conn, Sonar," a voice said over Pacino's headset, "we have a detect on Mark 12 Yo-Yo unit one thirty miles southwest of Yakushima Island. Detect is confirmed submerged submarine."

"Designate the contact Target One," Patton commanded. He walked across the room to the battle-control station zero, the first in line on the starboard side, and climbed in. Pacino followed suit, climbing into station four, the aft-most station. Lowering the canopy over his head down to waist level, he then pulled the helmet over his headset. A yellow screen came up, and the bluish orb of a contact, about a half mile away, appeared. "Switch to battle-control virtual display on Yo-Yo one." The amber background with its floating specs of red and blue vanished, replaced with the viewing point of the Yo-Yo: a cool blue world, the surface of the ocean overhead, the submarine a three-dimensional shape, not far away. "Switch to geographic plot, calibrated scale." The display changed to a god's eye view of the Naze-Yakushima Gap, the Yo-Yo's target on the upper section, their own ship on the lower right, the land appearing in detailed relief. Pacino whistled to himself. After seeing this, it would be impossible to go back to the old-fashioned two-dimensional consoles.

"Captain Patton, we need to launch the Mark 4s."

"Admiral, we're all set."

Within two minutes the first four Mark 4 missiles were away. The vertical-launching-system tubes in the forward ballast tank opened their upper doors, and a gas generator blew the missiles to the surface in a bubble of steam. The rocket motors lit and took the missiles skyward a half mile, then detached and fell back to earth. In the meantime, the onboard air-breathing jet engines had fired up and the missiles dived for the safety of low altitude. They skimmed the surface, barely twenty feet above the waves, until they arrived at their preordained splash-down positions. Abruptly, the missiles popped up toward the sky, rising by a thousand feet, then diving straight for the water. On the way down, the nose cones popped open in a flower-petal sequence, the missile airframes breaking apart. From each missile a package detached, a streamer trailing behind it for stability, a drogue parachute coming next, followed by the main parachute, deploying just a few hundred feet over the water. The Mark 4 payload, the Sharkeye sensor, drifted gently to the water and splashed down. The parachute was ditched as the main body of the sensor sank, leaving on the surface a transmitter connected by a cable.

Two minutes later, the second four missiles were away, and two minutes after that the final two Mark 4s were fired. All ten Mark 4 Sharkeye acoustic-daylight-imaging remote sensors survived their trips, sank to best listening depth, and began transmitting to satellites overhead.

SS-403 *ARCTIC STORM*

"Sir, we have a splash in the water, bearing zero nine five." Lo Sun sounded extremely nervous.

Chu stiffened in his command-console seat. He had taken the ship back deep to a depth of three hundred meters, the temperature profile indicating that to be the best listening depth.

"That's not all. We've got faint turbojet engines."

"Jets and splashes. What is that?"

"Sir," Lo Sun said, "we might have some incoming cruise missiles."

"Cruise missiles? What could a cruise missile do to us at three hundred meters?"

"For one thing, drop a plasma depth charge. Splash number two, sir. Now three. I've got a total of four now, all points of the compass."

Was that a coincidence, Chu thought, that the splashes were north, south, east, and west? Were they bracketing him, putting plasma depth charges around him? Or could they be sonobuoys, listening for his ship? Or were they cruise missile-delivered torpedoes?

He had the deepest feeling of unease he'd had during the operation. The Americans weren't afraid of him. They were marching in with aircraft and now missiles, undeterred that he'd shot down their planes. What would be next? And with the destructive power of plasma weapons, would he even know what happened?

Hurry, my little warrior, for they are coming for you, and they are strong. Finish quickly.

In his hour of uncertainty the dream returned to him, and he knew now what it meant. It had not been his father mysteriously speaking to him from the beyond, but his own mind putting the solution together for him, sounding a warning in the voice of the one man on earth he had always listened to. Except this time. He had not finished quickly. He had put the first convoy on the bottom, but it had not been enough. Perhaps he should have let one ship survive to tell the horrible tale—perhaps that would have made his power more real to the Americans. But there was no going back now.

The Americans were coming. They were coming without fear, with certainty and death. And they were strong. And he was going to die. Today was the day. And there would be no headstone, no bones to bury.

Chu had to admit to himself that he was deeply frightened.

His father's words came back to him yet again: *Courage is not the absence of fear, but actions taken from the heart while under the terrible grip of fear, actions taken for your men, your ship, your fleet, your country. Someday, my son, you will show your courage. For now just know that it is in you, that courage will come from your heart when it is time. Never doubt that.*

Pacino climbed into the position four battle-control station as soon as he heard that the first Sharkeye had detected a submerged contact.

He had to switch his display to the ship-centered virtual reality, to see the relative positions of the contacts as the onboard Cyclops computer analyzed the data rolling in. He allowed himself a smile as he looked at the sea and the contacts around them, even the land modeled in three-dimensional relief. He counted, not believing his eyes—four, five, six. They were all present and accounted for. He wanted to jump out and give Patton and White a high-five, but then he cautioned himself. The Cyclops system could cease functioning at any moment. Colleen had called it corrupt, ready to crash. Also, was it possible that it was misinterpreting the data? Did the computer see six when it should see only one?

He left the eggshell canopy and climbed to the elevated periscope platform. A look at the computerized chart display, which was linked to the Cyclops, displayed their position, the 688s' positions, and the position of the *Piranha*. There was good news here—they had in fact detected all six Rising Suns.

But there was bad news too. The six Rising Suns were outside weapons range. Attacking with aircraft was impossible with the P-5s shot down, and the Blackbeard squadrons and Seahawk helicopters were too far away onboard the carriers and destroyers of the backup Rapid Deployment Force. His sub force would have to take them down, but they were outside his Vortex Mod Charlie's range and outside of *Piranha*'s Mod Bravo's range. They were also outside the Mark 52 range of the 688s' weapons as well. Everyone would need to close range, which would bring them into range of the Rising Suns.

He dictated a message to the 688s and the *Piranha* and gave it to Patton to transmit. He'd given the subs the grid coordinates of the locations of the Rising Suns. The force would go in, *Piranha* and the 688s deep at moderate speeds, *Piranha* at seventeen knots, the 688s at ten, fast enough that they could make speed over ground, slow enough that their sonars would be able to strain for the enemy's noise over their own noise, and slow enough that they wouldn't rumble through the ocean like rattling old cars.

It seemed too easy, Pacino thought. What was he missing?

The answer came to him when the officer of the deck cursed.

"Loss of battle control," he called, picking up a microphone to the circuit one shipwide announcing system, shouting into it—despite it being a loudspeaker PA circuit—his voice mirroring the frustration of everyone aboard, "Loss of battle control."

The chart display table winked out, the surface black and featureless. The five eggshell screens at the positions of the battle-control system rolled up, their officers emerging like disoriented movie patrons coming out into bright sunshine. The door to sonar opened, and Senior Chief Byron DeMeers came in. The men gathered forlornly in the open space on the port side of the periscope stand.

Pacino debated with himself, then made a decision. He hurried forward down the centerline passageway to the computer room, punched the buttons to get inside.

There at the console sat Colleen O'Shaughnessy, the executive vice president of Cyclops Computer Systems, subsidiary of mighty DynaCorp Defense International, the chief architect of the Cyclops Mark 72 NSSN Battle-control System, with her head in her hands, tears silently running down her cheeks.

CHAPTER 33

Admiral Chu Hua-Feng stared at the sonar display in confusion and suspicion.

Twelve submarine contacts.

Twelve 688 submarines.

Sailing right into the Naze-Yakushima Gap as if he weren't there.

But that wasn't so odd, was it? They didn't know his position—he was being positively paranoid.

Still, twelve subs, all 688s, all clustered together at the entrance? What was going on?

"Sir," the navigator, Xhiu Liu, said from the sensor panel, urgency lacing his voice, "ten of the 688s are or have already opened bowcap torpedo-tube doors. Eleven, now twelve. Now we're getting second bow-cap door noises from each ship."

What the hell was going on? He wondered. All twelve coming in at once, directly toward him, all opening bow-cap doors. Did they sense him here or not? They had to know he was here; he was the easternmost submarine. Could this be some kind of deception? After all, didn't he have false periscopes being towed right now behind the sterns of his fleet of fishing trawlers? And weren't two dozen of those trawlers, to the west and southwest, pulling behind them noisemakers that attempted to simulate a nuclear submarine noise? Deception was an ancient Chinese tool of war.

But if it was an illusion, what was the purpose? To draw his fire? There was simply no way to know.

He made a decision. If they wanted to draw fire, by the heavens he would give them fire, and he'd do it decisively.

"Open bowcap doors to tubes 13 to 24. Arm gas generators 13 to 24. Set torpedoes in tubes 13 to 24 to high-speed transit, shallow trajectory."

"Aye, sir," Chen Zhu, the weapons officer said.

It took no time at all for the weapons to warm up.

"Set 13 for target ST-3, 14 for ST-4, and so on," Chu ordered.

"Thirteen and 14 ready, sir. Fifteen and 16 coming up now."

"Shoot 13 and 14," Chu ordered.

The difference between a high-impulse gas-generator torpedo launch and an ultraquiet slow swimout was dramatic. Under the action of a solid-rocket motor impinging a reservoir of water that instantly vaporized to high-pressure steam, the tube spat out the weapon like a cannon. The torpedo's engine lit off, and it soared into the sea at full throttle, the water jet pumping at maximum thrust, all provisions for stealth discarded. Within mere minutes Chu launched the torpedo battery at the twelve submarines of the American submarine wave, settling down to wait the fourteen minutes until torpedo impact.

It would be interesting to see if the target vessels took flight, or it they kept coming. Chu watched tensely from his command seat, wishing he could have a cup of tea, but there had been no time to fill the thermos since the aircraft contact had approached. Impatiently Chu waited.

"ST-3 through 14 remain inbound," the navigator reported.

They hadn't heard the torpedoes. Excellent. Chu waited, flipping through his displays, trying to think ahead to the next move. If this worked, perhaps there would be no next move required, because the Americans would give up and go home, as they should have since the beginning.

"ST-3 has detected the torpedo. Aspect change, he's turning, Admiral. Turning and speeding up. He's running, sir. Same with ST-5, ST-8, now ST-4. All across

the board, Admiral, the submarines have counter-
detected the torpedoes and are turning away."

"Very good." Was it? he asked himself. Or was this
part of an elaborate deception? And yet it wasn't good,
because the longer the fast 688s ran, the less chance they
had of being hit, the 85-click torpedo going up against
a 90-click submarine. All he could hope for was the termination plasma detonation of the weapons would kill
the running submarines.

The first explosion sounded in the room, audible to
the naked ear, although it was twenty kilometers away.
Then the second, the third and fourth explosions came.
Finally Chu lost count. The corner of his mouth rose
slightly. The Americans were paying for costing him so
many sleepless nights.

USS *DEVILFISH*, SSNX-1

"What the hell was that?"

Paully White stood in the ring of officers, waiting for
their battle-control system to come back up. The vessel
was blind without the Cyclops system. A single loud explosion had registered in the room, two more following
shortly afterward, then more, with uneven intervals between them.

Pacino arrived in the forward door to control in a
dead run.

"How many explosions?" he asked.

Patton gave him the bad news. "Twelve, Admiral. I
think the 688s took hits."

"Dammit," was all Pacino could say.

"Cyclops?"

"Down hard, Colleen thinks—" Just then the eggshell
canopies flickered, went dark, then flickered again, then
held, each one reconfiguring. The officers on the room's
port side ran back into their stations and donned their
helmets.

"Control, Computer Room, Cyclops is initializing now

and back on-line." Colleen's voice was low and measured, giving no trace of the hopelessness Pacino had seen twenty minutes before.

"Sonar, Captain," Patton's voice rang in Pacino's headset. "Report the situation."

"Captain, Sonar," DeMeers' answer came. "Still initializing, stand by. Captain, Sonar . . . we have six Rising Sun contacts, twelve unidentified large-diameter, low-density spheroids, and multiple objects—"

"What?" Patton was annoyed. "Do you have the twelve 688s?"

"Cap'n, Sonar, the twelve spheres are explosion zones from plasma weapons, and the multiple objects we interpret to be broken submarine hulls. Cyclops is showing them traveling vertically downward. They're sinking. All twelve show that they are now between two thousand and twenty-five hundred feet deep. Some are hitting the bottom and are disappearing from Cyclops as being bottom clutter. Captain, Sonar . . . as of now I only show six Rising Suns and the *Piranha.*"

"God *damn* that son of a bitch," Pacino spat. "That's almost two thousand of my men that bastard just killed." A murderous rage choked him. He wanted to kill the Red force commander with his bare hands.

"Admiral, *Piranha* is in range of three Rising Suns with his Vortex missiles."

USS *PIRANHA*, SSN-23

Captain Bruce Phillips stood on the conn and squinted down on the battle stations crew arrayed at the attack-center consoles.

"Sonar, Captain, status!" he barked into his boom microphone.

"Captain, Sonar," Master Chief Henry said in his baritone voice, the tone of it fitting perfectly with his shaved head, tree-trunk neck, and wide shoulders—the only thing missing his earring, which went on immediately when he left the ship. "We've got no contacts, just sonar blueouts at the previous bearings to the 688s."

"Sonar, Captain, I'm going upstairs and getting on the radio. Maybe Uncle Mikey on the *D-fish* can give me better information than you and your sonar girls."

The master chief's answer was as professional as Phillips' was casual: "Captain, Sonar, aye. Do you intend to clear baffles?"

"Sonar, Captain, no. Off'sa'deck, upstairs now!"

"Aye, sir," the officer of the deck snapped back, a twenty-eight-year-old lieutenant named Gustavson. "Dive, make your depth six six feet, steep angle. Helm, ahead full!"

"Sixty-six feet, aye, twenty-degree up bubble."

"Ahead full, Helm, aye. Maneuvering answers, all ahead full."

The deck inclined upward, and the crew grabbed for handholds. Their bodies strained against seat belts as the deck became a staircase-steep ramp.

"Eight hundred feet, sir."

"Very good," Gustavson said.

"Six hundred feet, sir."

"Sonar, Conn, coming to PD, no baffle clear," the OOD said to his boom mike. He was standing behind the number two periscope, which was still stowed in its well because the ship's speed was too high to raise it.

"Conn, Sonar, aye."

"Four hundred feet, sir."

"Helm, all back one-third. Dive, flatten the angle to up ten."

The deck trembled as the backing bell was answered. Phillips had to slow the ship before it emerged above the thermal layer, where a dangerously close surface contact could be lurking.

"Two hundred feet, sir!"

"Helm, all stop, mark speed seven knots."

"Helm, aye, maneuvering answers all stop. Speed ten knots."

"One five zero feet, sir," the diving officer barked.

"Mark speed seven knots, sir," the helmsman called.

"Lookaround number two scope," the OOD called, an order that required the diving officer and helm to report the ship's depth and speed to avoid shearing off a periscope and opening a huge hole in the hull.

"Depth, one one zero feet, sir."

"Speed, six knots, sir."

"Up scope!" Gustavson rotated the hydraulic control ring in the overhead, and the stainless steel pole lifted out of the well. He bent over to catch the optic module as it came out of the well, snapping down the grips as the module appeared.

"Dark, dark, dark," Gustavson said, training the periscope view upward to see the underside of any hulls that might be close enough to collide with. He rotated himself around in frantically fast circles. "No shapes, no shadows," he called.

"Eight zero feet, sir."

"Scope's breaking," Gustavson said as the periscope became awash in the phosphorescent foam of the sea at night. He continued driving the pole around in rapid circles, one per second. "Scope's breaking . . ."

"Seven five feet."

"Scope's breaking—"

"Seven zero feet!"

"Scope's clear, low-power surface search," Gustavson said, puffing from the exertion of spinning around the periscope.

The control room was silent, waiting for Gustavson to cry either "Emergency deep" or its functional equivalent, "Oh, shit!" which would be greeted with the same emergency actions to get the ship down fast, but finally Gustavson announced, "No close contacts."

Bruce Phillips reached for the red radio handset, the UHF satellite secure-voice tactical frequency named Nestor for some forgotten reason. He glanced at the call sign sheet, raising his eyebrows at his call sign and the *Devilfish*'s.

"Ricky, this is Lucy," he said into the red handset. "Ricky, this is Lucy, over."

The burst of blooping static immediately followed.

"Lucy, this is Ricky, flash message to follow from Fred. Message reads, coordinate readout, alpha at zero golf, bravo at eight hotel, charlie at two foxtrot, delta at nine mike, echo at six tango, foxtrot at five sierra." The Royal Navy executive officer, Roger Whatney, hurriedly scribbled the coordinates to the six Rising Sun submarines as fast as they were read off, then typed furiously, entering the data into the BSY-4 fire-control system. "Immediate release of all packages, break, break, acknowledge, over."

Phillips snapped his fingers at Whatney to get the data into the plot, and leaned over position two of the fire-control system. Three of the Rising Sun vessels were inside the range circle of the Vortex missiles. The ship was carrying them on the outside of the hull like a bandolier, since they were much too big to carry inside the ship. Plus, the launching mechanism for the old Mod Bravos was an external tube because the older missile could not be launched from a torpedo tube without rupturing the hull.

"Ricky, this is Lucy, tell Fred we are mailing packages. Lucy out."

"Sir," Roger Whatney said, "targets one, two, and four are in range."

Phillips had kept Vortex missile power applied ever since they'd entered the operation area. He'd risked the gyros overheating, but now he was glad he had, because now there would be no waiting.

"Weps, detach muzzle caps tubes ten, one, and nine. Lock in solutions as follows, target one to tube one, target two to tube ten, target four to tube nine."

"Locked in, Captain."

"Very well. Firing point procedures, tube one, target one."

"Ship ready," Gustavson called.

"Solution ready," Whatney said.

"Weapon ready, tube one, target one," the weapons officer said. "Launch auto-sequence start on tube one, target one. Computer has the countdown—"

"Sonar, Conn, Vortex launch!" Gustavson yelled,

warning the sonarmen to rip off their headsets or they would burst an eardrum.

"Three, two, one, igni—"

The rest of the weapons officer's countdown was cut off by the earthshaking roar of the huge Vortex missile solid-rocket fuel igniting and blasting the rocket away from the ship.

"Tube ten, target two, firing point procedures."

The same litany came again. The crew was a tightly orchestrated team, each with their own say in the sequence, until the computer was handed the task of coordinating the final weapon launch.

Ten seconds after receiving the Nestor radio information, Bruce Phillips had three Vortex missiles attacking three of the Rising Sun-class ships.

He pulled a fresh Havana cigar from his coverall breast pocket. "Now we're cooking," he said to no one in particular. He lit it with his USS *Greenville* lighter. The cigar came to life, and as he stoked it, the cloud from it grew a yard in diameter.

The first explosion seemed as if it had come from just next door. The second was more distant, the third farther out. After each explosion, a small cheer rose up in the room. Phillips did nothing to dampen the enthusiasm. His ears rang from the noise of the launches and the explosions. But this once he didn't care.

The ship had remained at periscope depth, and Phillips grabbed the red phone.

"Ricky, this is Lucy, over."

"Ricky, over."

"Three packages in the mail. You got receipts?" *Did we hit the bastards?*

"Lucy, this is Ricky, affirmative."

The roar of the crowd drowned out the next announcement on the Nestor.

SS-403 *ARCTIC STORM*

"What in heaven's name was that?" Chu asked.

"And where did it come from, Navigator?" Lo Sun joined in, his voice tinged with anger. Why hadn't either the explosions or the loud transients preceding them been detected by Lieutenant Commander Xhiu at the sensor panel?

"Yes, sir, checking now. The display is coming up, loud transients from bearing one one two. I have sonar blueouts on the bearings to the *Volcano, Lightning Bolt,* and *Tsunami,* Admiral."

How quickly the tide could turn, Chu thought bitterly. He'd just lost three of his ships, and his damned sensor operator was clueless.

"Navigator, feed the bearings to weps. Weps, program Nagasaki's 24, 23, and 22 for submerged targets ST-15, 16, and 17, all at bearing and range of transient starts."

Xhiu worked his panel frantically. Lo Sun leaned over Chu's shoulder and whispered, "Admiral, why three torpedoes?"

"Might be three ships," he answered.

"Sir, we only have eighteen fish left. You shoot three, we're down to fifteen. And if we lost the three ships, our squadron weapon load is lower. Do we really need three weapons?"

Chu glared at Lo. "Yes," he said, and Lo shut his mouth.

"Gas-generator high-impulse launches, high-speed search to the targets," Chu commanded.

It took six and a half minutes to get the three torpedoes out. Completely unsatisfactory, Chu thought. They were beginning to make mistakes, forgetting to flood tubes, apply torpedo power. The sooner the mission was over, the better. Only now, if he had lost three submarines, and he was fairly sure he had, he might be down a hundred Nagasaki torpedoes.

At least the weapons were away, he thought. Now on to the next nagging problem, and that was, how had three loud weapons been launched from a submarine

that he was not able to detect? He plotted the bearing
to the transients on the chart pad. Then he made a decision. He'd drive down the bearing line to the Americans,
confirm the kill, then get set up on the convoy.

CHAPTER 34

"Captain, Sonar, we have multiple torpedoes launched by the eastern Rising Sun toward the *Piranha.*"

Pacino sat up, startled. He found Patton standing outside the attack-center eggshell canopies. "We've got to warn Phillips," Pacino said, reaching for the Nestor handset himself.

"Lucy, this is Ricky, over!"

There was no reply.

"Lucy, this is Ricky, come in, over!"

Beads of sweat broke out on Pacino's forehead and ran down, one droplet hitting his eye and making it sting.

"Goddamn it, Bruce, pick up the phone," he said to no one.

USS *PIRANHA*, SSN-23

Phillips lit up his second cigar of the night, or the first of the day, since the local time chronometer had just clicked past midnight on the wee hours of Friday morning.

"Thank God it's Friday," Phillips mumbled to himself.

"Captain, two more in range," Whatney called, excited.

Phillips narrowed his eyes and addressed the crew. "Firing-point procedures, tube three, target three," he said, puffing the stogy.

"Lucy, this is Ricky, over."

Phillips rolled his eyes in annoyance. The radio blared insistently in the room. He kept giving orders and listening to reports as he reached distractedly for the phone.

"Ship ready," Gustavson called.

"Solution ready," Whatney reported.

"Weapon tube three, target five, and launch auto-sequence start. Computer has the countdown—"

"Ricky, this is Lucy, I copy, over," Phillips said to the phone, concentrating on the Vortex launch.

"Lucy, immediate execute. Clear datum to the east, emergency fl—"

The radio call was interrupted by the violent roar of the Vortex missile as it left tube number three on the starboard side, where the radio console was located. It took several seconds before Phillips could hear anything.

When he did, he clicked the transmit button and said, "Ricky, this is Lucy, say again?"

"He didn't hear you, Admiral."

"Lucy, this is Ricky! Immediate execute. Clear datum to the east, emergency flank! I say again, clear datum to the east, emergency flank, ASAP, ASAP, ASAP! Do you copy me, over?"

The reply was static-filled.

"Ricky, this is Lucy, say again, over."

"Lucy, this is Ricky, clear datum, dammit! Get out of there now! Withdraw! Do you copy?"

Bruce Phillips glared at the phone.

"Weps, tube eight, target five, firing-point procedures."

"Lucy, this is Fred, immediate execute, clear datum east, ASAP! Do you copy?"

Phillips made a face.

"Ship ready, sir."

Phillips made a decision. Micromanagement had its place, but he was two Rising Suns away from a Distinguished Submariners' Medal, and he'd be damned if he was going to clear datum. Yet ignoring the radio call wasn't his style. He'd confront the radio caller directly.

And this time he'd be damned if he'd use the stupid call signs.

"Admiral, this is Phillips, negative clear datum. I say again, negative negative negative. *Piranha* is at the firing point. I repeat, *Piranha* is at the firing point, negative clear datum. Phillips out."

He looked at his officer of the deck while turning the volume down on the radio.

"OOD, lower the periscope, take her deep, one thousand feet, best listening depth."

"Aye, sir," the officer of the deck acknowledged, making the orders to the helm and diving officer.

"Well," Phillips said to the weapons officer, peeved. "What are you looking at? Status on the weapon, let's go! Shoot eight!"

"Computer auto-sequence start at five, four, three . . ."

The three Nagasaki torpedoes soared through the water toward the target ahead, the one designated only as ST-15, the fifteenth submerged target encountered that campaign.

The weapons ate up the distance at eighty-five clicks, against a target moving at ten clicks at periscope depth, the range getting closer and closer.

Patton stared at Pacino.

"I don't believe it. He doesn't want to hear there are three plasma torpedoes on the way inbound," Patton sputtered.

"Shoot a Vortex at him," Pacino commanded.

"What?"

"Now, John, let's go, get a Vortex missile in the water, aim it for the *Piranha,* ceiling setting enabled, and make damned sure you disable the terminal-mode detonation. Move!"

A look of understanding dawned on Patton's face.

"Line up tube one, Vortex Mod Charlie, swimout mode, ceiling setting enabled, terminal detonation disabled, target—the USS *Piranha*. Firing-point procedures, *Piranha,* Vortex one. Report!"

"Sir, what are you doing?" XO Walt Hornick asked.

"Launch the damned thing now," Patton roared. The crew responded sluggishly, not understanding why they would be ordered to shoot at their own submarine, but Patton obviously did not have the time or the inclination to tell them.

It took fifty seconds for the Vortex Mod Charlie to clear the tube and ignite the solid-rocket fuel. Unlike Bruce Phillips' Mod Bravos, which left their launching sleeves under full thrust, the Mod Charlies had a torpedo-like booster engine to get the smaller missile clear of the tube and a few ship lengths away, allowing the solid-rocket fuel to ignite only when the missile was one thousand feet away going fifty knots.

Pacino ducked into station four to see what would happen. Would Phillips finally react?

"Sir," Hornick said, "why did we put friendly fire on the *Piranha*?"

"Think, XO," Patton said. "He didn't hear our order for him to clear datum; he wanted to keep shooting. He can't hear a Nagasaki torpedo, not even three, not while he's lighting off solid-rocket-fueled weapons, and I doubt he'd hear them anyway. So the next sound he'll hear is an *inbound* Vortex missile aimed at him. He'll go absolutely crazy and blow to the surface and shut the ship down. The Vortex is set with ceiling mode enabled, so anything it sees that is at a depth above two hundred feet it'll ignore. So Phillips will try to avoid the Vortex missile, and by doing that he'll avoid the Nagasakis he can't see. They'll completely miss him and swim on by, deep."

"Now all we need is to see what happens to the last two Rising Suns and Phillips," Pacino said on his boom mike.

"Loss of battle control!" came over on his headset just as the system flickered out and died.

Pacino climbed out of station four, miserable. It had crashed yet again.

The explosion that came next was deafening.

*   *   *

"Conn, Sonar, I have an incoming Vortex missile."

"Looks like *Devilfish* wants part of the action," Phillips said to Whatney.

"Conn, Sonar, this missile is constant bearing, decreasing range. Conn, Sonar, recommend evade!" The master chief's voice suddenly became distorted as he screamed into his circuit. "Captain, Sonar, the missile is targeting us! Recommend immediate emergency blow!"

Phillips didn't stop to wonder what was going on. He turned his head to the chief of the watch at the ballast-control panel and screamed, *"Emergency blow, both groups! Helm, ahead full! Dive, thirty-degree up angle!"*

No one needed to be told twice. The emergency-blow levers, two stainless steel levers in the overhead, put ultrahigh-pressure air to the ballast tanks. The draining was as quick and violent as if an explosion had happened in the tanks. The room was engulfed in a symphony of ear-splitting noise as the air blew into the ballast tanks. *Piranha* drove to the surface at a thirty-degree angle, the full bell and the blow and the angle bringing her up from a thousand feet to the surface in less than two minutes.

The ship was traveling at thirty-four knots when it broke the surface above. The parabolic cross-section nose cone penetrated the waves first, bringing with it tons of seawater. The cylindrical length of the ship followed, the sail emerging, then the aft cylinder, until the tail came out of the water. The giant submarine then crashed back into the ocean and vanished to a depth of two hundred fifty feet, then returned for the second time, bobbing and rolling on the surface.

"Scram the reactor!" Phillips ordered. "Shut down the ship!" The OOD passed the word aft to maneuvering, and within seconds the lights flickered and the air conditioning shut down. All but one console of the fire-control system went dead.

"Sonar, status of the missile?"

"Still inbound, sir, getting closer," the master chief said.

Phillips tossed the soggy cigar, started to pull out a

new one, but then put it back in his pocket. He tapped his feet, waiting.

Four hundred feet beneath the USS *Piranha* the Vortex Mod Charlie passed. Its detonation circuits told it to disregard targets shallower than two hundred feet, so it sailed by the *Piranha* and continued on until its fuel ran out forty seconds later. Then, as programmed, it shut down and sank to the bottom of the sea.

The three Nagasaki torpedoes became confused and sailed far beyond where their target should have been. They didn't have a ceiling setting, and were allowed to climb all the way to the surface. But at a depth of 178 feet lay a steep thermal layer. The water above was stirred by the wind and waves, heated by the sun. Below, the water temperature hovered a tenth of a degree above freezing. The Nagasaki torpedoes were deep, searching using passive sonar—listening only. As a result, any sound from above the layer reached downward only when the source was directly overhead. Sound waves out ahead of the torpedo, to the side, or behind bounced off the thermal layer like light bouncing off a mirror.

Waiting quietly above the layer, the *Piranha* confused the torpedoes. They drove back and forth and in circles before detonating in plasma explosions. But by that time they had drifted many miles away from the *Piranha*'s position.

The explosions that had come after the *Devilfish*'s battle-control system had crashed had been two Rising Sun submarines, put down by *Piranha*'s last Vortex shots. The sea was empty. Almost.

Piranha had survived. Yet there remained one last Rising Sun submarine, the *Arctic Storm*.

CHAPTER 35

USS *DEVILFISH*, SSNX-1

"Status of Cyclops?" Patton asked.

"Down hard," Colleen O'Shaughnessy said on the battle circuit.

"Can we launch Vortex missiles in manual?" Pacino asked.

"Should be able to," Colleen said.

"John, let's get fifteen of them out there in a saturation attack. And get someone on the horn to *Piranha*. Tell Phillips under no circumstances shall he submerge."

"Aye, sir."

Pacino leaned against the conn handrail, shutting his eyes, listening to the battle litany as they attempted to open the torpedo-tube muzzle doors to program the Vortex missiles to go out on a specific bearing line and look for contacts. A fan of fifteen Vortexes ought to do it, and if they didn't, perhaps by then the Cyclops system would be back and they could actually target the last Rising Sun.

The Vortex launches went on for a half hour, the solid-rocket motors igniting and flying off into space, looking for the Red sub. There was no way to tell if the missiles ever hit their target. Over the next hour, explosions started to be heard. That could just be their termination detonations, since the missiles were programmed to explode as they ran out of fuel, just in case by dumb luck they were close to a target.

Pacino felt a heavy weight of exhaustion fall on his shoulders. He had lost five Pegasus patrol planes, twelve

688s, and perhaps even the *Piranha,* all in a few hours' time.

He looked up to see Patton walking into the room from the forward centerline passageway.

"Colleen says she'll be up in about two minutes," he said.

Pacino donned his virtual-reality helmet and climbed into the darkened station four, waiting to see what had happened since they had gone blind and deaf.

SS-403 *ARCTIC STORM*

The missiles kept on coming.

Chu knew enough to turn tail and run, but before he did, he made sure he put out his last three high-speed Nagasakis to the bearing of the ship that had launched these miserable plasma missiles at him. Once the three weapons were away, Chu turned and ran west at maximum speed at maximum depth to try to evade the saturation attack.

It would turn out to be too little and too late. Plasma missile number six detonated a kilometer astern of his position, a termination detonation as it ran out of fuel. The explosion shock wave blasted through the water at sonic speed and hammered the *Arctic Storm*. If Chu hadn't been strapped into his console, he would have died, but as it was, the five-point harness held tightly, his body bruised by the G-forces, but not broken. But although Chu survived, the ship was not as lucky.

The reactor shut down.

The ship began to flood through a seawater cooling system.

The periscope no longer worked, nor would any of the masts or antennae.

All that was an easy day compared to the worst casualty. When the ship took the shock wave, the Second Captain died on impact.

The upper functions of the processing suites, the DNA parallel processors, ceased functioning as their cabinets broke open and the soup of DNA spilled to the decks. When the upper functions died, the lower functions of the neural network became confused and actually began working at cross purposes, a sort of machine equivalent to the convulsions of a headless chicken.

Although the ship was whole, the loss of the Second Captain meant they had to abandon ship.

And Chu couldn't abandon ship by surfacing it, because whoever had launched more than a dozen plasma missiles at him would not stop shooting because he was on the surface.

No, he'd get the crew out the escape hatch, then scuttle the ship. With luck they'd be picked up by one of his trawlers.

"Gentlemen, your attention, please," he said. "Leave your posts and assemble at the forward escape trunk. We are abandoning ship without surfacing. Any questions? Now!"

At the escape trunk, Chu found a dozen air hoods and surface survival kits, and he sent Xhiu for their own emergency radio transmitters and beacons. Once Chu opened the lower hatch, they climbed up into the chamber. The deck of the ship was starting to list slightly to port, taking on a more pronounced down angle. With his crew in the escape trunk, Chu shut the lower hatch, ordered the men into their hoods, and flooded the trunk. A hydraulic lever opened the upper hatch, leaving the men in a protected section separated from the upper hatch by an air pocket on the other side of a wall. Chu found the hose manifold, filled each man's hood with pressurized air, then shoved him out the open upper-escape trunk hatch. Last to go, he filled his own hood, ducked under the air barrier into the cold water, and climbed up out of the hatch.

For a passing second he regretted leaving the ship to die. He tapped twice on the hull in a gesture of farewell, and pulled himself out of the hatch. The buoyancy of the hood pulled him up to the surface, and Chu was careful to blow out all the way up. The air pressurized to one hundred twenty meters' depth would blow up his lungs if he didn't exhale hard.

In twenty seconds he broke the surface. The initial members of his crew had already inflated two rafts and were clicking the radios, trying to find help.

"Any luck, Lo?" he asked.

"I got through to Tianjin. They should be sending a seaplane for us. They'll be here in about two hours."

"Good."

"Admiral? Do you think we won?"

Chu considered the question. It had seemed so obvious to him that they had lost that the question almost seemed academic.

"We sank their first task force, then twelve of their submarines, five of their maritime-patrol planes, and they killed five of our subs and paralyzed our ship, forcing us to abandon her."

A booming roar sounded from beneath them, the sound muffled by the depth.

"That was either the ship imploding from the deep or someone finishing her off with a torpedo," Chu said. "Anyway, our success is to be measured by how well and how long we held off the American landing force. If the Americans decide this sea is still too risky to cross, then we will have won a huge victory. If they decide they have vanquished us and proceed to White China to fight our forces, then we will have suffered a tremendous defeat. My opinion? We did our best, and I owe each one of you a debt of thanks for your work, for risking your lives."

"Hear, hear," Lo Sun said.

USS PIRANHA, SSN-23

"Things are pretty quiet out here now," Master Chief Henry said.

"No missiles, no torpedoes, no Rising Suns."

"Correct."

"Let's restart the reactor, submerge, and get out of here," Bruce Phillips said.

USS DEVILFISH, SSNX-1

"Cyclops will be starting up in three, two, one—"

It would be a relief, Pacino thought, to be able to see the world around them. He was wrong.

The screens flickered to life again. Pacino strapped on his helmet.

"Goddamn it," one voice.

"Shit," a second.

"Torpedo in the water!" a third.

"Emergency flank!" Patton said. "Course one six zero!"

Pacino's display showed the *Piranha* on the surface, no one nearby, no Rising Suns, but one lonely incoming Nagasaki torpedo, less than one thousand feet from their position and targeted at the *Devilfish*.

The deck began to shake as the ship sped up to emergency flank. Pacino sincerely hoped that they could outrun it. He was thinking that thought when Patton made some odd orders.

"OOD, get on the circuit one and order all hands into emergency breathing masks."

"Aye, sir."

The circuit one announcing system blared out, "Torpedo in the water! All hands don EABs."

"OOD, arm the fire-suppression system."

"Aye, sir, um, Captain, won't that kill the Cyclops and all the other electronics aboard if we use that?"

"Better than dying in a fire," Patton said.

Pacino looked at him but decided not to interfere. Maybe it was just a quirk he had come upon after the *Annapolis* sinking.

Pacino strapped on his gas mask and plugged it into a receptacle. The air he found was dry and canned and hot.

The deck continued to vibrate beneath their feet as

they ran. Pacino wondered if this torpedo was programmed to execute a termination-run detonation. His
next thought was of Colleen, whether she was wearing
her gas mask, and what she was doing. He stood up and
reached for his hose connection at the manifold, planning to unplug it and walk forward to check on Colleen.

He never made it.

The termination detonation of the Nagasaki torpedo
knocked him to the deck. Then there was only darkness.

CHAPTER 36

The first few seconds after the torpedo impact seemed almost calm, due to the temporary deafness experienced by the crew.

Pacino found himself on the deck, lying on top of someone groaning in pain. He untangled his emergency-air-mask hose and pushed himself up. Seeing a handrail of the periscope stand above his head, he grabbed it and hauled himself to his feet. The lights overhead were flickering, but electrical bus fluctuations were normal after loss of the reactor. As the electrical turbines dropped off the grid, the battery's motor-generators picked up, dumping the nonvital buses and carrying the vital loads.

He looked over at the ship-control panel. The ship was maintaining depth. That meant the helmsman was still able to control the ship's angle and the planes. There didn't seem to be any immediate danger. They'd have to restart the reactor—that was strange, he thought, that the officer in maneuvering hadn't reported the reactor scram. The engine-order telegraph was set at ALL STOP. Pacino craned his neck to find Patton, who was pulling himself up from the other side of the commander's panel. He seemed okay, as did the officer of the deck. Each of them set about adjusting the rubber masks on their faces, then the hoses and regulators clipped to their belts.

Battle control was down again, but after a shock like they'd just experienced, Pacino expected it to be in trouble.

All told, they'd been able to outrun the Nagasaki torpedo, and they had come out whole. Pacino found Patton's eyes, and pointed at his gas mask. The masks were now unnecessary with the ship relatively safe. He was reaching for the straps when a booming voice stopped him dead.

The word came into the control room on the circuit four emergency voice line, which amplified a voice in any of the ship's phone circuits and broadcasted it over the ship-wide PA system. The man on the phone shouted:

"Fire in the torpedo room! Fire in the torpedo room, weapon-fuel fire!"

Pacino felt a surge of adrenaline slam him in the gut. A weapon-fuel fire was the death certificate of any nuclear submarine, because peroxide torpedo fuel, in the booster stages of the Vortex missiles and the main fuel for the two room-stowed Mark 52 torpedoes, burned without a source of oxygen, the oxidizer chemically contained in the fuel itself. While this made for ideal torpedo propellant, it meant disaster if a weapon broke open and began to burn, because there was no way to put the fire out. The peroxide would burn until it burned all the fuel, and the fumes from it were so toxic that a single breath would drop a two hundred fifty-pound man in his tracks. Pacino had been faced with this issue during the design phase of the SSNX, and had met the challenge two ways. He had installed a liquid nitrogen fire-suppression system in the room, a liquid nitrogen hose forward and one aft, and had stiffened the bulkheads of the torpedo room. With the hatches to the room shut, the room could be flooded by opening it up to sea and pumping seawater through the compartment. The water wouldn't stop the fuel fire, because it would simply keep burning underwater, but the water flowing through the flooded space could possibly cool the burning fuel enough to keep the hull from rupturing until the fire was burned out.

He had run simulations of a weapon-fuel fire, and every one had showed the ship sinking, the fuel fire too catastrophic to recover from. He had made a modification, ejecting the torpedoes that weren't on fire, and by doing that the nitrogen and flooding systems could handle the casualty, with skillful ship and depth control.

His thoughts flashed to Colleen. Her computer room was located just above the weapons. An image came to mind, of her struggling in a toxic-fuel fire, dropping to her knees and collapsing. Before he realized what he was doing, he took a deep breath and disconnected his hose and dashed through the aft door. Since he was not a member of ship's company, he had no assignment at battle stations or during a casualty, although U.S. Navy regulations were conflicted about his role at a time like this.

He didn't give a damn right now. He had to put out that fire. He dashed to the ladder outside the executive officer's stateroom. He slid down the slick stainless steel handrails, his feet dangling, until his shoes hit the lower-level deckplates. He raced through the berthing room to the forward door, the door to the torpedo room.

The door was a heavy steel hatch with a small window set at eye level. All he could see in the window was black smoke and the haphazard orange flash of flames. For a fraction of a second Pacino froze in place. If he opened the door, he would admit air and oxygen into the existing conflagration, making it worse. But then, he reasoned, what was burning inside didn't need the oxygen out here; it had plenty in liquid form.

He opened a locker marked OBA and pulled out a large contraption resembling a scuba buoyancy compensator, a sort of artificial lung with a gas mask—OBA stood for oxygen-breathing apparatus. He pulled it on, leaving the mask hanging by its hose, and grabbed a cartridge, a chemical oxygen generator, from the rack inside the cabinet. He inserted the canister, pulled the pin on it, and lit it off. The cartridge took thirty seconds to come up to temperature and generate the oxygen Pacino would need inside the space.

"Fire in the torpedo room," the circuit one PA system boomed from a speaker in the overhead. "Fire in the torpedo room. Casualty assistance team, lay forward.

Admiral Pacino is in charge at the scene. Ship is emergency-blowing to the surface. Prepare to flood the torpedo room."

Pacino was joined by a burly man, his shirt soaked in sweat.

"Who are you?" Pacino asked through his gas mask. Taking one last breath, he ditched the mask and put his face into the new mask of the OBA. The air in it was rubbery and hot, but he took a breath. It would keep him alive, if barely.

"Chief Hanson, torpedoman, sir," the burly man said. "I'm getting an OBA on myself."

"I'm going in and forward," Pacino said to the chief. "I'll hit the liquid-nitrogen suppression system. If I can, I'll get the LIN hose on the fire from forward, you get it on from aft. Then let's get the room empty. You know how to handle weapons from the aft panel?"

"Yessir," Hanson said.

Four more men showed up. Hanson had already donned his OBA, his canister lit off.

"Get them in OBAs and into the room, Chief. Let's get these missiles out of here! If we get a solid-rocket-fuel fire, we're all dead men!"

The solid-rocket fuel of a Vortex missile would put a four-foot hole in the hull, pressurize everything inside to a thousand pounds per square inch, and fill the ship with hydrogen cyanide, a gas capable of killing a man from a teaspoonful in a gymnasium.

"Sir, you've got to get into the steam suit or you'll be burned alive!"

"No time!" Pacino shouted.

"Take the gloves, then!"

Pacino strapped on the gloves the chief handed him. The chief hit the hatch lever and opened the hatch. Pacino stepped in, not believing what he saw or felt. It was as if someone had unlatched the gate of hell itself. Flames blasted at him through the hatchway as he ducked in. Rolling black smoke engulfed him. By feel Pacino ran around to the side, where the liquid-nitrogen suppression emergency button was. Like so many cures on the sub, this one was potentially as dangerous as the threat. The liquid nitrogen, or LIN, at minus 190 degrees was cold enough to kill human tissue on contact. A splash on a hand doomed it to amputation; a drop on the skin caused a cryogenic burn. In addition, as liquid nitrogen vaporized, it filled the space with nitrogen gas. A single breath of pure nitrogen could instantly shut down the functioning of the human respiration center of the brain. A breath of high-concentration nitrogen would kill a man, switching off his breathing like a switch. For that reason the liquid-nitrogen fire-suppression system was not entrusted to a computer or electrical system, but set off physically by a button. Pacino felt the cover over the button, yanked it off against a massive spring, and hit the mushroom cap,

The room hissed like a giant cat as liquid nitrogen hit the flames and weapons. The LIN system sprayed the room for a full two minutes, filling the space with the inert gas. Immediately, Pacino ducked under a hood beneath the button to avoid the fluid hitting his poorly protected skin. He could hear the hissing easing as the system ran out of LIN, and he stood.

Hanson's voice erupted behind him. "Forward, Admiral. I've got the aft hose. Jenson! Get the valve!"

Pacino advanced into the flames. Intense heat invaded every pore of his skin. His flame-resistant coveralls started to smolder, his sleeves smoking as the material caught. By the time Pacino reached the middle of the room, he realized he was on fire.

And there was absolutely nothing he could do about it. The first faint breeze of fear touched him, chilling him, slowing his steps. The alarm picked up until panic filled him, a gale force forcing away all logic and reason. The effect of the paralyzing panic was more frightening than the fact that his clothes were on fire.

He'd just about stopped moving when he felt a body beneath his right foot. The form lay facedown on the deck, dead. The scorched skin of the body crunched under Pacino's foot. Suddenly he wondered if the body was Colleen.

Colleen! his mind screamed. She would be directly over his head, and she might be dying right now. He had to get to her, he had to save her. With that thought the panic that had grabbed him by the throat was thrown off. Pacino ran to the forward bulkhead, his heart pounding, not with fear but with anger. He had finally found the one for him, and he wasn't going to be robbed of her before they even had a chance to get started.

At the panel, he grabbed the LIN hose, opened the valve. The liquid nitrogen blasted out at the hottest spot of the fire—he couldn't even see it, he could only feel it. The room seemed to cool for just a second, enough for him to scream at the chief:

"Jettison the weapons! Chief!"

"Mark 52s going now, Admiral," the chief called back.

The next sound was the crash of a torpedo tube launching a weapon. Pacino shut the LIN hose nozzle, waiting. Vaguely he was aware that the nitrogen around him was putting out the flames on his clothes. He couldn't feel any damage to his skin, but then, perhaps that was because he was numb. He pushed the thought away as a second crash sounded. The second torpedo tube had launched. A third and fourth tube-launch crash slammed his eardrums. The room grew hot again, and Pacino sprayed the LIN hose in spurts. The LIN in the aft section began to hiss as the supply ran low.

More torpedo tube doors opened. Vortex missiles rolled silently into the gaping maws on hydraulic rams as Hanson fed the tubes, then launched them into the sea. Pacino kept spraying, hoping the LIN would hold out until the weapons were jettisoned.

Finally the LIN hose ran out. Abandoning it, Pacino felt his way through the black smoke to a vertical runged ladder heading up to a hatch in the overhead.

"Chief, I'm out of LIN. Are you done yet?"

A torpedo tube-launch crash was his answer.

"Two more, sir!"

"Hurry, the flames are starting again!"

Hanson rammed in a Vortex, shut the breech door,

and launched the tube. Then he opened the final breech door on the port side.

But it might be too late, Pacino thought as the fire roared out at him with renewed fury. The sound of it was enough to stop a man's heart. A vibration started jangling at his breastbone—the timer on the canister. It had been set for fifteen minutes, the unit only good for eighteen. Pacino had to wait, though, because if he went through the hatch now, the flames would spread up into the computer room, and the toxic gas of the smoke would kill Colleen within a few seconds. But if he stayed, the flames would kill him. He could already feel his lungs straining to pull the oxygen out of the rubber lungs.

The final torpedo crash came as the flames licked up into the overhead. Pacino could feel his hair starting to singe, his rubber mask melting, the oxygen going, going. He began to feel dizzy, dim words coming into his mind, the words swimming slowly at him, his grip on the ladder becoming tentative.

"Flooding the space, Admiral! Get out the hatch! I'm going aft!"

Pacino heard the mighty roaring of water flooding the space. Within moments he felt the cool of something at his feet, the water. It rose quickly to his chin, cooling him, mercifully cool after walking through hell. The OBA gave up then, and Pacino ditched the mask. The toxic smoke of the fire invaded his lungs. A black dizziness overcame him, sapping his mental strength. He forgot what he was about to do. He knew it was important, but it seemed to float just out of reach. The water level was now just two feet below the hatch to the computer room.

Pacino's head collided with the hatch-release wheel. That made him remember, he had to turn to spin the hatch. But he was too weak. The water kept rising as he tried to get a grip on the wheel. *Counterclockwise, you have to turn the wheel counterclockwise to open it.* He pulled as hard as he could, and the hatch undogged. He pushed on the hatch to open it, but succeeded only in pushing himself into the water. The water had grown hot from the fire. The fuel was still burning even under a roomful of seawater. They would need to flush water through the space to keep it cool, he thought, keep the fire from eating through the hull. At last he found a ladder rung, and with one last push of his hand and foot, he opened the hatch.

Up into the opening he put his hand, but he couldn't seem to get a grip. The water level rose fully over his head, claiming him, the air gone. As he sank back into the water, he thought that maybe it just didn't matter anymore.

USS *PIRANHA*, SSN-23

"Aircraft noises from bearing two seven zero, Captain," Master Chief Henry called.

"Take her upstairs, Off'sa'deck," Bruce Phillips commanded.

The ship came shallow, Phillips himself taking the periscope as the ship came up. Water and foam washed over the lens until the scope broke through, the film of water washing away. It was pitch black outside, with no close contacts.

Phillips did an air search, but he saw nothing.

"Sonar, Captain, jet or prop?"

"Turboprop, Captain. Be careful, it could be maritime patrol. Maybe the Reds have MPA planes."

"OOD, arm the SLAAM 80," Phillips ordered. The Mark 80 missile, called a SLAAM, was a submarine-launched anti-air missile, mounted in the sail, capable of finding a heat source on an aircraft and bringing it down.

"Shifting to infrared," Phillips said. Immediately he picked out an airplane flying low on the horizon toward them. The effect was strange, the infrared showing heat sources as patterns of light, allowing Phillips to see inside the plane at the interior consoles and equipment, a sort of X-ray vision. The plane came down lower, then hit the water.

"Seaplane!" Phillips called. "The plane's landed, bearing mark!"

"Two one zero."

"Helm, right full rudder, steady course two one zero, all ahead two-thirds."

The ship came around, closing on the seaplane rolling in the swells, its propellers stopped, quiet on the water. Phillips shifted to high-power magnification, making out the form of men leaning out a hatch to pull other men in from the water.

"He's doing a rescue. it's the Reds," he said, not quite believing it. "OOD, take the scope, surface the ship, take it over to the seaplane at full. Use HP air, no time to use the blower, and rig the bridge for surface. Move it!"

Phillips grabbed Whatney and ran to the middle level, to the small-arms locker in the centerline passageway. Whatney fiddled with his key, finding the right one. The locker opened, and Phillips loaded Whatney with weapons. Grabbing an automatic M-20 rifle and a Bereta 9mm pistol, he ran for the upper level.

At the ladder going up into the tunnel to the bridge on top of the sail, he bolted upward, making the thirty steps to the bridge in record time. He emerged through the grating at the top of the hatch to the night air, crisp and cool and smelling wonderful after he'd been locked in the ship for so long.

A bow wave washed up the bulbous shape of the cigar of the hull, splashing spray up into the bridge. Phillips grabbed binoculars and hoisted them to his eyes. There, dead ahead by five hundred yards, the massive Red Chinese seaplane was hauling floating survivors into the hatch. The men seemed in no hurry. Phillips aimed the M-20 at the men in the hatchway, the rifle set to full automatic.

"Hey, assholes!" he shouted, then let loose with a burst of automatic-rifle fire. The bullets slammed into the tail of the seaplane, into the water, the racket loud and furious. Whatney, joining him on the bridge, aimed his M-20 and let loose with a burst of automatic rounds.

Under the hail of bullets, the raft exploded and sank.
Bullets stitched curving lines in the aluminum airframe
of the plane. The night was split by the roaring of a
turbojet engine spinning its propeller. The plane was attempting to get away. Phillips shouted down the tunnel,
"Ahead flank." The second prop roared to life. Closer
now, he aimed his rifle and hit the trigger, but the clip
was empty.

"Clip," he shouted in frustration. Then Whatney's rifle
clicked impotently. Phillips pulled his 9mm handgun out
and fired it out over the water, but he was still too far
away to guarantee a hit. "Dammit," he cursed as the
9mm clicked in his hand, out of ammo. The two props
came to full revolutions. The seaplane rolled on the sea,
the wake behind it white and phosphorescent as the
plane sailed off to the west.

"Let's shoot it down," Phillips said to Whatney. "Get
down there and tell them to shoot a Mark 80 at that son
of a bitch. He's getting away."

"Sir, it won't fire from the surface. It's a gas generator—come on, we've got to submerge so we can launch
a missile."

Phillips slid down the ladder, pausing only to shut the
hatch. "Go on, get this tub submerged, quick!"

But as he emerged into the control room, the OOD
shook his head from the periscope.

"We can't get her down. Sir, even with max bow
planes at flank, the buoyancy's too high. All main ballast
tank vents are open, and the SLAAM 80s will just explode in their tubes if we try to launch them dry. He's
gone, sir. I can't even see him anymore."

"Dammit," Phillips cursed. "After all that mess those
idiots caused, and now they get away scot free."

Then he looked at Whatney—both men said the word
at the same time:

"Air strike."

Phillips stepped to the radio panel, yelling into the
overhead open microphone to the radiomen to bring up
the convoy aircraft carrier. A couple F-22s could put the
seaplane into the ground, Phillips thought.

Minutes later, four F-22s lifted off the deck of the USS *Douglas MacArthur* at full throttle, full afterburners, shrieking skyward and soaring over the East China Sea.

CHAPTER 37

The hands that grabbed him and pulled him out of the hatch were strong and many. Pacino had the impression that a single person with six arms had pulled him from the gaping maw of the submerged torpedo room.

He coughed, spitting up the water in his stomach, coughing up more that had reached his lungs, then vomiting, his body convulsing and heaving. His frame was folded up in a fetal position, his eyes shut, tears squeezing out. When the convulsions ended, his breath wheezed in and out of him frantically. Finally that too slowed. The dizziness ended, the room's spinning coming to a slow stop, his eyes able to focus.

He took a deep breath, and it seemed to clear his mind. He was lying in a puddle on the deck of the middle level. His coveralls were soaked—what was left of them, the fire having eaten gaping holes. He opened his eyes, blinking against the glare from the overheads. His retinae had been burned by the flames in the torpedo room. A face floated above his own, the bone structure narrow, with pronounced cheekbones, deep eye sockets, heavy black eyebrows beneath the diesel-oil black hair. Captain John Patton was staring down at him, frowning. Now why, Pacino thought, would he be frowning?

"Colleen," Pacino said, his voice a croak. "Where is . . . Colleen?"

"I'm right here, Michael," her voice came, low and sweet. "Captain Patton sent one of his officers in here.

I was on the floor coughing my face off, but they got a mask on me and got me out of here."

"Are you okay?"

"I'm fine, I'm fine."

"Are you sure?" His arm rose to reach up to her, but her hands put his arm back. At her touch pains shot up his arm. Pacino looked over at Patton, then back at Colleen, both of them staring at him.

"What is it, John? Am I okay? Did I get burned?"

An image of himself—horribly burned and disfigured, his skin mottled and stretched too tightly across his skull, his hair gone. Did he look like that? Why were they staring?

"You look like the day I first met you, Admiral," Colleen said, smiling.

"Why are you looking at me like that?"

"You saved the ship, sir. We'd have gone down if not for you." Patton was talking dazedly, as if in a trance. "It would have been just like the *Annapolis* sinking— the smoke—it smelled the same. It was a torpedo-fuel fire. That's what happened to us!"

"Two torpedo-room fires in one operation," Pacino said, struggling to sit up. "No one should have to go through that."

"I can't believe you went in there, sir. It was . . . amazing."

"Didn't have a lot of choice, John. It was go into the torpedo room or go down with the ship."

"How do you feel?"

"Terrible. Am I burned?" He looked down at his skin—most of his legs was red or blistering. His hands were blistered, his face feeling sunburned.

"Minor, Admiral. You look like you've been to Club Med."

"John, I need to talk to Colleen. Could I have a minute?"

After Patton excused himself, Pacino leaned against the equipment cabinet, his eyes half shut, feeling more exhausted than at any time in his life.

"Don't try to talk, honey," Colleen said.

"I have to," he said. "I need to tell you. I—"

"I know," she said, one finger over her mouth. "Hush, we'll do that later. It's not right here, not inside a sub with all these Navy guys and all this equipment. Give a woman some romance."

"I'd be happy to," he said. He felt her arms go around him, supporting him. The feel of her, the smell of her skin, was deeply relaxing. He fell asleep instantly, without realizing he was utterly spent.

The seaplane had struggled to get airborne, one of the turbines damaged from the fired bullets. The American fighters had flown high overhead, searching for them while the seaplane hugged the coastline, almost on the water. Eventually, the fighters had given up and flown back to wherever they came from.

Admiral Chu Hua-Feng sat in the canvas seat, holding the bleeding and dying form of his second in command, Lieutenant Commander Lo Sun, in his arms. Lo was bleeding from his chest, and Chu was covered with his blood.

"I'm so sorry, Lo," Chu said, low enough that no one else could hear him. "I lost your brother, I lost him. He was my best friend, the best weapons officer a pilot could have. He was my friend when no one else would be because I was the admiral's son. And he's gone. Now, Lo, you are my friend, the best friend in the world. You've gone into two hot submarine hijackings with me. You've been my first officer. You've taken down a whole convoy with me. We fought for the ship together, and we escaped when it was lost. Lo, please don't leave, don't go, don't die. You are my friend. Please, Lo, I'm so sorry."

Why did it have to be Lo? He prayed. Why couldn't he have taken the bullet?

"Chu," Lo Sun said, his eyes half open. "I'm dying. I can feel it. I'm cold. But there is a light. You must talk to . . . my mother. Tell her—"

"What?"

Lo's eyes shut. His lungs hissed, a rasping rattle, and

his body was still. And Admiral Chu Hua-Feng, Red Dagger mission commander, wept, his tears washing over the younger man's face.

Hours later, when they landed in Tianjin, he stepped out of the hatch, carrying Lo's body like that of a child's. A crew of paramedics took Lo Sun from him. Gently laying his corpse on a white-sheeted gurney, they loaded it into a van and drove off. Chen Zhu and Xhiu Liu came by, putting their hands on his shoulders, then walking off down the pier. The rest of the crew followed them, all the others of his unit surviving except Lo.

For what seemed an hour Chu stood on the pier after the van with Lo's body drove off. The cold eased as the sun rose in the east, shining out over Bo Hai Bay, and he realized he wasn't alone.

"I waited for you," she said, the voice music. "I heard that one crew survived, and I was hoping it was you. But no one knew. You're alive."

"Mai," he said, his tone saying everything he wanted to say to her. He stood, looking at her, the weight of the world on his shoulders, the mission behind him, but still vivid in his memory. Impulsively he walked to her and hugged her hard, her arms wrapping around him. He could feel her heart beating through her tunic, her slim body small in his arms.

"What happened?" he asked. "What is the news? Did we succeed?"

The sadness in her eyes told him all, all of it. "All of the Rising Suns were sunk. The American backup force headed into the East China Sea. Chairman Yang watched them on the news. I was with him when he saw."

"What did he do?"

"I'm sorry, Chu. He said, 'Sue for peace. Give the Whites whatever they want. Just don't let the Americans on Chinese soil, whether Red or White.'"

"Then what?"

"Phone calls were made. Our PLA is withdrawing from all fronts. The Whites have taken more territory to the west. We still have Beijing. Peace talks start tomorrow, but the American fleet is ten kilometers off Shanghai, their guns and missiles pointed across White China at us. It's over. It almost worked, Chu. Almost."

"Almost is never good enough," he said.

"Who cares?" She said, burying her head in his shoulder. "At least you're safe."

He held her, thinking about Lo Sun, the submarine, the Americans, and what the future would bring. Somehow, none of it seemed so bad with Mai Sheng beside him.

"Let's go," he said. "I want to get away from the water. All water."

EPILOGUE

FRIDAY
NOVEMBER 8

East China Sea

As the sun rose over the sea, the nuclear submarine *Arctic Storm* rose slowly to the surface, her buoyancy just slightly positive. The fin penetrated the sea's surface, then the hull. The empty ship was silent and abandoned, the last fact underscored by the open forward escape-trunk hatch through which the Red Dagger platoon had left.

An American destroyer arrived a half hour later when the radar contact had been classified a surfaced submarine. The USS *Princeton* pulled alongside and threw over eight lines, made up from the destroyer's deck cleats to the sub's. Slowly the ship towed the shut-down submarine back home.

When *Princeton* docked at Yokosuka Naval Seaport, a man named Akagi Tanaka was waiting on the ridge, looking down on the channel. The submarine being towed in represented the fruit of many late nights. As it sailed by, he waved at it, sniffing as it vanished around the corner of the ridge and out of sight.

Yokosuka Naval Seaport
Yokosuka, Japan

As the USS *Piranha* first came into view around the corner of the ridge, cheers burst out, a band began to play, confetti and ribbons started flying. On her bow and stern a hundred sailors and officers stood at rigid attention. Dressed in pressed service dress blues, the men faced the pier. The wind whipped around the dark uniforms, and the American flag flying on the sail flapped in the stiff breeze.

As she pulled up, a hundred ships in the bay began sounding their horns in salute. On the flying bridge, a set of stainless steel handrails on top of the sail, Captain Bruce Phillips, in his dress blues with full medals, stood tall. As the horns blared, he raised his hand to his forehead, the salute not required, but seeming to come of its own volition. *Piranha* threw over the first line to the pier, the ship back from the mission, the party only beginning.

He looked down on the crowd milling on the pier, the SNN reporters, the cameras, the women, the children, the families flown over by the Navy for this homecoming, particularly celebrated since a dozen submarines would not be returning today. Phillips searched the crowd, looking for her, but Abby O'Neal wasn't among them.

He pulled out a cigar from the inside pocket of his dress blue jacket and lit it with his USS *Greenville* lighter. He puffed it to life and took one lingering look down at the pier. No sign of her. Abby had not come.

"Your loss, toots," he said to no one, his mouth half curled in a smirk.

"Excuse me, sir?" the officer of the deck said.

"Nothing. Never mind," Phillips said, looking down on the crowd.

A female reporter waved up at him. "Captain! Captain Phillips! Would you agree to an interview? Satellite News Network? I can get you on prime time!"

The reporter was pretty and vivacious, her smile either genetically perfect or the subject of a huge dental invoice.

"How about in my stateroom?" he shouted down to her. "I have champagne!"

"Great!" she shouted back.

Bruce Phillips straightened his tie, clamped the Havana cigar between his teeth, and climbed over the bridge coaming to the sail's welded-in ladder rungs. The officer of the deck watched as Phillips shook the reporter's hand and led her to the hatch, holding out his elbow to escort her along the hull.

The *Devilfish* came around the ridge ten minutes later. Her crew was also dressed in crisp dress blues, manning the rails, facing the pier, at rigid attention.

As the band struck up again and the horns sounded, the two dozen fireboats in the channel started their pumps. Arcs of water climbed four hundred feet into the sky. A rain of confetti and ribbons came sailing down from the hill overlooking the piers. As the ship came closer, white block letters could be made out mounted on the black sail:

SSNX
USS *DEVILFISH*

High above the sail, on a stainless steel mast, the American flag flapped in the wind, partially obscured by the flag in front of it, with a white skull and crossbones on the black field, the Jolly Roger.

Hanging below the Jolly Roger was an old-fashioned straw broom, swaying in the breeze.

A television cameraman framed a reporter before the tall black sail of the *Devilfish* as she slowly hove into view. The reporter spoke into his microphone: ". . . can be seen flying a broom from the yardarm, which we've been told is a tradition passed down from the days of square-rigged sailing vessels, pronouncing that the ship has done 'a clean sweep,' the enemy ships all at the bottom. And as you can see, Brett, the SSNX has almost single-handedly won the battle of the East China Sea . . ."

The television wide-screen was playing in the Oval Office in the White House. President Jaisal Warner watched as the SSNX drew up to the pier.

"You know," Admiral Richard O'Shaughnessy said, "Pacino did that for you, the letters reading SSNX. He knew you'd been taking heat about it, and he wanted them to remember that the SSNX was your baby."

Warner smiled at O'Shaughnessy. "Oh, shut up, Dick. You don't have to push him on me anymore. I'll accept your recommendation. Pacino for Chief of Naval Operations. Number one admiral in the navy."

O'Shaughnessy smiled back. "I hate to leave this job, but it's okay if I'm leaving it to him."

"Oh, I don't think you'll mind too much, Dick, seeing as how you'll be stepping up to Chairman of the Joint Chiefs. Hey, you know, that girl standing next to Pacino, she looks like your daughter."

O'Shaughnessy stared. There on the television screen Colleen and Pacino were side by side as they left the ship, the two of them talking, both of them animated, both smiling and laughing.

"I'll be goddamned," he stammered. "He took Colleen to sea? On a *combat* mission?"

"Sorry, Dick, too late to change your recommendation. But I think you'd better plan for more than just having Pacino be your Chief of Naval Operations. You'd better think about what it would be like having him as a son-in-law."

PACIFIC OCEAN
ALTITUDE: 51,000 FEET

"Cyclops won this war," Pacino said. They were airborne in the supersonic SS-12, making its way back to Pearl Harbor

"It did okay," Colleen O'Shaughnessy said, her tone modest, but brimming with happiness that he would say that.

"No, I mean it. Without Cyclops and the acoustic daylight, we'd still be out there looking for those damned Rising Suns."

"Maybe it was in the right place at the right time,"

she said, her deep brown eyes looking into Pacino's. "Like me."

He smiled at her. "I like to think we would have come together one way or another, timing be damned."

She reclined in her seat, shutting her eyes, her breathing deep. Pacino looked at her for a full minute, then reclined his seat next to hers.

The video phone beeped insistently. Pacino half opened one eye and clicked the video on. The face of Mason Daniels, Number Four, came up in the view screen.

"Number Four. Good to hear from you," Pacino said.

Daniels grinned. "I got you a present for winning the war," he said, laying into Pacino immediately. The video view moved from Daniels to an object right beside him.

"It's a grill. I figure you're an expert at it now. What are you, well done?"

"Go to hell, Daniels," Pacino said, clicking off but smiling.

As he shut his eyes, he thought about Dick Donchez, and about what he would have said if he had seen Pacino today.

PEARL HARBOR, HAWAII
UNIFIED SUBMARINE COMMAND
PACIFIC SQUADRON SUBMARINE PIERS

Pacino got out of the staff car and slowly walked to the end of the piers where the twelve 688-class submarines had been berthed before they had sailed for the East China Sea mission. For some time he watched the water washing against the piers. Then he turned and accepted a wreath from Colleen, dropping it into the water. The flowers of the wreath floated on the gentle waves of the harbor. Pacino stood there for several minutes before finally drawing himself to attention, his hand coming up in a ruler-straight salute, then dropping it by his side.

Reluctantly he turned and walked back to the staff

car. He was still staring at the piers as the car roared off to return to the airport, where the SS-12 waited to take the next Chief of Naval Operations back to Washington.